Stories

Scott Baker
Robert Bloch
Pat Cadigan
Harlan Ellison
John M. Ford
Charles L. Grant
Lucius Shepard
S. P. Somtow
Karl Edward Wagner
Gene Wolfe

and many more . . .

RIPPER!

—— Edited by ——

Gardner Dozois
and
Susan Casper

A TOM DOHERTY ASSOCIATES BOOK
NEW YORK

RIPPER!

A TOR Book
Published by Tom Doherty Associates, Inc.
49 West 24 Street
New York, NY 10010

ISBN: 0-812-51700-8   Can. ISBN: 0-812-51701-6

Library of Congress Catalog Card Number: 88-50334

First edition: September 1988

Printed in the United States of America

0 9 8 7 6 5 4 3 2 1

ACKNOWLEDGMENTS

Foreword by Robert Bloch. Copyright © 1971 by Robert Bloch.

"Yours Truly, Jack the Ripper," by Robert Bloch. Copyright © 1943 by *Weird Tales*. "The Prowler in the City at the Edge of the World," by Harlan Ellison. Originally appeared in *Dangerous Visions*; copyright © 1967 by Harlan Ellison. Reprinted by arrangement with, and permission of, the author and the author's agent, Richard Curtis Associates, Inc., New York. All rights reserved.

For Christopher Casper

The editors would like to thank the following people for their help and support:

Jack Dann, Lucius Shepard, Charles L. Grant, Robert Bloch, Karl Edward Wagner, Howard Waldrop, George R.R. Martin, Lewis Shiner, Dennis Etchison, Harlan Ellison, Gene Wolfe, Somtow Sucharitkul, Tim Sullivan, Sarah Clemens, Pat Cadigan, Scott Baker, Greg Frost, Steve Rasnic Tem, John M. Ford, Cooper McLaughlin, Stephen Gallagher, Harry Turtledove, Alan Ryan, Edward Bryant, Michael Swanwick, Gregory Nicoll, Janet and Ricky Kagan, Tess Kissinger, Bob Walters, Michael Emyrs, Virginia Kidd, Patrick Delahunt, Merilee Heifetz, Mark Van Name, and special thanks to our own editor, Melissa Ann Singer

Contents

FOREWORD

Who was Jack the Ripper?

For almost a century this question has challenged criminologists, plagued psychologists, intrigued investigative reporters, authors, playwrights, and the general public throughout the world. Millions of words have been expended in speculation, a thousand theories propounded, scores of theories and solutions offered in books, articles, essays, stories, drama on stage or screen. But the identity of Jack the Ripper remains a mystery.

And an even greater mystery is this: Why, after a hundred years of hypotheses, do we still seek an answer?

Consider the facts.

On the face of it, the victims of the elusive murderer were scarcely such as to inspire interest. In London's slum of Whitechapel, during the fall of 1888, the Ripper killed five prostitutes. Four were women in their forties who, from descriptions, medical reports, and photographs, were hardly glamorous sex objects. Destitution and dissipation had aged them beyond their years to a point where they resembled the bag ladies of today. The fifth victim was twenty-four, but no beauty; big and burly, she was over three months pregnant at the time of her untimely death. So continuing interest in these crimes cannot be connected with the physical charms of the females who met their fate at the hands—and knife—of their mysterious assailant.

True, his methods inspired morbid imaginations. The blade that cut throats also slashed bodies, and each successive slaying involved increasing mutilation, even the removal of internal organs. The third and fourth murders occurred within the space of an hour on the same night. The fifth—the only one which took place indoors—culminated in carving up the corpse so hideously as to defy description.

But the history of homicide abounds with accounts of atrocities accompanying murder: prolonged torture, dismemberment, cannibalism, necrophilia, and other embellishments.

It can be argued that mass murder was a shock to Victorian sensibilities; aside from historical horrors perpetrated by Gilles de Retz, Countess Báthory, and a few others plus the perhaps apocryphal atrocities of a Sawney Bean or Sweeney Todd, there seemed little precedent for serial slayings.

Still, since that time multiple homicides have become commonplace. Only three years later, an exploration of the so-called Murder Castle in Chicago yielded ghastly hints of perhaps as many as two hundred killings over a period of eighteen months. Their perpetrator, a man who called himself H. H. Holmes, was also believed to have done away with many other victims prior to that time. Holmes was apprehended following his callous and calculated murder of a partner and his three young children.

In their heyday Henri Landru, Peter Kurten, Fritz Haarmann, Neville Heath, Reginald Christie, Albert Fish, and a dozen others horrified newspaper readers, but their fame or infamy faded in the mists of passing time. In our own era came a multiplicity of multiple murderers—a sniper atop a tower shooting down dozens of innocent victims at random, the savage slayer of eight nurses in a single night of nightmare, the serial slaughters committed by the Hillside Strangler, the Son of Sam, the Skid Row Slasher, and scores of others whose murders and methods exceed the Ripper's both in number and in nature.

But it's the Ripper we remember.

He came silently out of the midnight shadows on August 31, 1888, emerged again on September 8, reappeared on September 30, then made his final fearsome bow on the night of November

9. He vanished afterward, but the shadows remain; the shadows cloaking his deeds, his motives, his identity.

Perhaps this is why we continue to remember him. We can identify the other mass murderers, for they were caught and punished. But though he was hunted by hundreds of police, sought by thousands of self-appointed avengers, and dreaded by millions of potential victims, the monster with the knife escaped without a trace. His trail of blood led nowhere, and to this day we do not know his name.

Thus the Ripper remains as a symbol of all our secret fears—the fear of the stranger on a darkened street, fear of the neighbor whose commonplace exterior may conceal the beast within, even the fear of a friend we *think* we know; a friend who may become a fiend once the mask comes off and the knife comes out.

The mystery of the Ripper's identity was constantly challenged, both during his reign of terror and ever since. An entire literature of explanations has been created by those whom my learned colleague Colin Wilson calls "Ripperologists." In a fascinating treatise, the pseudonymous Alexander Kelly lists over fifty types of suspects who have been proposed as the killer in both fact and fiction, including a Druid, a black magician, an invisible man, a time-traveler, an orangutan, and even a gorilla.

And not all seeming solutions have been so fanciful. More reasonable choices involve members of the medical profession—doctors, students, veterinarians, abortionists, midwives—persons whose comings and goings in the nighted slums would attract scant notice, but all of whom would be skillful in wielding a knife. Other candidates include police, military men, sailors, lunatics, syphilitics, and a catalog of citizenry ranging from nonentities to the nobility.

There, perhaps, lies a clue within a clue. Can it be we continue to seek the Ripper not just as a symbol of our secret fears but also as a symbol of our innermost hatreds?

Does the Ripper serve as a scapegoat?

If we are prejudiced against any profession, any class of society, any race or religion, we can probably find a candidate for our convictions among the suspects. If we dislike Russians, Poles, Jews, Americans, Spaniards, Latin Americans, Frenchmen, Norwegians, Asiatics, or even Texans, we may take comfort in knowing that each in turn has been suggested as the mass murderer. Jack is all things to all men.

Of course many of the allegations are fanciful and farfetched, but over the years various students of Ripperology have advanced more detailed and serious theories of identification.

One of the best known concerns a "Dr. Stanley," whose son was infected with syphilis by a prostitute and died of the disease. Bent on vengeance, the good doctor tracked down the guilty party, Mary Jane Kelly, killing the other whores to prevent them from warning her. Kelly was his last victim, and after butchering her he disappeared. Before his death in Buenos Aires he supposedly confessed his crimes in a Spanish newspaper story. But the news item has never been found, and none of the "factual" details hold water. It normally takes ten to twenty years for syphilis to cause death, and since Mary Jane Kelly was only twenty-four when she was murdered, it seems unlikely that she cohabited with the doctor's son when she was between the ages of four and fourteen. More to the point, medical reports show that Mary Jane Kelly didn't have syphilis.

Another and more startling accusation is leveled against none other than Edward, the Duke of Clarence, a grandson of Queen Victoria. It is claimed that hints of his guilt were found in the private papers of the Queen's physician, Sir William Gull. According to the story, Clarence was syphilitic and died in a mad house rather than during the 1892 flu epidemic. But Clarence was reputedly homosexual. And even if he chose to murder whores out of hatred, his excursions into Whitechapel would involve many difficulties, for he was an easily recognized public figure. Yet none of the self-proclaimed witnesses who insisted they'd seen the Ripper near the scene of his crimes ever mentioned a resemblance to Clarence. And on the dates of several of the slayings his whereabouts are listed and accounted for in the official Court Calendar.

His former tutor and supposed lover, James Stephen, also is proposed as the killer, but semi-invalidism after a head injury tends to cast doubt on his ability to perform the killings. And the motives attributed to him, including a weird conspiracy involving high-ranking members of the Masonic Order, are a bit hard to accept. Moreover, he, too, would have encountered great problems visiting the slums and committing multiple slayings without detection.

A Polish Jew named Kosminski—not to be confused with Severin Klosowski, a Russian who committed other types of murders in the 1890s under the name of George Chapman and lived with a woman named Chapman who was no relative of the Annie Chapman killed earlier by the Ripper—is sometimes named as a suspect, along with another Russian, Michael Ostrog. Klosowski, in turn, may or may not have been the alias of another Russian, Alexander or Alexei Pedachenko, whose real name was Vasili Konovalov, but who also called himself Andrei Luiskovo. If this is a trifle difficult to follow, so is the convoluted "evidence" regarding the reputed barber-surgeon or medical doctor who may or may not have been planted in London as a secret agent to stir up anarchist elements in Whitechapel. Explanations also involve the existence of a "double," allegations of homicidal mania, and even statements made years later by Rasputin—purportedly written in French, a language he didn't know—which were found in the basement of Rasputin's house after his death. But Rasputin's house didn't have a basement, and the theories themselves lack a solid foundation.

One of the most popular suspects is Montague J. Druitt, a barrister who failed at law, became a tutor at a private school in Blackheath, and voiced fears that he was going insane. Shortly after the last of the five slayings credited to the Ripper, Mr. Druitt weighted his pockets with stones and drowned himself in the Thames, from which his body was recovered a month or so later. Since the killings stopped at the time of his suicide, it is most convenient to propose him as the guilty party. But nomination isn't election, and the trouble with Druitt's candidacy—aside from the fact that there's no evidence linking him to the crimes—is his ability as a cricketer. On the mornings following two of the Whitechapel murders, Druitt was playing his heart out on cricket fields many miles away from London. That he could kill and mutilate two women in the city slums shortly before dawn, then board a train and go directly to join his team in contest matches in the country is hardly plausible. To do so just isn't cricket.

None of these or other suspects seem likely sources for the flood of mail which inundated police and newspaper offices during the seventy-day period of slaughter—confessions, taunts, threats, even verse, pouring in from all over England and beyond. Graphology, psychology, and just plain common sense indicate that the bulk of this correspondence was obviously the product of hoaxers and/or the mentally ill.

But how to explain the handwritten letter received by the Central News Agency on September 28 in which the writer promises that "the next job I do shall clip the lady's ears off and send them to the police officers"—and signs himself as "Jack the Ripper"?

What makes it interesting is that two days later the same pen-pal sent a postcard warning, "You'll hear about Saucy Jack's work tomorrow. Double event this time . . . Had not time to get ears for the police." And it was on that date that the Ripper did indeed perform a "double event," which was not publicized in the press until the following day. The writer also offers his thanks for "keeping last letter back until I got to work again"—a fact which only the writer of the first letter would know.

It has been argued that both letters were the work of a journalist bent on sensationalism to increase newspaper circulation, and that the second letter, dated September 30, might not have been mailed until the following day, at which time the press had news of the "double event."

But on October 16 another disturbing missive was received by George Lusk, head of the newly formed Whitechapel Vigilance Committee—enclosed in a parcel which contained "half the Kidne I took from one woman." The other half "I fried and ate it was very nise."

One of the "double event" victims was missing a kidney, and examination proved that the condition of the mailed fragment matched the kidney which remained, and had probably come from the same corpse. Very "nise" indeed.

So the letters, with their disguised handwriting, their seemingly contrived grammatical errors, their inconsistent misspelling and use of slang, cannot in these instances be arbitrarily dismissed as hoaxes.

The trouble is that none of them seem likely to be the work of the most popular suspects. It's hard to imagine a revenge-ridden doctor, a Russian secret agent, a royal personage, a classical tutor, or a barrister-turned-tutor managing to master colloquialisms correctly and employing elaborately disguised handwriting merely to mystify police. Nor does it explain the mysterious message chalked on a Whitechapel wall following the "double event." It read, "The Juwes are not the men that will be blamed for nothing," and if that sounds ambiguous it cannot be clarified by any handwriting analysis or comparison—because Sir Charles Warren, in charge of the investigation, rubbed it out before daylight permitted a photograph to be taken. He claimed he feared inciting anti-Semitic riots in Whitechapel, but whatever his reason, he destroyed a possibly important piece of evidence. Conceivably it could have been the work of someone trying to stir up dissension for political reasons, but if so, why didn't that person include inflammatory remarks in the two letters and postcard which seem genuine?

But these questions are merely samples of literally hundreds of puzzles, riddles, and mysteries-within-mysteries. Small wonder, then, that a century of controversy and conjecture has revolved around the Ripper's elusive identity.

From time to time the public has been enlightened by various self-styled "experts." Though particulars may differ, they all tell approximately the same story. Each one claims to have been the recipient of confidences from some highly placed member of the Metropolitan Police, Scotland Yard, or even the Home Office. This anonymous source assured them that of course the "authorities" knew exactly who Jack the Ripper really was—and knew it almost immediately after the time of the final slaying. In other words, although choosing not to name names, they had the correct answer and there was really no "mystery" left to solve.

But if the "authorities" really believed that Kosminski, Montague J. Druitt, or the Duke of Clarence or any of a dozen others was truly Jack the Ripper, then why were more than fifty extra plainclothes police officers still detailed to Whitechapel from other districts for over a full year after the 1888 murders?

I submit that they were still searching for Jack the Ripper.

And, a hundred years later, so are we.

Hence this book, this collection of fact and fancy, which may perhaps furnish clues with which you, the reader, can come up with a final solution. If so it would be a great victory, and I wish you luck in that endeavor.

Let's win this one for the Ripper!

—ROBERT BLOCH

JACK'S DECLINE

Lucius Shepard

Jack the Ripper murdered five women, and, with only one exception (a victim from whom he was probably frightened away before he could finish his work), the mutilations he performed became more terrible with each successive murder. Terrible beyond belief. The last victim was so badly mutilated that a grainy black-and-white photograph of the scene can still jolt even our jaded modern sensibilities—can shock even someone hardened and inured to gore by the endless recent stream of slasher movies and splatter flicks. Then, abruptly, the murders stopped. The Ripper was never heard from again. One popular theory, then and now, was that the murders had stopped because the Ripper was dead—that he had committed suicide, in fact, overcome by remorse at last. Perhaps even the Ripper found the ultimate atrocities of that final murder too much to take—too much to live with, too much to bear.

And yet, suppose the Ripper did survive. How would he be able to live with the knowledge of what he had done, of what he had become?

It would take a writer with a deep and profound understanding of the true nature of evil to answer that question . . . and, as the disturbing story that follows deftly proves, Lucius Shepard is just such a writer.

Lucius Shepard began publishing in 1983, and in a very short time has become one of the most popular and prolific writers to come along in many years. In 1985, Shepard won the John W. Campbell Award as the year's best new writer, as well as being on the Nebula Award final ballot an unprec-

*edented three times in three separate categories. Since then,
he has turned up several more times on the final Nebula ballot, and has been a finalist for the Hugo Award, the British
Fantasy Award, the John W. Campbell Memorial Award, the
Philip K. Dick Award, and the World Fantasy Award. In 1987,
he finally picked up his first (though probably not his last)
award, winning the Nebula for his landmark novella ''R&R.''
His acelaimed first novel,* Green Eyes, *was an Ace Special.
His most recent books are the novel* Life During Wartime *and
the collection* The Jaguar Hunter. *He is currently living somewhere in the wilds of Nantucket, where he is at work on two
new novels.*

AT FIRST THEY STRAPPED HIM TO THE BED AND LET
him howl, let him try to vomit out the red, raw thing
inside his hate. He would scream until his voice became a hoarse, scratchy chord, and then he would lapse into
a fugue, his mind gone as blank as the gray stone walls.
Often during these quiet times, the man who washed and fed
him would bring strangers into the room, charging them a
fee to have a peek at the greatest villain of the age, and they
would stand beside the bed, shadows in the half light, and
say, ''*That's* the Ripper? Why, that poor sod couldn't butter
his own toast, let alone do murder. I want me money back!''
And their disbelief would rankle the demon within him, and
he would scream louder than ever, shaking the bed and de-
lighting in his visitors' fearful attitudes.

Later, after dozens of therapies—torments, really—and
doctors whose manner was unanimously neutral, years and
years later when he began to suffer guilt and wanted to atone,
he realized there was no possibility of atonement, that his
demon was not accessible to moral remedies. For a while he
tried to deny the horrors of his past, to steep himself in the
genteel associations of his childhood, in memories of gra-

cious estates and garden parties. But he found that more vivid memories possessed him. Those five slatternly faces going slack when they saw the blade, their scent of sweat and cheap perfume, and the hot true perfume of their blood bubbling over his fingers. He yearned to engage once again in those terrible *amours*; yet he was also repelled by that yearning, and these contrary pressures drove him to consider suicide. But it did not seem a sufficient punishment: death for him would be surcease, and he could think of no means of extinction vile enough to earn him absolution. And so, despairing, dulled by despair, he wandered the corridors of his family's keep, becoming—as the years passed and the century turned—a numb meat of a man with graying hair and a gray pallor, whose fingers would sometimes clench spasmodically, and whose eyes would sometimes appear to grow dark and lose their animation, like pools in which the fish had long since ceased to spawn.

In 1903 there was a reawakening of interest in the murders, new clues and rumors that struck close to the bone, and his family—none of whom he had seen since the beginning of his confinement—gave orders that he be moved from England, fearing that their awful secret would be brought to light. He was issued a German passport under the name of Gerhard Steigler, and one night in the autumn of that year, along with his warders, his doctor of the moment, and a trunkful of the drugs that kept his demon tame, he crossed the English Channel to Calais, and there entrained for Krakow in Poland. From Krakow he was transported by coach to a hunting lodge in the northeast of the country, a rambling structure of whitewashed walls and pitch-coated beams, set among rumpled hills thicketed with chokecherry, forested with chestnuts and stunted water oaks. Travel had rekindled his spirits somewhat, and during his first year at the lodge, he came again to derive a mild pleasure from life. He liked the isolation of the place, and he would walk for hours through the woods, often winding up atop a hill from which he could look westward over a checkerboard of cultivated fields, of wheat and barley and sorghum. Here he would sit and watch cloud shadows rushing across the land, great shafts of light piercing down and fading, the golden fields dappling with an alternation of bright and dark, and it seemed to him that this constant shifting display was an airy machinery, an immaterial clockwork that registered the inner processes of time. He realized that but for a brief, bloody season, his life had evinced this same insubstantiality, this same lack of true configuration, and as the years slipped away, he returned each afternoon to commune with that vast, complicated emblem of light and shade, believing that therein he could perceive the winnowing of his days.

If he were to look eastward from the hilltop—something he rarely permitted himself to do—his eye would encounter a smallish town of thatch and whitewash and curling chimney smokes, its church steeple poking up like a rifle sight. There, he knew, would be women of the sort he fancied. The thought of their bellies gleaming pale, the neatly packaged meats of their sex awaited a knife to reveal their mysteries, that would start him trembling, and for days thereafter he would be overborne by his demon's urges and have to be restrained.

During that first winter, in order to perfect his role as a member of the German aristocracy, he immersed himself in the study of the language. He had always been adept at learning, and by the time the spring thaw had arrived, he had become fluent in the spoken tongue and was capable of reading even the most difficult of texts. He enjoyed the works of Schiller and Nietzsche, but when he came to *Faustus* and its humanistic depiction of evil, he was so nettled by the author's dearth of understanding that he hurled the book out the window. Demons were not nearly as personable as Goethe had described them. They were parasites, less creatures unto themselves than the seepage of a dark force that underlay all creation, that—presented with an opening—would pour inside you, seducing not your soul but your blood, your cells, feeding upon you and growing to assume hideous shapes. He had seen the nesting places of such demons in the bodies of the women he had slain, had caught brief glimpses of them as they scurried for cover deeper into their bloody caves.

Turning from literature, he developed an interest in gardening, and would work from dawn until dusk in his plot, exerting himself so strenuously that his sleep was free of nightmares. But in the end this, too, failed him. Things grew to obscenely feminine proportions in that rich soil. Beneath heart-shaped leaves, the snap beans dangled like a bawd's earrings, and he would unearth strange hairy roots that with their puckered surfaces bore an uncanny resemblance to the female genitalia. Once again he despaired, considered suicide, and sank into a torpor.

In December of 1915, when he was fifty-six years old, a new doctor came to the lodge: a dapper little man in his forties, brimming with energy and good humor and talk of subconscious drives, neuroses, and the libido. The doctor treated him as if he were a man and not an aberration, and through hypnosis, several childhood traumas were revealed, notable among them a humiliating evening spent at a brothel when he was twelve, brought there by the family coachman and left alone in the common room, a target for the taunts of the whores. The doctor believed these incidents were seeds that had grown to fruition and inspired his murderous acts; but he rejected this theory.

"You claim, Doctor," he said, "that once I accept the connection between my childhood pain and the murders, a cure will be forthcoming. But those experiences only weakened me, made me susceptible to the demon and allowed him to enter and take possession of my body. There were supernatural forces in play. Witness the arrangements I made of the viscera . . . like some sort of cabalistic sign. I was driven to create that arrangement by my demon. It was the mark of his triumph over the demons encysted within the women.''

The doctor sighed. ''It seems to me you have invented this demon in order to shift blame to its shoulders.''

''You think I am denying guilt?''

''Not entirely, but . . .''

''Believe me, Doctor,'' he said, ''despite my inability to exorcise the demon, I am expert at guilt.''

He enjoyed these exchanges not for their intellectual content, but because he felt the doctor liked him. He had been self-absorbed for so long that he had forgotten even the concept of friendship, and the hope that he could actually have a friend caused him no end of excitement. He had become a decent chef over the years, and he would prepare the doctor special dinners accompanied by fine wines and venerable brandies. He honed his chess game so as to provide worthy opposition for the doctor, who had been a schoolboy champion; he took renewed interest in worldly affairs in order to make better conversation. Things, he believed, were going swimmingly. But one afternoon as they walked along the crest of a wooded hill, in a companionable moment he threw his arm about the doctor's shoulder and felt the man stiffen and shrink away from his touch. He withdrew his arm, looked into the doctor's eyes, and saw there fear and revulsion. What he had taken for friendship, he realized, had merely been a superior form of bedside manner.

''I . . .'' The doctor came a step toward him, contempt and pity vying for control of his expression. ''I'm sorry. It's just . . .''

The eviscerated flesh, the severed organs, the blood.

''I understand, Doctor,'' he said. ''It's quite all right.'' He spun on his heel and walked back to the lodge alone, back to despair. It was, he knew, no less than he deserved. But he could not help feeling betrayed.

* * *

His seventieth birthday passed, his seventy-fifth, and with the decline of his flesh, it seemed his menace also declined, for his family stopped sending doctors and he came to believe that the men who cared for him were no longer warders but merely servants. This slackening of concern unsettled him, and like a good madman he continued to take his drugs and sleep in a bed with leather restraints. He had hoped senility would erode his memories, but he retained an uncommon clarity of mind and his body remained hale, albeit prone to aches and pains. It was, he thought, his demon that kept him strong, that refused to permit a collapse into peaceful decay. He still felt the violent urges that had destroyed his life and others, and to quell them he would spend hours each day maintaining a surgical sharpness to the edges of the kitchen knives, thinking that this pretense would convince the demon that its bloodlust would soon be sated.

Not long after his eightieth birthday, he received a visitor from the town: a doddering priest older than himself, who had come to warn him of imminent danger. The Nazis were massing on the border, and rumor had it an invasion was near. He invited the priest into the main hall, a high-ceilinged room centered by a long table and lorded over by a chandelier of iron and crystal, and he asked who these Nazis were, explaining that it had been years since he had paid any attention to politics.

"Evil men," the priest told him. "An army of monsters ruled by a madman."

Intrigued, he asked to hear more and listened intently to tales of outrage and excess, of Hitler and his bloody friends. He thought it would be interesting to meet these men, to learn if their demons were akin to his.

"I sense in you a troubled soul," said the priest as he made to leave. "If you wish I will hear your confession."

"Thank you, Father," he said. "But I have spent these

past fifty years in confession and it has served no good purpose.''

''Is there anything else I might do?''

He considered asking for the rite of exorcism, but the notion of this frail old man contending with the fierce horror inhabiting his flesh was ludicrous in the extreme. ''No, Father,'' he said. ''I fear my sins are beyond your precinct. I'm more likely to receive comfort from the Nazis.''

One morning a month or so after the priest's visit, he waked to find himself alone. He went through the house, calling the names of his servants, to no avail; then, more puzzled than alarmed, he walked to his hilltop vantage and looked east. Dozens and dozens of tanks were cutting dusty swaths across the fields, rumbling, clanking, at that distance resembling toys run wild on a golden game board. Black smoke billowed from the little town, and the church steeple was no longer in evidence. When dusk began to gather, he returned to the lodge, half expecting to find it reduced to rubble. But it was intact, and though he waited up most of the night to greet them, no soldiers came to disrupt the peace and quiet.

The next afternoon, however, a touring car pulled up to the lodge and disgorged seven young men, all wearing shiny boots and black uniforms with silver emblems on the collar shaped like twin lightning bolts. They were suspicious of him at first, but on seeing his proof of German citizenship, they treated him as if he were a fine old gentleman, addressing him as ''Herr Steigler'' and asking permission to billet in the lodge. ''My home is yours,'' he told them, and he set before them his finest wines, which they proceeded to swill down with not the least appreciation for their nose or bouquet.

They propped their feet on the table, scarring its varnish, and they told crude jokes, hooting and slapping their thighs, spilling the wines and breaking glasses, offering profane toasts to their venerable host. Watching them, he found it difficult to believe that these louts were creatures of evil; if they were possessed, it must be by demons of the lowest order, ones that would quail before his own. Still, he withheld final judgment, partly because their captain, who remained aloof from the carousing, was of a different cut. He was a thin, black-haired man with pale, pocked skin and a slit of a mouth . . . Indeed, all his features seemed products of a minimalist creator, being barely raised upon his face, lending it an aspect both cruel and disinterested. His behavior, too, was governed by this minimalism. He sipped his wine, conversed in a monotone, and displayed an economy of gesture that—to his host's mind—appeared to signal a pathological measure of self-discipline.

"What do you do here, Herr Steigler?" he asked at one point. "I assume, of course, that you are retired, but I have seen no evidence of previous occupation."

"Poor health," said the old man, "has precluded my taking up a profession. I read, I walk in the woods and meditate."

"And what do you meditate upon?"

"The past, mostly. That, and the nature of evil."

The rigor of the captain's expression was disordered by a tick of a smile. "Evil," he said, savoring the word. "And have you arrived at any conclusions?"

The old man gave thought to bringing up the subject of demons, but instead said, "No, only that it exists."

"Perhaps," said the captain, with a superior smile, "you believe we are evil."

"Are you?"

"If I were, I would hardly admit to it."

"Why not? Even were I disposed against evil, I am old and feeble. I could do nothing to menace you."

"True," said the captain, running his finger around the mouth of his glass. "Then I will tell you that I may well be evil. Evil is a judgment made by history, and history may judge us as such."

"That is a fool's definition," said the old man. "To think that evil is not self-aware is foolish to the point of being evil. But you are not evil, Captain. You merely wish to be."

The captain dismissed this comment with a haughty laugh. "I am a soldier, Herr Steigler. A good one, I believe. This may call for a repression of one's conscience at times, but I would scarcely deem that evil. And as for my wishing to be so, my only wish is to win the war. Nothing more."

The old man made a gesture that directed the captain's attention toward his uniform. "Black cloth and patent leather and silver arcana. These are not the lineaments of a good soldier, Captain. They are designed to inspire dread. But apart from being psychological weapons, they are ritual expressions. Invocations of evil. You had best beware. Your invocations may prove effective and allow evil to possess you. Should that occur, you will have no joy in it. Take my word."

For an instant the captain's neutral mask dissolved, as if the old man's words had disconcerted him, and the old man could see the symptoms of insecurity: parted lips and twitching nerves and flicking tongue. But then the mask re-formed and the captain said coldly, "I fear your long solitude has deluded you, Herr Steigler. You speak with the confidence of expertise, yet by your own admission you have little knowledge of the world beyond these hills. How can you be expert upon anything other than, say, regional wildlife?"

The old man was weary of the conversation and merely said that being widely traveled was no prerequisite to wisdom.

Later that afternoon, a second touring car containing five women under guard arrived at the lodge. They were all young and lovely, with dusky complexions and doe eyes, and seeing them, the old man felt a dissolute warmth in his groin, a joyous rage in his heart.

"Jews," said the captain by way of explanation, and the old man nodded sagely as if he understood.

That night the house echoed with the women's screams, and the old man sat in his room ablaze with arousal, fevered with anger, his knees jittering, hands clenching and unclenching. He was barely able to restrain himself from taking a knife and hunting through the dark corridors of the lodge. Though wantonness had been imposed upon the women, it was in their nature to be wanton, alluring, and oh how he wanted to fall prey to their allure! Perhaps, he thought, he would ask the soldiers to give him one. No, no! He would *demand* one. As payment in lieu of rent. It was only fair.

The following morning, after the soldiers had locked the women in the basement and gone about their business, the old man crept down the stairs and peered through the barred window of the basement door. When they saw him, the women pressed themselves against the bars, pleading for his help. They were bruised, their dresses ripped, and they stank of sex. The sight of their breasts and nipples and ripely curved bellies made him faint. He would have liked to batter down the door and flash among them, drawing secret designs of blood across their soiled flesh.

"I cannot help you," he said. "They have taken the key."

They intensified their pleading, reaching through the bars, and he jumped back from their touch, fearing that it would further inflame him. "Perhaps there is a way," he said, his voice thick with urgency. "I will think on it."

He went back up the stairs and returned with wine, bread, and cheese. As they ate, he asked them about their lives; he felt a childlike curiosity about them, just as he had with the five women in Whitechapel. Three were farm wives, the fourth a butcher's daughter. The fifth, whom he thought the most beautiful, tall, with high cheekbones and full breasts, was the local schoolteacher. Her eyes were penetrating, and it was those eyes, their look of stern accusation, as if she knew his guilty soul, that made him aware of the magical opportunity with which he had been presented.

There were *five*!

Just as in Whitechapel, there were five, and one would be handy with a knife.

Here was the perfect resolution, the arc that would complete his mad journey and release him from his demon's grasp.

"I have a plan," he said. "But should it succeed, you must do something for me."

There was a chorus of eager assent from four of the women, but the schoolteacher stared at him with distaste and said, "I you wish to sleep with us, why not take your turn with the Germans?"

"It's not that, not that at all," he said, trying to inject wealth of sincerity into his voice. "I promise you, you will not be harmed."

Again a chorus of assent, and again the schoolteacher favored him with a disdainful stare.

"You must swear you will do as I ask," he said to her "No matter how repellent the task."

"Tell me what you want," she said.

"I will tell you afterward," he said. "Now swear!"

"Very well," she said, following a lengthy pause. " swear."

Excited beyond measure, he hurried up the stairs, went t his desk, and wrote page after page of explicit instructions Then he busied himself in the kitchen, preparing a feast fo the soldiers. There would be veal and chicken, artichokes an asparagus, home-baked bread, and a delicate soup. And wine Oh, yes. The wine would be the soul of the meal. As he wer about these preparations, he whistled and sang, gleeful to th point of hysteria. His limbs trembled with anticipation, h heart pounded. Glasses and cutlery and china seemed to shir with unnatural brilliance as if they were registering and, in deed, sharing in his joy. Once the pots had been set to sin mer, he returned to his room, stripped off his clothes, an with his best pen, traced the mystic designs upon his gro and abdomen. He set half a dozen candelabra about the bed, and—satisfied with these arrangements—he opened his medicine chest and emptied his vials of the drugs with which he would treat the wine.

The soldiers had told him they would return by dusk, and six of them were true to their word—the captain, they said, had been held up in town. The old man could see that they were eager to be at the women again, but he begged and cajoled, and on beholding the sumptuous table he had laid, they could not reject his hospitality. Loosening their belts, they set to with hearty appetites, washing down every mouthful with liberal drafts of wine.

Oh, the old man was happy, he was sad, he was beset by storms of emotion, knowing that peace was soon to be his. Just as had happened in the kitchen, it was as if everything were in sympathy with his poignant moods. The room was giddy with light. The glaze on the veal shimmered, the varnished wood rippled like a grainy dark river, the chandelier glittered, and the silver lightning bolts twinkled on the collars of the doomed men as if accumulating the runoff of their vital charge. Three of the men keeled over almost immediately; two others managed to stagger to their feet, groping for their sidearms as they fell. The sixth actually succeeded in drawing his weapon. He fired twice, but the bullets ricocheted off the floor and he toppled facedown at the feet of the old man, who finished him with a knife stroke across the throat, switched off the lights, and went to wait for the captain.

Waiting grew long, and several times he nearly decided to go ahead with his plan; but at last he heard a motor, followed by footsteps in the foyer. "Uwe!" called the captain. "Horst!" The old man flattened against the wall, saw a shadow moving past, and swung his knife. Some sound must have given his presence away, for the shadow turned and the knife penetrated the captain's shoulder, not—as he had intended—the back. There was a shriek, and then the scrabbling of the captain trying to drag himself away. The old man eased along the wall, unable to locate the captain, not daring to switch on the lights for fear of posing a target. But darkness had always been his friend, and he was unconcerned. He held still and heard the captain's whistling breath and felt a joy so rich that it seemed to tinge the darkness with a shade of crimson.

"Herr Steigler?" said the captain. "Is that you?"

Ah! The old man spotted a lump of shadow huddled by a chair.

The captain fired at random—three distinct spearpoints of flame. "Why are you doing this?" Voice atremble with desperation. "Who *are* you?"

I am Red Jack, the old man said to himself. I am fear made flesh.

"Who are you?" the captain repeated, and fired again.

The old man inched closer; he could make out the shape of the gun in the captain's hand.

"For God's sake!" said the captain.

Moving a step closer, the old man kicked the gun. Heard it skitter across the floor. He kneeled beside the captain, who had slumped onto his back, and pricked his throat with the knife.

"Please," said the captain.

With his free hand, the old man felt for the pulse in the captain's neck. It was strong and rapid, and he kept his finger there, liking the heady sense of potency it transmitted. "Evil, Captain," he said. "Do you remember?"

"Herr Steigler! Please! What are you doing?"

"Killing you."

"But why? What have we done to you?" The captain tensed, and the old man pressed harder with the knife.

"You have a stringy neck, Captain," he said. "Necks should be soft and smooth. I may have to saw with the edge a little to do the job right." He prolonged the moment, exulting in the quiver transmitted along the blade by the man's straining muscles.

"Please, Herr Steigler!"

"I am not Herr Steigler," said Red Jack. "I am mystery." Then he nicked the carotid artery and jerked his hand away before the first jet could escape the wound. Male blood did not excite him.

The women rushed forward when he opened the basement door, but on seeing the bloody knife, they shrank back, their faces going slack in a most familiar way. He had waited up-stairs for an hour after killing the captain, letting the hungers of his demon subside; but despite that, they looked so vulnerable with their rags and bruises, it took all his self-control to keep from attacking them. "I have freed you," he said at last. "Now you must free me."

He led them to his room, lit the candelabra, and explained what must be done. To the butcher's daughter he handed his written instructions, detailing the depth of each incision and the precise order in which they should be made. Then he removed his clothing to display the bizarre template he had sketched on his body. The women were horror-struck, and the butcher's daughter flung down the papers as if they were vile to the touch. "I cannot do this," she said.

"You swore," he said to the schoolteacher.

She said nothing, fixing him with her black stare.

"Do you know who I am?" he asked them. "I am the Ripper! Red Jack!"

The name was lost on them.

"I have killed women!" He pointed to the papers. "Killed them exactly in the manner I have described. You must give me justice." They edged away. "You swore!" he said, hearing the petulance in his voice.

They turned to leave, and he clutched at the schoolteacher's arm. "You must help me!" he cried. Then he realized he was still holding the knife. He gripped it more tightly. In his mind's eye he saw her belly sliced open, its red fruit spilling into his hands. But before he could strike, she reached out and took the knife. Took it! Like a mother forbidding her child a dangerous toy. His fingers uncurled from the hilt as if she had worked magic to calm him.

He fell to his knees, eyes brimming with tears. "Please don't abandon me," he said. "Help me, please!"

The schoolteacher regarded him soberly, then looked to the butcher's daughter. "Can you manage it?" she said.

"No." The butcher's daughter lowered her eyes.

"Look at him!" The schoolteacher forced the butcher's daughter to face the old man. "This is what he most desires. What he needs. We owe him our lives, and if you can find the strength, you must do as he asks . . . no matter what toll it takes."

"I can't!" cried the butcher's daughter, turning away; but the schoolteacher grabbed her by the shoulders, shook her, and said, "Do you see his pain? He is an old, mad creature torn by some cancer, one you must excise. If we deny him release, we condemn him to far worse than the knife."

The butcher's daughter stared at him for long seconds, and her face hardened as if she had seen therein some blameful thing that would make the chore endurable. "I will try," she said.

Babbling his thanks, he lay down upon the bed and told them to fasten the straps about his wrists and ankles. As they cinched them tight, he felt a trickle of fear, but when they had done, he knew a vast sense of relief. "Stand at the foot of the bed," he said to the schoolteacher. "And you"—he nodded at one of the farm wives—"stand beside her"—he nodded at the butcher's daughter—"and hold the instructions in a good light." He positioned the two remaining women on the other side of the bed.

"Do you wish to pray?" asked the schoolteacher.

"No god would hear me," he said; then, to the butcher's daughter: "I will scream, but you must not heed the screams. They will be merely reflex and no signal of a desire for you to stop." He gazed up at the women ringing the bed. In the flickering light, with their widened eyes and parted lips, their secret flesh gleaming through rents in their dresses, they looked like the souls of his victims beatified by death, yet still sensual and sullied after years of phantom life. Eerie wings of shadow played across their faces. He drew a deep breath and said, "I am ready."

He had steeled himself against the pain of the first incision, but even so he was astonished by its enormity. His body arched, his tendons corded, and hearing himself scream, he was further astonished by how shrill and feminine was the voice of his agony. Pain became a medium in which he floated, too large to understand, and he knew only that it contained him, that he had gone forever inside it. Biting her lower lip, the butcher's daughter wielded the knife with marvelous deftness, and he could tell by the thin, hot trickles down his thighs that she was cutting neither too deeply nor too haphazardly, that he would survive the completion of the design. Once his eyes filmed over with redness and he nearly lost consciousness, but the schoolteacher's unswerving gaze centered him and pulled him back from oblivion. Reflected in her eyes, he saw the crimson light of his dying, and—growing numb to pain, able again to conjure whole thoughts—he reckoned her stern beauty a gift, a beacon set to guide him through the act.

Finally the butcher's daughter straightened and let fall the knife; on beholding the full extent of her work, she covered her face with her stained hands. Two of the farm wives had averted their eyes, and the other stood agape, her hand outstretched as if in a gesture of gentle restraint. Only the schoolteacher was unmoved. She engaged his stare unflinchingly, her voluptuous mouth firmed into cruel lines: the image of judgment.

"Lift my head!" he gasped as their lovely faces began to waver and recede, like angels passing ahead of him into the accumulating dark. It seemed he could feel an evacuation taking place, a lightening, a lessening of perverse cravings and violent urges, and he wanted to learn what manner of demon, what beast or wraith, was crawling from his guts. He needed sight of it to validate the fullness of his atonement, to assure himself that he would have a niche not in heaven, but in some less terrifying corner of hell, where he might from time to time secure a few moments' grace from the process of damnation. But his demon—if it existed—must have been invisible or otherwise proof against the eye, for when he looked down into the great cavity of the wound, he felt only the sick despair with which his every attempt to seek salvation had been met, and saw there nothing more demonic than his red, wrong life pulsing quick to the last.

GENTLEMEN OF THE SHADE

HARRY TURTLEDOVE

This is a field in which reputations can be made fast, and that is just what Harry Turtledove is currently engaged in doing. In only a handful of years (writing both as Turtledove—his real name—and as Eric G. Iverson), he has become a regular in Analog, Amazing, *and* Isaac Asimov's Science Fiction Magazine, *and has become particularly well known for his two popular series of magazine stories: the Basil Argyros Series, detailing the adventures of a "Magistrianoi" in an alternate Byzantine Empire, and the Sim series, which takes place in an alternate world in which European explorers find North America inhabited by homonids instead of Indians. Turtledove is just starting to make his work at longer lengths as well. A novel called* Agent of Byzantium *appeared in 1987, and a tetralogy called* The Videssos Cycle *will be appearing one volume at a time over the next few years. Upcoming is another novel,* A Different Flesh, *which will be part of the Isaac Asimov Presents line from Congdon & Weed. Turtledove has a Ph.D. in Byzantine history from UCLA and lives in Canoga Park, California, with his wife and two daughters.*

Here he shows us that real class will always tell, no matter what you do for a living . . .

HE GAS FLAME FLICKERED EVER SO SLIGHTLY WITHIN its mantle of pearly glass as Hignett opened the door to fetch us in our port and cheeses. All five of us were in the lounge that Friday evening, an uncommon occasion in the annals of the Sanguine Club and one calling therefore for a measure of celebration.

As always, the cheeses went untouched, yet Hignett will insist on setting them out; as well reverse the phases of the moon as expect an English butler to change his habits. But some of us quite favor port, I among them. I have great relish for the fashion in which it makes the sweet blood sing through my veins.

Bowing, Hignett took his leave of us. I poured the tawny port with my own hand. For the toast to the Queen, all of us raised glasses to our lips, as is but fitting. Then, following our custom, we toasted the Club as well, after which those of us who care not for such drink may in honour decline further potations.

Yet whether or not we imbibe, the company of our own kind is precious to us, for we are so few even in London, the greatest city the world has known. Thus it was that we all paid close heed when young Martin said, "I saw in the streets last evening one I reckon will make a sixth for us."

"By Jove!" said Titus. He is the eldest of us, and swears that oath from force of habit. "How long has it been since you joined us, Martin, dear chap?"

"Myself?" Martin rubbed the mustache he has lately taken to wearing. "I don't recollect, exactly. It has been some goodish while, hasn't it?"

"Six!" I exclaimed, suddenly finding new significance in the number. "Then two of us can be away and still leave enough for the whist table!"

Amid general laughter, Titus said, "Ah, Jerome, this unwholesome passion of yours for the pasteboards does truly make me believe you to have Hoyle's blood in you."

"Surely not, after so long," I replied, which occasioned

fresh mirth. I sighed in mock heaviness. "Ah, well, I fear me even so we may go without a game as often as not. But tell us more of the new one, Martin, so as to permit me to indulge my idle fancy."

"You will understand I was upon my own occasions, and so not able to make proper inquiry of him," Martin said, "but there can be little doubt of the matter. Like calls to like, as we all know."

"He noted you, then?" Arnold asked, rising to refill his goblet.

"Oh, I should certainly think so. He stared at me for some moments before proceeding down Buck's Row."

"Buck's Row, is it?" said Titus with an indulgent chuckle. "Out chasing the Whitechapel tarts again like a proper young buck, were you?"

"No denying they're easy to come by there," Martin returned. In that he was, of course, not in error. Every one of us in the Club, I am certain, has resorted to the unfortunate "widows" of Whitechapel to slake his lusts when no finer opportunity presented itself.

"A pity you did not think to have him join you, so you could hunt together," remarked Arnold.

The shadow of a frown passed across Martin's countenance. "I had intended to do so, my friend, yet something, I know not what, stayed my hand. I felt somehow the invitation would be unwelcome to him."

"Indeed!" Titus rumbled indignantly. "If this individual spurns the friendship of an honoured member" ("You honour me, sir," Martin broke in. "Not at all, sir," our Senior replied, before resuming) "—an honoured member, as I say, of what is, if I may speak with pardonable pride, perhaps the most exclusive club in London, why, then, this individual appears to me to be no gentleman, and hence not an appropriate aspirant for membership under any circumstances."

Norton had not taken part in the discussion up to this time, contenting himself with sitting close to the fire and observing the play of the flames. As always when he did choose to speak, his words were to the point. "Nonsense, Titus," he said. "Martin put it well: like calls to like."

"You think we shall encounter him again, then, under circumstances more apt to let us judge his suitability?"

"I am certain of it," Norton replied, nor in the end did he prove mistaken. I often think him the wisest of us all.

The evening passed most pleasantly, as do all our weekly gatherings. Our practice is to meet until midnight, and then to adjourn to seek the less cerebral pleasures the night affords. By the end of August, the sun does not rise until near on five of the clock, granting us no small opportunity to do as we would under the comforting blanket of night.

For myself, I chose to wander the Whitechapel streets. Past midnight, many London districts lie quiet as the crypt. Not so Whitechapel, which like so much of the dissolute East End of the city knows night from day no more than good from evil. The narrow winding streets that change their names from block to block have always their share of traffic. I sought them for that, as I have many times before, but also, I will not deny, in the hope that I might encounter the personage whom Martin had previously met.

That I did not: I supposed him to have sated himself the night before, and so to be in no need of such peregrinations now—here again, as events transpired, I was not in error. Yet this produced in me only the mildest of disappointments, for, as I have said, I had other reasons for frequenting Whitechapel.

The clocks were just striking two when I saw coming toward me down Flower and Dean Street a likely-seeming wench. Most of the few lamps such a small, dingy lane merits were long since out, so she was nearly upon me before realizing I was there. She drew back in startlement, fearing me to be some footpad, I suppose, but then decided from my topper, claw hammer, and brocaded waistcoat that such was not the case.

"Begging your pardon, guvnor," she said, smiling now, "but you did give me 'arf a turn, springing from the shadows like that." She smelled of sweat and beer and sausage.

I bowed myself nearly double, saying, "It is I who must apologize to you, my dear, for frightening so lovely a creature." This is the way the game is played, as it has been from time immemorial.

"Don't you talk posh, now!" she exclaimed. She put her hands on her hips, looking saucily up at me. She was a fine strong trollop, with rounded haunches and a shelflike bosom that she thrust my way; plainly she profited better from her whoring than so many of the skinny lasses who peddle their wares in Whitechapel. Her voice turned crooning, coaxing. "Only sixpence, sir, for a night to remember always."

Her price was more than that of the usual Whitechapel tart, but had I been other than I, I daresay I should have found her worth the difference. As it was, I hesitated only long enough to find the proper coin and press it into her hand. She peered down through the gloom to ensure I had not cheated her, then pressed her warm, firm body against me. "What's your pleasure, love?" she murmured in my ear, her tongue teasing at it between words.

When I led her to a wall in deeper darkness, she gave forth a tiny sigh, having, I suppose, hoped to ply her trade at leisure in a bed. She hiked up her skirts willingly enough, though, and her mouth sought mine with practiced art. Her hands fumbled at my trouser buttons while my teeth nibbled her lower lip.

" 'Ave a care," she protested, twisting in my embrace. "I'd not like for you to make me bleed." Then she sighed again, a sound different from that which had gone before, and stood stock-still and silent as one made into a statue. Her skirts rustled to the ground once more. I bent my head to her white neck and began to feed.

Were it not for the amnesic and anesthetic agent contained within our spittle, I do not doubt that humans should have hounded us vampires to extinction a long age ago. Even as is, they remain uneasily aware of our existence, though less so, I own to my relief, in this teeming faceless metropolis of London where no one knows his neighbor, or cares to, than in the hidden faraway mountains and valleys whence our kind sprang and where folk memory and fear run back forever.

When I had drunk my fill, I passed my tongue over the twin wounds I had inflicted, whereupon they healed with the same rapidity as does my own flesh. The whore stirred then. What her dreams were I cannot say, but they must have been sweet, for she declared roundly, "Ah, sir, you can do me anytime, and for free if you're hard up." Greater praise can no courtesan give. She seemed not a whit perplexed at the absence of any spunk of mine dribbling down her fat thighs; doubtless she had coupled with another recently enough beforehand so as not to miss it.

She entreated me for another round, but I begged off, claiming adequate satisfaction, as was indeed the case. We went our separate ways, each well pleased with the other.

She had just turned down Osborn Street toward Christ Church and I was about to enter on Commercial Street when I spied one who had to be he whom Martin had previously encountered. His jaunty stride and erect carriage proclaimed him recently to have fed, and fed well, yet somehow I found myself also aware of Titus' stricture, delivered sight unseen, that here was no gentleman. I could find no concrete reason for this feeling, and was about to dismiss it as a vagary of my own when he also became aware of my presence.

His grin was mirthless; while his cold eyes still held me, he slowly ran his tongue over his lips, as if to say he was fain to drink from my veins. My shock and revulsion must have appeared on my features, for his smile grew wider yet. He bowed so perfectly as to make perfection itself a mockery, then disappeared.

I know not how else to put it. We have of course sometimes the ability briefly to cloud a mere man's mind, but I had never thought, never imagined, the occasion could arise, to turn this power upon my own kind. Only the trick's surprise, I think, lent it success, but success, at least a moment's worth, it undeniably had. By the time I recovered full use of my faculties, the crass japester was gone.

I felt angry enough, nearly, to go in pursuit of him. Yet the sun would rise at five, and my flat lay in Knightsbridge, no small distance away. Reluctantly I turned my step toward the Aldgate Station. As well I did; the train was late, and morning twilight already painting the eastern horizon with bright colors when I neared home.

The streets by then were filling with the legions of wagons London requires for her daily revictualing. Newsboys stood on every corner hawking their papers. I spent a penny and tucked one away for later reading, time having grown too short for me to linger.

My landlady is of blessedly incurious nature; so long as the rent is promptly paid and an appearance of quiet and order maintained, she does not wonder at one of her tenants not being seen abroad by day. All of us of the Sanguine Club have digs of this sort: another advantage of the metropolis over lesser towns, where folk of such mercenary nature are in shorter supply. Did they not exist, we should be reduced to squalid, hole-and-corner ways of sheltering ourselves from the sun, ways in ill accord with the style we find pleasing once night has fallen.

The setting of the sun having restored my vitality, I glanced through the paper I had purchased before. The headlines screamed of a particularly grisly murder done in Whitechapel in the small hours of the previous day. Being who and what

I am, such does not easily oppress me, but the details of the killing—for the paper proved to be of the lurid sort—did give me more than momentary pause.

I soon dismissed them from my mind, however, being engaged in going up and down in the city in search of profit. Men with whom I deal often enough for them to note my nocturnal habit ask no more questions on it than my landlady, seeing therein the chance to mulct me by virtue of my ignorance of the day's events. At times they even find their efforts crowned with success, but, if I may be excused for boasting, infrequently. I have matched myself against their kind too long now to be easily fooled. Most of the losses I suffer are self-inflicted.

I could be, I suppose, a Croesus or a Crassus, but to what end? The truly rich become conspicuous by virtue of their wealth, and such prominence is a luxury, perhaps the one luxury, I cannot afford. My road to safety lies in drawing no attention to myself.

At the next gathering of the Club, that being Friday the seventh, only four of us were in attendance, Martin having business similar to mine or the need to replenish himself at one of the multitudinous springs of life abounding in the city. By then the Whitechapel slaying was old news, and occasioned no conversation: none of us, full of the wisdom long years bring though we are, yet saw the danger from that direction.

We spoke instead of the new one. I added the tale of my brief encounter to what Martin had related at the previous meeting, and found I was not the only one to have seen the subject of our discussion. So also had Titus and Norton, both in the East End.

Neither appeared to have formed a favorable impression of the newcomer, though as was true with Martin and myself, neither had passed words with him. Said our Senior, "He may eventually make a sixth for us, but no denying he has a rougher manner than do those whose good company now serves to warm these rooms.''

Norton being Norton was more plain-spoken: "Like calls to like, as I said last week, and I wish it didn't.''

Of those present, only Arnold had not yet set eyes on the stranger. He now inquired, ''What in him engenders such aversion?''

To that none of the rest of us could easily reply, the more so as nothing substantial backed our hesitancy. At last Norton said, ''He strikes me as the sort who, were he hungry, would feed on Hignett.''

''On our own servant? I should sooner starve!''

''So should we all, Arnold, so should we all,'' Titus said soothingly, for the shock in our fellow's voice was quite apparent. Norton and I gave our vigorous agreement. Some things are not done.

We decided it more prudent for a time not to seek out the newcomer. If he showed any greater desire than heretofore for intercourse with us, he could without undue difficulty contrive to make his path cross one of ours. If not, loss of his society seemed a hardship under which we could bear up with equanimity.

Having settled that, as we thought, to our satisfaction, we adjourned at my urging to cards, over which we passed the balance of the meeting, Arnold and I losing three guineas each to Norton and Titus. There are mortals, and not a few of them, too, with better card sense than Arnold's. Once we broke up, I hunted in Mayfair with good enough luck and went home.

Upon arising on the evening of the eighth, my first concern was a paper, as I had not purchased one before retiring and as the newsboys were crying them with a fervor warning that something of which I should not be ignorant had passed during the hours of my undead sleep. And so it proved: at some time near five-thirty that morning, about when I was going up to bed, the Whitechapel killer had slain again, as hideously as before, the very least of his atrocities being the cutting of his victim's throat so savagely as almost to sever her head from her body.

Every one of the entrepreneurs with whom I had dealings that evening mentioned of his own accord the murders. An awful fascination lay beneath their ejaculations of horror. I had no trouble understanding it. A madman who kills once is frightening, but one who kills twice is far more than doubly so, the second slaying portending who could say how many more to come.

This fear, not surprisingly, was all the worse among those whom the killer had marked for his own. Few tarts walked the streets the next several evenings, and such as did often went in pairs to afford themselves at least what pitiful protection numbers gave. I had a lean time of it, in which misfortune, as I learned at the next meeting of the Club, I was not alone. For the first time in some years we had not even a quorum, three of our five being absent, presumably in search of sustenance. The gathering, if by that name I may dignify an occasion on which only Arnold and I were present, was the worst I remember, and ended early, something hitherto unknown among us. Nor did my business affairs prosper in the nights that followed. I have seldom known a less pleasant period.

At length, despite our resolutions to the contrary, I felt compelled to visit the new one's haunts in the East End. I suspect I was not the first of us driven to this step. Twelve hundred drabs walk the brown-fogged streets of Whitechapel and hunger works in them no less than in me. Fear of the knife that may come fades to insignificance when set against the rumbling of the belly that never leaves.

I did, then, eventually manage to gain nourishment, but only after a search long and inconvenient enough to leave me rather out of temper despite my success. Not to put too fine a point on it, I should have chosen another time to make the acquaintance of our new associate. The choice proved not to be mine to make: he hailed me as I was walking toward St. Mary's Station on Whitechapel Road.

Something in the timbre of his voice spoke to me, though I had not heard it before; even as I turned, I knew who he was. He hurried up to me and pumped my hand. We must have made a curious spectacle for those few people who witnessed our meeting. Like all members of the Sanguine Club, I dress to suit my station; moreover, formal attire with its stark blacks and whites fits my temperament, and I have been told I look well in it.

My new companion, by contrast, wore a checked suit of cut and pattern so bold as to be more appropriate for the comedic stage than even for a swell in the streets of Whitechapel. Of his tie I will say nothing save that it made the suit stodgy by comparison. His boots were patent leather, with mother-of-pearl buttons. On his head perched a low-crowned billycock hat as evil as the rest of the rig.

I should not have been surprised to smell on his breath whiskey or more likely gin (the favored drink of Whitechapel), but must confess I could not. "Hullo, old chap," he said, his accent exactly what one would expect from the clothes. "You must be one o' the toffs I've seen now and again. The name's Jack, and pleased t'meetcher."

Still a bit nonplussed at such heartiness where before he had kept his distance, I rather coolly returned my own name.

"Pleased t'meetcher," he said again, as if once were not enough. Now that he stood close by, I had the chance to study him as well as his villainous apparel. He was taller than I, and of younger seeming (though among us, I know, this is of smaller signification than is the case with mankind), with greasy side-whiskers like, you will, I pray, forgive me, a pimp's.

Having repeated himself, he appeared to have shot his conversational bolt, for he stood waiting for some response from me. "Do you by any chance play whist?" I asked, lacking any better query.

He threw back his head and laughed loud and long. "Blimey no! I've better games than that, yes, I do." He set a finger by the side of his nose and winked with a familiarity he had no right to assume.

"What are those?" I asked, seeing he expected it of me. In truth I heartily wished the encounter over. We have long made it a point to extend the privileges of the Sanguine Club to all our kind in London, but despite ancient custom I would willingly have withheld them from this Jack, whose vulgarity disbarred him from our class.

This thought must have been plain on my face, as he laughed again, less good-naturedly than before. "Why, the ones wiv dear Polly and Annie, of course."

The names so casually thrown out meant nothing to me for a moment. When at last I did make the connection, I took it to be no more than a joke of taste similar to the rest of his character. "Claiming yourself to be Leather Apron, sir, or whatever else the papers call that killer, is not a jest I find amusing."

"Jest, is it?" He drew himself up, offended. "I wasn't jokin' wiv yer. Ah, Annie, she screamed once, but too late." His eyes lit in, I saw, fond memory. That more than anything else convinced me he spoke the truth.

I wished then the sign of the cross were not forbidden me. Still, I fought to believe my fear mistaken. "You cannot mean that!" I cried. "The second killing, by all accounts, was done in broad daylight, and—" I forbore to state the obvious, that none of our kind may endure Old Sol.

"Oh, it were daylight, right enough, but the sun not up. I 'ad just time to do 'er proper, then nip into my 'idin' place on 'Anbury Street. The bobbies, they never found me," he added with scorn in his voice for the earnest bumbling humans who sought to track him down. However much I found the thought repugnant, I saw he was truly one of us in that regard, his sentiment differing perhaps in degree from our own, but not in kind.

I observed also once more the relish with which he spoke of the slaying, and of his hair's breadth escape from destruction; the sun is a greater danger to us than ever Scotland Yard will be. Still, we of the Sanguine Club have survived and flourished as we have in London by making it a point never to draw undue attention to ourselves. Being helpless by day, we are hideously vulnerable should a determined foe ever set himself against us. I said as much to Jack, most vehemently, but saw at once I was making no impression upon him.

"Aren't you the toffee-nose, now?" he said. "I didn't ask for no by-your-leave, and don't need one of you neither. You bloody fool, they're only people, and I'll deal wiv 'em just as I please. Go on; tell me you've not done likewise."

To that I could make no immediate reply. I have fed innumerable times from victims who would have recoiled in loathing if in full possession of their senses. Nor am I myself guiltless of killing; few if any among us are. Yet with reflection, I think I may say I have never slain wantonly, for the mere sport of it. Such conduct must inevitably debase one who employs it, and in Jack I could not help noting the signs of that defilement. Having no regard for our prey, he would end with the same emptiness of feeling for his fellows (a process I thought already well advanced, by his rudeness toward me) and for himself. I have seen madness so many times among humanity, but never thought to detect it in one of my own.

All this is, however, as I say, the product of rumination considerably after the fact. At the time I found myself so very unnerved as to fasten on utter trivialities as if they were matters of great importance. I asked, then, not that he give over his cruel sport, but rather where he had come by the apron that gave him his sobriquet in the newspapers.

He answered without hesitation: "Across the lane from where I done the first one is Barber's 'Orse Slaughter 'Ouse— I filched it there, just after I 'ad me bit o' fun. Fancy the fools thinkin' it 'as some meanin' to it." His amusement confirmed what I had already marked, that he found humanity so far beneath him that it existed but for him to do with as he wished.

Again I expostulated with him, urging him to turn from his course of slaughter.

"Bloody 'ell I will," he said coarsely. " 'Oo's to make me, any road? The bobbies? They couldn't catch the clap in an 'orehouse."

At last I began to grow angry myself, rather than merely appalled, as I had been up to this point. "If necessary, my associates and I shall prevent you. If you risked only yourself, I would say do as you please and be damned to you, but your antics threaten all of us, for if by some mischance you are captured you expose not only your own presence alone but reveal that of your kind as well. We have been comfortable in London for long years; we should not care to have to abandon it suddenly and seek to establish ourselves elsewhere on short notice."

I saw this warning, at least, hit home; Jack might despise mankind, but could scarcely ignore the threat his fellows might pose to him. "You've no right to order me about so," he said sullenly, his hands curling into fists.

"The right to self-preservation knows no bounds," I returned. "I am willing to let what is done stay done; we can hardly, after all, yield you up to the constabulary without showing them also what you are. But no more, Jack. You will have us to reckon with if you kill again."

For an instant I thought he would strike me, such was the ferocity suffusing his features. I resolved he should not relish the attempt if he made it. But he did not, contenting himself instead with turning his back and wordlessly taking himself off in the rudest fashion imaginable. I went on to the station and then to my home.

At the next meeting of the Club I discovered I had not been the only one to encounter Jack and hear his boasts. So also had Norton, who, I was pleased to learn, had issued a warning near identical to mine. If anything, he was blunter than I; Norton, as I have remarked, is not given to mincing words. Our actions met with general approbation, Martin being the only one to express serious doubt at what we had done.

As the youngest among us (he has been a member fewer than two hundred years), Martin is, I fear, rather more given than the rest of us to the passing intellectual vagaries of the mass of humanity, and has lately been much taken with what they call psychology. He said, "Perhaps this Jack acts as he does because he has been deprived of the company of his own kind, and would be more inclined toward sociability in the world as a whole if his day-to-day existence included commerce with his fellows."

This I found a dubious proposition; having met Jack, I thought him vicious to the core, and not likely to reform merely through the good agency of the Club. Norton confined himself to a single snort, but the fashion in which he rolled his eyes was eloquent.

Titus and Arnold, however, with less acquaintance of the newcomer, eagerly embraced Martin's suggestion: the prospect of adding another to our number after so long proved irresistible to them. After some little argument, I began to wonder myself if I had not been too harsh a judge of Jack, nor did Norton protest overmuch when it was decided to tender an invitation to the Club to him for the following Friday, that is to say, September 21.

I remarked on Norton's reticence as we broke up, and was

rewarded with a glance redolent of cynicism. "They'll find out," he said, and vanished into the night.

It was with a curious mingling of anticipation and apprehension that I entered the premises of the Club for our next meeting, an exhilarating mixture whose like I had not known since the bad nights when all of mankind was superstitious enough to make our kind's every moment a risk. Titus was there before me, his features communicating the same excitement I felt. At that I knew surprise afresh, Titus having seen everything under the moon: he derives his name, after all, from that of the Roman Augustus in whose reign he was born.

"He'll come?" I asked.

"So Martin tells me," replied our Senior.

And indeed it was not long before good Hignett appeared at the lounge door to announce the arrival of our guest. Being the perfect butler, he breathes discretion no less than air, yet I could hear no hint of approval in his voice. What tone he would have taken had he known more of Jack I can only imagine. Even now his eyes lingered doubtfully on the newcomer, whose garments were as gaudy as the ones in which I had first met him, and which contrasted most strikingly with the sober raiment we of the Sanguine Club commonly prefer.

After leaving the port and the inevitable cheeses, Hignett retired to grant us our privacy. We spent some moments taking the measure of the stranger in our midst, while he, I should think, likewise took ours. He addressed us first, commenting, "What a grim lot o' sobersides y'are."

"Your plumage is certainly brighter than ours, but beneath it we are much the same," said Martin, still proceeding along the lines he had proposed at our previous session.

"Oh, balls," Jack retorted; he still behaved as though on the Whitechapel streets rather than in one of the more refined salons London boasts. Norton and I exchanged a knowing glance. Titus's raised eyebrow was eloquent as a shout.

Martin, however, remained as yet undaunted, and persisted. "But we are. The differences between you and us, whatever they may be, are as nothing when set against the difference between the lot of us on the one hand and those among whom we dwell on the other."

"Why ape 'em so, then?" asked Jack, dismissing with a sneer our crystal and plate, the overstuffed chintz chairs in which we sat, our carpets and our paneling of carved and polished oak, our gaslight which yields an illumination more like that of the sun (or so say those who can compare the two) than any previously created, in short all the amenities that serve to make the Sanguine Club the pleasant haven it is. His scorn at last made an impression upon Martin, who knew not how to respond.

"Why should we not like our comforts, sir?" Titus, as I have found in the course of our long association, is rarely at a loss for words. He continued, "We have been in straitened circumstances more often than I can readily recall, and more than I for one should care to. Let me remind you, no one compels you to share in this against your will."

"An' a good thing, too—I'd sooner drink 'orseblood from Barber's, I would, than 'ave a digs like this. Blimey, next 'ou'll be joinin' the bleedin' Church o' Hengland."

"Now, you see here!" Arnold, half rising from his seat in anger, spoke for all of us. Horseblood is an expedient upon which I have not had to rely since the Black Death five and a half centuries ago made men both too scarce and too wary to be easily approached. To this night I shudder at the memory of the taste, as do all those of us whom mischance has at one time or another reduced to such a condition. I almost found it more shocking than the notion of entering a church.

Yet Jack displayed no remorse, which indeed, as should by this point be apparent, played no part in his character. "Get on!" he said. "You might as well be people your own selves, way you carry on. They ain't but our cattle, and don't deserve better from us than they give their beasts.''

"If what Jerome and Norton say is true, you give them rather worse than that," Titus said.

Jack's grin was broad and insolent. "Aye, well, we all have our sports. I like making 'em die monstrous well, better even than feeding off 'em." He drew from his belt a long, sharp blade, and lowered his eyes so as to study the gleaming, polished steel. Did our reflections appear in mirrors, I should have said he was examining his features in the metal.

"But you must not act so," Titus expostulated. "Can you not grasp that your slayings endanger not you alone, but all of us? These cattle, as you call them, possess the ability to turn upon their predators and hunt us down. They must never suspect themselves to be prey."

"You talk like this bugger 'ere," said Jack, pointing in my direction. "I were wrong, guvnor, an' own it—it's not men the lot of yez are, it's so many old women. An' as for Jack 'e does as 'e pleases, an' any as don't fancy it can go play wiv themselves for all 'e cares."

"Several of us have warned you of the consequences of persisting in your folly," said Titus in a voice like that of a magistrate passing sentence. "Let me say now that you may consider that warning to come from the Sanguine Club as a whole." He looked from one of us to the next, and found no dissent to his pronouncement, even Martin by this time having come to realize our now unwelcome guest was not amenable to reason.

"You try an' stop me and I'll give yer what Polly an' Annie got," Jack shouted in a perfect transport of fury, brandishing the weapon with which he had so brutally let the life from the two poor jades. We were, however, many to his one, and not taken by surprise, as had been his earlier victims. Norton seized the knife that sat among Hignett's despised cheeses. Of the rest of us, several, myself included carried blades of our own, if not so vicious as the one Jack bore.

Balked thus even of exciting terror, Jack foully cursed us all and fled, being as I suspected too great a coward to attack without the odds all in his favor. He slammed the door behind him with violence to make my goblet of port spring from the end table where it sat and hurtle to the floor. Only the quickness of my kind enabled me to save it from destruction and thus earn, though he would never know of it, Hignett's gratitude.

The crash of Jack's abrupt departure was still ringing in our ears when Martin most graciously turned to me and said, "You and Norton appear to have been correct; my apologies for doubting you."

"We shall have to watch him," Titus said. "I fear he will pay no heed to our advice."

"We shall also have to keep watch over Whitechapel as a whole, from this time forth," Arnold said. "He may escape our close surveillance, yet be deterred by observing our vigilance throughout the district."

"We must make the attempt, commencing this very night," Titus declared, again with no disagreement. "That is a mad dog loose on the streets of London, mad enough, I fear, to enable even the purblind humans of Scotland Yard eventually to run him to earth."

"Which will also endanger us," I put in.

"Precisely. If, however, we prevent his slaying again, the hue and cry over this pair of killings will eventually subside. As we are all gathered here now, let us agree on a rotation that will permit at least three of us to patrol Whitechapel each night, and" (here Titus paused to utter a heavy sigh) "all of us on our Fridays. Preservation here must take precedence over sociability."

There was some grumbling at that, but not much; one thing our years confer upon us is the ability to see what must be done. Hignett evinced signs of distress when we summoned him from downstairs long before the time usually appointed, and more upon being informed we should not be reconvening for some indefinite period. Not even the promise that his pay would continue heartened him to any great extent; he had grown used to our routine, and naturally resented any interruption thereof.

Having decided to patrol Whitechapel, we walked west along the south bank of the Thames past the Tower of London and the edifice that will upon its completion be known as Tower Bridge (and which would, were it complete, offer us more convenient access to the northeastern part of the city) to London Bridge and up Gracechurch Street to Fenchurch Street and Whitechapel. Once there, we separated, to cover as much ground as our limited numbers permitted.

Jack had by this time gained a considerable lead upon us; we could but hope he had worked no mischief while we were coming to the decision to pursue him. Yet the evening was still relatively young, and both of his previous atrocities had taken place in later hours, the second, indeed, so close to sunrise as to seem to me to display a heedlessness to danger suitable only to a lunatic among our kind.

I prowled the lanes near Spitalfields Market, not far from where I had first set eyes on Jack after supping off the young whore, as I have already related. I should not have been sorry to encounter her there once more, since, I having in a manner of speaking made her acquaintance, she would not have shied from my approach, as did several ladies of the evening, and I was, if not yet ravenous, certainly growing hungry.

It must have been nearing three when I spied Jack in Crispin Street, between Dorset and Brushfield. He was coming up behind a tart when I hailed him; they both turned at the sound of my voice. ''Ah, cousin Jack, how are you these days?'' I called cheerily, pretending not to have noticed her.

In my most solicitous tones, I continued, "The pox troubles you less, I hope?"

"Piss off!" he snarled. The damage to his cause, however, was done, for the whore speedily took herself elsewhere. He shook his fist at me. "You'll pay for that, you bugger. I only wanted a bit of a taste from 'er."

"Starve," I said coldly, our enmity now open and undisguised. Would that keeping him from his prey might have forced that fate upon him, but we do not perish so easily. Still, the hunger for blood grows maddening if long unsatisfied, and I relished his suffering hardly less than he the twin effusions of gore he had visited upon Whitechapel.

He slunk away; I followed. He employed all the tricks of our kind to throw me off his track. Against a man they would surely have succeeded, but I was ready for them and am in any case no man, though here I found myself in the curious position of defending humanity against one of my own kind gone bad. He failed to escape me. Indeed, as we went down Old Montague Street, Arnold fell in with us, and he and I kept double vigil on Jack till the sky began to grow light.

The weakness of our plan then became apparent, for Arnold and I found ourselves compelled to withdraw to our own domiciles in distant parts of the city to protect ourselves against the imminent arrival of the sun, while Jack, who evidently quartered himself in or around Whitechapel, was at liberty to carry out whatever outrage he could for some little while before finding it necessary to seek shelter. A similar period of freedom would be his after every sunset, as we would have to travel from our homes to the East End and locate him afresh each night. Still, I reflected as I made my way out of the slums toward Knightsbridge, in the early hours of the evening people swarmed through the streets, making the privacy and leisure required for his crimes hard to come by. That gave me some small reason, at least, to hope.

Yet I must confess that when nightfall restored my vitality

I departed from my flat with no little trepidation, fearing to learn of some new work of savagery during the morning twilight. The newsboys were, however, using other means to cry their papers, and I knew relief. The concern of getting through each night was new to me, and rather invigorating; it granted a bit of insight into the sort of existence mortals must lead.

That was not one of the nights assigned me to wander through Whitechapel, nor on my next couple of tours of duty there did I set eyes on Jack. The newspapers made no mention of fresh East End horrors, though, so the Sanguine Club was performing as well as Titus could have wished.

Our Senior, however, greeted me with grim and troubled countenance as we met on Fenchurch Street early in the evening of the twenty-seventh, preparatory to our nightly Whitechapel vigil. He drew from his waistcoat pocket an envelope which he handed to me, saying, ''The scoundrel grows bolder. I stopped by the Club briefly last night to pay my respects to Hignett, and found this waiting there for us.''

The note the envelope contained was to the point, viz.: ''You dear chums aren't as clever as you think. You won't catch me if I don't want that. And remember, you haven't found my address but I know where this place is. Give me trouble—not that you really can—and the peelers will too. Yours, Jack the Ripper.''

''The Ripper, is it?'' My lip curled at the grotesque sobriquet, and also at the tone of the missive and the threat it conveyed. Titus perfectly understood my sentiments, having no doubt worked through during the course of the previous night the thought process now mine.

He said, ''We shall have to consider harsher measures than we have contemplated up to this point. A menace to the Club is a menace to us all, individually and severally.''

I nodded my affirmation. Yet to suppress Jack we had first to find him, which proved less easy than heretofore. Norton and I met in the morning twilight of the twenty-eighth at St. Mary's Station without either one of us having set eyes on him. "He may be staying indoors for fear of our response to his note," I said, having first informed Norton of the letter's contents.

My dour colleague gloomily shook his head. "He fears nothing, else he would not have sent it in the first place." Norton paused a while in silent thought—an attitude not uncommon for him—then continued, "My guess is, he is merely deciding what new atrocity to use to draw attention to himself." I did not care for this conclusion but, in view of Jack's already demonstrated proclivities, hardly found myself in position to contradict it.

The night of Saturday the twenty-ninth found me in the East End once more. (Most of the previous evening, when under happier circumstances the Sanguine Club would have met, I spent beating down a most stubborn man over the price of a shipment of copra, and was sorely tempted to sink teeth into his neck afterward to repay him for the vexation and delay he caused me. I had not thought the transaction would take above an hour, but the wretch haggled over every farthing. Titus was most annoyed at my failure to join our prearranged patrol, and I counted myself fortunate that Jack again absented himself as well.)

Early in the evening I thought I caught a glimpse of Jack by London Hospital as I was coming down Mount Street from Whitechapel Road, but though I hastened up and down Oxford Street, and Philpot and Turner, which come off it, I could find no certain trace. Full of vague misgivings, I turned west onto Commercial Road.

Midnight passed, and I still had no idea of my quarry's whereabouts. I had by chance encountered both Martin and Arnold, who shared the night with me, and learned of their equal lack of success. "I believe he must still be in hiding, in the hope of waiting us out," Arnold said.

"If so," I replied, "he is in yet another way a fool. Does he think us mortals, to grow bored after days or weeks and let down our guard?"

The answer to that soon became all too clear. At one or so a great outcry arose on Berner Street, scarcely a hundred yards from Commercial Road where I had walked but a short while before. As soon as I heard the words, "Leather Apron," I knew Jack had chosen to strike again in defiance not only of human London, but also of the Sanguine Club, and also that he had succeeded in evading us, making good on the boast in his recent note.

I started to rush toward the scene of this latest crime, but had not gone far before I checked myself. I reasoned that Jack could scarcely strike again in or close to such a crowd, if that was his desire, but would take advantage of the confusion this murder engendered, and of the natural attraction of the constabulary in the area to it. It was Norton's reasoning that made me fear Jack would not be content with a single slaying, but might well look at once for a fresh victim to demonstrate everyone's impotence in bringing him to heel.

My instinct proved accurate, yet I was unfortunately not in time to prevent Jack's next gruesome crime; that I came so close only served to frustrate me more thoroughly than abject failure would have done. I was trotting west along Fenchurch Street, about to turn down Jewry Street to go past the Fenchurch Street Station, as the hour approached twenty of two, when suddenly there came to my nose the thick rich scent of fresh-spilled blood.

Being who I am, that savory aroma draws me irresistibly, and I am by the nature of things more sensitive to it by far than is a man, or even, I should say, a hound. Normally it would have afforded me only pleasure, but now I felt alarm as well, realizing that the large quantity required to produce the odour in the intensity with which I perceived it could only have come from the sort of wounds Jack delighted in producing.

I followed my nose up Mitre Street to a courtyard off the roadway, where, as I had feared, lay the body of a woman. Despite the sweetness of the blood tang rising intoxicatingly from her and from the great pool of gore on the paving, I confess with shame to drawing back in horror, for not only had she been eviscerated, but her throat was slashed, her features mutilated almost beyond identity, and part of one earlobe nearly severed from her head.

I had time to learn no more than that, or to feed past the briefest sampling, for I heard coming up Mitre Street the firm, uncompromising tread likely in that part of the city to belong only to a bobby, footpads and whores being more circumspect and men of good conscience in short supply. I withdrew from the court, thankful for my ability to move with silence and not to draw the eye if I did not wish it. Hardly a minute later, the blast of a police whistle pierced the night as humanity discovered this latest piece of Jack's handiwork.

As I once more walked Mitre Street, I discovered the odour of blood to be diminishing less rapidly than I should have expected. Looking down, I discovered a drop on the pavement. I stooped to taste of it; I could not doubt its likeness to that which I had just tried. A bit farther along the street was another. I hastened down this track, hoping also to discover one of my fellows to lend me assistance in overpowering Jack. As if in answer to my wish, up came Martin from a side street, drawn like me by the pull of blood. Together we hastened after Jack.

The drippings from his hand or knife soon ceased, yet the alluring aroma still lingering in the air granted us a trail we could have followed blindfold. I wondered how Jack hoped to escape pursuers of our sort, but soon found he knew the

East End better than did Martin or myself, and was able to turn that knowledge to his advantage.

On Goldstone Street, in front of the common stairs leading to numbers 108 and 119, stood a public sink. It was full of water, water which my nose at once informed me to be tinctured with blood: here Jack had paused to rinse from his hands the traces of his recent deeds. Martin found also a bit of bloodstained black cloth similar to that of a garment the latest unfortunate victim had worn.

Martin and I attempted to resume our pursuit, but unsuccessfully. In washing himself and, I believe, cleansing his blade on the rag from his victim's apron, he removed the lingering effluvium by which we had followed him, and forced us to rely once more on chance to bring us into proximity to him. Chance did not prove kind, even when we separated in order to cover more ground than would have been possible in tandem. Just as he had bragged, Jack had slain again (and slain twice!), eluding all attempts to stay his hand.

I was mightily cast down in spirit as I traveled homeward in the morning twilight. Nor did the clamour in the papers the next evening and during the nights that followed serve to assuage my anxiety. "Revolting and mysterious," "horrible," and "ghastly" were among the epithets they applied to the slayings; "Whitechapel Horrors," shrieked *The Illustrated Police News*. It was, however, a subhead in that same paper which truly gave me cause for concern: it spoke of the latest "Victim of the Whitechapel Fiend," a designation whose aptness I knew only too well, and one which I could only hope would not be literally construed.

Titus must also have seen that paper and drawn the same conclusion as had I. When I came to myself on the evening of the second I found in my postbox a note in his classic hand. "Henceforward we must all fare forth nightly," he wrote, "to prevent a repetition of these latest acts of depravity. We owe this duty not only to ourselves but to our flock, lest they suffer flaying rather than the judicious shearing we administer.''

Put so, the plea was impossible to withstand. All of us prowled the sordid streets of Whitechapel the next few nights, and encountered one another frequently. Of Jack, however, we found no sign; once more he chose to hide himself in his lair. Yet none of us, now, was reassured on that account, and when he did briefly sally forth he worked as much mischief, almost, without spilling a drop of blood as he had with his knife.

We failed to apprehend him in his forays, but their results soon became apparent. The lunatic, it transpired, had written not merely to us of the Sanguine Club, but also, in his arrogance, to the papers and the police! They, with wisdom unusual in humans, had suppressed this earliest missive, sent around the same time as the one to us, perhaps being uncertain as to its authenticity, but he sent another note after the horrid morning of the thirtieth, boasting of what he termed his ''double event.'' As the police had not yet announced the murders, not even men could doubt its genuineness.

Once more the press went mad, filled with lurid rehashes and speculations, some claiming the Ripper (for so he had styled himself also in his public letters) to be a man seeking to stamp out the vice of prostitution (presumably by extirpating those who plied the trade), others taking varying psychological tacks which intrigued our faddish Martin with their crackbrained ingenuity and left the rest of us sourly amused, still others alleging Jack a deranged *shochet*.

''Your work takes credit there, Jerome,'' Titus remarked to me as we chanced upon each other one evening not far from the place where Jack's last victim had died. ''A madman of a ritual slaughterer fits the particulars of the case well.''

''The Jews always make convenient scapegoats,'' I replied.

''How true,'' Titus murmured, and again I was reminded of the Caesar for whom he had been named.

Other, darker conjectures also saw print, though, ones I could not view without trepidation. For those Jack himself was responsible, due to a bit of sport he had had with the police after his second killing: after slaying Annie Chapman, he had torn two rings from her fingers and set them with some pennies and a pair of new-minted farthings at her feet. This he had wasted time to do, I thought with a *frisson* of dread, as the sun was on the point of rising and ending his amusements forever! It naturally brought to mind black, sorcerous rituals of unknown but doubtless vile purpose, and thoughts of sorcery and of matters in any way unmundane were the last things I desired to see inculcated in the folk of London.

I did my best to set aside my worries. For all Jack's dark skill, murder no longer came easy in Whitechapel. Aside from us of the Sanguine Club, the constabulary increased their patrols in the district, while a certain Mr. George Lusk established a Whitechapel Vigilance Committee whose membership also went back and forth through the area.

Neither constables nor Committee members, I noted during my own wanderings, refrained from enjoying the occasional streetwalker, but the women themselves took more pleasure from those encounters than they should have from a meeting with Jack. The same also holds true for the whores we of the Club engaged. As I have previously noted, the wounds we inflicted healed quickly, the only aftereffect being perhaps a temporary lassitude if one of us fed overdeep because of unusual hunger.

Jack may have taken a hiatus from slaughter, but remained intent on baiting those who so futilely pursued him. October was not yet a week old when he showed his scorn for the Whitechapel Vigilance Committee by means of a macabre gift to its founder: he sent Mr. Lusk, in a neatly wrapped cardboard box, half the kidney of his latest victim, with a mocking note enclosed.

"He will be the ruin of us all," I said gloomily to Martin

upon the papers' disclosure of this new ghoulery. "Would you had never set eyes on him."

"With that I cannot take issue," replied my colleague, "yet this lapse, however revolting humans may find it—and I confess," he added with a fastidious shudder, "to being repelled myself at the prospect of eating a piece from a woman's kidney—however revolting, I say, it does not add to any fears directed toward us, for none of our kind would do such a deed, not even Jack, I should say."

"One never knows, where he is concerned," I said, and Martin's only response was a glum nod.

As October wore on, more letters came to the papers and police, each one setting off a new flurry of alarm. Some of these may indeed have been written by Jack; others, I suspect, sprang from the pens of men hardly less mad than he, and fully as eager for notoriety. Men have so little time to make their mark that such activity is in them at least faintly comprehensible, but for Jack, with years beyond limit before him, I offer no explanation past simple viciousness. In his instance, that was more than adequate.

Still, despite sensations such as I have described, the month progressed with fresh slayings. Once I dashed a couple of furlongs down Old Montague Street into Bakers Row, drawn as on the night of the "double event" by the scent of blood, but discovered only a stabbed man of middle years with his pockets turned out: a matter in which the police were certain to take an interest, but not one, I was confident, that concerned me.

My business affairs suffered somewhat during this period, but not to any irreparable extent; at bottom they were sound, and not liable to sudden disruption. I thought I would miss the weekly society of the Sanguine Club to a greater degree than proved to be the case. The truth is that we of the Club saw more of one another in our wanderings through Whitechapel than we had at our meetings.

October passed into November, the nights growing longer but less pleasant, being now more liable to chill and to wet fogs. These minor discomforts aside, winter has long been our kind's favorite season of the year, especially since coming to this northern latitude where around the December solstice we may be out and about seventeen hours of the twenty-four, and fifteen even in the midautumnal times to which my narrative now has come. Yet with Jack abroad, the increased period of darkness seemed this year no boon, as I was only capable of viewing it as a greater opportunity for him to sally forth on another murderous jaunt.

On the evening of the eighth, then, I reached Whitechapel before the clocks struck five. By the time they chimed for six, I had already encountered in the narrow, gridless streets Norton, Arnold, and Titus. We tipped our hats to each other as we passed. I saw Martin for the first time that night shortly after six. We were complete, as ready as we might be should the chance present itself.

The night gave at the outset no reason for supposing it likely to prove different from any other. I wandered up toward Bishopsgate Station, having learned that the whore who was Jack's latest victim had been released from there not long before her last, fatal encounter. "Ta-ta, old cock, I'll see you again soon!" she had called drunkenly to the gaoler, a prediction that, unfortunately for her, was quickly proven inaccurate.

Wherever Jack prowled, if indeed he was on the loose at that hour, I found no trace of him. Seeing that so many prostitutes passed through the station, I made it a point to hang about: Jack might well seek in those environs an easy target. Whores, indeed, I saw in plenty thereabouts but, as I say, no sign of Jack. When the clocks struck twelve, ushering in a new day, I gave it up and went to hunt elsewhere.

Walking down Dorset Street near twelve-thirty, I heard a woman with an Irish lilt to her voice singing in a room on one of the courtyards there. I paused a moment to listen; such good spirits are rarely to be found in bleak Whitechapel. Then I continued east, going by London Hospital and the Jews' Cemetery, my route in fact passing the opening of Buck's Row onto Brady Street, close to the site of Jack's first killing.

That area proved no more profitable than had been my prior wanderings of the night: no more profitable, indeed, than the whole of the past five weeks' exertions on the part of the Sanguine Club. True, I am more patient than a man, but even patience such as mine desires some reward, some hint that it is not employed in pursuit of an *ignis fatuus*. As I lacked any such hint, it was with downcast mien that I turned my steps westward once more.

My nostrils began to twitch before I had any conscious awareness of the fact. I was on Wentworth Street between Commercial and Goulston, when at last my head went suddenly up and back, as I have seen a wolf's do on taking a scent. Blood was in the air, and had been for some little while. Yet like a wolf, which scents its prey at a distance, I had to cast about to find the precise source of the odour.

In this search I was unsurprised to encounter Norton, who was coming down Flower and Dean Street toward Commercial. His features bore the same abstracted set I knew appeared on my own. "Odd sort of trail," he said without preamble, as is his way.

"It is." I tested the air again. "The source lies north of us still, I am certain, but more precise than that I cannot be. It is not like the spoor I took from Jack's last pleasantry."

"A *man* could have followed that, from what you said of it," Norton snorted, and though he spoke in jest I do not think him far wrong. He continued, "Let us hunt together."

I agreed at once, and we proceeded side by side up Commercial (which in the dark and quiet of the small hours belied its name) to a corner where, after deliberation, we turned west onto White Street rather than east onto Fashion. Well that we did, for hurrying in our direction from Bishopsgate came Titus. His strides, unlike our own, had nothing of doubt to them. Being our Senior, he is well supplied with hunters' lore.

"Well met!" he cried on recognizing us. "This way! We have him, unless I miss my guess!" Practically at a run, he swept us north along Crispin Street to Dorset, the very ground I had patrolled not long before.

The scent trail was stronger now, but remained curiously diffuse. "How do you track with such confidence?" I asked.

"That is much blood, escaping but slowly to the outside air," Titus replied. "I think our quarry has taken his atrocious games indoors, in hopes of thwarting us. He has been—you will, I pray, pardon the play on words—too sanguine in his expectations."

His proposed explanation so precisely fit the spoor we were following that I felt within me the surge of hope I recently described as lacking. A much-battered signboard on the street read "Miller's Court"; it was the one from which I had earlier heard song. A light burned in number 13. From that door, too, welled the scent which had drawn us; now that we had come so close, its source could not be mistaken.

As our tacit leader, Titus grasped the doorknob, Norton and I standing behind him to prevent Jack from bursting past and fleeing. Jack evidently had anticipated no disturbances, for the door was not locked. On Titus' opening it, the blood smell came forth as strongly as ever I have known it, save only on the battlefield.

The scene I glimpsed over Titus' shoulder will remain with me through all my nights. Our approach had taken Jack unawares, he being so intent on his pleasure that the world beyond the squalid little room was of no import to him. A picture nail in his hand, he stared at us in frozen shock from his place by the wall.

Both my eyes and nose, though, drew me away from him to the naked flesh on the bed. I use that appellative in preference to "body," for with leisure at his disposal Jack gained the opportunity to exercise his twisted ingenuity to a far greater and more grisly extent than he had on the streets of Whitechapel. The chamber more closely resembled an abattoir than a lodging.

By her skin, such of it as was not covered with blood, the poor wretch whose abode this presumably had been was younger than the previous objects of his depravity. Whether she was fairer as well I cannot say, as he had repeatedly slashed her face and sliced off her nose and ears to set them on a bedside table. The only relief for her was that she could have known none of this, as her throat was cut; it gaped at me like a second, speechless mouth.

Nor had Jack contented himself with working those mutilations. Along with her nose and ears on that table lay her heart, her kidneys (another offering, perhaps, to George Lusk), and her breasts, his gory handprints upon them. He had gutted her as well.

Not even those horrors were the worst. When we interrupted him, Jack was engaged in hanging bits of the woman's flesh on the wall, as if they were engravings the effect of whose placement he was examining.

The tableau that held us all could not have endured above a few seconds. Jack first recovered the power of motion, and waved in invitation to the blood-drenched sheets. "Plenty there for the lot o' yez," said he, grinning.

So overpowering was the aroma hanging in the room that my tongue of itself ran across my lips, and my head swung toward that scarlet swamp. So, I saw, did Titus'. Norton, fortunately, was made of sterner stuff, and was not taken by surprise when Jack tried to spring past us. Their grapple recalled to our senses the Senior and myself, and I seized Jack's wrist as he tried to take hold of his already much-used knife, which, had it found one of our hearts, could have slain us as certainly as if we were mortal.

In point of fact, Jack did score Norton's arm with the blade before Titus rapped his hand against the floor and sent the weapon skittering away. Norton cursed at the pain of the cut, but only for a moment, as it healed almost at once. The struggle, being three against one, did not last long after that. Having subdued Jack and stuffed a silk handkerchief in his mouth to prevent his crying out, we dragged him from the dingy cubicle out into Mitre Court.

Just then, likely drawn by the fresh outpouring of the blood scent from the newly opened door of number 13, into the court rushed Martin, and the stout fellow had with him a length of rope for use in the event that Jack should be captured, an eventuality for which he, perhaps inspirited by youthful optimism, was more prepared than were we his elders. We quickly trussed our quarry and hauled him away to obtain more certain privacy in which to decide his fate.

We were coming out of Mitre Court onto Dorset Street when I exclaimed, "The knife!"

"What of it? Let it be," Titus said. Norton grunted in agreement.

On most occasions, the one's experience and the other's sagacity would have been plenty to persuade me to accede to their wishes, but everything connected with Jack, it seemed, was out of the ordinary. I shook my head, saying, "That blade has fleshed itself in you, Norton. Men in laboratories are all too clever these days; who knows what examination of the weapon might reveal to them?"

Martin supported me, and my other two colleagues saw the force of my concern: why stop Jack if we gave ourselves away through the mute testimony of the knife? I dashed into number 13 once more, found the blade, and tucked it into the waistband of my trousers. I found coherent thought in that blood-charged atmosphere next to impossible, but realized it would be wise to screen the horrid and pathetic corpse on the bed from view. Accordingly, I shut the door and dragged up a heavy bureau to secure it, only then realizing I was still inside myself.

Feeling very much a fool, I climbed to the top of the chest of drawers, broke out a pane of glass, and awkwardly scrambled down outside. I hurried to catch up to my comrades, who were conveying Jack along Commercial Street. As he was most unwilling, this would have attracted undue attention from passersby, save that we do not draw men's notice unless we wish it.

We turned off onto Thrawl Street and there, in the shelter of a recessed doorway, held a low-voiced discussion. "He must perish; there is no help for it," Martin declared. To this statement none of us dissented. Jack glared mute hatred at us all.

"How, then?" said I. I drew forth Jack's own knife. "Shall I drive this into his breast now, and put an end to it?" The plan had a certain poetic aptness I found appealing.

Martin nodded approvingly, but Titus, to my surprise, demurred. He explained, "Had I not observed this latest outrage, Jerome, I should have no complaint. But having seen it, my judgment is that the punishment you propose errs in the excessive mercy it would grant."

"What, then?" I cast about for some harsher fate, but arrived only at the obvious. "Shall we leave him, bound, for the sun to find?" I have never seen the effects of sunlight on the flesh of our kind, of course; had I been in position to observe it, I should not now be able to report our conversation. Yet instinctively we know what we risk. It is said to be spectacularly pyrotechnic.

Jack's writhings increased when he heard my proposal. He had dared the sun to kill for his own satisfaction, but showed no relish for facing it without choice. Our Senior coldly stared down at him. "You deserve worse."

"So he does," Norton said. "However much the sun may pain him, it will only be for a little while. He ought instead to have eternity to contemplate his failings."

"How do you propose to accomplish that?" asked Martin. "Shall we store him away in the basement of the Sanguine Club? Watch him as we will, one day he may effect his escape and endanger us all over again."

"I'd not intended that," replied Norton.

"What, then?" Titus and I demanded together.

"I say we take him to the Tower Bridge now building, and brick him up in one of its towers. Then every evening he will awaken to feel the traffic pounding close by, yet be powerless to free himself from his little crypt. He will get rather hungry, by and by."

The image evoked by Norton's words made the small hairs prickle up at the nape of my neck. To remain forever in a tiny, black, airless chamber, to feel hunger grow and grow and grow, and not to be able even to perish . . . were he not already mad, such incarceration would speedily render Jack so.

"Ah, most fitting, indeed," Titus said in admiration. Martin and I both nodded; Norton's ingenuity was a fitting match for that which Jack had displayed. Lifting the miscreant, we set off for the bridge, which lay only a couple of furlongs to the south of us. Our untiring strength served us well as we bore Jack thither. His constant struggles might have exhausted a party of men, or at the least persuaded them to knock him over the head.

Although we draw little notice from mortals when we do not wish it, the night watchman spied our approach and turned his lantern on us. " 'Ere, wot's this?" he cried, seeing Jack's helpless figure in our arms.

We were, however, prepared for this eventuality. Martin sprang forward, to sink his teeth into the watchman's hand. At once the fellow, under the influence of our comrade's spittle, grew calm and quiet. Titus, Norton, and I pressed on to the unfinished span of the bridge and into its northern tower, Martin staying behind to murmur in the watchman's ear and guide his dreams so he should remember nothing out of the ordinary.

The other three of us fell to with a will. The bricklayers had left the tools of their trade when they went home for the night. "Do you suppose they will notice their labour is farther advanced than when they left it?" I asked, slapping a brick into place.

Titus brought up a fresh hod of mortar. "I doubt they will complain of it, if they should," he said, with the slightest hint of chuckle in his voice, and I could not argue with him in that.

Norton paused for a moment from his labour to stir Jack with his foot. "Nor will this one complain, not while the sun's in the sky. And by the time it sets tomorrow, they'll have built well past him." He was right in that; already the tower stood higher than the nearby Tower of London, from which the bridge derived its name. Norton continued, "After that, he can shout as he pleases, and think on what he's done to merit his new home."

Soon, what with our unstinting effort, Jack's receptacle was ready to receive him. We lifted him high, set him inside, and bricked him up. I thought I heard him whimpering behind his gag, but he made no sound loud enough to penetrate the masonry surrounding him. That was also massive enough to keep him from forcing his way out, bound as he was, while the cement joining the bricks remained unset. He would eventually succeed in scraping through the ropes that held him, but not before daybreak . . . and the next night would be too late.

"There," said Norton when we had finished, "is a job well done."

Nodding, we went back to reclaim Martin, who left off

charming the night watchman. That worthy stirred as he came back to himself. He touched his grizzled forelock. "You chaps 'ave a good evenin', now," he said respectfully as we walked past him. We were none too soon, for the sky had already begun to pale toward morning.

"Well, my comrades, I shall see you this evening," Titus said as we prepared to go our separate ways. I am embarrassed to confess that I, along with the rest of us, stared at him in some puzzlement over the import of his words. Had we not just vanquished Jack? Seeing our confusion, he burst out laughing: "Have you forgotten, friends, it will be Club night?" As a matter of fact, we had, having given the day of the week but scant regard in our unceasing pursuit of Jack.

On boarding my train at St. Mary's Station, I found myself in the same car as Arnold, who as luck would have it had spent the entire night in the eastern portion of Whitechapel, which accounted for his nose failing to catch the spoor that led the rest of us to Jack; he had entered the train at Whitechapel Station, half a mile east of my own boarding point. He fortunately took in good part my heckling over his absence.

After so long away, our return to the comforts of the Sanguine Club proved doubly delightful, and stout Hignett's welcome flattering in the extreme. Almost I found myself tempted to try eating cheese for his sake, no matter that it should render me ill, our kind not being suited to digest it.

Despite the desire I and, no doubt, the rest of us felt to take the opportunity to begin to return to order our interrupted affairs, all of us were present that evening to symbolize the formal renewal of our weekly fellowship. We drank to the Queen and to the Club, and also all drank again to an unusual third toast proposed by Titus: "To the eternal restoration of our security!" Indeed, at that we raised a cheer and flung our goblets into the fireplace. A merrier gathering of the Club I cannot recall.

And yet now, in afterthought, I wonder how permanent our settlement of these past months' horrors shall prove. I was not yet in London when Peter of Colechurch erected Old London Bridge seven centuries ago, but recall well the massive reconstruction undertaken by Charles Lebelye, as that was but a hundred thirty years gone by; and there are still men alive who remember the building of New London Bridge in its place by John Rennie, Jr., from the plans of his father six decades ago.

Who can be certain Tower Bridge will not someday have a similar fate befall it, and release Jack once more into the world, madder and more savage even than before? As the French say, *"Tout passe, tout casse, tout lasse"*—everything passes, everything perishes, everything palls. We of the Sanguine Club, to whom the proverb does not apply, know its truth better than most. Still, even by our standards, Jack surely will not find freedom soon. If and when he should, that, I daresay, will be time for our concern.

DEAD AIR

Gregory Nicoll

Did you ever turn on the radio late at night and get nothing but dead air? Did you ever think that there may be a reason why they call it that . . . ?

Gregory Nicoll is a popular new writer whose work has appeared in Omni, The Twilight Zone Magazine, Pulpsmith, Southline, *and elsewhere. He contributed to* The Penguin Encyclopedia of Horror and the Supernatural, *and has adapted stories by Poe and Lovecraft for the Atlanta Radio Theatre. He drinks Heileman's Old Style and plays Telsco Del Rey guitars. He can also write some very scary stuff.*

SCREAMIN' LORD SUTCH—Lord David Sutch was the Fifth Earl of Harrow, a full-blooded member of English nobility who also hacked out a reputation for himself as a hardworking rock 'n' roll revivalist during the 1960s. As Screamin' Lord Sutch and the Savages, Dave and his band were noted for spectacular and macabre shows which frequently started with Dave emerging from a coffin carried onstage by hooded monks. His recorded output is unfortunately rather spotty. Dave's best-known American release is Hands of Jack the Ripper *(Cotillion Records, SD 9049, out of print), a live LP featuring members of the Who and the Jimi Hendrix Experience. A standout tune is the title track, over nine minutes' worth of delirious sonic mayhem which some listeners claim can . . .*

—Carlton and Wood, Weird Heroes of Rock 'n' Roll, *vol. 2 (DB Press, 1989)*

THE BROADCASTING STUDIO, LONG AND NARROW LIKE a coffin, had soundproofed walls unbroken by windows. A torn and wrinkled poster for Mötley Crüe's *Shout at the Devil* was their only decoration.

This place is a tomb, Mary thought. *Feels like I'm buried alive.*

She struck a match and touched it to the end of a Marlboro, her fifth since she'd started her air shift. She was alone in the radio station, a squat building full of tiny, cramped offices and racks of old record albums in tattered covers.

Jimmy Page's fuzzy guitar screeched from enormous speakers overhead as Led Zeppelin's *Presence* rotated on the left-hand turntable at an even, digitally verified 33⅓ rpm. The room was damp and cold and smelled like cigarette smoke. It was almost a quarter to four in the morning, and Mary grimaced at the thought of staying there another three hours.

Maybe Neil will come in early and I can sweet-talk him into running the end of the shift for me . . .

She shivered, drawing the collar of her silver W-H-O-R satin jacket up around her neck. *Good ole Bert,* she thought sarcastically. *He spends a fucking fortune on these jackets for us, but won't shell out a nickel for some heat.*

As the Led Zep tune faded out, Mary quickly pulled on her headphones, potted up her mike, and set her hands on the knobs which controlled the right-hand turntable. The next song was Pink Floyd's "Another Brick in the Wall, Part 2," and fading it on cue was tricky enough when you did it as a straight segue—much more so when you had an ID and a back-sell to lead in with.

"That was the sizzling sound of Led Zeppelin," she announced as the song ended. "Comin' up we've got a lot more rock 'n' roll for you here on the Home of Rock—W-H-O-R, Atlanta, Georgia! A little later we'll be rollin' up to four A.M. with a Blue Oyster Cult superset, but right now let's each mix up a batch of mortar and pour ourselves a tall glass of Amontillado. It's time to help the Floyd put another brick . . . in the wall.''

She punched the button, starting the right-hand turntable spinning, while at the same time she rotated the potentiometer all the way to maximum. The sound of the song rolled in precisely on cue.

And the two lights on the telephone began to flash like the eyes of a winking demon.

Here come the geeks, she thought, picking up her cigarette for one quick drag before she replaced the Led Zep LP in its sleeve. *Well, they can wait a minute.*

She took her time filing the album in the rack and had yet another hit on the Marlboro before she answered the first of the incoming calls.

"W-H-O-R! You're rockin' with Mary. It's your dime."

There was a snicker on the line. *"Yeah,"* said a deep male voice, blurry with alcohol.

"Somethin' I can do for you?" she asked, trying hard to feign enthusiasm. *God, does anyone listen to this station when they're sober?*

"Y-you're new there, ain't you?"

"*Um-hmm.* I started the night before last."

"I th-thought so." There was a long pause. "What do you look like?"

"What do you *think* I look like?"

"I bet you're one *fine*-lookin' lady. One *damn* fine-lookin' fox."

Mary shook her head. "You just might be right. Now, is there a song I can play for you?"

The drunk chuckled quietly. "What are you wearing right now?"

"My W-H-O-R jacket."

"And *nothing* else?"

She punched the button for the other extension, cutting off

the first caller. "You're rockin' with Mary on W-H-O-R, the Home of Rock 'n' Roll. What can I do for you?"

"Uh, er . . ."

"Go ahead. Spit it out."

There was a moment's pause. Then a timid male voice, possibly belonging to a teenage boy, asked, "You takin' requests for that superset?"

"Sure," she said. "What d'you want to hear?"

"How about 'Smoke on the Water'?"

She rolled her eyes. " 'Fraid not. Like I said, the superset is by the Blue Oyster Cult. I'll play you something—but it's gotta be a BOC cut or nothin' at all."

"Oh."

Mary cued up "Don't Fear the Reaper" as she waited for the kid to make a choice.

"I know," he said at last. "How about 'Veteran of the Psychic Wars'?"

"That's a good one," she admitted, flipping through a nearby stack of Blue Oyster Cult albums to verify that she had a copy of *Fire of Unknown Origin*. "I'll be glad to play it for you. You're gonna be listenin', aren't you?"

"Damn straight," he answered, his tone firm with conviction. "Say, what's with your voice, Mary?"

"My voice?"

"It sounds real different tonight."

She smiled. "I'm new here. My name's Mary Clark. You must be thinking of Mary Kelly, the D.J. who used to have this shift."

"Ohhhhhh . . . Gee . . . Uh, what happened to her?"

Mary shrugged. "Beats me. The station owner didn't say."

"Well, I hope you stay around awhile. I like your voice."

"*Thanks*. And thanks for calling in. G'bye."

"G'bye."

The huge Favag dial clock overhead displayed the time as just shy of a quarter to four.

Mary sighed. *Another three hours, give or take a few minutes, depending on when Neil gets here. How the hell am I gonna make it?*

She massaged the back of her eyelids.

It had been a long night—and a rough one—starting at seven when Bert had picked her up at her apartment. His ancient Austin-Healey was probably a lot of fun in warm weather, she conceded, but in the autumn chill it had been intensely uncomfortable to ride in the ragtop. The wind sliced her cheeks, and the broken springs in the passenger seat impaled her fanny. Add to that a broken heater and you had the recipe for a ruined evening.

Of course, she thought, *Bert did his best to warm me up.*

She smirked. *Well, at least he tried . . . Poor guy. He probably couldn't get it up if he tied it to a toothbrush.*

Mary lifted the cigarette to her lips and drew deeply from it.

The first phone line lit up again.

"W-H-O-R, Rock 'n' Roll Radio. What's your pleasure?"

Silence came over the line.

"Hello? Anybody there?"

"I-I'll tell you wh-what my pleasure is," sniggered the same drunken voice that had called before. "I'm comin' over to that there radio station to see you in a minute, and I'm gonna bring a jar full of wet, squishy—"

She slammed down the handset.

The second line lit up.

Sure hope this is somebody else . . .

She balanced her Marlboro on the edge of the ashtray and lifted the handset to her ear again. "Hello. You're rockin' with Mary on W-H-O-R, the Home of—"

"Mary?"

Though it had said but a single word, the voice was instantly familiar. There was no mistaking that rich, deep English accent with its heavy suggestion of Big Ben,

Buckingham Palace, the Tower of London, Prince Charles and Lady Diana, and all other veddy, veddy British things.

It was Bert.

"Oh," she said, her voice stopping cold in genuine surprise. "Ah, I didn't expect to hear from you so soon, Bert."

"Look, Mary," he said briskly, "about this evening. I'm frightfully embarrassed by what happened and I'd truly like to make it up to you—"

"Bert, there's really no call for that. I'm sorry for the way things worked out, and I want you to know that I'll never tell anyone wh—"

"Of course," he interrupted. "But I'd truly appreciate the opportunity to sit down with you and to explain why I couldn't—"

"Bert, I—"

"I don't want you to think it had anything to do with *you*; I mean with you *personally*."

"Bert—"

"It's just that I—"

"Bert!"

He finally stopped talking.

"Bert," she said, *"please!* I feel bad enough about the whole thing already. Yes, we can talk about it sometime, but not *now*—I'm in the middle of my air shift, fer Chrissakes. Maybe tomorrow afternoon we could meet for breakfast or—"

"No, Mary, no. Not tomorrow. Tonight."

"Tonight? Oh, Bert," she protested. "There's just no way. I've been up for over fifteen hours straight now and I already feel like I've got rigor mortis. When my shift is over I'm going straight home and collapsing into bed. And let no man stand in my way!"

The line was silent for a few moments. Then Bert said one word. He said it quietly, but with an air of gentle persistence that she found irresistible. He said her name.

"Mary . . ."

She raised the cigarette back to her lips. "All right, Bert. You can come by here."

"Gracious thanks, Mary," he said. "You're sure it's all right?"

"Um-hmm." She rubbed her temples. "The question is, am *I* all right?"

"Whatever do you mean?"

She grimaced. "My head hurts like crazy. How many drinks did I have over at your place?"

"Only two, I'm afraid."

"Well, I'm sure feeling zonked. Maybe you oughta bring me some aspirin . . . and, uh, maybe a little hair o' the dog?"

"You've got it, Mary dear. I'll be there directly."

She hung up and swiveled back to face the console.

The speakers went dead. The song was over.

Damn, she thought, her eyes racing across the board in a panic, *I can't remember what I was going to do next!*

The station was broadcasting nothing but silence, the empty, lonely sound of dead air.

Tapping a button nearby, she activated her microphone. Using it without the headphones to monitor her own voice was difficult but it could be done. The trick was staying close to the mike and watching the needles on the VU meters to regulate her volume.

"Hope you en*joyed* the *Floyd*," she quipped, "and now, from that *rhyme*, we shift to the *time*!"

She glanced up at the Favag. It was almost four.

"Well, well, well, the clock here at H-O-R, the Home of Rock Radio, says it's time for the Blue Oyster Cult's superset . . . *after this*!"

She tapped the button which triggered the first audiocart deck. A waterbed store commercial—one of Neil's editing room wonders—squawked from the speakers.

Massaging her temples with one hand, Mary used the other to pluck a BOC album from the pile near her feet and slap it on the turntable. She cued it with the little monitor built into the console. When the waterbed spot ended a few seconds later, her headphones were on her head, her fingers poised on the controls of the turntable.

"Creeping up on four o'clock in the mornin' here at 1300 on your AM dial. You're rockin' with Mary Clark, and right now we're gonna kick off our salute to the Soft White Underbelly—*better known as the Blue Oyster Cult*—with their classic 'Don't Fear the Reaper'!"

She started the song, its haunting guitar lines chiming from the speakers at exactly the right instant.

The telephone extensions lit up again.

"Fuck you," she muttered. It was safe now—the mike was switched off. "Gimme a chance to pull my music."

She thumbed through the other BOC albums, selecting the ones she'd need. "Burnin' For You" would follow "Don't Fear the Reaper." That'd carry the set up to the station ID at the top of the hour. Then she'd come out of the ID with "Veteran of the Psychic Wars"—the trouble was that it was on *Fire of Unknown Origin*, the same album as "Burnin' For You," and they only had one copy of it.

"Well," she said, thinking aloud, "I guess I could always play it off the *Heavy Metal* soundtrack album . . . if we've got a copy of that around here."

She checked the card file. Sure enough, it was there—two of its songs, one by Don Felder and another by Sammy Hagar, were still in infrequent rotation on W-H-O-R's playlist.

Sliding back her chair to the record rack behind her, she located the *Heavy Metal* jacket and slipped the two discs out.

"Veteran of the Psychic Wars" was scratched. A deep gouge ran completely through all its grooves.

So much for that, she thought. *Unless . . . unless there's another copy back in the disc library . . .*

Glancing over at the turntables, she saw that "Don't Fear the Reaper" was less than a third of its way through. The flashing phone extensions, she decided, could wait—there was just enough time to go back to the stacks and hunt down another record with "Veteran of the Psychic Wars" on it. Mary stuck her cigarette back on the edge of the ashtray and got up, hastily making the circuit around the console to the door at the far end of the little room.

Her feet clicked on the slick floor of the hall outside. *Damnedest thing*, she thought. *Every other station I've worked at had carpeting at least a coupla inches thick. Guess Bert doesn't mind the background noises and echoes around here.*

Hell, who'd ever hear 'em? This is AM, after all. Ain't even stereo unless they've got one of those special receivers . . .

The record library was at the far end of the hall, two doors past Bert's office. Racks of albums ran from floor to ceiling, and piles of unsorted discs cluttered the tabletops around the room. A turntable set up in one corner bore a large sign, scrawled on a legal pad sheet, which warned, *"Do not use this record player. The needle is shot."*

Underneath, in a different handwriting, was scribbled, *"Then fix it, dammit!"*

Mary found a sealed copy of the *Heavy Metal* LP in the stacks. She tried to pick open the plastic, but her fingernails weren't up to the task.

Now, where the hell is that knife they keep around here?

It was on top of a carton containing twenty-five copies of the new Black Sabbath album. The knife had a slender, eight-inch blade with a slight curve at its tip. It was mounted in a stout wooden handle.

Mary slipped it into the edge of the record jacket, and the plastic seal melted away. She tossed the knife back on the carton of records.

Something creaked in a faraway room.

"Hello?" she called. "Is that you, Bert?"

There was no response.

Instinctively she picked the knife back up. Then, feeling foolish, she replaced it on the box.

"Neil?"

There was a thump, as of a door closing.

The front door—I wonder if I forgot to lock it . . . Gee . . . I was pretty upset when I came in . . . I might've forgot all about it . . .

Another sound, fainter, indistinct—footsteps on the hall floor?

Christ! It might be that drunk asshole who called in! He said something about "comin' over" here . . .

Her heart beat faster.

"Hello?" she called. "Who is it?"

Still nothing.

Carefully placing the *Heavy Metal* album on a nearby table, she stepped out into the hall. She did her best to mute the clicks of her boots against the hall floor as she headed up to the reception area at the front door of the station. The mysterious sounds seemed to have come from there.

When she turned the corner, she discovered that the room was empty. The secretary's desk, a few chairs, and the huge pair of monitor speakers were the only things in the wood-paneled room, aside from the usual assortment of gold records and autographed photos hung on the walls.

Right now the speakers were kicking out the final bars of "Don't Fear the Reaper." The song was only seconds from its finale.

"Dammit!" Mary grunted, her professional training overcoming her personal terror. *I better get my ass back in the booth*.

She didn't make it.

For almost ten full seconds the station broadcast nothing but dead air.

Fuckin' terrific. And with Bert probably on his way over here right now, no doubt listening to all this and wonderin' what the hell is goin' on.

Dammit dammit dammit.

He'll probably fire me the minute he walks in the door.

"Burnin' For You" was spinning on the right-hand turntable. To play "Veteran of the Psychic Wars" next, she'd have to go back to the record library and pick up that *Heavy Metal* LP she'd left there. For a few seconds she considered substituting another song.

No, she finally decided, *I promised that kid who called in that I'd play it next . . .*

Mary picked up her cigarette and discovered that it had burned out.

Jesus. This just ain't my night.

She went back into the hall and started toward the library.

Hey—what's that smell?

She stopped, turned around—and noticed a light under the closed door to Bert's office. There was a faint odor which seemed to be coming from that direction, the smell of something sour.

"Bert?"

She knocked tentatively on the door. "Bert, are you in there?"

Mary tried the handle. It turned, and the door swung open slowly to reveal—

Nothing. There's nobody here.

The sour smell was stronger inside the little room, but she couldn't see anything that might be causing it.

Bert probably left a milk carton in his wastebasket or something . . .

She reached over to the light switch on the far side of the desk, silently cursing whatever inconsiderate architect or electrician had positioned the switch so far from the door. To reach it she had to lean around the large bookcase which stood at a right angle to Bert's desk. In the process of bending her arm around the expanse of bookshelves she couldn't help but notice the long row of leather-bound volumes lining the space.

She chuckled.

Neil and some of the other W-H-O-R jocks had a running series of jokes about Bert's eclectic reading habits. Most of the staff, however, decided that Bert's book collection was just there for show—a form of wallpaper that must've cost nine dollars per square inch. The titles were certainly impressive enough—*Remembrance of Things Past, Best Plays of Shakespeare, Of Human Bondage, Gray's Anatomy, Beowulf, Discourses on Livy,* and *Farewell to Arms*—although they kept strange bedfellows. On the shelf below were *The Book of Rock Lists, Up and Down with the Rolling Stones,* and *Elvis and Me*.

She flicked the light switch. It snapped down with a resounding *click*.

Mary shook her head as she shut the office door behind her. *Coulda sworn that light was already off the last time I passed by it . . .*

A minute later with the album in her hands, she was heading back up the hall when another sound stopped her short.

Water?

It sounded like a tap running—possibly the one in the rest room up near the reception area.

"Bert? Neil? *Anybody?*"

She walked to the other end of the hall but couldn't hear the sound any better there. *"Hello?"*

"Burnin' For You" was blasting from the reception room speakers. The song was into its final chorus.

Mary spun in place and ran back into the booth. She was in her seat, headphones in hand, when it ended.

Dead air again, dammit all!

She opened the mike. "It's just past four o'clock and time

to rock—on the Home of Rock 'n' Roll Radio, W-H-O-R, Atlanta, 1300 AM!''

As she spoke, she slapped the *Heavy Metal* disc onto the left-hand turntable and lowered the tone arm to the appropriate groove. Then, holding her breath, she rotated the potentiometer up to full as the record began to spin.

Christ, I sure hope the needle fell in the right place!

The song began *in medias res*. Missing was a part of the opening instrumental, though not a significant portion.

Mary let her breath out slowly and switched off her mike. *Well*, she decided, *that coulda been a lot worse* . . .

She looked around at the stacks of records. What to play next? A superset was supposed to have at least four songs by the featured artist.

Noticing that the phone lines were both still flashing, she answered the first of the incoming calls.

"Home of Rock. What can I do you for?"

The voice was young, slightly nervous. "Uh, is this Mary?"

"You got me."

"Uh, can you, uh, can you play 'Godzilla' in this set?"

"Sure can."

"Er, *gee*, uh, you're really gonna play it?"

"Be happy to. It'll be right after 'Veteran of the Psychic Wars.' "

"Oh . . . okay. Great. Thanks!"

She switched over to the second call. "H-O-R, the Home of Rock 'n' Roll. What can I do you for?"

It was quiet on the line, although a faint hiss of presence indicated that someone was there.

"This is Mary. Hello? Is there somethin' I can play for you?"

"Yes," said a hesitant male voice. It sounded suspiciously like the drunk who'd called earlier, but she couldn't be sure. "I want you play . . . 'Hands of Jack the Ripper.' "

Mary rolled her eyes. "Is that by the Blue Oyster Cult?"

There was no answer, only the vague sound of presence.

"I'm not familiar with 'Hands of Jack the Ripper.' Is that one of those import-only tracks, or is it something off the first live album?"

The caller *laughed*. It was a low, murky, horrible laugh. Then he whispered, "I'm coming for you now, Mary Clark."

The line went dead.

"Fuck you, too," she huffed, dropping the handset back on its cradle.

She lit another Marlboro and practiced blowing smoke rings at the microphone. Several of them successfully encircled its knoblike end before disappearing in the air.

The phone flashed again.

"Mary on the Rock. What's your pleasure?"

There was a twitter on the line. An *English* twitter.

"Bert?"

"Yes, yes. It's me." He chuckled. "*Really,* my dear, surely you knew before you answered."

"And how could I do *that*?" she asked, slightly annoyed.

"Oh, come on, then. Surely you were having me on! You don't always answer the phone like that, do you?"

"Not always, Bert, but I do try to be personable."

"Very well, then. I'll speak no more of it. I just rang over to tell you I'm on my way."

"Check. I'll see you when you get here. And by the way— hurry it up, okay? Some weirdo keeps calling me up, and he's starting to give me the heebie-jeebies. Maybe you could answer the phone for me for a while."

"I'd be delighted to, Mary. Fret not. I'll be there . . . And one more thing—a small favor, if you will."

"You're the boss."

"Play me a song for the drive over. 'Roll Over, Beethoven' would be nice."

"Sorry, chief. That one's scratched. I was gonna use it in

the Beatles superset at two A.M. but there was an awful gash
right through the grooves. By the way, there seems to be a
lot of that going on around here. Some other song I could
swap for it, maybe?''

''Well—we do have another version of it.''

''That's news to me, Bert. Who's it by?''

''Screamin' Lord Sutch.''

''Never heard of the dude. Is he one of those Brit rockers
you've added to the playlist?''

''Well, actually I haven't added him yet, but the album's
on my desk. You can't miss it. It's called *Hands of Jack the
Ripper*. See you soon!''

She lowered the handset slowly to the cradle. *So that's
what that asshole caller was asking for! Some obscure
Limey wax which he must've heard Bert play on the oldies
show . . .*

She took a drag on her cigarette and checked the turntable.
''Veteran of the Psychic Wars'' had about another two minutes to play. Plenty of time to zip down to Bert's office and
pick up that LP he wanted her to use. She left the Marlboro
in the ashtray and made a beeline down the hall.

The light in the office was on again.

What the fuck is going on?

She turned around and yelled up the hall, ''Whoever's in
here and running around playing games better cut it out *right
now*! This shit isn't funny anymore!''

*Probably Neil. If I hadn't had so much booze tonight, I'd
probably think all this was funny as hell . . .*

Bert's desk was cluttered with promo albums, wadded
W-H-O-R T-shirts, Post-It notes of uncertain vintage, back-
stage passes from a half-dozen recent rock shows, and a Mc-
Donald's fish sandwich that looked at least three days old.

It was, without *any* further doubt, the source of the sour
smell in the office.

''Phew!'' Mary gasped. She felt an urge to puke and fought

hard to suppress it. *The mayo on that thing must be blue-green by now.*

She groaned as she discovered that *Hands of Jack the Ripper* by Lord Sutch and His Heavy Friends lay beneath the sandwich.

''The things I do for Rock 'n' Roll,'' Mary muttered as she cautiously separated the LP from its noxious burden.

Back in the control room the Blue Oyster Cult was still singing as Mary resumed her seat. She relit her Marlboro and stuck it in her lips as she examined *Hands of Jack the Ripper*.

It was a gatefold album, its rather innocuous front cover opening to reveal a photo of a man dressed as Jack the Ripper stalking a woman in Victorian garb. There were also several photos of Lord Sutch and various musicians rehearsing in a small studio. Mary recognized Keith Moon of the Who in one shot and smiled at his goofy expression.

Then she remembered that Moon was dead.

Helluva loss, she thought. *The Who sure wasn't the same without him . . .*

Another picture showed Noel Redding, the bass guitarist of the Jimi Hendrix Experience.

Hunh . . . Hendrix is dead, too . . .

She squinted at the liner notes, a column of ultra-fine print on the right edge of the gatefold. Skimming them quickly, she spotted a reference to John Bonham of Led Zeppelin.

Another dead musician . . .

Shuddering, she flipped the record jacket over to its back cover where the song list was printed. ''Roll Over, Beethoven'' was the second song on side one. *Beethoven,* she noted with amusement, *still another dead man—although he's a lot colder than the others.*

The last song on side one was the title track, ''Hands of Jack the Ripper.'' She raised an eyebrow as she noticed that it was 9¼ minutes long.

Must be a whole lotta rippin' goin' on in that one.

Beside the song list was a large photo of Lord Sutch. He was devastatingly handsome, his blond hair trimmed to a perfect Brian Jones pageboy, ruffled shirt hanging open to reveal a chest that would've made Tarzan proud.

He looked like he'd be a lot better in bed than Bert.

"Veteran of the Psychic Wars" neared its conclusion.

Mary dropped *Hands of Jack the Ripper* on the console and reached for the control board. It was too late. The record ended and her broadcast fell silent.

Dead air dead air dead air. All night long. Dead air dead air.

Tapping the controls, she set "Godzilla" spinning.

Dammit. This has been the worst shift of my life. What I need is some fresh air. Maybe during this song . . .

She was playing the long version of "Godzilla" off the live album. With a little fast work to get things in order, cueing up the next song and picking out a few more to follow it, she felt she could earn a brief fresh-air break. A stroll to her Mustang in the sandlot outside would be just what she needed. And if, while she was out that way, there happened to be any Jack Daniel's left in that bottle on the passenger seat . . .

Well, why not?

It'll be okay . . . I'll switch on the car's radio so I can keep tabs on the broadcast . . .

She cued up "Roll Over, Beethoven" from *Hands of Jack the Ripper* as the next song. With deep regret she eyed the running time of the title tune. "Beethoven" was only 2½ minutes long; the 9¼-minute "Hands of Jack the Ripper" would've made an even better cocktail song than "Godzilla."

But, she reminded herself, *I promised Bert I'd play "Roll Over, Beethoven" . . . and he* is *my boss.*

Unless he fires me over all that dead air that's been fouling up my shift.

Cigarette in hand, Mary walked out of the studio and around to the front door, which she propped open with a chair to expedite getting back inside when the time came.

I can just imagine fumbling for my key here in the dark while the record plays out on the turntable!

It was cold outside. She zipped her W-H-O-R jacket up as tightly as it would go.

Her Mustang was parked close to the door. She shook her head in disbelief when she saw the acute angle at which she had pulled it up to the edge of the lot.

Christ! Was I that blitzed when I got here tonight? How many gins did I drink over at Bert's?

She unlocked the door and flopped into the driver's seat. The car smelled of cigarettes and stale beer. The bottle of J.D.'s was right where she'd left it, and she was in luck— there was almost a pint left. She unscrewed the cap, letting its bracing aroma strike her nostrils with its delicious impact. The burning sweet scent easily cut through the car's odor. Mary raised the bottle to her lips and took a deep swallow.

It felt good going down. She could feel the warmth spreading through her chest.

She switched on the radio. "Godzilla" came blasting from the dashboard speakers. Mary turned it down so that it was just barely audible.

"Heavy metal," she muttered, "is *not* what my headache needs."

The radio station stood just a few hundred years off North Druid Hills Road, and from the front seat of her car she could watch the occasional early morning vehicle pass by. At this hour the traffic was mostly newspaper carriers and dairy trucks. Even in a sprawling metropolis like Atlanta, people had to sleep *sometime*.

To the southwest she could see the city itself, skyscrapers and industrial centers interlaced with ribbons of expressway. A million tiny lights gave proof through the night that her listening audience was still there. Her *target* audience. It was still too early in her tenure at W-H-O-R to know if she was hitting it.

Of course, she thought wryly as she leaned back on the car seat, *any of 'em with even a lick of sense should be asleep right now.*

She looked up at the starlit sky.

Rising high into the air behind the station was the massive antenna tower. It loomed like a gallows against the starry night.

Smiling contentedly, she took another hit on the Marlboro, another hit on the bottle. "Godzilla" thundered along on the radio, showing no sign of concluding. Mary let out a peaceful sigh.

She turned east. North Druid Hills Road rose slightly as it rolled that way. Beyond the curving hill, past the lone telephone booth at its crest, the road stretched toward the outlying communities of Toco Hills and Decatur. Life was a lot different in that direction. Not two miles from the chic uptown boutiques of Lenox Square and Phipps Plaza, some people still lived in clapboard shacks and plowed their fields with mule teams.

She put them quickly out of her head.

After all, she thought, *certainly none of those people listen to my show.*

"Godzilla" ended.

Dead air!

She dropped the bottle of Jack Daniel's and tossed the cigarette aside, scrambling out of the Mustang and sprinting for the station door. Reaching the doorway, she tripped over the chair she'd used to prop it open and fell forward, hitting her head on the bare concrete floor.

Mary got up slowly. Her hands were shaking.

Damn it all . . .

It took a great deal of effort and willpower—and she was

dangerously short of both—to crawl around to the studio and get back into her seat behind the console. Her head was spinning and her eyes found it hard to focus. Somehow the console—that standard radio station control board so familiar from fifteen years in the business—now looked as foreign as the dashboard of a 747.

She slipped on her headphones and stared idiotically at the buttons and dials and meters and switches in front of her.

Dead air dead air dead air. The story of my life!

She lit another cigarette, but with difficulty—her hands were still shaking. Mary inhaled. The tobacco restored her to her senses.

She opened her mike. "Here's a rare version of a rock 'n' roll classic for you on W-H-O-R, 1300 AM," she said. "This is 'Roll Over, Beethoven' as interpreted by Screamin' Lord Sutch!"

She tapped the button.

Nothing happened.

Dead air. Dammit. What the hell is—?

A voice shouted from the speakers. It was saying something about the next song.

Mary shook her head. The headphones fell off and clattered against the surface of the console, then plopped to the floor.

The voice coming from the speakers introduced the upcoming song as "Hands of Jack the Ripper."

What the hell?! Hey!!!

She swiveled in her chair and eyeballed the turntable. Reading a record's center paper as it rotates is a skill every D.J. has to master. A disc spinning at 45 rpm can be pretty tricky, but catching one at 33⅓ is not exceptionally difficult.

Sure enough, the needle was planted on the last track of side one, the title tune—"Hands of Jack the Ripper."

Satanic laughter and spookhouse horn effects boomed from the speakers.

Dammit. I know I cued up "Roll Over, Beethoven," not this song. That means . . . Well, I guess it means that . . .

That there's somebody else here in the station . . .

Its Halloween-show introduction over, the song began with a ¾-time rock 'n' roll beat. It was a standard chord progression, the classic "Woolly Bully" riff. The music proceeded for a few bars before a female chorus joined in, chanting every few seconds.

This is just too weird for me, Mary thought. She stood up and walked to the studio door. The hand which held her Marlboro was shaking so hard that she dropped the cigarette on the hall floor. She mashed it under her boot heel.

"Neil? *Bert?* Are you here, Bert?"

She stuck her head in his office and switched on the light. No—nothing there but his piles of junk, old records, and putrid fish sandwich.

Footsteps sounded in the distance—from the reception area?

"Bert?"

It had to be Bert. Neil certainly wouldn't be *this* early even if he had a whole stack of audiocarts to dub for tomorrow.

She moved in the direction of the sound, trying hard not to stumble. Her head hurt even worse than before.

The footsteps continued. It sounded like someone was strolling all around the secretary's desk by the front door.

Who is it? And where the hell are they walking to?

She remembered the drunk who'd called and said he'd come over.

Christ! I sure as hell hope it isn't him . . .

She reached the source—the small room at the front of the building.

There was nobody there. Just the reception desk and monitor speakers. Two *silent* monitor speakers.

The footsteps proceeded around the room.

Mary's brow creased. *Is . . . is that sound on the record?*

A woman's voice, her accent a thick cockney, called out a greeting.

That's what it is, Mary decided. *It's a sound effect on the album . . . and those footsteps must've been in stereo, moving from speaker to speaker. I think . . .*

The woman with the cockney accent started gasping, "No! No!"

I wonder where the hell Bert is, Mary thought. *He should've been here by now . . .*

The woman on the record was screaming. The vocalist began to sing about a London physician who chased and butchered the local ladies of the night.

I better have another drink . . .

The song continued, Lord Sutch assuming the part of Jack the Ripper as he called out for the blood of his next victim, a woman named *Mary . . .*

Better not go out to the car again, though. Guess I'll just wait on Bert.

She walked back to the booth.

Maybe he hasn't left his apartment yet . . .

She found Bert's home phone number on the list posted beside the console and picked up the phone to dial it.

The line was dead.

What the—?

Mary tapped the plungers a few times, but the phone could not be resuscitated. She slammed down the handset angrily.

Goddam Southern Bell piece a shit!

One of the extensions flashed. Somehow, some way, *a call was coming in.*

Mary lifted the receiver to her ear. "Hello?"

Nothing.

"This is W-H-O-R," she said firmly. "Is anybody there?"

There was a sound—a *laugh*. A laugh she'd heard before—low, murky, horrible.

Mary looked back at the base of the telephone. Her eyebrows rose as she saw that both of the lights for the two incoming extensions were unlit.

But there *was* a light—a tiny one at the opposite end of the phone's base.

The call was coming from *inside* the station.

She dropped the handset. *Oh. My. God.*

The doorknob at the far end of the broadcasting booth began to turn. It clicked softly as the bolt slid back, freeing the latch.

"Hands of Jack the Ripper" continued to boom from the booth's speakers. The gleeful, demented laughter of Screamin' Lord Sutch filled the air as the song rumbled along.

"Wh-who is it?" Mary shouted at the door.

It swung open—and Bert stepped in.

He was wearing an English-style overcoat and heavy boots. His expression was pleasant, though he seemed a bit puzzled.

"What's afoot here, Mary?" he asked. "The light was on down the hall."

"I went into your office to get that record," she said. Her heartbeat began to slow. "But I turned it off. I swear I did."

"Well, then, who—?"

She fumbled with the cigarette pack until she discovered that it was empty. She crumpled it and cast it aside.

"Bert, there's somebody *in* here. He called me on the internal line, and he's been playing tricks on me all night." She brushed her hair back and let out a long breath. "He even recued this record—I'd set it up to play 'Roll Over, Beethoven.'"

Bert glanced down at the spinning disc. "Looks like it's got a good five minutes to go. What say we look around together?"

She nodded. "Okay . . . Uh, did you bring me that drink?"

Bert smiled reassuringly. "I did indeed. But let's inspect the premises before we indulge."

"Okay. We can start with the record library."

There was nobody in the record library.

"Here," said Mary, picking up the knife the staff used to open new records. "You might need this."

He chuckled. *"O happy dagger . . ."*

She looked at him, her eyebrows knitted in confusion. "What?"

"Um?"

"What's that you were saying?"

He held the knife up. *"O happy dagger . . ."* He smiled. "It's from Shakespeare. *Romeo and Juliet.*" There was a faraway look in Bert's eyes.

Mary smiled. "I keep forgetting that you're such a big reader."

Bert stepped closer to her. "Yes," he said, "From *Human Bondage* to human anatomy."

He raised the knife in front of her face.

"Put that down, Bert. You're scaring me—and my nerves are frazzled enough as it is."

He smiled again and moved the knife slowly downward, toward her chest.

"Hey," she said, taking a step back. "Will you cut that out?"

"Precisely my intention—to cut something out, Mary Clark."

"What?"

Bert laughed. It was a horrible laugh—the laugh she'd heard on the phone.

All Mary could do was run.

She fled up the hall, her boot heels scraping the floor as she went. She ran through the reception area, the cries of Screamin' Lord Sutch from the speakers blending with the laughter of Bert right behind her.

At last reaching the door, she flung it open hard and stumbled awkwardly out toward her car, her right hand digging in her pocket for the ignition key.

But her pocket was gone. She was wearing a white dress.

Her car was gone, too.

And even North Druid Hills Road was gone. There was a fence or a wall or something where it should have been.

And the city lights of Atlanta were also missing, replaced by a solitary row of antique gaslights. They spread their amber glow across the cobblestones of the narrow street in which Mary stood.

Alone.

Bert's footsteps clattered on the cobblestones.

She turned to face him.

He was dressed in what looked like a Sherlock Holmes costume, complete with elegant cape and a deerstalker hat. There was a small black bag in his right hand.

And a knife in his left.

Eight inches of glistening steel, curving slightly at the tip.

She stumbled back against the fence. "No!" she screamed. *"No! No!"*

The blade entered her like a lover. Its thrusts were slow and careful at first, but they built to a climactic frenzy, plunging deeper and deeper . . .

On the left-hand turntable of the broadcast booth of W-H-O-R, "Hands of Jack the Ripper" rolled to its finale precisely 9¼ minutes after it had started. The record continued to spin, and with each rotation the tip of the diamond needle fell back into the closed groove at the edge of the center paper. To virtually everyone listening, the station seemed to be broadcasting nothing but dead air; but to a scattered few who, puzzled by the sudden silence, turned their stereos up louder, there was a faint but rhythmic scraping in the speakers.

Scritch . . .

Scritch . . .
Scritch . . .
Scritch . . .
Scritch . . .
The sound continued, straight on till morning.

STREET OF DREAMS

JOHN M. FORD

A hundred years have gone by since the Ripper murders, so you'd think that it would be much too late for any kind of vengeance. And so it would be . . . unless you're willing to take the chance of walking on the Street of Dreams . . .

One of the most respected writers of his generation, John M. Ford won the prestigious World Fantasy Award in 1984 for his brilliant alternate-world fantasy novel The Dragon Waiting. *His other books include the underrated novels* Web of Angels *and* The Princes of the Air, *and a Star Trek adventure,* The Final Reflection. *His most recent book is a comic Star Trek extravaganza,* How Much for Just the Planet? *which may well be the weirdest Star Trek novel ever written. Ford doesn't write a lot of short fiction (although he has sold a fair amount of what he does write to* Isaac Asimov's Science Fiction Magazine *over the years—under three different editors, so far—as well as* Omni, Liavek, Under the Wheel, *and elsewhere), but when he does produce a short piece, it is likely to be elegant, oblique, subtle, challenging, and strange—as is the story that follows.*

WHEN RAINES'S MOTHER DIED, THERE WAS NOTHing left but the house and the money. Raines could not live in the house, too empty of life, too full of memory. He had no notion of what to do with the money. But there was still the London matter in his mind; so he moved the few things he might wish to return to—the books, the butterflies—into the small cottage, and arranged for the solicitors, Cheyne and Cheyne, to let the house and provide Raines with funds as he desired them, through a City bank.

The younger Cheyne, upon hearing that Raines was bound for London with no supervision and a liberal fortune, wished him well in extraordinarily coarse terms and gave him several names and addresses related to the dissipation of wealth and health.

Raines thanked young Cheyne and told him that he meant to make use of this information, and this he did, after a fashion. For three years he followed one name to another, purchasing revelations and purchasing silences, and because he was a normal man in his late twenties, purchasing pleasures as well—though even that was in the pursuit of his final end, building trusts and opening doors that money could not.

By the end of the Year of Grace 1894, Raines had had at least a glimpse of every facet of London's night world.

He had been party to the blackmail of an M.P. and a Peer of the Realm who had enjoyed one another's company in a specially equipped room.

He had smoked opium.

He had been a hooded observer at a Black Mass.

And at last he was given an address that was sworn to be what he had come to London to find.

The cabman let Raines off at a dingy alley off Ropemaker Street near Moorgate: it was some distance from Whitechapel, but this hardly surprised Raines. He had learned well how devious are the lines of corruption.

There was a Black Smog in London; eight had been found dead, and more were likely to appear when the visibility improved. The cabdriver accepted his fare with thanks muttered through a mask and drove on, disappearing in a moment, leaving only the clatter of hooves on stone, which soon faded as well.

Something was wrong with the light. As Raines walked toward the streetlamp, he saw that one of its panes was broken, making the flame (already half-smothered by the bad air) waver in the faint draft. The effect was most theatrical, like a canvas heath in a tuppenny *Macbeth*.

Raines found the shop. Nothing was displayed in its windows; it showed no sign but a tarnished brass number 9 on the door. There was a small light from within. Raines tapped on the door with his stick, and after a moment there was a rattle and the door swung open.

The man in the door was old, and small, though not at all bent; he wore a red cap and a scarlet doctor's gown. "Good evening, sir," he said, as one man might greet another at their club. "I have been expecting you. Come in."

Raines went in. "I am—"

"Names are the lies of Adam," the old man said. "We do not use them here."

"There is a man I am seeking. May I name him?" Raines spoke patiently. The quest had occupied three years, the obsession three more than that. He was in no special hurry now.

"No need, sir. I know whom you want. I know all the names he has been called. I even know his true name."

"A great number of people have told me that they knew his name," Raines said, still patient.

"Yes," said the old man, "and some of them may have been right; but it is not really the name you want, is it, sir? It is the man that you desire. Am I not right?"

Raines looked around the shop. It was dark, but he could see oddly shaped furniture, iron candlesticks, African masks, and what seemed to be his own image in a small round glass— though when he looked again, there was nothing but a faint shimmer. He said, "Yes. The man. He is alive?"

"He still lives."

"And how much will his name cost me?"

The old man shook his head. "I do not trade in names, young sir. If you must have a name, call him Jack; it is what he calls himself now. But the name is given without charge. For my price, I offer you the man himself.''

A clock chimed six times. Raines knew it was not the hour, and certainly well after six. ''Very well. What is your price?''

''One pound ten, sir. And a few words from you.''

''*What?*'' Raines said, and reached for the revolver in his coat.

''Calm yourself, sir,'' said the old man. ''The words are all I really desire. The money is simply a necessary part of the bargain.'' He smiled; his teeth were very white and even.

''Thirty shillings?'' Raines said.

''It is the going price of betrayal, sir.''

Raines controlled himself. The man might be mad; he did not care. ''Very well. What are the 'words' you want from me?''

''The reason, sir.''

''Reason of what?''

''The reason you want the man, sir.''

Raines said flatly, ''To kill him.''

The old man laughed. ''I did not suppose you wanted to put him into Parliament, though I daresay he would do better there than some. But I did not ask your *end* in seeking him, sir. I asked your *reason*. What set you on the quest?''

''Good God, man, you have to ask that?''

''I do.''

Raines paused. His chest felt tight. In three years this was the first time anyone had asked him that particular question, and it made him falter. ''If I tell you, you will give him to me? My answer—whatever it is—will not cancel the bargain?''

''If the answer you give me is true, then you will have what you want. If you lie, the bargain is forfeit.''

''Very well. One of the—one of his victims—''

''No names, sir. Now go ahead; what was she to you?''

Again the tightness, the loss of resolve. "She was—she would have been my fiancée. We were childhood friends, until her family fell upon hard times. She went to London in search of—employment."

"Found it, too, I daresay."

"Sir!"

"Merely an observation. How did you discover her . . . position?"

"She sent me a letter . . . telling me that she had changed her name upon taking up her . . . trade."

"A very bold girl, " the old man said, then continued in a cool tone, "Did she do this in the hope that you would seek her out? Rescue her from durance vile?"

Raines said in a rush of breath, "I believe she wanted me to think well of her despite her state."

"But you did not . . . go to her, I mean."

"I lived with my mother at the time. It would have been . . . very complicated . . . It was not long after this that the Whitechapel murders began. And I never again heard from the young lady."

"Her assumed name was among those of the victims?"

"She didn't—her letter did not tell me what name she had chosen, only that she had changed it. But the assumption . . ."

"Made in good faith," the old man said. "Yes. Do go on."

"For some time after that, I thought that the police must surely bring the killer to justice. But they have not."

The old man nodded. He reached into a cabinet and produced a dusty book with a thick binding. He held it out to Raines. "Now, young sir, would you swear on the memory of your murdered lover that what you have told me is the true cause of your seeking this particular man, known as Jack?"

Raines felt anger flare inside him. He had not been angry in longer than he could remember; all that he had done and endured to this point had been cold with purpose. He determined that, if this lead proved false, he would return and give the old man a thorough beating.

He put his hand on the book, which was curiously warm. "I swear," he said.

"By the violated body that once you knew and possessed as your own?"

"*Yes!*"

The old man put the book away. "Thirty shillings to conclude the bargain."

Raines counted them out, coin by silver coin. "And now? You promised me the man—not the name, you said, the man himself, and living. Where is he? And I warn you, if you tell me that he is to be found upon Tigris and Euphrates, or living in the bosom of Christ, I shall—"

"He is in the cellar of the house beyond this one," the old man said. "You may enter through the back. I'll show you the door."

Raines felt a flash of rage—but controlled himself. This at least made sense, that the man should be hiding in a cellar, not seeing the light for months, perhaps years, even his madness not strong enough to break the prison of his infamy.

The old man led Raines through cluttered back rooms to the door, a small, plain door with a round top. "Here," he said. "I warn you, I shall lock it behind you."

"There is another way out?"

"That is the truth."

The old man opened the door. It was dark beyond. "There will be light," the old man said, and closed the door behind Raines.

As he passed through, Raines turned quickly, to thrust his stick into the doorway and prevent its closing.

But he found no door. There was no wall behind him; only a darkness, and a mist, dense and slow. The mist seemed to be red in colour, though that might have been only a trick of the absence of light.

Raines turned again. His eyes had begun to adapt to the dark, and he saw that he was in a broad alley, buildings rising out of sight on either side. At the far end a haze of light was visible.

Raines examined the buildings lining the alley. There seemed to be no openings at street level, though in the gloom above he thought he discerned dull windows. There was the explanation: the old man's door was in one of those walls, cleverly concealed. Doubtless he received stolen property through it.

His anger against the old man had passed. Raines was swindled again—but only of a few coins and a small secret. There was no ground for blackmail, even had Raines a position to ruin. As for his momentary humiliation—whatever his other sins, Raines had never been a proud man.

He began to walk toward the light at the end of the alley. It was very quiet for this time of night; distantly Raines heard wheels on pavement, and a faint high whistling sound. The smog seemed to have lightened, though the air was sulfurous as always.

Raines reached the street. It was unfamiliar, but he had long ago learned that the back streets of London were no more knowable than the features of the Deity. He was surprised to see that there were no streetlights, but an overall hazy glow. The buildings lining the street were all shuttered, and none showed a light or a sign.

There was a man a few yards away from Raines; he was trying to peer into one of the closed shops.

Raines held still. Perhaps the old man had not swindled him after all? He put a hand on his pistol and took a step.

The other man turned to face him. He was tall, clean-shaven, not foreign-looking though the cut of his clothes was definitely strange. "Hello, mister," he said. "Can I get a cab around here?"

An American, Raines thought. That did not make him innocent, though Raines was certain the man he sought was an Englishman, probably a Londoner. The casting of blame upon foreigners or Jews was typical mob foolishness, fanned by the newspapers.

But this man had no look of the murderer about him. "I doubt that a cab is to be had in this side street, sir. If you'll walk with me to someplace better lighted, I should be glad to share one with you."

"That'd be jus' fine. This way?"

"Are you lost, sir?"

The American looked wary. Then he laughed, said, "Yeah. I sure am. Thought I'd got to know this part of town, too."

"As did I," Raines said. "I believe we are in the same predicament."

They began walking. The American said, "How come you t'be down here? Lookin' for a little action?"

There was no mistaking the man's meaning; it was a brash but not unreasonable question. Raines said, "I was looking for a particular chap. I was told I might find him here."

The American stopped. "Yeah? Same here." He reached inside his jacket, showed a star-shaped badge. "Mind tellin' me who it is you're after?"

Surely, Raines thought, he would have known if another man—especially a foreigner—had been following the same trail he had. And if it were true, then the grinning old man had sent the American through his door only minutes before Raines had arrived at the shop—perhaps even while Raines was knocking at the door.

Was it possible that, after all his careful work, he had come full circle to the simplest of confidence games? Was East London full of amateur detectives who had paid the old fence thirty shillings and their secret dreams to be bustled through his back door?

Raines said, "I don't know his name. Not his true name, at any rate."

"Keep talkin'."

"I'll talk or not as it pleases me," Raines said crisply. "And I do not wish any further words with you, sir. Good night, sir." He turned to go.

"Wait a minute. I didn't mean to be rude. I'm sorry."

"Very well. My name is Raines."

"I'm Deke Hammond, Texas State Police." He hesitated. "I'm lookin' for the Moonlight Man."

It was a nickname Raines had not heard before; an invention of the American newspapers, he supposed. "I believe," he said slowly, "that we are looking for the same man. Was your informant an old man, in a cluttered shop, very hard to find?"

"That's the fella."

"Then I think that we have both been made proper fools of. I am seeking the same man as you—and clearly he is not here."

"What the hell do *you* know about him?"

"He killed someone I . . . cared for." It was no secret any longer.

"Izzat so." There was disbelief in the words, and contempt.

"Yes. Yes, Mr. Deke Hammond, it is so. I should like very much to ask what your interest in the case is, to bring you all the way to London; but I suspect that I know it only too well. You may want fame, or a reward—'bounty hunter,' is that the American term?—but I am after vengeance, blood vengeance, and—"

"What did you say?"

Raines's thought was interrupted. "I beg your pardon?"

"What did you say about goin' to London?"

"That is where you are, Mr. Hammond."

"Funny," Hammond said, "when I got up this mornin', it was New Orleans." There was a quick motion of his hand, and suddenly he held an enormous revolver, pointed at Raines's head. "Tell you what, mister. Let's go for a walk together, and soon's we find a fomeboof we can call some of the local po-lice to take a look at you."

Whatever the American's madness (and whatever a "fomeboof" was) there was no denying the argument of his weapon; Raines made no move toward his own revolver. They began to walk up the misty street; Raines hoped that upon reaching a better-traveled street he might find a policeman, or at least be able to flee.

The lane opened out onto a wide cobbled way. There were still no streetlamps, only the faint silvery glow from above. And all the building fronts were closed and dark. This was wrong, Raines thought. Even with the Black Smog, there should still be a taproom open, a light on in a private house. There should have been *someone* on the street.

A cry came from up the street, a woman's voice, surely less than fifty yards away. *"Help! Murderrr—"* The word dissolved into a horrifying scream.

Raines said to Hammond, "I am going to that woman's aid. You may shoot me if you like."

Hammond lowered his gun. "Let's go." Together they ran up the street.

The woman was lying in an alley barely wider than the span of a man's arms. She was on her back, her head almost against one wall, one arm beneath her, the other thrown out straight. Her legs were spread wide, and her skirts had been pushed up to display the killer's handiwork.

There was more blood than Raines had ever imagined possible. He had read the accounts, he had seen the dreadful photographs, and they had been no preparation at all for the quantity of blood, the incredible colours, and bloated wormy shapes of the human body opened like a sausage casing. He had gone to slaughterhouses and to autopsies, both to steel himself to the cutting of flesh and to search for suspects— and they meant nothing, nothing now with blood soaking his shoes and a woman's bald kneecap wreathed in gut—

"I could have saved her!" Raines shouted at the American who was staring at the body, his gun hand hanging at his side, his jaw clenched. "If I had not allowed you to distract me, *I could have saved her*—and now the city will know another season of terror, because of *you*, Mr. Hammond—"

Hammond looked up, from the awful pit of violation to the victim's face. He spoke an obscenity mixed with the name of Christ.

Raines looked. His knees nearly gave way beneath him. No. No. After all these years, no, not with him only a few steps, a few seconds behind. It was too cruel a joke for a world with a living God in it, a wilder darkness than took Cordelia in her cell.

He took a step through the mucky blood, bent down to close her eyes.

"Get away from her!" the American shouted.

"I'll disturb no clues, Officer."

"I said, *don't touch her*." Hammond had his pistol leveled.

"I've known this woman since we were children together."

"I think I'd'a remembered you. Texarkana ain't that big a place."

The man was clearly deranged; had they not been together at the time of the murder, Raines could have easily supposed him the killer, and the old man truthful—

"The old man," Raines said. "He asked you for thirty shillings, and a question, is that correct?"

"Liberty dimes," Hammond said. "I try everything from the FBI to an ol' gypsy conjure woman, go all the way t'New

Orleans so this old fool can ask me for three dollars in change and—'' Then the thought reached him. "The old bastard! It's *him*, ain't it?"

"We have been more than made fools of," Raines said.

"I'll kill the old bastard," Hammond said. Then he pointed his pistol at Raines again. "Don't you try to get in my way, or get at him first. He's mine, you understand, fella?" He began to back away.

Raines held still. When they were a few yards apart, the American turned and began running up the street, into the mist. Raines let him go. He could not know London as well as Raines. Hammond would get there too late.

He looked down at the dear ruined thing on the ground. He could not call for a policeman now; if he were found by the body, there would be suspicions, questions, time wasted— and in truth his only alibi for the night was Hammond. With a shake of his head Raines turned away.

Ahead of him, not far at all, there was another woman's scream.

Raines drew his revolver and ran. Once in his earlier rampage the killer had struck twice in one night; now, free again after so long quiet, how many lives might the monster take before he was stopped?

Shortly he found the body. The mutilations were even worse than the last, the face stabbed and sliced at, the breasts severed and tossed aside like half-eaten fruit—though for Raines it brought only revulsion; no unknown victim could match the sick horror of *recognition*.

Raines began to search in the grainy light for some trail— surely the man must have left a bloody footprint.

"Awright, *freeze*, sucker!"

Raines turned. A few steps behind him stood a huge coloured man, holding a revolver; the weapon seemed tiny in his hands. "Drop the gun, man." There was no Indies in his voice—*another* American?

Raines said, "Do you think I am responsible for this?"

"That's not for me to decide, friend. But I'll tell you this: There's a guy in the Georgia Penitentiary who's gonna be watching the papers *real* close . . . Now, I asked you to drop the gun."

The night was utterly mad, Raines thought. There was no appeal to reason; he decided to bluff it out. "I am a policeman, sir. Raines of Scotland Yard."

"You're kidding."

"I assure you I am not, sir. May I show you my credentials?"

"Get them out. Slowly."

Raines reached inside his coat, removed his wallet with care. He extended his arm, and then, with a snap of his wrist, threw it into the other man's face, and on the instant turned and ran. A gun cracked, a bullet flew past Raines's ear. He turned the first corner that appeared and kept running, into the night, into the fog.

His arm was grasped; he was slammed bodily into a wall. Briefly he thought that he had found his quarry, only to have it turn on him; he would be the killer's first male victim. Then cold metal was pressed against his lips; he looked down what must have been the barrel of a pistol, though it was flat in shape, with no cylinder—perhaps a dueling pistol, then, with but a single shot.

The man who held the gun wore a kind of uniform—more a boilersuit with military insignia. He looked Slavic. *"Prikazyvat?"* he shouted.

"I don't understand," Raines said, ready to weep with rage and frustration and fear.

The Slav pressed Raines even harder against the wall. "American? You American? Sequence! Code sequence—missiles! You gave!"

"English! Not American—I! Am! English!"

The man drew the pistol back. He spat into Raines's face.

He turned and walked away, leaving Raines against the wall, slowly sinking down, rubbing his palms against his face, trembling.

When the female scream came, Raines nearly screamed along with it. Without volition he stumbled along the street toward the sound.

There was another scream.

And a man's voice, murmuring.

Raines found him still at work, holding his victim pressed upright against a wall, his left hand spread like a monstrous white spider against her poor cut face, his right hand going in, out, in, out, sewing stitches of dull light and blood.

Raines's pistol was gone; he had not even a penknife. There were no ready clubs to hand. He had only the weapons his Maker had given him, needed only the will to use them.

He put his hand on the killer's shoulder, spun him round. There seemed to be no mass to the man at all. Raines looked into the face he had come so far to see.

One eye was loose in its lidless socket; the other was gone. Flesh peeled like paper from a moldering wall, and the lips were curled back to show blackened gum and white bone. Raines's hand tightened involuntarily, and beneath it, within the tattered clothing, something crumbled.

The jaw worked, and a scallop-edged tongue flicked behind the teeth. A sound came from the thing; after a few repetitions, Raines understood the words.

"Kill me," it said. "Kill me kill me."

Raines's hand slipped from the killer's shoulder. The single eye rolled; Raines saw its pupil was huge with more than the darkness. The thing was afraid.

"Kill me killmekillme," it chattered. "Pleasssse."

It held up the bloody knife in its infested hands.

Raines tore his gaze from the thing, to look at its victim. She slumped against the wall. From the wounds in her throat and belly, mischievous eyes looked back at him.

Raines fled.

He ran through the bewildered cries of children.

He ran through the rattle of guns in a cold garage.

He ran through the light that was brighter than a thousand suns.

He ran until he found himself at a door, and pounded a it, unable to draw the breath to speak, until it opened, and he tumbled through into candlelight and clutter.

"I told you there was another way out," the old man said

"That place—it was—"

"A principality of my realm. Though it goes by many names."

"Yet I—escaped." It was at least partly a question.

"This particular snare. There will be others."

"But how am I free of—Judgment—"

"You had not been judged, young sir. You entered as par of a bargain; but you did not conclude that bargain. You die not kill the man. No 'value received,' in lawyers' language.'

"And if I had killed him?"

"Your exit would have closed, and he would have been free—not in that other realm, you understand, but free o mine."

"It has a strange logic . . ."

"Logic is a common entry to my realm, but rarely an exit Now you must be on your way, young sir. The shop is clos ing." The old man took Raines's arm, guided him toward the door.

Raines stopped. "The lady—it was not her that I saw, then but some illusion? She is still—alive, somewhere?"

The old man said, "I will answer that question, young sir but I warn you—the answer will be costly."

"Whatever the price, I will pay it."

"Very well." The old man had the smile of a plaster saint "The master of lies tells you that your woman can be found."

Raines was frozen for a moment; then he laughed once, a dry, dead sound. "Well. You did warn me."

"Many things am I called, sir," the old man said, "but always a gentleman."

The door closed, and Raines was outside, alone in the cold and the poison air.

YOURS TRULY, JACK THE RIPPER

Robert Bloch

Robert Bloch is perhaps best known as the author of Psy
cho, from which Alfred Hitchcock made one of the most fa
mous films in the history of cinema. A decade or two later
Bloch came up with the book version of Psycho II. In additio
to detailing the antic goings-on at the Bates Motel, Bloch ha
written hundreds of short stories and dozens of novels, sca
tered across the closely related genres of horror, fantasy, an
mystery/thriller. Bloch has truly done it all. His career span
over half a century. He was a member of the famous Love
craft Circle, contributed many stories to the original Weir
Tales in the thirties and forties and is still appearing regu
larly in the horror fiction markets today, at the tag end of th
eighties. Bloch's most recent books include American Gothic
Cold Chills, Strange Eons, and Night of the Ripper, a nove
about you-know-who. In 1975 he won the World Fantas
Award, being presented with the prestigious Life Achievemer
Award.

"Yours Truly, Jack the Ripper" may be the most famou
Ripper story ever written. Certainly it's the one that mo
people remember if you ask them if they've ever read anythin
about Jack—and deservedly so. If you've read it before
you're probably eager to reread it already. If you haven
read it yet—well, we'll step out of your way now, withou
further ado, and let you get to it. (Bob is considered a
international authority on the Ripper, by the way, and, i
case you hadn't noticed, wrote the Foreword for this book.

I LOOKED AT THE STAGE ENGLISHMAN. HE LOOKED AT ME.

"Sir Guy Hollis?" I asked.

"Indeed. Have I the pleasure of addressing John Carmody, the psychiatrist?"

I nodded. My eyes swept over the figure of my distinguished visitor. Tall, lean, sandy-haired—with the traditional tufted mustache. And the tweeds. I suspected a monocle concealed in a vest pocket, and wondered if he'd left his umbrella in the outer office.

But more than that, I wondered what the devil had impelled Sir Guy Hollis of the British Embassy to seek out a total stranger here in Chicago.

Sir Guy didn't help matters any as he sat down. He cleared his throat, glanced around nervously, tapped his pipe against the side of the desk. Then he opened his mouth.

"Mr. Carmody," he said, "have you ever heard of—Jack the Ripper?"

"The murderer?" I asked.

"Exactly. The greatest monster of them all. Worse than Springheel Jack or Crippen. Jack the Ripper. Red Jack."

"I've heard of him," I said.

"Do you know his history?"

"Listen, Sir Guy," I muttered. "I don't think we'll get any place swapping old wives' tales about famous crimes of history."

Another bull's-eye. He took a deep breath.

"This is no old wives' tale. It's a matter of life or death."

He was so wrapped up in his obsession he even talked that way. Well—I was willing to listen. We psychiatrists get paid for listening.

"Go ahead," I told him. "Let's have the story."

Sir Guy lit a cigarette and began to talk.

"London, 1888," he began. "Late summer and early fall. That was the time. Out of nowhere came the shadowy figure of Jack the Ripper—a stalking shadow with a knife, prowling through London's East End. Haunting the squalid dives of Whitechapel, Spitalfields. Where he came from no one knew. But he brought death. Death in a knife.

"Six times that knife descended to slash the throats and bodies of London's women. Drabs and alley sluts. August seventh was the date of the first butchery. They found her body lying there with thirty-nine stab wounds. A ghastly murder. On August thirty-first, another victim. The press became interested. The slum inhabitants were more deeply interested still.

"Who was this unknown killer who prowled in their midst and struck at will in the deserted alleyways of night-town? And what was more important—when would he strike again?

"September eighth was the date. Scotland Yard assigned special deputies. Rumors ran rampant. The atrocious nature of the slayings was the subject for shocking speculation.

"The killer used a knife—expertly. He cut throats and removed—certain portions—of the bodies after death. He chose victims and settings with a fiendish deliberation. No one saw him or heard him. But watchmen making their gray rounds in the dawn would stumble across the hacked and horrid thing that was the Ripper's handiwork.

"Who was he? What was he? A mad surgeon? A butcher? An insane scientist? A pathological degenerate escaped from an asylum? A deranged nobleman? A member of the London police?

"Then the poem appeared in the newspapers. The anonymous poem, designed to put a stop to speculations—but which only aroused public interest to a further frenzy. A mocking little stanza:

I'm not a butcher, I'm not a Yid
Nor yet a foreign skipper,
But I'm your own true loving friend,
Yours truly—Jack the Ripper.

"And on September thirtieth, two more throats were slashed open."

I interrupted Sir Guy for a moment. "Very interesting," I commented. I'm afraid a faint hint of sarcasm crept into my voice.

He winced, but didn't falter in his narrative.

"There was silence, then, in London for a time. Silence, and a nameless fear. When would Red Jack strike again? They waited through October. Every figment of fog concealed his phantom presence. Concealed it well—for nothing was learned of the Ripper's identity, or his purpose. The drabs of London shivered in the raw wind of early November. Shivered, and were thankful for the coming of each morning's sun.

"November ninth. They found her in her room. She lay there very quietly, limbs neatly arranged. And beside her, with equal neatness, were laid her head and heart. The Ripper had outdone himself in execution.

"Then, panic. But needless panic. For though press, police, and populace alike waited in sick dread, Jack the Ripper did not strike again.

"Months passed. A year. The immediate interest died, but not the memory. They said Jack had skipped to America. That he had committed suicide. They said—and they wrote. They've written ever since. Theories, hypotheses, arguments, treatises. But to this day no one knows who Jack the Ripper was. Or why he killed. Or why he stopped killing."

Sir Guy was silent. Obviously he expected some comment from me.

"You tell the story well," I remarked. "Though with a slight emotional bias."

"I've got all the documents," said Sir Guy Hollis. "I've made a collection of existing data and studied it."

I stood up. "Well," I yawned, in mock fatigue, "I've enjoyed your little bedtime story a great deal, Sir Guy. It was kind of you to abandon your duties at the British Embassy to drop in on a poor psychiatrist and regale him with your anecdotes.''

Goading him always did the trick.

''I suppose you want to know why I'm interested?'' he snapped.

''Yes. That's exactly what I'd like to know. Why are you interested?''

''Because,'' said Sir Guy Hollis, ''I am on the trail of Jack the Ripper now. I think he's here—in Chicago!''

I sat down again. This time I did the blinking act.

''Say that again,'' I stuttered.

''Jack the Ripper is alive, in Chicago, and I'm out to find him.''

''Wait a minute,'' I said. ''Wait—a—minute!''

He wasn't smiling. It wasn't a joke.

''See here,'' I said. ''What was the date of these murders?''

''August to November, 1888.''

''1888? But if Jack the Ripper was an able-bodied man in 1888, he'd surely be dead today! Why, look, man—if he were merely born in that year, he'd be fifty-seven years old today!''

''Would he?'' smiled Sir Guy Hollis. ''Or should I say, 'Would she?' Because, Jack the Ripper may have been a woman. Or any number of things.''

''Sir Guy,'' I said. ''You came to the right person when you looked me up. You definitely need the services of a psychiatrist.''

''Perhaps. Tell me, Mr. Carmody, do you think I'm crazy?''

I looked at him and shrugged. But I had to give him a truthful answer.

''Frankly—no.''

''Then you might listen to the reasons I believe Jack the Ripper is alive today.''

"I might."

"I've studied these cases for thirty years. Been over the actual ground. Talked to officials. Talked to friends and acquaintances of the poor drabs who were killed. Visited with men and women in the neighborhood. Collected an entire library of material touching on Jack the Ripper. Studied all the wild theories or crazy notions.

"I learned a little. Not much, but a little. I won't bore you with my conclusions. But there was another branch of inquiry that yielded more fruitful return. I have studied unsolved crimes. Murders.

"I could show you clippings from the papers of half the world's great cities. San Francisco. Shanghai. Calcutta. Omsk. Paris. Berlin. Pretoria. Cairo. Milan. Adelaide.

"The trail is there, the pattern. Unsolved crimes. Slashed throats of women. With the peculiar disfigurations and removals. Yes, I've followed a trail of blood. From New York westward across the continent. Then to the Pacific. From there to Africa. During the World War of 1914–18 it was Europe. After that, South America. And since 1930, the United States again. Eighty-seven such murders—and to the trained criminologist, all bear the stigma of the Ripper's handiwork.

"Recently there were the so-called Cleveland torso slayings. Remember? A shocking series. And finally, two recent deaths in Chicago. Within the past six months. One out on South Dearborn. The other somewhere up on Halsted. Same type of crime, same technique. I tell you, there are unmistakable indications in all these affairs—indications of the work of Jack the Ripper!"

I smiled. "A very tight theory," I said. "I'll not question your evidence at all, or the deductions you draw. You're the criminologist, and I'll take your word for it. Just one thing remains to be explained. A minor point, perhaps, but worth mentioning."

"And what is that?" asked Sir Guy.

"Just how could a man of, let us say, eighty-five years commit these crimes? For if Jack the Ripper was around thirty in 1888 and lived, he'd be eighty-five today."

Sir Guy Hollis was silent. I had him there. But—

"Suppose he didn't get any older?" whispered Sir Guy.

"What's that?"

"Suppose Jack the Ripper didn't grow old? Suppose he is still a young man today?"

"All right," I said. "I'll suppose for a moment. Then I'll stop supposing and call for my nurse to restrain you."

"I'm serious," said Sir Guy.

"They all are," I told him. "That's the pity of it all, isn't it? They know they hear voices and see demons. But we lock them up just the same."

It was cruel, but it got results. He rose and faced me.

"It's a crazy theory, I grant you," he said. "All the theories about the Ripper are crazy. The idea that he was a doctor. Or a maniac. Or a woman. The reasons advanced for such beliefs are flimsy enough. There's nothing to go by. So why should my notion be any worse?"

"Because people grow older," I reasoned with him. "Doctors, maniacs, and women alike."

"What about—*sorcerers*?"

"Sorcerers?"

"Necromancers. Wizards. Practicers of Black Magic?"

"What's the point?"

"I studied," said Sir Guy. "I studied everything. After a while I began to study the dates of the murders. The pattern those dates formed. The rhythm. The solar, lunar, stellar rhythm. The sidereal aspect. The astrological significance."

He was crazy. But I still listened.

"Suppose Jack the Ripper didn't murder for murder's sake alone? Suppose he wanted to make—a sacrifice?"

"What kind of sacrifice?"

Sir Guy shrugged. "It is said that if you offer blood to the dark gods that they grant boons. Yes, if a blood offering is made at the proper time—when the moon and the stars are right—and with the proper ceremonies—they grant boons. Boons of youth. Eternal youth."

"But that's nonsense!"

"No. That's—Jack the Ripper."

I stood up. "A most interesting theory," I told him. "But Sir Guy—there's just one thing I'm interested in. Why do you come here and tell it to me? I'm not an authority on witchcraft. I'm not a police official or criminologist. I'm a practicing psychiatrist. What's the connection?"

Sir Guy smiled. "You are interested, then?"

"Well, yes. There must be some point."

"There is. But I wished to be assured of your interest first. Now I can tell you my plan."

"And just what is that plan?"

Sir Guy gave me a long look. Then he spoke.

"John Carmody," he said, "you and I are going to capture Jack the Ripper."

That's the way it happened. I've given the gist of that first interview in all its intricate and somewhat boring detail, because I think it's important. It helps to throw some light on Sir Guy's character and attitude. And in view of what happened after that—

But I'm coming to those matters.

Sir Guy's thought was simple. It wasn't even a thought. Just a hunch.

"You know the people here," he told me. "I've inquired. That's why I came to you as the ideal man for my purpose. You number among your acquaintances many writers, painters, poets. The so-called intelligentsia. The Bohemians. The lunatic fringe from the Near North Side.

"For certain reasons—never mind what they are—my clues

lead me to infer that Jack the Ripper is a member of that element. He chooses to pose as an eccentric. I've a feeling that with you to take me around and introduce me to your set, I might hit upon the right person."

"It's all right with me," I said. "But just how are you going to look for him? As you say, he might be anybody, anywhere. And you have no idea what he looks like. He might be young or old. Jack the Ripper—a Jack of all trades? Rich man, poor man, beggar man, thief, doctor, lawyer— how will you know?"

"We shall see." Sir Guy sighed heavily. "But I must find him. At once."

"Why the hurry?"

Sir Guy sighed again. "Because in two days he will kill again."

"Are you sure?"

"Sure as the stars. I've plotted this chart, you see. All of the murders correspond to certain astrological rhythm patterns. If, as I suspect, he makes a blood sacrifice to renew his youth, he must murder within two days. Notice the pattern of his first crimes in London. August seventh. Then August thirty-first. September eighth. September thirtieth. November ninth. Intervals of twenty-four days, nine days, twenty-two days—he killed two this time—and then forty days. Of course there were crimes in between. There had to be. But they weren't discovered and pinned on him.

"At any rate, I've worked out a pattern for him, based on all my data. And I say that within the next two days he kills. So I must seek him out, somehow, before then."

"And I'm still asking you what you want me to do."

"Take me out," said Sir Guy. "Introduce me to your friends. Take me to parties."

"But where do I begin? As far as I know, my artistic friends, despite their eccentricities, are all normal people."

"So is the Ripper. Perfectly normal. Except on certain

nights." Again that faraway look in Sir Guy's eyes. "Then he becomes an ageless pathological monster, crouching to kill, on evenings when the stars blaze down in the blazing patterns of death."

"All right," I said. "All right. I'll take you to parties, Sir Guy. I want to go myself, anyway. I need the drinks they'll serve there, after listening to your kind of talk."

We made our plans. And that evening I took him over to Lester Baston's studio.

As we ascended to the penthouse roof in the elevator I took the opportunity to warn Sir Guy.

"Baston's a real screwball," I cautioned him. "So are his guests. Be prepared for anything and everything."

"I am." Sir Guy Hollis was perfectly serious. He put his hand in his trousers pocket and pulled out a gun.

"What the—" I began.

"If I see him I'll be ready," Sir Guy said. He didn't smile, either.

"But you can't go running around at a party with a loaded revolver in your pocket, man!"

"Don't worry, I won't behave foolishly."

I wondered. Sir Guy Hollis was not, to my way of thinking, a normal man.

We stepped out of the elevator, went toward Baston's apartment door.

"By the way," I murmured, "just how do you wish to be introduced? Shall I tell them who you are and what you are looking for?"

"I don't care. Perhaps it would be best to be frank."

"But don't you think that the Ripper—if by some miracle he or she is present—will immediately get the wind up and take cover?"

"I think the shock of the announcement that I am hunting the Ripper would provoke some kind of betraying gesture on his part," said Sir Guy.

"You'd make a pretty good psychiatrist yourself," I conceded. "It's a fine theory. But I warn you, you're going to be in for a lot of ribbing. This is a wild bunch."

Sir Guy smiled. "I'm ready," he announced. "I have a little plan of my own. Don't be shocked at anything I do," he warned me.

I nodded and knocked on the door.

Baston opened it and poured out into the hall. His eyes were as red as the maraschino cherries in his Manhattan. He teetered back and forth regarding us very gravely. He squinted at my square-cut Homburg hat and Sir Guy's mustache.

"Aha," he intoned. "The Walrus and the Carpenter."

I introduced Sir Guy.

"Welcome," said Baston, gesturing us inside with over-elaborate courtesy. He stumbled after us into the garish parlor.

I stared at the crowd that moved restlessly through the fog of cigarette smoke.

It was the shank of the evening for this mob. Every hand held a drink. Every face held a slightly hectic flush. Over in one corner the piano was going full blast, but the imperious strains of the March from *The Love for Three Oranges* couldn't drown out the profanity from the crap game in the other corner.

Prokofiev had no chance against African polo, and one set of ivories rattled louder than the other.

Sir Guy got a monocleful right away. He saw LaVerne Gonnister, the poetess, hit Hymie Kralik in the eye. He saw Hymie sit down on the floor and cry until Dick Pool accidentally stepped on his stomach as he walked through to the dining room for a drink.

He heard Nadia Vilinoff, the commercial artist, tell Johnny Odcutt that she thought his tattooing was in dreadful taste, and he saw Barclay Melton crawl under the dining room table with Johnny Odcutt's wife.

His zoological observations might have continued indefinitely if Lester Baston hadn't stepped to the center of the room and called for silence by dropping a vase on the floor.

"We have distinguished visitors in our midst," bawled Lester, waving his empty glass in our direction. "None other than the Walrus and the Carpenter. The Walrus is Sir Guy Hollis, a something-or-other from the British Embassy. The Carpenter, as you all know, is our own John Carmody, the prominent dispenser of libido liniment."

He turned and grabbed Sir Guy by the arm, dragging him to the middle of the carpet. For a moment I thought Hollis might object, but a quick wink reassured me. He was prepared for this.

"It is our custom, Sir Guy," said Baston loudly, "to subject our new friends to a little cross-examination. Just a little formality at these formal gatherings, you understand. Are you prepared to answer questions?"

Sir Guy nodded and grinned.

"Very well," Baston muttered. "Friends—I give you this bundle from Britain. Your witness."

Then the ribbing started. I meant to listen, but at that moment Lydia Dare saw me and dragged me off into the vestibule for one of those Darling-I-waited-for-your-call-all-day routines.

By the time I got rid of her and went back, the impromptu quiz session was in full swing. From the attitude of the crowd, I gathered that Sir Guy was doing all right for himself.

Then Baston himself interjected a question that upset the applecart.

"And what, may I ask, brings you to our midst tonight? What is your mission, O Walrus?"

"I'm looking for Jack the Ripper."

Nobody laughed.

Perhaps it struck them all the way it did me. I glanced at my neighbors and began to *wonder*.

LaVerne Gonnister. Hymie Kralik. Harmless. Dick Pool. Nadia Vilinoff. Johnny Odcutt and his wife. Barclay Melton. Lydia Dare. All harmless.

But what a forced smile on Dick Pool's face! And that sly, self-conscious smirk that Barclay Melton wore!

Oh, it was absurd, I grant you. But for the first time I saw these people in a new light. I wondered about their lives—their secret lives beyond the scenes of parties.

How many of them were playing a part, concealing something?

Who here would worship Hecate and grant that horrid goddess the dark boon of blood?

Even Lester Baston might be masquerading.

The mood was upon us all, for a moment. I saw questions flicker in the circle of eyes around the room.

Sir Guy stood there, and I could swear he was fully conscious of the situation he'd created, and enjoyed it.

I wondered idly just what was *really* wrong with him. Why he had this odd fixation concerning Jack the Ripper. Maybe he was hiding secrets, too . . .

Baston, as usual, broke the mood. He burlesqued it.

"The Walrus isn't kidding, friends," he said. He slapped Sir Guy on the back and put his arm around him as he orated. "Our English cousin is really on the trail of the fabulous Jack the Ripper. You all remember Jack the Ripper, I presume? Quite a cutup in the old days, as I recall. Really had some ripping good times when he went out on a tear.

"The Walrus has some idea that the Ripper is still alive, probably prowling around Chicago with a Boy Scout knife. In fact"—Baston paused impressively and shot it out in a rasping stage whisper—"in fact, he has reason to believe that Jack the Ripper might even be right here in our midst tonight."

There was the expected reaction of giggles and grins. Baston eyed Lydia Dare reprovingly. "You girls needn't laugh," he smirked. "Jack the Ripper might be a woman, too, you know. Sort of a Jill the Ripper."

"You mean you actually suspect one of us?" shrieked LaVerne Gonnister, simpering up to Sir Guy. "But that Jack the Ripper person disappeared ages ago, didn't he? In 1888?"

"Aha!" interrupted Baston. "How do you know so much about it, young lady? Sounds suspicious! Watch her, Sir Guy—she may not be as young as she appears. These lady poets have dark pasts."

The tension was gone, the mood was shattered, and the whole thing was beginning to degenerate into a trivial party joke. The man who had played the March was eyeing the piano with a *Scherzo* gleam in his eye that augered ill for Prokofiev. Lydia Dare was glancing at the kitchen, waiting to make a break for another drink.

Then Baston caught it. "Guess what?" he yelled. "The Walrus has a gun."

His embracing arm had slipped and encountered the hard outline of the gun in Sir Guy's pocket. He snatched it out before Hollis had the opportunity to protest.

I stared hard at Sir Guy, wondering if this thing had carried far enough. But he flicked a wink my way and I remembered he had told me not to be alarmed.

So I waited as Baston broached a drunken inspiration.

"Let's play fair with our friend the Walrus," he cried. "He came all the way from England to our party on this mission. If none of you is willing to confess, I suggest we give him a chance to find out—the hard way."

"What's up?" asked Johnny Odcutt.

"I'll turn out the lights for one minute. Sir Guy can stand here with his gun. If anyone in this room is the Ripper he can either run for it or take the opportunity to—well, eradicate his pursuer. Fair enough?"

It was even sillier than it sounds, but it caught the popular fancy. Sir Guy's protests went unheard in the ensuing babble.

And before I could stride over and put in my two cents' worth, Lester Baston had reached the light switch.

"Don't anybody move," he announced, with fake solemnity. "For one minute we will remain in darkness—perhaps at the mercy of a killer. At the end of that time, I'll turn up the lights again and look for bodies. Choose your partners, ladies and gentlemen."

The lights went out.

Somebody giggled.

I heard footsteps in the darkness. Mutterings.

A hand brushed my face.

The watch on my wrist ticked violently. But even louder, rising above it, I heard another thumping. The beating of my heart.

Absurd. Standing in the dark with a group of tipsy fools. And yet there was real terror lurking here, rustling through the velvet blackness.

Jack the Ripper prowled in darkness like this. And Jack the Ripper had a knife. Jack the Ripper had a madman's brain and a madman's purpose.

But Jack the Ripper was dead, dead and dust these many years—by every human law.

Only there are no human laws when you feel yourself in the darkness, when the darkness hides and protects and the outer mask slips off your face and you feel something welling up within you, a brooding shapeless purpose that is brother to the blackness.

Sir Guy Hollis shrieked.

There was a grisly thud.

Baston had the lights on.

Everybody screamed.

Sir Guy Hollis lay sprawled on the floor in the center of the room. The gun was still clutched in his hand.

I glanced at the faces, marveling at the variety of expressions human beings can assume when confronting horror.

All the faces were present in the circle. Nobody had fled. And yet Sir Guy Hollis lay there . . .

LaVerne Gonnister was wailing and hiding her face.

"All right." Sir Guy rolled over and jumped to his feet. He was smiling. "Just an experiment, eh? If Jack the Ripper *were* among those present, and thought I had been murdered, he would have betrayed himself in some way when the lights went on and he saw me lying there.

"I am convinced of your individual and collective innocence. Just a gentle spoof, my friends."

Hollis stared at the goggling Baston and the rest of them crowding in behind him.

"Shall we leave, John?" he called to me. "It's getting late, I think."

Turning, he headed for the closet. I followed him. Nobody said a word.

It was a pretty dull party after that.

I met Sir Guy the following evening as we agreed, on the corner of Twenty-ninth and South Halsted.

After what had happened the night before, I was prepared for almost anything. But Sir Guy seemed matter-of-fact enough as he stood huddled against a grimy doorway and waited for me to appear.

"Boo!" I said, jumping out suddenly. He smiled. Only the betraying gesture of his left hand indicated that he'd instinctively reached for his gun when I startled him.

"All ready for our wild-goose chase?" I asked.

"Yes." He nodded. "I'm glad that you agreed to meet me without asking questions," he told me. "It shows you trust my judgment."

He took my arm and edged me along the street slowly.

"It's foggy tonight, John," said Sir Guy Hollis. "Like London."

I nodded.

"Cold, too, for November."

I nodded again and half shivered my agreement.

"Curious," mused Sir Guy. "London fog and November. The place and the time of the Ripper murders."

I grinned through darkness. "Let me remind you, Sir Guy, that this isn't London, but Chicago. And it isn't November, 1888. It's over fifty years later."

Sir Guy returned my grin, but without mirth. "I'm not so sure, at that," he murmured. "Look about you. These tangled alleys and twisted streets. They're like the East End. Mitre Square. And surely they are as ancient as fifty years, at least."

"You're in the colored neighborhood off South Clark Street," I said shortly. "And why you dragged me down here I still don't know."

"It's a hunch," Sir Guy admitted. "Just a hunch on my part, John. I want to wander around down here. There's the same geographical conformation in these streets as in those courts where the Ripper roamed and slew. That's where we'll find him, John. Not in the bright lights of the Bohemian neighborhood, but down here in the darkness. The darkness where he waits and crouches."

"Is that why you brought a gun?" I asked. I was unable to keep a trace of sarcastic nervousness from my voice. All of this talk, this incessant obsession with Jack the Ripper, got on my nerves more than I cared to admit.

"We may need a gun," said Sir Guy, gravely. "After all, tonight is the appointed night."

I sighed. We wandered on through the foggy, deserted streets. Here and there a dim light burned above a gin-mill doorway. Otherwise, all was darkness and shadow. Deep, gaping alleyways loomed as we proceeded down a slanting side street.

We crawled through that fog, alone and silent, like two tiny maggots floundering within a shroud.

When that thought hit me, I winced. The atmosphere was beginning to get *me*, too. If I didn't watch my step I'd go as loony as Sir Guy.

"Can't you see there's not a soul around these streets?" I said, tugging at his coat impatiently.

"He's bound to come," said Sir Guy. "He'll be drawn here. This is what I've been looking for. A *genius loci*. An evil spot that attracts evil. Always, when he slays, it's in the slums.

"You see, that must be one of his weaknesses. He has a fascination for squalor. Besides, the women he needs for sacrifice are more easily found in the dives and stewpots of a great city."

I smiled. "Well, let's go into one of the dives or stewpots," I suggested. "I'm cold. Need a drink. This damned fog gets into your bones. You Britishers can stand it, but I like warmth and dry heat."

We emerged from our side street and stood upon the threshold of an alley.

Through the white clouds of mist ahead, I discerned a dim, blue light, a naked bulb dangling from a beer sign above an alley tavern.

"Let's take a chance," I said. "I'm beginning to shiver."

"Lead the way," said Sir Guy.

I led him down the alley passage. We halted before the door of the dive.

"What are you waiting for?" he asked.

"Just looking in," I told him. "This is a tough neighborhood, Sir Guy. Never know what you're liable to run into. And I'd prefer we didn't get into the wrong company. Some of these Negro places resent white customers."

"Good idea, John."

I finished my inspection through the doorway. "Looks deserted," I murmured. "Let's try it."

We entered a dingy bar. A feeble light flickered above the

counter and railing, but failed to penetrate the further gloom of the back booths.

A gigantic Negro lolled across the bar—a black giant with prognathous jaw and apelike torso. He scarcely stirred as we came in, but his eyes flicked open quite suddenly and I knew he noted our presence and was judging us.

"Evening," I said.

He took his time before replying. Still sizing us up. Then, he grinned. "Evening, gents. What's your pleasure?"

"Gin," I said. "Two gins. It's a cold night."

"That's right, gents."

He poured, I paid, and took the glasses over to one of the booths. We wasted no time in emptying them. The fiery liquor warmed.

I went over to the bar and got the bottle. Sir Guy and I poured ourselves another drink. The big Negro went back into his doze, with one wary eye half-open against any sudden activity.

The clock over the bar ticked on. The wind was rising outside, tearing the shroud of fog to ragged shreds. Sir Guy and I sat in the warm booth and drank our gin.

He began to talk, and the shadows crept up about us to listen.

He rambled a great deal. He went over everything he'd said in the office when I met him, just as though I hadn't heard it before. The poor devils with obsessions are like that.

I listened very patiently. I poured Sir Guy another drink. And another.

But the liquor only made him more talkative. How he did run on! About ritual killings and prolonging the life unnaturally—the whole fantastic tale came out again. And of course, he maintained his unyielding conviction that the Ripper was abroad tonight.

I suppose I was guilty of goading him.

"Very well," I said, unable to keep the impatience from

my voice. "Let us say that your theory is correct—even though we must overlook every natural law and swallow a lot of superstition to give it any credence.

"But let us say, for the sake of argument, that you are right. Jack the Ripper was a man who discovered how to prolong his own life through making human sacrifices. He did travel around the world as you believe. He is in Chicago now and he is planning to kill. In other words, let us suppose that everything you claim is gospel truth. So what?"

"What do you mean, 'so what'?" said Sir Guy.

"I mean—so what?" I answered. "If all this is true, it still doesn't prove that by sitting down in a dingy gin mill on the South Side, Jack the Ripper is going to walk in here and let you kill him or turn him over to the police. And come to think of it, I don't even know now just what you intend to *do* with him if you ever did find him."

Sir Guy gulped his gin. "I'd capture the bloody swine," he said. "Capture him and turn him over to the government, together with all the papers and documentary evidence I've collected against him over a period of many years. I've spent a fortune investigating this affair, I tell you, a fortune! His capture will mean the solution of hundreds of unsolved crimes, of that I am convinced.

"I tell you, a mad beast is loose on this world! An ageless, eternal beast, sacrificing to Hecate and the dark gods!"

In vino veritas. Or was all this babbling the result of too much gin? It didn't matter. Sir Guy Hollis had another. I sat there and wondered what to do with him. The man was rapidly working up to a climax of hysterical drunkenness.

"One other point," I said, more for the sake of conversation than in any hopes of obtaining information. "You still don't explain how it is that you hope to just blunder into the Ripper."

"He'll be around," said Sir Guy. "I'm psychic. I know."

Sir Guy wasn't psychic. He was maudlin.

The whole business was beginning to infuriate me. We'd been sitting here an hour and during all this time I'd been forced to play nursemaid and audience to a babbling idiot. After all, he wasn't a regular patient of mine.

"That's enough," I said, putting out my hand as Sir Guy reached for the half-emptied bottle again. "You've had plenty. Now I've got a suggestion to make. Let's call a cab and get out of here. It's getting late and it doesn't look as though your elusive friend is going to put in his appearance. Tomorrow, if I were you, I'd plan to turn all those papers and documents over to the FBI. If you're so convinced of the truth of your wild theory, they are competent to make a very thorough investigation, and find your man."

"No." Sir Guy was drunkenly obstinate. "No cab."

"But let's get out of here anyway," I said, glancing at my watch. "It's past midnight."

He sighed, shrugged, and rose unsteadily. As he started for the door, he tugged the gun free from his pocket.

"Here, give me that!" I whispered. "You can't walk around the street brandishing that thing."

I took the gun and slipped it inside my coat. Then I got hold of his right arm and steered him out of the door. The black man didn't look up as we departed.

We stood shivering in the alleyway. The fog had increased. I couldn't see either end of the alley where we stood. It was cold. Damp. Dark. Fog or no fog, a little wind was whispering secrets to the shadows at our backs.

The fresh air hit Sir Guy just as I expected it would. Fog and gin fumes don't mingle very well. He lurched as I guided him slowly through the mist.

Sir Guy, despite his incapacity, still stared apprehensively at the alley, as though he expected to see a figure approaching.

Disgust got the better of me. "Childish foolishness," I

snorted. "Jack, the Ripper, indeed! I call this carrying a hobby too far."

"Hobby?" He faced me. Through the fog I could see his distorted face. "You call this a hobby?"

"Well, what is it?" I grumbled. "Just why else are you so interested in tracking down this mythical killer?"

My arm held his. But his stare held me.

"In London," he whispered. "In 1888—one of those nameless drabs the Ripper slew—was my mother."

"What?"

"Later I was recognized by my father, and legitimatized. We swore to give our lives to find the Ripper. My father was the first to search. He died in Hollywood in 1926—on the trail of the Ripper. They said he was stabbed by an unknown assailant in a brawl. But I know who that assailant was.

"So I've taken up his work, do you see, John? I've carried on. And I will carry on until I do find him and kill him with my own hands.

"He took my mother's life and the lives of hundreds to keep his own hellish being alive. Like a vampire, he battens on blood. Like a ghoul, he is nourished by death. Like a fiend, he stalks the world to kill. He is cunning, devilishly cunning. But I'll never rest until I find him, never!"

I believed him then. He wouldn't give up. He wasn't just a drunken babbler anymore. He was as determined, as relentless as the Ripper himself.

Tomorrow he'd be sober. He'd continue the search. Perhaps he'd turn those papers over to the FBI. Sooner or later, with such persistence—and with his motive—he'd be successful. I'd always known he had a motive.

"Let's go," I said, steering him down the alley.

"Wait a minute," said Sir Guy. "Give me back my gun." He lurched a little. "I'd feel better with the gun on me."

He pressed me into the dark shadows of a little recess.

I tried to shrug him off, but he was insistent.

"Let me carry the gun, now, John," he mumbled.

"All right," I said.

I reached into my coat, brought my hand out.

"But that's not a gun," he protested. "That's a knife."

"I know."

I bore down on him swiftly.

"John!" he screamed.

"Never mind the 'John,' " I whispered, raising the knife. "Just call me—Jack."

ANNA AND THE RIPPER OF SIAM

S. P. SOMTOW

One of those little-known facts that make History Fun is that Anna Leonowens—the heroine of The King and I, *and a real historical personage—was Boris Karloff's aunt. It's tempting to imagine that when Boris was just a wee lad she used to tell him the grisly and gonzo story that follows, perhaps as she tucked him in at night. That could explain a lot . . .*

Born in Bangkok, Thailand, Somtow Sucharitkul has lived in six countries and was educated at Eton and Cambridge. Multitalented as well as multilingual, he has an international reputation as an avant-garde composer, and his works have been performed in more than a dozen countries on four continents. Among his compositions are "Gongula 3 for Thai and Western Instruments" and "The Cosmic Trilogy." His book publications include the novels Starship and Haiku, Mallworld, *and* Light on the Sound. *His most recent books are the novels* Vampire Junction *and* The Shattered Horse, *written as S. P. Somtow, and* The Darkling Wind *and* The Fallen Country. *In 1986 he received the Daedalus Award for* The Shattered House. *A resident of the United States for many years, he now makes his home in Van Nuys, California, and is at work on a new novel,* Moondance.

THE SLATTERTHWAITE WING OF ST. _____'s COLlege, Cambridge, is remarkable mostly for its singularly unprepossessing architecture. Although attributed to Christopher Wren, it was undoubtedly designed by someone else; or if indeed by that worthy, he was surely under the influence of some mind-altering chemical. Because of its ugliness, and because it contains no documents of note, the collection is rarely visited by scholars. It is said that, in the 1860s, Lord Slatterthwaite used to repair to this room to smoke opium. When I was up at Cambridge, in the late 1960s, its purpose had changed but little. The only outward expansion consisted in the variety and, it must be said, the price of the substances obtainable there.

On the pretext of researching Lord Slatterthwaite's papers, I had obtained a late night key for the wing from my director of studies, Dr. Blavatsky. In fact, on my arrival, a party was in full swing. I retired behind a bust of the Founder to indulge myself. In my zeal, I knocked over the bust. Fortunately, there was no damage to the Founder; but tucked between the bust and the plinth, I uncovered the manuscript which now follows. The date is not legible, but for internal reasons must be in the early 1860s, approximately a quarter century before its principal subject made himself known in Whitechapel.

For reasons that I shall reveal in my scholarly afterword, it seems all too clear that the manuscript is a forgery, albeit, perhaps, one contemporaneous with the events it describes and foreshadows. Nevertheless, whether or not it is so, it remains a fascinating glimpse into the psychosexuality of Victorian England.

It is not without a certain *frisson* of anguish within my breast that I venture to set forth these words, my dear Lord Slatterthwaite. It is my express hope that, having read, digested, and been duly appalled by the facts which I am about to reveal, which cannot fail to elicit the utmost revulsion and disgust within the heart of every Englishman of character, you will treat them with that gentlemanly respect for a lady's privacy that I have sorely missed since the beginning of my sojourn in this magnificent, barbaric kingdom of Siam; that is to say, that you will instantly consign this missive to the flames.

I shall think of you, Lord Slatterthwaite, and all those delightful tea parties; I shall imagine that, while these dark words shrivel to ashes in your fireplace, you are sipping a cup of good English tea and enjoying the delicate flavor of a crumpet smothered in butter. Ah, could you but know how I constantly dream of these simple English pleasures! Nightly these natives force devilish concoctions down my throat: fiery curries made of meats whose origin I fear to question, ungainly fruits whose appearance gives no clue as to their taste, soups so spicy as to evoke the flames of hell itself; food, in short, such as might be expected in a land of idolaters and heathens. Ah, what would I give to be magically transported from these decadent orgies to your lordship's country estate, there to consume a steak and kidney pie!

But lest you assume from these lamentations that the lack of a good boiled ham is the only horror of these parts, let me proceed to the matter at hand. I assure you, Lord Slatterthwaite, that the lack of proper tea has been the least of my worries. Nevertheless, it was this aforementioned lack of tea that caused me to seek an audience with His Majesty that fateful day.

Having but lately arrived in this kingdom to act as governess to His Majesty's children, I was still not inured to the mosquitoes and the sweltering heat. I was staying in a wing of the women's quarters of the palace. I had not, at that stage, learned that all the women therein served but a single function; viz., to satiate the loathsome lusts of that being whom the Siamese idolatrously elevate to a position of godhood! Imagine, my dear Lord Slatterthwaite: all these hapless young women—ruined, without hope of a decent Christian marriage! Later I was most shocked of all to discover that none of them seemed remotely perturbed by their shameful condition. So prevalent is the licentiousness of this kingdom that the many concubines of His Majesty actually seemed honored in their position, and vied with each other for their lord's attention like so many lapdogs!

I first saw evidence of their lax moral standards at the first soirée to which I was invited. There I was treated to the sight of more than a dozen young women, *each with her ankles completely unbared*, in a wanton exhibition which could undoubtedly stir sordid passions even in the breast of a gentleman. Furthermore, these Siamese eat while sitting on the floor in a most discomfiting position. Luckily, the burning sensation aroused by the chilies, which are liberally used in every recipe, had a tendency to numb me, so that I viewed the world through a veil of gustatory agony that did much to disguise the true horror that I ought, as an Englishwoman, to have felt.

By day I taught English to the palace children. The poor dears, I was the one civilizing influence in their lives. But every evening came one of those terrifying dinners. At last, after several months without tea, I thought that I should surely die. I was unable to complain to the British consulate, for men were forbidden to enter the women's quarters of the palace on pain of death; but finally I convinced Nang Sobha, one of the King's favorites and one of the few women to befriend me, to bear His Majesty a message. She undertook to do so when next she was summoned to the King's pleasure; and to my surprise, I received the next morning a summons to a tea party by the river.

What a party it was, though! There was but a single chair in the entire pavilion, and that was occupied by His Majesty; all the other guests were seated on the floor in various states of prostration; and the teapot was being pushed along the polished wooden floors by a slave who crawled abjectly from guest to guest, not daring to raise her hand more than a foot from the ground! At my entrance, the Siamese ladies actually averted their gaze, and one or two even held their hands in front of their noses. It was probably yet another arcane native custom.

Though I had seen the King on a number of occasions, this was the first time I had had an extended visit. I had, of course, formed my own impression of him from that which I witnessed daily about me. I assumed that so barbaric a monarch would be a gibbering, spineless creature, able to utter but a few words in the noble tongue of Shakespeare and Milton before relapsing into the cacophonous argot of these parts. I was somewhat shocked to find that His Majesty spoke English with barely a trace of accent, and that he betrayed astonishing intelligence for one not privileged to be born a subject of Her Britannic Majesty.

"Oh, I say, Miss Leonowens," he said jovially, "enjoying the tea, eh, what?"

I had not yet drunk a drop, so astounded was I by the spectacle of it all. For the pavilion in which we sat, a thing of pointed eaves covered in gold leaf, stood on stilts within a canal, or *klong*, which joined the great river Menam, athwart which rose a vast edifice of pagodas and pyramidal roofs, all glittering with gold, gems, and brilliantly colored tiles. Slaves with fans and fly whisks surrounded us on all sides, while others tended the bowls of the incense used to dispel mosquitoes.

His Majesty's question aroused me from my reverie, and I lifted the cup to my lips. It tasted terrible. Suddenly I realized what the matter was. "May it please Your Majesty," I said, trying to be as tactful as possible, "in England we drink our tea with milk."

"We see," he said, folding his arms across his chest.

"You fool!" Nang Sobha, my confidante, whispered. "One doesn't contradict the King."

In vain I tried to retract my complaint, fearful that my innocent remark would cause me to be beheaded.

"Well, there aren't any cows here, and in any case the heat makes milk spoil rather easily," said the King mildly. "But I do have an alternative."

He beckoned to another of the palace women, who was heavy with child. She kowtowed humbly as she approached him. He issued an imperious command; she crawled away on her hands and knees; in a few minutes a servant came crawling up to me, bearing a silver platter in which rested a small cup of milk.

"Your Majesty is indeed generous," I said, hoping to rectify my error and to stave off my putative decapitation for a few more hours.

"We should say so," said the King. "That milk was intended for Our unborn child."

I had already drunk half a cup of the tea when I realized what His Majesty meant. I looked up in horror to see that the entire court was either stifling laughter or looking steadfastly at the floor. My dear Lord Slatterthwaite, I was ten thousand miles from England, being made the butt of an obscene joke! Even the pregnant woman was leering at me from a corner of the pavilion!

"But then, my dear Miss Leonowens, you foreigners are a very childlike race."

"We are the most magnificent race on earth!" I countered hotly.

"But you *are* like children. You have the overweening self-confidence that only children have, for they have not yet learned that the world is not a mere extension of themselves. Besides, like certain children, you are stubborn, and you don't bathe."

"But it's unhealthy to—" I began. But my words were drowned in a burst of applause from the court. What sycophants! I thought. What miserable beings, to perceive every minuscule utterance of their lord and master as a profound witticism!

"Never mind," His Majesty opined. "But there is another of your kind joining us for tea today. We hear from the court women that you've not been terribly happy here. Today, as it happened, a Dutch ship, the *Groote Koning*, came in from Indonesia. There was a Dr. Gaunt aboard. I asked whether he might remain in Bangkok as my guest for a while, thinking that perhaps the sight of a fellow barbarian would cheer you up."

I was taken aback at His Majesty's gross distortion of the truth. Fellow barbarian indeed—and these words from a heathen despot! But so relieved was I to hear that an Englishman would soon be present that I did not mind. I realized that His Majesty was, in his own way, demonstrating his concern for me. So flushed with gratitude was I that I downed the entire cup of tea.

It was at that moment that Dr. Zebediah Gaunt entered the pavilion. He was a young man, debonair, of a leonine and aristocratic demeanor. To my surprise, he groveled to the King, performing the prostration with practiced grace. Clearly he was a man accustomed to Oriental potentates, and comfortable in their presence. At first I was afraid he might have gone native. But my fears were soothed when he clapped his hands and a manservant entered with a small pitcher of milk. Dr. Gaunt crawled into position beside me. "I come prepared," he whispered. "Would you care to share my milk, madam?"

"Oh!" I said. I was overwhelmed at this small token of civility, and my thoughts were instantly transported to England, where my mind rejoiced with images of verdant meadows and foggy streets, of stalwart gentlemen in frock coats . . . the air ringing with the music of great English composers like Sullivan and Balfe.

"Perhaps, my dear Madam, you would care to dine with

me next Friday at my quarters? I can dispatch a gondola for your convenience. Not for nothing is this fair city known as the Venice of the East.''

''I would be most delighted, Dr. Gaunt. And yet . . . perhaps the impropriety of a woman going alone to dine at a gentleman's boudoir . . .''

''We are in a strange country, madam, among foreigners to whom our little civilities must seem as quaint as their own exotic customs do to us. I think that under the circumstances a slight breach of protocol might be considered not unacceptable.''

''In that case, sir, I will gladly accept your invitation . . . if His Majesty will permit me to leave the women's quarters of the palace.''

The King, who had been listening to our conversation, said, ''Jolly good! Dear Miss Leonowens, We are most graciously pleased to grant you the freedom of the city. Besides, the children need a holiday from their conjugations and recitations; We fear that the intractability of your language has taken its toll on their delicate sensibilities.''

I pursed my lips at this insult to the tongue of Wordsworth and Chatterton, reminding myself forcibly that this was no European monarch. As though I could ever forget that fact, seeing him covered from head to toe in silks, his breeches of heavily embroidered brocade held tenuously together with a belt of solid gold links, with slaves and minions prostrate at his feet.

''Thank you, Your Majesty,'' I said.

He smiled. ''Do have another crumpet, Miss Leonowens, old thing,'' he said. ''The recipe was sent to Us by your very own Lord Slatterthwaite. Alas, they were somewhat bland, so I have added a few Siamese embellishments to the formula.''

The platter was passed round to me. I munched decorously on the crumpet, being careful to scrape away the chilies that so liberally garnished it. Inwardly, I cursed the accident of fate which had led me to this godless kingdom, and I prayed fervently for Friday to come soon, for at least I would then be able to sup in the company of Englishmen.

That evening His Majesty asked me to remain behind to help him construe a particularly difficult passage of Shakespeare. "Come to the *hong bantom*" was the message delivered to me by the beautiful Nang Sobha. I was glad of some diversion, and came willingly. I was startled to discover that the *hong bantom* was nothing more or less than a bedchamber, and that His Majesty was occupying it entirely alone!

"May it please Your Majesty," I said, "would it not be better to have me chaperoned? A woman in my position cannot risk being compromised."

His Majesty laughed. "You English are absolutely out of your minds," he said. "I suppose you thought I was going to have your head chopped off when you had the temerity to demand milk at tea time."

"I—"

"Think nothing of it." He motioned me to sit on the floor at his feet; there was a triangular cushion to support me in the *phraphrieb* position, which the natives find comely in a woman. He himself began to pace up and down. "I admire spirit in a woman," he said, "provided, of course, she does not forget her place too frequently."

I was afraid of where this conversation might lead. I thought it best to turn the conversation in a more edifying direction. "Your Majesty wished to consult me about Shakespeare?" I inquired, pulling a volume of the collected works from my satchel.

"Ah, Shakespeare . . . a very good poet . . . though not as fine, I think, as he who penned the epic poem *Phra Law*." He paused and began reciting: "Shall I compare thee to a summer's day? Thou art—"

"More lovely and more—" I stumbled. "Contemplate? Disparate? Desquamate?"

"Temperate!" the King roared with such ferocity that I shrank into my silken cushion. "You English are such hypocrites! Why is it that your ancient poets speak with such passion, such rich lasciviousness, about the art of carnal love, and yet you people are all so prudish?"

"Surely Your Majesty does not impute craven lusts to the great Shakespeare—" I began.

"Ha! You do not even see it, then!"

"I most certainly do not," I said, drawing myself up with what little dignity that remained to me.

The King began to caress my hair. I started to shudder. "What is the matter?" he said. "Are you afraid of me? I have never been known to be anything less than gentle to the fair sex."

"Your Majesty . . ." I was overcome. Lord Slatterthwaite, never had England seemed so far from me. I began to weep with a passion I did not know I had.

"Ah," he said soothingly, "at least you are capable of some emotion. But why are you weeping?"

"Oh, Your Majesty . . . I am afraid of . . . what my mother once called 'a fate worse than death.' I am so terrified that it may happen to me. I know that you are used to practicing the most indecent liberties on the defenseless forms of young women, but I *am* English, and entitled to a little consideration in that regard . . ."

The King did not relent, but continued to stroke the nape of my neck. His fingers actually began to explore that part of my skin which lay beneath the confines of my ruff collar. A feeling of astonishing abandon swept over my entire being. "Did your mother," the King said, "inform you as to the exact *nature* of this 'fate worse than death'?"

"She only said that it would be too horrible to contemplate."

"Well, on Our honor as King of a sovereign nation, Miss Leonowens, We assure you that We shall perform no act upon your body that could be construed as too horrible to contemplate."

Much reassured, I allowed His Majesty's hands to rove all over my body. In only a few minutes he was unclasping stays, unbuttoning buttons, and disentangling hooks with astonishing skill, considering that our English manner of dressing was alien to him. I was too stunned to resist; as a member of the weaker sex, I had no alternative but to submit. Still suspicious, however, I said, "Are you sure, Your Majesty, that your intentions are honorable? My mother told me that this dread act involved a certain loosening of the undergarments, a certain . . . immodesty."

"Well, my dear Miss Leonowens, that proves it! The act I was intending to perform cannot be the same one that you fear so much. The one involves the undergarments, whereas this involves removing every stitch of clothing completely. To quote your own John Donne, 'Full nakedness! All joys are due to thee.' "

I had not heard the quotation, but did not want to reveal my ignorance. If a great English poet had indeed condoned it, this must not be the thing my dear mama had warned me against, and my reputation would not suffer.

All thoughts of England, however, were swept away in the delicious pleasure that followed. I cast all caution aside, for night had come and in the dark I could not quite tell what was going on. I only knew that some rapturous device was being inserted into me. When it was over, His Majesty said, panting heavily, "Was that not infinitely preferable to your 'fate worse than death,' madam? I trust so."

The heat . . . the confusion . . . my mind was awhirl with new and wild sensations. Surely what we had done was something that could only be accomplished in the tropics, where the great heat boils the blood and gives rise to most un-

English emotions. It was then, lying beside His Majesty beneath the enormous mosquito net on sheets of sheerest silk, that I resolved to compose a memoir of my adventures in this exotic land. Indeed, I was writing the first few sentences in my head, a description of this bizarre Oriental communion I had just undergone, when I heard a bloodcurdling scream from somewhere in the palace.

Shrieking, I sat up on the bed. "What's wrong, Miss Leonowens?" His Majesty said.

"A scream!" In the half dark I saw nothing. A tendril of mosquito incense; a shaft of light through a distant doorway; nothing else.

"Oh, it's probably just a slave being whipped or something," said His Majesty in a decidedly bored tone.

The scream came again; this time there were footsteps. "The Lord Buddha preserve Us!" said the King. "We're being assassinated!" With astonishing alacrity he leaped from the bed and donned a pair of Chinese silk pajamas. "Lights! Guards!"

In an instant the room had filled with people. Luckily, they had prostrated themselves, and were therefore unable to gaze on my immodest appearance; I was able to squeeze into my things before I was noticed. By then, the entire crowd was already moving off, and I followed them; for if I was indeed to write the memoir I had decided upon, I must make myself into a veritable Pepys, observing every detail with uncompromising objectivity.

By then, screams were coming from everywhere. We hurried down corridor after corridor, our way lit up by guards armed with swords and bearing oil lamps. To my astonishment, we appeared to be going toward the women's wing of the palace.

We crossed a courtyard lit by pale moonlight. The scent of jasmine was in the air. There was the women's wing. The guards stopped at the threshold; they could not enter on pain of death. Instead, one of the *khlon*, the withered old women who policed the harem, emerged, prostrated herself, and led us on. Women, many in a shocking state of dishabille, regarded us from every side. At last we were led to one of the private bedchambers reserved for the King's favorites. When the door was flung open, I beheld a sight of such unmitigated horror that it will remain with me for the rest of my life.

Lying on a mat of woven straw, resting against one of the triangular pillows of brilliant green silk, was a severed head. The face had been completely removed, revealing strips of flesh that hung upon her skull; eyeballs dangled from the sockets. Beside it—I mistook it at first for a serpent—was her bloody tongue, which had been ripped out by the roots.

An odor of decaying flesh—for rot sets in fast in the tropics—was already filling the air. Panicking, I stared at the rest of the chamber. The torso lay a little farther beyond; it was completely naked, and covered with crisscross lacerations. The abdomen had been sliced open, and a twirl of intestine emerged from it, dripping an odious dark rheum onto the floor. A human heart was displayed upon an elegantly embroidered sarong.

"It is the sarong of Nang Sobha," His Majesty said. I could see that he, too, was struggling to overcome his grief and horror. As an Englishwoman I could not fail to do likewise, for I could not have it said that my self-control was less than that of a foreigner. However, my stiff upper lip was unequal to the occasion; my gorge rose, and I regurgitated all over myself and His Majesty.

Such was my embarrassment at this solecism that I fainted and was, presumably, borne away by the servants.

I had barely recovered from the shock of finding my one friend viciously murdered, when the time came for me to dine at the lodgings of Dr. Gaunt. Relieved to be absent from the scene of violence, I boarded the boat and journeyed about a mile downriver. His Majesty had provided the good doctor a small house on one of the smaller *klongs* that fed off the Menam; the house rose on stilts from the water's edge, and rested above an orchard of mango and banana trees. A gibbon, chained to the veranda, screeched as I approached.

As I climbed the wooden steps, there was a familiar odor blended with the sultry smells of the river and the orchard. I sniffed as I lifted my skirts over the threshold of the house. In the antechamber, a table was set for two; and from farther within came the alluring scent of English food! Filled with gratitude at the trouble Dr. Gaunt was taking to remind me of dear, dear England, I began to sob.

"My dear Miss Leonowens," said Dr. Gaunt, emerging from the back, "what a pleasure."

We talked of relatives and acquaintances for a while; and then dinner was served by a lad in the uniform of a cabin boy.

"Jan! Een beetje wijn voor de vrouw," Dr. Gaunt commanded. I realized then that the boy was a Hollander, probably his servant aboard the *Groote Koning* on which he had so lately traveled. The boy poured wine for me.

"Are there no other guests?" I asked, wary of Dr. Gaunt's intentions.

"Alas, none, madam. But in a foreign land—"

I wept again. I had to tell someone of the horrifying events of the previous day, and Dr. Gaunt was the only Englishman I knew. I did not tell him of my adventures in the *hong bantom*, for the matter did seem extremely personal. But our discovery of the remains of Nang Sobha seemed to fascinate the doctor, and he begged me to describe all the details of the corpse's condition, which I did to the best of my ability, lacking as I did Dr. Gaunt's acquaintance with the subject.

I was explaining how the face seemed to have been lifted off the skull, leaving behind a mass of bone and gelatinous tissue, when Dr. Gaunt interposed, "Goodness gracious!

Whoever did that must surely have a good knowledge of the finer points of the surgical art!''

I went on to describe the torso, shuddering as I relived the vision of the handmaiden's heart lying upon the silken sarong.

''And the internal organs? The duodenum? The kidneys?'' Dr. Gaunt said. ''What of them?'' Seeing that I was quaking, he continued, ''But I see that my professional interest in the matter has outstripped common courtesy. *Jan, wij moeten toch eeten!*'' The boy returned with a steaming plate. To my delight I recognized the aroma of a steak and kidney pie. ''We shall have no more discourse on this unpleasant subject, Miss Leonowens. Pray fall to.''

Nothing loath, I attacked the pie with most unladylike gusto. ''It is undoubtedly the best steak and kidney pie I have ever tasted!'' I said. Nor was this flattery; I could not remember partaking of so succulent a dish, not even in England.

''Ah, but I am rather proud of my recipe,'' Dr. Gaunt said, ''and I use only the finest ingredients.''

I was a little chagrined to find the conversation shifting back once more to the subject of the murder of Nang Sobha. ''Were any suspects in evidence at the scene of the crime?'' the doctor asked.

''None to my knowledge,'' I said, ''save the *khlon* on duty, and various other handmaidens and harem girls. I fail to believe that any of them could be the guilty one. They are but defenseless women like myself, for all that they are foreigners. Ah, that unfortunate Nang Sobha! To die in so perfectly horrid a manner!''

''You sympathize with her? Ah, but you were her friend. What a fine soul you have, Miss Leonowens, to be able to feel compassion even for a harlot!''

''My dear Mr. Gaunt! I had hardly thought to hear such filth from your lips.''

"But alas, it is true . . . your friend was one of the King's *nang snom phra od*, and as such her duties consisted entirely of . . . ah . . ."

I nodded sagely, realizing that he was referring to the "fate worse than death," which I myself had but narrowly eluded the previous night. "What a terrible thing!" I exclaimed. "And yet she seemed a civilized woman."

"Such bizarre mutilations," Dr. Gaunt said. "Do you think it might be connected with some heathen rite?"

I trembled. "Perhaps I can do a little investigation," I said. For in truth I found the matter fascinating, in a macabre sort of way; and it would alleviate the boredom and the heat.

"I, with my medical abilities, can perhaps do some research myself," Dr. Gaunt said, winking conspiratorially at me. "Perhaps, together, we can solve the case. *Meer wijn!*" The boy refilled our cups—I must confess to having become a little tipsy by then—"A toast! To the detective team of Gaunt and Leonowens!"

"We'll have the killer's identity long before the King's constabulary can figure it out. We'll show these savages," I said grimly, "what superior British intelligence and cunning can achieve."

"Another toast! To England! To our good Queen Victoria!"

We lifted our glasses. "To the Queen!" I said, and then burst into a rousing rendition of "God Save the Queen." He joined in in a rich baritone. Exhausted, I said, "Thank God we're English."

"Thank God for that," Dr. Gaunt sighed. What a pleasant evening it had turned out to be! I now had a purpose other than the English lessons—to defend the honor of England by finding the miscreant responsible for the death of my friend. I was forever indebted to Dr. Gaunt; for in his abode, surrounded though it was by the alien sounds of Asia, I was able to forget for a few hours that I was far from home, my very life dependent on the whims of an Eastern potentate.

For the next few days I tried to keep my eyes and ears open. Not knowing the language made matters rather difficult. I also began keeping a journal of these happenings. What astonished me most was the equanimity with which the Siamese appeared to accept their lot. When I questioned them about it, they would invariably affirm that Nang Sobha's *karma* had somehow been bad, and that they hoped she would improve her fate in her next life; for these natives, sadly, believe in the transmigration of souls. An attendant who had failed to observe anyone enter or leave the bedchamber was summarily flogged; but apart from this, no further action was taken, and the event was dismissed as an unhappy anomaly in the otherwise idyllic life of the court. I was invited to tea again, and this time His Majesty did not play any cruel pranks on me, though he became very interested when I described Dr. Gaunt's steak and kidney pie to him, and he asked me to send him a copy of the recipe.

In the days to come, however, it was reported that the ghost of Nang Sobha had visited the concubines' dormitories on a number of occasions. I scoffed—in this age of scientific wonders, it seemed inappropriate to give credence to the idle superstitions of pagans—but the stories were repeated.

A week later, I was sound asleep in my bedroom when I heard a scuffling sound in the corridor outside. I put on my nightgown, lit a candle, and went out.

The hall was dark. My candle cast strange shadows on the wall. I heard something drop. I whirled. A figure darted across the flame's penumbra. I could barely make out the face, but it seemed to be . . . indeed . . . it seemed to be Nang Sobha! I tried to scream, but only a gurgle escaped my throat. I backed away, trying to pull myself together.

Courage! I told myself. Ghosts do not exist.

I resolved to settle the matter once and for all by going to Nang Sobha's chamber, which by then had been inherited by a certain Nang Methini, a new favorite of His Majesty's. I stalked down the corridor and flung open the doorway to the boudoir of my old friend.

"Excuse me!" My hand flew to my mouth. For there was His Majesty himself, and beside him, naked, was the Nang Methini!

"Oh, I say, dear Miss Leonowens; do come in," His Majesty said in a languorous voice. In the candlelight I saw that he had a most extraordinary deformity between his legs; I wondered whether so prodigious a protuberance characterized all members of the darker races. It made me wonder whether the machine that I had felt being inserted into me was in reality . . . quickly I dismissed the distasteful thought from my mind.

At first—remembering Dr. Gaunt's callous remarks about harlotry—I thought I had stumbled upon something I should not have seen. But when His Majesty bade me approach, and began the same ministrations upon my person that he had initiated that other night, my qualms evaporated. When Nang Methini joined in, I rested secure that this could not possibly have anything to do with the nasty goings-on of the conjugal union; for in all my mother's warnings she had never mentioned the notion that the "fate worse than death" might involve more than two persons. Besides, this second occurrence was so pleasurable that I was hard pressed to think it could be something calculated to revolt me. By the time our thrashings, caressings, and thrustings were done, I was in no condition to tell His Majesty what I had witnessed. It must have been a trick of the light; it were well I did not show myself to be a victim of heathen superstitions.

At length I took my leave of His Majesty and retired to my own chamber, where I made a glorious entry in my journal, and lay dreaming of its publication in England and my subsequent fame.

I was awakened by a piercing shriek—

This time it was the lovely Nang Methini who had been slain. Aghast, I stood among the other women as His Majesty came to inspect the scene of horror. The killing was even more elaborate than that of poor Nang Sobha; for the body had been dissected, the interior of the body exposed, the flaps of skin splayed out and fastened to the floor with hooks such as might be used in an anatomy lesson. The stomach and divers other organs had been removed; and from within the cavity stared the young woman's head, crowned with a turban fashioned entirely from her small intestine. The floor of the entire bedchamber was soaked with blood.

The women were all jabbering away in their heathen tongue, but I was able to make some sense of it. It seemed that they considered these women victims of a *phii krasue*.

"What is that, Your Majesty?" I asked him, as we left the scene of carnage.

"Oh, it is a kind of spirit. By day it is an ordinary, harmless corpse; but by night the head detaches itself from its body, and, dragging its entrails behind it, propels itself along the ground with its tongue."

"Surely you cannot countenance such superstition, Your Majesty!"

He sighed. "What can We do? Have you a better explanation, Miss Leonowens?"

"Not at the moment. But we must in all things proceed logically." I then told him of the rumors about the sightings of Nang Sobha, and that I myself had had a hallucinatory encounter with that lady.

"Ah, perhaps our barbaric superstitions are beginning to get to you," he said wryly as he left me.

* * *

As the day progressed I became aware of a sharp pain in the nether region of my body, which confined me to my chamber. This area of my being, whose precise location I have not the indecency to pinpoint to you, Lord Slatterthwaite, seemed as much on fire as though it had been flagellated and the open sores rubbed with chilies. I did not know what to do—I could hardly bring such a personal matter to the attention of the natives—until I remembered that I was dining with Dr. Gaunt again that evening. Of course I could tell him everything; he was a doctor.

I made notes in the journal about the few scraps of evidence that had come to light. One: I had most definitely seen Nang Sobha about the hallways; and the first of the two corpses had had its face removed in a peculiarly skillful manner. Perhaps the killer needed to conceal the true identity of his victim . . . perhaps Nang Sobha was indeed still alive. Adding two and two together, I had come up with one prime suspect at least. But why would she wish to kill the other women of the harem? Suddenly it all became clear to me . . . for were not all these women vying for the attentions of their sovereign, and scheming to be elevated to the position of queen? It was not every concubine that attained the status of a *phranangjao*, as their queens were known. Most never rose above a *nang snom phra od*, and of these only a few became a *jao jom manda*, let alone queen. (Living as I did within the very confines of the harem, I had not failed to learn the elaborate system of rank among these women.) Jealousy, then . . . that was the answer!

That lady whom I had thought so full of charm, who had sought out my friendship and been my confidante . . . was a wicked murderess! But what other answer was there? The only man allowed within these walls was His Majesty himself, so the killer had to be a woman. I was revolted that Nang Sobha had been able to so pervert the normal gentleness of her sex; but I reminded myself that she was an Oriental and by nature inscrutable. Doubtless she had befriended me only because I was an Englishwoman, and she hoped to learn from me a few of the attributes of civilization, the better to exert her wiles upon His Majesty. I was so furious that I forgot even the aching in my nether vitals.

I resolved to inform Dr. Gaunt of my theory without delay.

"Absolutely fascinating!" said Dr. Gaunt as we settled down to an apéritif that evening. "You arrived at these conclusions purely through the exercise of logic?"

"I'm afraid so, dear Doctor," I said ruefully.

"Well, His Majesty will have to be informed at once."

"I intend to seek an audience at the earliest opportunity."

"What a sad state of affairs!" Dr. Gaunt said. "But come; the table has been set, and little Jan is coming in with a tray of delicacies. Did you know, my dear Miss Leonowens, that today is St. Andrew's Day?"

I confessed that I had not known; for in the tropics the days went by, each one sultrier than the next, and I had ceased to keep track of the saints' days as we do in England. "Thank you, Dr. Gaunt, for informing me."

"More than that! I have prepared a Scottish feast in honor of that day; we shall begin with a haggis."

Once again we dined on fine British food; once again I was astonished at the doctor's culinary skill, and devoured my portion as though I had been starved these past few days. Dr. Gaunt viewed my enthusiasm with pride. "Once again, I have used only the best ingredients," he told me.

"How you could have obtained a sheep's stomach of such freshness in this forsaken land, Dr. Gaunt, I will never guess."

"To tell the truth, Miss Leonowens, one sometimes cannot find the exact ingredients necessary for a truly fine haggis or a steak and kidney pie; at times perforce one must improvise.'' He called to the cabin boy, who poured more wine. The boy was rather jumpy, and I remarked on it.

"Alas, I was forced to thrash him within an inch of his life," sighed the good doctor, "for I caught him trying to steal from me!"

"An old English remedy," I said severely, "spare the rod and spoil the child." I wagged a finger at him as he cowered in the shadows. "You naughty boy." The boy went to the back of the house; I was left alone with Dr. Gaunt. It was time for me to tell him of my affliction, and I did so.

He cluck-clucked in concern. "I'm afraid I shall have to examine it, Miss Leonowens," he said. "But rest assured; am a doctor."

At the conclusion of the repast, Dr. Gaunt led me into an inner chamber, and directed me to lie down upon a certain couch. He bound my arms with cords and told me to raise my legs so that he could more readily unfasten my nether garments.

"Never!" I said, offended.

"Ah, Miss Leonowens, I am a doctor."

Reluctantly I agreed. He poked at me with a cold metal instrument for a while; then he shook his head gravely. He made no move to release me from bondage.

"Madam, I am afraid—" He suddenly began to palpitate all over. Sweat poured down his brow, and a slight froth came bubbling from his mouth. "Filth! Obscenity! Dirty, filthy, filthy, dirty—"

"I say, Dr. Gaunt! Are you quite all right?" I said anxiously.

"Whore! Slut! Strumpet!" he shouted. His words became cries of inchoate rage.

"My dear Dr. Gaunt! This is hardly the place to allow a woman to give ear to such language!"

"I have the evidence that you are as filthy as all the others!" Dr. Gaunt screamed. "You should have been pure . .

but you have allowed yourself to be compromised . . . to be violated . . . to suffer a fate worse than death!''

"That is not so!" I protested. "His Majesty assured me—"

"It is so!" he screamed, his face purple with indignation.

"Rubbish," I said, with a last vestige of defiance. "It cannot be so, because the act that His Majesty performed required the use of a tubelike deformity situated between his legs; and I am quite certain that no Englishman possesses such a prodigy!"

Wordlessly, Dr. Gaunt began to unbutton his trousers. I squeezed my eyes shut, but he forced them open with his fingers. And I saw, emerging rampant from the fly of my captor, that same fleshy engine that I had seen on His Majesty!

Slowly it dawned upon me that perhaps I had been the victim of a cruel delusion. The "fate worse than death" and the night of rapture I had experienced were one and the same! I twisted and struggled against my bonds to no avail. Why did I even bother? I was a ruined woman. "Please tell me it isn't so," I whimpered. "Oh, please, Dr. Gaunt."

"It is so, alas," he said. He was no longer angry; a grim sadness was in his features. "As a doctor, I must insist that that has indeed been your fate. You enjoyed it, didn't you, you brazen hussy! In the degradation of your moral condition, you failed to be revolted by the horror inflicted upon you . . . you actually reveled in it . . . may you be damned in your sin, madam!"

"Is there no remedy?" I wailed.

"Yes, my dear Miss Leonowens. It will be possible to purge you, to erase all traces of this mishap from your flesh."

"Oh, please, Dr. Gaunt! Any emetic, any potion, any number of leeches . . ."

"Unfortunately it will take more than leeches to drive the taint from your flesh. I shall be forced to take direr measures

. . . just as I did with the others. In vain I preached to them of the virtues of purity; but they laughed at me. And so I punished them, as was the will of God Almighty. I must now do the same to you, Miss Leonowens. At least feel some satisfaction that you now die at the hand of an Englishman rather than a godless native."

He bent down over me. If his anger had been terrifying, his calm was even more so. His eyes were completely lifeless. He was utterly detached as he tightened the ropes and began methodically to tear off my clothing. I spat, I screamed, I importuned; in response he slapped my face again and again until blood spurted from my nose into my mouth and eyes. He opened a black leather bag and feverishly dumped its contents onto the floor. My eyes widened as I spied lancets, scalpels, pincers, hacksaws . . . all the paraphernalia of the surgeon's trade. He pored over the instruments and finally selected a scalpel.

"Have you heard of vivisection, Miss Leonowens?" My only response was a strangled cry. He lifted up the scalpel and touched it to my breast, sending a sliver of cold pain through my body. "Ah, but you will soon learn all about it at first hand," he said. He began to whistle to himself. I recognized it as a melody from one of the Savoy operas. It was now all too apparent that Dr. Gaunt was not a sane man.

I screamed as the scalpel penetrated the skin of my breasts and the blood began streaming down my stomach and sides—

At that moment, an eerie music sounded outside the house . . . xylophones, the plaintive wailing of an oboe, the alien rhythms of the Siamese drum . . . it was the music for the royal progress! I heard footsteps. I screamed all the more as the door to the inner chamber was flung open—and His Majesty stood before us, in full court regalia, brandishing a pistol!

"Save me!" I cried.

To my astonishment, His Majesty marched over to where

I was lying and held the pistol to my forehead. "We have you now," he said. He turned to Dr. Gaunt, and continued, "We must thank you, kind sir, for assisting Us in the investigation. Our Siamese system of justice must now take over, and We will see that Miss Leonowens is suitably punished for the terrible crimes she has committed."

Dr. Gaunt was now pacing the room with a look of satisfaction on his face. Weakly I tried to protest. "Your Majesty, I am innocent . . . indeed, it was Dr. Gaunt who—"

"Rubbish!" Dr. Gaunt said, shrugging. "You know very well, madam, that it is forbidden for any man to enter the women's wing of the palace."

His Majesty surveyed me with a look of utter opprobrium. Indeed, my fate would be to die among savages! He had tricked me into giving away that which is most precious in a woman . . . doubtless he had committed the murders himself, to satisfy some dread Oriental rite, and I was now the luckless scapegoat!

"We suspected you from the first," His Majesty said, "for you were ignorant of those facts of life that are known to every peasant in the kingdom. You English are a very peculiar bunch. You deny this knowledge to your daughters, cloaking it in lies and filth; yet beneath this seeming innocence seethes a cauldron of guilt and repression. It is the fact that you cannot express your natural desires that has given you this relentless drive for world domination. You hide your passions and choose instead to lord it over hapless natives from Ireland to India. You are a sick, sick people, you English! It is not surprising to me that, having had your sexual illusions stripped from you in a single night of wanton pleasure, you would seek vengeance on those who do not share your repressions. Your years of self-denial, Miss Leonowens, were swept away in a single instant; the dam of your sanity burst; and you were transformed from a gentlewoman into an insane monster. It is obvious that you slipped away from Our side while we slept, performed the heinous act, and returned black-heartedly to Our *hong bantom* without suffering the slightest pangs of remorse. The second murder you effected even more easily, since the chamber of Nang Methini was but a stone's throw from your own. Perfidious monster! We pity you, Miss Leonowens, We pity you.''

''Your Majesty is the most compassionate of men,'' Dr. Gaunt said.

''Your information was most valuable to Us,'' the King said, ''and We are glad that We had Miss Leonowens followed, as you advised.''

''Perhaps Your Majesty would care for a piece of leftover haggis?''

I cannot describe the complex feelings that warred within my hapless breast at that moment. I was the only one who knew that Dr. Gaunt was the killer; yet here I lay, strapped and bleeding, accused of these foul acts myself, with no means of redress! Words were useless now. I would not be believed. In these moments, which I was sure were my last (for His Majesty still pointed his pistol in my direction, and, convinced as he was of my guilt, might at any time do away with me), I prayed for deliverance. Since this world held nothing more for me, I steadfastly and resolutely set my eyes on the next; and though I would die unshriven in an alien land, yet I trusted that the Lord Jesus Christ would see me in my ultimate anguish and lead me to that final paradise that is the lot of all stout-hearted members of the Church of England.

It was at that moment that Nang Sobha entered the room.

Something was clearly the matter with her, for she no longer walked with the natural grace that she used to have, but minced, as though her sarong ill fitted her; indeed, she seemed in pain, and rubbed her hinder parts as if they had recently been flagellated.

She said to Dr. Gaunt: *"Moet ik evetjes naar de paleis gaan, meneer?"*

"Get back, you idiot!" Dr. Gaunt shouted. "The King's here!"

The King whirled round and pulled the trigger. Clutching her stomach, Nang Sobha fell forward. Her silken blouse tore open and two bloodstained half coconut shells came bouncing forth. A hairpiece began to slide down her face, revealing short, blond locks beneath. Most horrible of all, the face itself began to peel, and I perceived that it was a mask of human skin stretched over a rattan frame; and beneath it, mouth agape in an unborn death cry, was the visage of little Jan, the cabin boy!

The boy's dead body thudded on the floor.

His Majesty then turned his weapon on Dr. Gaunt. "Back to the wall, Dr. Gaunt!" he said, groping around on the couch for the scalpel with which the doctor had tortured me. He sliced the cords that bound me. "We apologize, my dear Miss Leonowens, for using you as bait. But We think you will agree that the criminal has been caught red-handed. Now, if you would please assist Us in incapacitating Dr. Gaunt?"

Too stunned to protest this new turn of events, I obeyed blindly, and soon we had the doctor tied to the couch. He mumbled obscenities and imprecations at us, none of which dear Lord Slatterthwaite, I dare set to paper for fear of sinking even further in your estimation.

"It remains only to wait for the arrival of the palace guards," the King said. "Perhaps, Miss Leonowens, you would not care to stay in the same room as this madman."

I heartily agreed. We quit the chamber. As we descended from the house, the royal orchestra began to play, and I saw one of the royal barges on the water, a nine-headed serpent covered with beaten gold, which glimmered magically in the twilight. Rowers in uniform plied their oars to the accompaniment of mystical chants. His Majesty invited me to join him on the barge; he sat enthroned while I leaned on the cushions at his feet.

"Your Majesty knew it was the doctor all this time?" I said, wondering.

"Ah, Miss Leonowens, We admit that at first We did suspect you, for We had no explanation for how a man could have entered the harem. And you do have that strange English ingenuousness about carnal matters. We knew it was an Englishman, for no Siamese would have so dishonored the decapitated head of a corpse by placing it lower than the corpse's feet." He shuddered. "We began to suspect the doctor, however, when you mentioned the steak and kidney pie over tea."

"My goodness, Your Majesty," I said. A most disquieting thought had just struck me. "Do you mean to say that—"

"Just so," said the King, shaking his head. "No one was ever able to find Nang Sobha's kidneys. Alas, she will be cremated without them. And as for poor Nang Methini's stomach . . ."

"The haggis!" I exclaimed, sickened to the core.

"Ah, the haggis," said the King. "When the doctor came to Us, detailing his suspicion of you, We played along. We knew that—if he chanced to be right in his accusation—it would be simple to apprehend you; and if Our own theory was correct, that the doctor would be playing right into Our hands." So much, my dear Lord Slatterthwaite, for British ingenuity and cunning! How stupid I felt in the presence of this positively Machiavellian intellect!

The constables boarded the vessel now, laden with evidence from the doctor's house . . . dozens of masks made from real human faces, sections of the nether parts of women which had been cured and tanned on wooden frames . . . women's breasts, flayed and stretched out over coconut shells . . . horror upon horror until I was too numb to show revulsion.

"He and the boy, apparently, have been at work in the

courts of Java and Sumatra as well,'' the King said, as he examined the grisly trophies. "It was the boy, you see, disguised as Nang Sobha, whom you saw that night. He was scouting out the premises for his master, who would arrive later, also attired as a woman, to perform the actual killing. Well, their dastardly partnership is no more."

"I trust you will punish him severely," I said, when all the offending objects had been removed, and we began to move upstream, the chanting punctuated by the slap of oars on water. The stars were beginning to emerge. Across the river, in Bangkok's sister city of Dhonburi, the moon shone over the Temple of Dawn. The air buzzed with mosquitoes and with the chirpings of exotic reptiles, and was fragrant with night-blooming jasmine. "Will you have him executed?" I said, wondering whether the spectacle of an Oriental beheading would be as interesting to watch as an English hanging.

"On the contrary, Miss Leonowens, We intend to let him go."

"But that is positively immoral!" I said.

"We are a king," said His Majesty, "and the interests of the entire country must come before any personal satisfaction or revenge. You English have conquered India, are sinking your teeth into Burma and Malaya; your rivals the French are daily making further incursions into IndoChina. Where will all this end? Already you have extraterritoriality in our country; We could not execute this man, as a British subject, even though he killed two of Our favorite wives in cold blood."

"But you will yield him up to the British Ambassador, will you not? And he will be tried in England, and hanged."

"Why?" His Majesty said. "We shall just send him home. We intend to eradicate all records of this matter. Perhaps, in the years to come, he will grow more careful, more difficult to catch. We can only hope that he will give you English so hard a time that you will no longer think of trying to invade Siam.''

"I am sure that such a thing is farthest from the mind of Her Britannic Majesty,'' I said indignantly.

"Ah,'' His Majesty said, stroking my arm. I did not resist—how could I? I was a ruined woman now, capable of any depravity—but allowed him every liberty with me. "You have so much to learn about us, my dear Miss Leonowens. You come here, thinking to civilize a barbarian monarch with your superior ways. Has it never occurred to you that we barbarians might think wholly otherwise? That to us it is *you* who are the uncivilized upstarts? We shall let this man go, Miss Leonowens, not only because it is politically expedient to Us . . . but also because We are a disciple of the Lord Buddha, who taught compassion above all things. Our *karma* has caused Us to be born a king, and it is in the nature of kings to be merciful. May Dr. Gaunt's tormented soul find release in some other incarnation.''

I have just come from the funeral of the two concubines. I have listened to the chanting of bonzes; I have watched the funeral flames rise toward the night sky. As I write these words to you, Lord Slatterthwaite, my thoughts are constantly of England. I confess that I am plagued by doubts. Perhaps they could be assuaged by a cup of tea. I shall summon a servant to bring me some. His Majesty has graciously assigned a servant to me whose only function is to brew tea, and he has had a cow brought in for the sole purpose of providing my tea with milk.

I realize now, Lord Slatterthwaite, that my journal contains many incidents that do not show the English in an entirely perfect light. But the public will doubtless demand some account of my sojourn in this country; and they will expect to read the heartwarming tale of an Englishwoman, who managed to win the heart and tame the spirit of a cruel, inscrutable despot. I shall have to give them what they want. For, though I have been compromised, England must never be. The good name of England must be preserved at all costs.

I therefore urge you to burn this epistle at once, my dear Lord Slatterthwaite. I am confident that, once Dr. Gaunt has breathed our purifying English air, he will no longer feel the urge to kill. The matter is closed now, or will be with the destruction of this letter. I am forced to believe that an Englishman perpetrated these atrocities; yet there were mitigating circumstances. The tropics can drive the sanest man into madness; and besides, the doctor's accomplice was Dutch! Who knows what role the boy may have played in corrupting his master? But the cabin boy is no more, and cannot tell us.

As for me, I shall hide my dishonor from the world, and write a memoir that will demonstrate to everyone's satisfaction that it is the God-given right of the English to rule over all the races of men. It is the least I can do to still the doubts that yet rage within my palpitating breast.

Your Lordship, I remain

    Your most humble and obedient servant,

    Anna

                March 186__ [illegible]

It was, of course, necessary to try to prove the manuscript's authenticity by assiduous research. Fortunately, the following Sunday, *The King and I* was shown on the BBC, and I was not too drunk to notice that Anna Leonowens is shown, in this unchallengeable source, not only to be a widow, instead of a dewy virgin, but to have a young son! Alas, the creator of the bogus document at hand did not have the perseverance for even the minimal research of watching television! Of course, there *was* no telly in Victorian England.

I was having tea at the Copper Kettle with a certain Sheffield, who is doing his Ph.D. in astrophysics and ought to know a thing or two. He has an interesting theory, which, mathematically, derives from Hoyle's steady-state theory of the universe; namely, that the manuscript may in fact be quite genuine, but have been deposited in our space-time continuum from another, *alternate* universe in which the facts occurred just as the document describes them. Although I am not qualified to speculate about the scientific basis of all this, I must say that the old fellow's hypothesis does grant the whole thing a kind of shaky legitimacy. As such, it is to be heartily applauded.

—St. _____'s College, Cambridge
Michaelmas Term, 1967

THE EDGE

Pat Cadigan

Pat Cadigan was born in Schenectady, New York, and now lives in Overland Park, Kansas. One of the best new writers in SF, Cadigan made her first professional sale in 1980 to New Dimensions, *and soon became a frequent contributor to* Omni, The Magazine of Fantasy and Science Fiction, Isaac Asimov's Science Fiction Magazine, *and* Shadows, *among other markets. She was the coeditor, along with husband Arnie Fenner, of* Shayol, *perhaps the best of the semiprozines; it was honored with a World Fantasy Award in the "Special Achievement, Non-Professional" category in 1981. She has also served on the Nebula Award jury. Her first novel,* Mindplayers, *was released in 1987, to excellent critical response, and she's at work on a new novel called* Sinners.

In the razor-edged look at the world of Style that follows, she shows us that it's getting all the accessories right that gives a man the Edge . . .

NOT A CURIO SHOP, NOTHING SO PICTURESQUE IN A *mall.* A knife store, a place that sold edges. Cutting edges. Hunting knives, bowie knives (David assumed; he had no idea what a bowie knife really was), serrated knives, knives with intricately-worked hilts, knives with designs engraved in their blades; pocket knives; daggers; antique-looking cavalry sabres; a samurai sword that was certainly a reproduction; some lethal-looking letter openers. No steak knives or tableware. This was not a place to buy anything so prosaic as something to cut a steak with. Or saw on a steak with; David thought of the steak knives at home in the drawer, which had gone dull after their first use. But the tastefully-lettered sign in the window display said they would sharpen any and all knives, scissors, or other edges. That was how they put it—not blades, edges. Interesting point of view in there, he thought. But then anyone who was so involved with knives—

The more he thought about it, the stranger it seemed. *Only* knives? Only *knives*. Could anyone really make a living selling knives only?

Someone walked past behind him with a crackle of shopping bags. "Ugh, *knives*," said a woman's voice. "I *hate* knives. It's like a phobia . . ." Her voice faded into the general mall babble just as a little boy ran up beside him and put both chubby hands on the window.

"Look, Mommy, *knives*!"

"Bobby, *please*." The voice, presumably Mommy's, was very tired.

"They're *shiny*!" The boy looked up at David as though looking for agreement. David smiled at him. The boy's eyes narrowed slightly and then he gave David a grin too knowing for a child's face. David took a step back just as a tired-looking woman with drooping frizzy hair and too many packages swept the boy away in a crackle of shopping bags. He stared after them as they dwindled into the mall traffic. The expression on the boy's face had been shockingly old, as though there were some ancient entity looking out the windows of the boy's eyes, a hint of humanity as it had been in a less civilized, more elemental state. Racial memory; ghosts in the DNA.

David shook his head. The child was trotting helplessly along in his mother's grip, his free arm flailing the air. He was just a toddler. There you have it, David thought bemusedly. Get divorced and the next thing you knew, you were hanging around shopping malls finding sinister things in children's faces. What could a toddler know about racial memory or less pleasant things that might sleep in the blood.

Blood. His attention went back to the window display. Enough knives there to instigate a blood flood. But not the right knife, not the one for him.

Light flashed on a hundred separate blades as he went inside.

"Everyone has, of course, knives in their homes." The shop owner was some kind of exotic but David couldn't tell what. Something about his face made David think of Australian aborigines but his eyes seemed oriental and his black hair was straight.

"I'm tempted to say something like 'Knives don't kill people, people kill people.' " The man smiled at his own indulgence. "You have to understand that the knife was probably the first tool—the first deliberate tool, I mean, the first tool primitive man made—crafted—on purpose. A man with a knife could cut through undergrowth, kill game for food, skin it for pelts, carve new tools. And cut another man's throat. Though by the time man achieved the knife, I'm sure murder was old news." He paused, holding out a smooth eight-inch blade with a flat black handle.

"Oh, right, sure," David said, pretending to give serious consideration to the knife. "It looks good, but—" He shrugged.

The man looked from the knife to David and back again. "You're right, this isn't the one. It's important to get the right one."

David felt a small chill at hearing his thoughts echoed aloud by this stranger. "The right one? The right knife?"

"The right anything, sir," the man said, almost purring. He replaced the knife in a drawer behind the counter. "You don't buy a car you don't feel comfortable driving or a suit that doesn't fit. Nor do you buy a suit which fits perfectly but which doesn't reflect your true self." He turned to examine the stacks of wooden drawers against the wall behind him.

"You carry a lot of stock."

"In order to sell the right knife to the right person, it's necessary to have a large inventory." He looked over his shoulder at David, frowning a little. "I'm not quite sure which knife would be right for you."

David gave a self-conscious laugh. "Well, I'm five-eleven, a hundred and sixty pounds, sandy hair, brown eyes. Libra." He laughed again. "If that helps."

The man smiled. "Libra. Yes, quite humorous." Mayans, David thought suddenly. Incas. They'd liked knives, hadn't they? But he knew instinctively this man wasn't either one but something else, something that didn't exist anymore except for the odd stranger here and there where the genes, scattered among the general population, came together in a chance combination that was exactly right.

He blinked, shoving the thought away. What a strange thing to think, and about someone he didn't even know. The divorce had given him plenty to think about but here he was daydreaming little nothings.

"Sir? I said, How many knives do you own?" The man was studying him with mild concern.

"Oh, sorry," David said with embarrassment. "I've had a lot on my mind lately. How many knives? You mean besides the dull steak knives my in-laws gave us?"

The man raised one eyebrow. "You're married?"

"Well. The divorce was final a couple of days ago. But I did get custody of the steak knives, which wouldn't cut warm butter."

"Ah." The man nodded. "Some people will try that, thinking it will 'defuse,' so to speak, the situation. For some, I'm sure it does. But others, no; they come looking, eventually."

"Pardon? I don't—"

"Come looking for their knives. Some people try to avoid the issue of knives by owning large and expensive collections of cutlery. Claiming they cook, of course. They mistake the satisfaction of owning expensive things for the satisfaction of owning an edge. There are even some knife people who try to be gun people. Very frustrating for them; they confuse the concept of weapon with the weapon itself."

"Well, I'm definitely against guns," David said stoutly.

"Quite right. Noisy, filthy things, requiring no talent, no skill, no subtlety. A bullet could never give you an edge."

David laughed without humor. "I know some people who'd probably give you an argument on that point. Anyway, I wouldn't exactly call a knife wound subtle."

"Ah, but it must be inflicted at close range—"

"What about throwing knives?" David interrupted.

"Cheap carnival tricks. If you care for that sort of thing." The man made a disgusted noise. "The knife was meant to be held in the hand. It is personal, intimate. And it takes great skill to get close enough to do that. Someone capable of it certainly would have an edge on other people, wouldn't you say?"

David put his hands on the glass counter, feeling a little ill. God, how had they gotten into such a discussion? This guy had to be sick. The people who were allowed to run around loose, he thought. But he didn't push himself away from the counter full of knives and the nut who was peddling them. It was not that he couldn't, he just didn't.

"You know," the man went on, "there are some people as repelled by knives as there are those drawn to them."

"Oh, yeah, I did know that. It's like a phobia," he said, thinking of the woman who had passed him just before that little boy with that awful grin—obviously he knew a fellow enthusiast—

But the man was still talking. "—just like a phobia, yes. Some people will smoke, drink to excess, poison themselves with all manner of strange drugs, but show them a naked edge—they become quivering wrecks.'' He smiled serenely. ''Knife people are a breed apart.'' His gaze seemed to go right through David without losing any of its serenity. ''And I believe I know exactly which edge is right for you now.''

Before David could say anything, the man went down to the opposite end of the counter and pulled out a drawer beneath the display case. He sorted through several boxes carefully and then returned with a long, skinny box that had been taped and retaped several times to keep it together. There was no brand name or trademark symbol on it.

''The edge itself,'' the man said, removing the lid, ''is very, very old.''

The blade flashed under the lights with the brilliance of new steel. ''Doesn't look it,'' David said.

''Oh, it's been very well cared for. And there seems to be a certain peculiarity in the metal. I believe it's a special alloy, not the usual kind. Metalworking is not my particular area of knowledge but I do know this knife is, well, different.''

The knife was undistinguished to David's eye. The blade was plain; the handle was ivory, yellowed with age. But a good handle, he noticed. It looked like you'd be able to keep a grip on it no matter what.

''Pick it up,'' the man said softly. ''It's not for butchers.''

David reached for the knife, and there was the briefest moment before he touched it when he wondered why he was blindly obeying this knife-fixated fruitcake who probably regarded knives as phallic symbols; yeah, he should have terminated this conversation and left long ago.

Then he picked up the blade.

The handle was cold, as though it had been in a refrigerator. David felt the chill spread through his hand and run up his arm like a stream of water to his neck, encircling it and then striking the base of his brain like a fist.

He stared at the reflection of his eyes in the gleaming blade. *A certain peculiarity in the metal.*

Those were not his eyes.

The eyes were ebony, slanted. As David watched, they closed with pleasurable slowness; a fine spray dotted the eyelids, ran down from a corner like a tear. Blood.

The scene changed; like several dreams melting one into the other, he saw the blade pass from hand to hand in a Far Eastern court; it was wielded only by one chosen and the one chosen used it with skill bordering on elegance. When the blood flowed, it made patterns that spoke to the one chosen and to David; there was art in everything if you knew the right way to do it.

The blade passed from hand to hand and from generation to generation. The court vanished and he saw country he didn't know, semitropical landscape that changed to ocean and then to desert. Pyramids. The one chosen was no longer one chosen with any formality; the knife chose. He saw the face of a man who stole it and traded it for food, and the knife knew the hand it had come to. When the man turned away, there was a red line drawn skillfully across his neck with one good stroke. The image of the man's face was replaced by several more, one dissolving into another but each with the same well-drawn line through blood vessels and windpipe.

The knife went to a woman who kept it up a long, embroidered sleeve, where it slid down to her hand whenever she wanted.

Edge, said the man behind the counter. *Not just a blade or a knife but an* edge. *It's important to have an edge and to know when to use it.*

There was darkness for a long time until someone in seventeenth-century finery discovered the knife locked in a cabinet. The teenaged boy kept it with him all the time, polishing it, fondling it, and finally using it, just once, on his wedding night.

A brief moment of discovery in a lady's hands—David could feel the shock, the pleasure and disgust mingling with the realization that she must never touch it again. Darkness once more; David thought it would go on forever.

And then someone laid claim to the edge again, touching it with care and appreciation. Of all the people who had had the edge, this was a connoisseur—an edge connoisseur—who knew the small secret of there being a right edge for all knife people, and this was *his*. David sensed the intricate patterns the knife cut through the air, through the world, through life. And it was not to question the rightness or wrongness, only to know that the knife was being used the way it had been *meant* to be used, an extension of the body, of the self. The subtlety was in the dance before and the retreat after, while the moment of the edge was a frenzy of sensation that stretched across the centuries, from the one chosen who had masked his edge with intrigues and assignments from the ruler of the Far Eastern court, to the damp, foggy evenings of London in 1888, where a man described sometimes as saucy and sometimes as spring-heeled hid his edge just with darkness.

The eyes gazed into his, the recognition unmistakable.

His head cleared and he found himself holding the knife over the counter in an experienced grip.

"What happened?" David asked.

"No one knows. Perhaps he lost his edge and emigrated to the land of opportunity and started over again. Married, raised a family." The man took the knife carefully from David's hand and placed it in the box again. "Thirty dollars."

"Oh." David slipped his wallet out of his back pocket and dug out some bills. "What's the tax on that?"

"No tax." The man smiled. "Not this time. You have an

edge now.'' He presented the box to David, who took it with both hands and stared down at it.

"Uh—I don't think—I mean, are you sure—"

"This merchandise cannot be returned. It's *your* edge. Take it home. Live with it, take care of it. Get used to it. You'll see how good it is to have an edge."

David walked out of the store, out of the mall, into the fading afternoon, and it was just a little while later, only a matter of two nights, when he discovered that the man had been right, and he knew the pleasure of having the edge; of going over the edge.

AN AWARENESS
OF ANGELS

Karl Edward Wagner

One of the most intriguing things about the Ripper murders is that nobody has any clear idea why they were committed. Many theories have been advanced over the years, without any real evidence to support any of them. Were the murders the crazed act of a woman-hating madman . . . or were they perhaps the cold and calculated machinations of a rather radical social reformer, designed to call attention to the truly appalling conditions in the Whitechapel slums? It has even been suggested that the murders were committed as part of a sinister Masonic conspiracy to cover up a royal indiscretion! In the chilling tale that follows, though, Karl Edward Wagner gives us a motivation for the killings unlike any we have ever seen before . . .

Karl Edward Wagner is one of the true giants of the modern horror genre. As editor of The Year's Best Horror Stories, *Wagner's choices have been extremely influential in publicizing what is happening on the cutting-edge of horror, while as editor of the small press imprint Carcosa, he has at the same time been instrumental in preserving the best work of old masters such as Manly Wade Wellman and Hugh B. Cave. It is as a writer, though, that Wagner has had his biggest impact, and his unsettling stories—frequently set in a beautifully-evoked Rural American South, often drenched with explicitly-sexual imagery, always controversial—are prized by connoisseurs of the genre. He has won the British Fantasy Award four times and the World Fantasy Award twice;*

the best of his short fiction has been collected in In a Lonely Place, *a cornerstone book for any horror library. His other books include* Darkness Weaves, Death Angel's Shadow, Bloodstone, Dark Crusade, Night Winds, *and* The Road of Kings.

H E SURRENDERED SO MEEKLY. IT WAS OVER SO QUI-
etly. It was anticlimactic.

Sheriff Jimmy Stringer certainly thought so. "Please." And there were tears quavering his voice, but his hand with the .357 was steady. "Please. Just try something. Please try something."

But the killer just stood there placidly in the glare of their lights, blood-smeared surgical gloves raised in surrender.

In the back of his van they could see the peppermint-stripe body of the fourteen-year-old hooker, horribly mutilated and neatly laid out on a shower curtain. Another few minutes, and all would be bundled up tidily—destined shortly thereafter for a shallow grave in some pine-and-scrub wasteland, or perhaps a drop from a bridge with a few cinder blocks for company. Like the other eleven they had so far been able to find.

"Please. Do it," begged Stringer. One of the eleven had been an undercover policewoman, and that had been Stringer's idea. "Come on. *Try* something."

But already there were uniformed bodies crowding into the light. Handcuffs flashed and clacked, and someone began reading the kid his rights.

"Steady on there, Jimmy. You're not Clint Eastwood." Dr. Nathan Hodgson's grip on his shoulder was casual, but surprisingly strong.

His own hand suddenly shaking, Stringer slowly lowered his Smith & Wesson, gently dropped its hammer, and returned the revolver to the holster at his side. His belt was a notch tighter now, needed one more. He'd lost fifteen of his two hundred pounds during the long investigation, despite a six-pack every night to help him sleep.

More sirens were curdling the night, and camera flashes made grotesque strobe effects with the flashing lights of police and emergency vehicles. They'd already shoved the killer—the suspect—into one of the county cars.

Stringer let out a shuddering breath and faced the forensic psychiatrist. Dr. Hodgson looked too much like a television evangelist for his liking, but Stringer had to admit they'd never have nailed this punk tonight without the shrink's help. *Modus operandi* was about as useful as twenty-twenty hindsight; Hodgson had been able to study the patterns and to predict where the psycho most likely would strike again. Like hunting a rabbit with beagles: wait till it runs around by you again—then, *bang*.

"Suppose now that we caught this little piece of shit, you'll do your best to prove he's crazy, and all he needs is some tender loving care for a couple months."

Stringer's freckled face was sweaty, and he looked ready to hit someone. "Dammit, Nate! They'll just turn the fucker loose and call him a responsible member of society. Let him kill and kill again!"

Dr. Hodgson showed no offense. "If he's guilty, then he'll pay the penalty. I don't make the laws."

An old excuse, but works every time. Stringer tried to spit, found his mouth too dry. The bright flashes of light hurt his eyes. Like kicking over a long-dead dog on the side of the road. Just a bunch of wriggling lumps, all bustling about a black Chevy van and the vivisected thing in its belly. Lonely piece of two-lane blacktop, an old county road orphaned by the new lake. Old farm fields overrun with cedar and briar and a couple years' growth of pine and sumac. Probably a good place to hunt rabbits. He had half a beer in his car.

"Neither do I," Stringer said heavily. "I just try to enforce them."

Right off the TV reruns, but he was too tired to be clever. He hoped some asshole deputy hadn't used his beer can for an ashtray.

His name was Matthew Norbrook, and he wanted to make a full confession. So they'd only found a dozen? He'd show them where to look for the rest. If he could remember them all. The ones in this end of the state. Would they like to know about the others? Maybe the ones in other states?

Too easy, and they weren't taking chances on blowing this case due to some technicality. The judge ordered a psychiatric examination for the next morning.

Dr. Nathan Hodgson was in charge.

There were four of them in the observation room, watching through the two-way mirror as Dr. Hodgson conducted his examination. Morton Bowers was the court-appointed defense attorney—a gangling black cleanly dressed in an off-the-rack mill-outlet suit that didn't really fit him. Cora Steinman was the local D.A., and her businesswoman's power suit fit her very well indeed. Dr. something Gottlieb—Stringer hadn't remembered her first name—was wearing a shapeless white lab coat, and alternated between scribbling notes and fooling with the video recording equipment. Stringer was wearing his uniform for a change—none too neat, and that wasn't a change—partly to show that this was official business, but mainly to remind these people that he was in charge here, at least for now. A further reminder, two of Stringer's deputies were standing just outside in the hallway. In charge for now: the state boys would be crowding in soon, and probably the FBI next.

Stringer sipped on his coffee. It reminded him of watching some bad daytime drama on the big projection TV they had in the bar at the new Trucker's Heaven off I-40—actually their sign read "Haven," but try to tell that to anyone. Stringer wished for a smoke, but they'd all jumped on his case when he'd earlier pulled out a pack. It had all been boring thus far: preliminaries and legal technicalities. Stringer supposed it all served some purpose.

Trouble was, you could be damn sure that the purpose was to make certain this murdering little pervert got off scot-free. Stringer just wished they'd leave him alone in a room with the filthy creep—two-way mirrors or not. He might be pushing fifty, but . . .

"Before we go any further," Norbrook was saying, "I want it perfectly understood that I consider myself to be entirely sane."

He was wearing orange county-jail coveralls—Dr. Hodgson had insisted that they remove the handcuffs—but he still managed the attitude of having kindly granted this interview. His manner was condescending, his speech pedantic to the point of arrogance.

Some bright little college punk, Stringer judged—probably high on drugs most of the time. About thirty, and tall, dark, and handsome, just like they say. He'd have no problem picking up girls: Let's climb into my van and snort a little coke. Here, try on this gag while I get out my knives. Stringer knotted his heavy fists and glared at that TV-star nose and smiling mouth of toothpaste-ad teeth.

"Are you sometimes concerned that other people might not think that you are entirely sane?" Dr. Hodgson asked him.

The psychiatrist was wearing a three-piece suit that probably cost more than Stringer's pickup truck. He was almost twice the age of the suspect—of his patient—but had the distinguished good looks and gray-at-the-temples pompadour that seemed to turn on women from teeny-boppers to golden-agers. Stringer had heard enough gossip to know that Hodgson was sure no fairy, and maybe there was a dent or two in the old Hippocratic oath back up North that had made the doc content to relocate here in a rural southern county.

Norbrook's smile was supercilious. "Please, Dr. . . . Hodgson, is it? We can dispense with the how-do-you-feel-about-that? routine. My concern is that the story I propose to tell may at first sound completely mad. That's why I asked for this interview. I had hoped that a psychiatrist might have the intelligence to listen without preconception or ignorant incredulity. All Sheriff Andy of Mayberry and his redneck deputies here seem capable of understanding is a body count, and that rather limits them to their ten fingers."

Stringer dreamed of sharing Norbrook's ten fingers with a sturdy brick. Afterward they'd slip into those surgical gloves just like Jell-O going into a fancy mold.

"This story you want to tell me must seem very important to you," Dr. Hodgson said.

"Important to the entire human race," Norbrook said levelly. "That's why I decided to surrender when I might have escaped through the brush. I didn't want to risk the chance that a bullet would preserve their secrets."

"Their secrets?"

"All right. I'm perfectly aware that you're fully prepared to dismiss everything I'm about to tell you as paranoid fantasy. And I'm perfectly aware that paranoid schizophrenics have no doubt sat here in this same chair and offered this same protest. All I ask is that you listen with an open mind. If I weren't able to furnish proof of what I'm about to tell you, I'd never have permitted myself to be captured. Agreed?"

"Suppose you begin at the beginning."

"It began a hundred years ago. No, to be precise, it began before history—perhaps at the dawn of the human race. But my part of the story begins a century ago in London.

"My great-grandfather was Jack the Ripper."

Norbrook paused to study the effect of his words.

Hodgson listened imperturbably. He never made notes during an interview; it was intrusive, and it was simpler just to play back the tape.

Stringer muttered, "Bullshit!"—and crumpled his coffee cup.

"I suppose," continued Norbrook, "that many people will say that madness is inherited."

"Is that how you sometimes feel?" Hodgson asked.

"My great-grandfather wasn't mad, you see—and that's the crux of it all."

Norbrook settled back in his chair, smiling with the air of an Agatha Christie detective explaining a locked-room murder.

"My great-grandfather—his identity has defied discovery all these years, although I intend to reveal it in good time—was a brilliant experimental surgeon of his day. Because of his research, some would have condemned him as a vivisectionist."

"Can you tell me how all of this was revealed to you?"

"Not through voices no one else can hear," Norbrook snorted. "Please, Doctor. Listen and don't interrupt with your obvious ploys. My great-grandfather kept an extensive journal, made careful notes of all of his experiments.

"You see, those prostitutes—those creatures—that he killed. Their deaths were not the random murders of a deranged fiend. On the contrary, they were experimental subjects for my great-grandfather's early researches. The mutilation of their corpses was primarily a smoke screen to disguise the real purpose for their deaths. It was better that the public know him as Jack the Ripper, a murderous sex fiend, rather than as a dedicated scientist whose researches were destined to expose an unsuspected malignancy as deadly to humanity as any plague bacillus."

Norbrook leaned forward in his chair—his face tense with the enormity of his disclosure.

"You must understand. They aren't *human*."

"Prostitutes, do you mean—or women in general?"

"Damn you! Don't mock me!"

Stringer started to head for the door, but Norbrook remained seated.

"Not all women," he continued. "Not all prostitutes. But *some* of them. And they're more likely by far to be hookers or those one-night-stand easy lays anyone can pick up in singles bars. Liberated women! I'm certain that *they* engineered this so-called sexual revolution."

"They?"

"Yes, *they*. The proverbial *they*. The legendary *they*. They really are in legend, you know."

"I'm not certain if I follow entirely. Could you perhaps . . . ?"

"Who was Adam's first wife?"

"Eve, I suppose."

"Wrong." Norbrook leveled a finger. "It was Lilith, so the legend goes. Lilith—a lamia, a night creature—Adam's mate before the creation of Eve, the first woman. Lilith was the mother of Cain, who slew Abel, the first child born of two human parents. It was the offspring of Lilith that introduced the taint of murder and violence into the blood of mankind."

"Do you consider yourself a Creationist, Mr. Norbrook?"

Norbrook laughed. "Far from it. I'm afraid I'm not your textbook religious nut, Dr. Hodgson. I said we were speaking of legends—but there must be a basis for any legend, a core of truth imperfectly interpreted by the minds of those who have experienced it.

"There's a common thread that runs through legends of all cultures. What were angels really? Why are they generally portrayed as feminine? Why was mankind warned to beware of receiving angels unawares? Why are witches usually seen as women? Why was mankind told not to suffer a witch to live? Why were the saints tormented by visions of sexual lust by demonic temptresses? What is the origin of the succubus—a female demon who copulates with sleeping men?''

''Do you sometimes feel threatened by women?''

''I've already told you. They aren't *human*.''

Norbrook leaned back in his chair and studied the psychiatrist's face. Hodgson's expression was impassively attentive.

''Not *all* women, of course,'' Norbrook proceeded. ''Only a certain small percentage of them. I'm aware of how this must sound to you, but consider this with an open mind.

''Suppose that throughout history a separate intelligent race has existed alongside mankind. Its origin is uncertain: parallel evolution, extraterrestrial, supernatural entities—as you will. What is important is that such a race does exist—a race that is parasitic, inimical, and undetectable. Rather, *was* undetectable until my great-grandfather discovered their existence.

''They are virtually identical to the human female. Almost always they are physically attractive, and always their sexual appetites are insatiable. They become prostitutes not for monetary gain, but out of sexual craving. With today's permissive society, many of them choose instead the role of a hot-to-trot pickup: two beers in a singles bar, and it's off to the ball. Call them fast or easy or nymphos—but they won't be the ones complaining about it on your couch, Doctor.''

Dr. Hodgson shifted himself in his chair. ''Why do you think these women are so sexually promiscuous?''

''The answer is obvious. Their race is self-sterile. Think of them as some sort of hybrid, and you'll understand—a hybrid of human form and alien intelligence. To reproduce they require human sperm, and constant inseminations are required before the right conditions for fertilization are met.

It's the same as with other hybrids. Fortunately for us, reproduction is difficult for them, or they'd have reduced humanity to mere breeding stock long ago.

"They use mankind as cuckoos do other birds, placing their eggs in nests of other species to be nurtured at the expense of natural hatchlings. This is the truth behind the numerous legends of changelings—human-appearing infants exchanged in the crib for natural offspring, and the human infant carried away by malevolent elves or fairies. Remember that elves and fairies are more often objects of fear in the older traditions, rather than the cutesy cartoon creatures of today. It's hardly coincidence that elves and fairies are usually thought of as feminine."

"This is a fucking waste of time!" Stringer muttered—then responded: "Beg pardon, ladies," to Dr. Gottlieb's angry "Shh!"

To Stringer's disgust, Dr. Hodgson seemed to be taking it all in. "Why do you think they only take the shape of women?"

"We've considered that," Norbrook said. "Possibly for some reason only the female body is suited for their requirements. Another reason might be a genetic one: only female offspring can be produced."

"When you say 'we' do you sometimes feel that there are others who have these same thoughts as you do?"

"All right, I didn't really expect you to accept what I've told you as fact. I asked you to keep an open mind, and I ask that you continue to do so. I am able to prove what I'm telling you.

"By 'we' I mean my great-grandfather and those of our family who have pursued his original research."

"Could you tell me a little more about what you mean by research?"

"My great-grandfather made his initial discovery quite by accident—literally. A prostitute who had been run over by a carriage was brought into his surgery. She was terribly injured; her pelvis was crushed, and she was unconscious from skull injuries. Her lower abdomen had been laid open, and he worked immediately to try to stop the profuse bleeding there. To his dismay, his patient regained consciousness during the surgery. His assistant hastened to administer more ether, but too late. The woman died screaming under the knife, although considering the extent of her injuries, she could hardly have noticed the scalpel.

"Her uterus had been ruptured, and it was here that my great-grandfather was at work at the moment of her death. His efforts there continued with renewed energy, although by now his surgical exploration was clearly more in the nature of an autopsy. When his assistant set aside the ether and rejoined him, my great-grandfather described a sort of lesion which he characterized as an 'amoeboid pustulance' that had briefly appeared under his blade at the moment of her death agony. The lesion had then vanished in the welter of blood—rather like an oyster slipping from the fork and into the tomato sauce, to use his expression—and subsequent diligent dissection could reveal no trace of it. His assistant had seen nothing, and my great-grandfather was forced to attribute it all to nervous hallucination.

"He might have dismissed the incident had not he been witness to a railway smashup while on holiday. Among the first to rush to the aid of the victims, he entered the wreckage of a second-class carriage where a woman lay screaming. Shards of glass had virtually eviscerated her, and as he tried to staunch the bleeding with her petticoats, he again saw a glimpse of a sort of ill-defined purulent mass sliding through the ruin of her perineum just at the instant of her final convulsion. He sought after it, but found no further trace—these were hardly ideal conditions—until other rescuers drew him to the aid of other victims. Later he conducted a careful autopsy of the woman, without success. It was then that he learned the victim had been a notorious prostitute.

"Despite my great-grandfather's devotion to medical research, he was a man of firm religious convictions. In deliberating over what he had twice seen, he considered at first that he had witnessed physical evidence of the human soul, liberated in the instant of death. I won't bore you with details of the paths he followed with his initial experiments to establish this theory; they are all recorded in his journals. It soon became evident that this transient mass—this entity—manifested itself only at the moment of violent death.

"Prostitutes seemed natural subjects for his research. They were easily led into clandestine surroundings; they served no good purpose in the world; they were sinful corrupters of virtue—undeserving of mercy. Moreover, that in both cases when he had witnessed the phenomenon the victims had been prostitutes was a circumstance not lost upon my great-grandfather—or Jack the Ripper, as he was soon to be known.

"He was unsuccessful in most of his experiments, but he put it down to imprecise technique and the need for haste. Fortunately for him, not all of his subjects were discovered. Mary Ann Nichols was his first near-success, then nothing until Catherine Eddowes. With Mary Jane Kelly he had time to perform his task carefully, and afterward he was able to formulate a new theory.

"It wasn't the human soul that he had glimpsed. It was a corporeal manifestation of evil—a possession, if you prefer—living within the flesh of sinful harlots. It was an incarnation of Satan's power taken seed within woman—woman, who brought about mankind's fall from grace—for the purpose of corrupting innocence through the lure of wanton flesh. This malignant entity became fleetingly visible only at the instant of death through sexual agony—rather like rats fleeing a sinking ship, or vermin deserting a corpse."

Norbrook paused and seemed to want to catch his breath.

"I use my great-grandfather's idiom, of course. We've long since abandoned that Victorian frame of reference."

Dr. Hodgson glanced toward the two-way mirror and adjusted his tie. "How did you happen to come into possession of this journal?"

"My great-grandfather feared discovery. As quickly as discretion allowed, he emigrated to the United States. Here, he changed his name and established a small practice in New York. By then he had become more selective with his experimental subjects—and more cautious about the disposal of their remains.

"He was, of course, a married man—Jack the Ripper was, after all, a dedicated researcher and not a deranged misogynist—and his son, my grandfather, grew up to assist him in his experiments. After my great-grandfather's death shortly before the First World War, my grandfather returned to England in order to serve as an army field surgeon in France. The hostilities furnished ample opportunity for his research, as well as a cover for any outrage that may have occurred. Blame it on the Hun.

"It was my grandfather's opinion that the phenomenon was of an ectoplasmic nature, and he attempted to study it as being a sort of electrical force. He married an American nurse at the close of the war and returned to New York, where my father was born. By now, my grandfather's researches had drifted entirely into the realm of spiritualism, and his journals, preserved alongside my great-grandfather's, are worth reading only as curiosa. He died at the height of the Depression—mustard gas had damaged his lungs—discredited by his peers and remembered as a harmless crank.

"It was intended that my father should follow the family tradition, as they say. He was working his way through medical school at the time of Pearl Harbor. During his college days, his pro-Nazi sentiments had made him unpopular with some of his classmates, but like many other Americans he was quick to enlist once bombs and tanks replaced political rhetoric. His B-17 was shot down over France early on, and he spent the remainder of the war in various prison camps. After the fall of Berlin, my father was detained for some time by the Russians, who had liberated the small prison camp where he was assisting in the hospital. There was talk of collaboration and atrocities, but the official story was that the Russians had grabbed him up along with all the other German scientists engaged in research there. My father was a minor Cold War hero when the Russians finally released him.

"He left the Army and resettled in southern California, where he married my mother and spent his remaining reclusive years on her father's citrus farm. His manner was that of a hunted fugitive, and he had a great fear of strangers—eccentricities the locals attributed to the horrors of German and Russian prison camps. His journals recounting his wartime experiences, fragmentary as they are, show that he had good reason to feel hunted. By the time I was born, a decade after the war, there were rumors of newly declassified documents that linked my father to certain deplorable experiments regarding tests for racial purity—performed under his direction. I'm afraid my father was rather obsessed with the concept of Aryan superiority, and his research was vitiated by this sort of tunnel vision. It was about the time they got Eichmann when they found him hanging in the orange grove. They ruled it suicide, although there was talk of Nazi-hunters. I know better.

"So did my mother. She sold the farm, bundled me up, and left for Oregon. I heard that afterward the whole place was burned to the ground. My mother never told me how much she knew. She hardly had the chance: I ran off to San Francisco early in my teens to join the Haight-Ashbury scene. When I hitched my way home five years later, I found that my mother had been murdered during a burglary. There was insurance money and a trust fund—enough for college and a medical education, though they threw me out after my third year. Her lawyers had a few personal items as well, held in trust for my return. My great-grandfather's Bible didn't interest me, until I untied the cord and found the microfiche of the journals tucked into a hollow within.

"I suppose they got the originals and didn't concern themselves with me. In any event, I covered my tracks, got a formal education. Living on the streets for five years had taught me how to survive. In time I duplicated their experiments, avoided all the blind alleys their preconceptions had led them down, formed conclusions of my own.

"It's amazing just how really easy it is these days to pick up a woman and take her to a place of privacy—and I assure you that they all came willingly. After the first it was obvious that the subjects had to *want* to be fucked. No, kidnaping was counterproductive, although I had to establish a few baselines first. They're all the same wherever you go, and I should know. Over the past few years I've killed them all across the country—a few here, a few there, keep on moving. In all this time I've been able to establish positive proof in about one case out of twenty."

"Proof?"

"Portable VCRs are a wonderful invention. No messy delays with developing film, and if you draw a blank, just record over it on the next experiment. You have to have the camera exactly right; the alien presence—shall we consider it an inhuman ovum?—exudes from the uterus only in the instant of violent death, then dissipates through intracellular spaces within the dead tissue. I've come to the conclusion that this inhuman ovum is a sentient entity on some level, seeking to escape dissolution at the moment of death. Or is it trying to escape detection? I wonder."

"There were videocassettes found in your van."

"Useless tapes. I've put the essential tapes in a safe place along with the microfiches."

"A safe place?"

"I've already told my attorney how to find them. The judge tried to appoint a woman attorney to defend me, you know, but I saw the danger there."

"You say you allowed yourself to be captured. Wasn't some part of you frightened?"

"I have the proof to expose them. My forebears lacked the courage of their misguided convictions. Personal safety aside, I feel that I have a duty to the human race."

"Do you see yourself as handing this trust on to your son?"

"I have no children, if that's what you mean. Knowing what I do, I find the idea of inseminating any woman totally abhorrent."

"Tell what you remember most about your mother?"

Norbrook stood up abruptly. "I said no psychiatric games, Dr. Hodgson. I've told you all I need to in order to establish my sanity and motives. That's all a part of legal and medical record now. I think this interview is terminated."

The door opened as Norbrook arose. He turned, with cold dignity permitted the deputies to cuff his wrists.

Stringer stopped the psychiatrist as he followed the others into the hallway. The sheriff scowled after Norbrook as his deputies led him away to the car.

"Well, Doc—what do you think?"

"You heard it all, didn't you?"

Stringer dug out a cigarette. "Craziest line of bullshit I ever listened to. Guess he figures he can plead insanity if he makes up a load of crap like that."

Dr. Hodgson shook his head. "Oh, Matthew Norbrook's insane—no doubt about it. He's a classic paranoid schizophrenic: well-ordered delusional system, grandiosity, feelings of superiority, sense of being persecuted, belief that his actions are done in the name of a higher purpose. On an insanity scale of one to three, I'd have to rate him as four-plus. He'll easily be found innocent by reason of insanity."

"Damn!" Stringer muttered, watching Norbrook enter the elevator.

"The good news, at least from the patient's point of view," Hodgson went on, "is that paranoid schizophrenia so easily responds to treatment. Why, with the right medication and some expert counseling, Matthew Norbrook will probably be out of the hospital and living a normal life in less than a year."

Stringer's hand shook as he drew on the cigarette. "It isn't *justice*, Nate!"

"Perhaps not, Jimmy, but it's the way the law works. And look at it this way—the dead don't care whether their murderer is executed or cured. Norbrook may yet live to make a valuable contribution to society. Give me one of those, will you?"

Stringer hadn't known the doctor smoked. "The dead don't care," he repeated.

"Thanks, Jimmy." Hodgson shook out a Marlboro. "I know how you must feel. I saw a little of what was on that one videocassette—the one where he tortured that poor policewoman, Sherri Wilson. Hard to believe she could have remained conscious through it all. Guess it was the cocaine he used on her. Must have really been tough on you, since you talked her into posing as a hooker to try to trap him. It's understandable that you're feeling a lot of guilt about it. If you'd like to come around and talk about it sometime . . ."

Hodgson was handing back the cigarettes, but already Stringer had turned his back and walked off without another word.

Cora Steinman, the district attorney, stepped out from the doorway of the observation room. She watched the elevator doors close behind Stringer.

"I hope you know what you're doing," she said finally.

Dr. Hodgson crushed his unsmoked cigarette into the sand of a hallway ash can. "I know my man."

From the parking lot, the report of the short-barreled .357 echoed like cannonfire against the clinic walls.

"Morton, you've taken care of the journals?" Hodgson asked.

The black defense attorney collected his briefcase. "I took care of *everything*. His collection of evidence is now a couple of books on Jack the Ripper, a bunch of S&M porno, and a couple of snuff films."

"Then it's just a matter of the tape from the interview."

"I think there's been a malfunction in the equipment," Dr. Gottlieb decided.

"It pays to be thorough," Steinman observed.

A deputy flung open the stairway door. He was out of breath. "Norbrook tried to escape. Had a knife hidden on him. Jimmy had to shoot."

"I'll get the emergency tray!" Dr. Hodgson said quickly.

"Hell, Doc." The deputy paused for another breath. "Just get a hose. Most of the sucker's head is spread across your parking lot."

"I'll get the tray anyway," Hodgson told him.

He said to the others as the deputy left: "Must keep up appearances."

"Why," Steinman wondered, as they walked together toward the elevator, "why do you suppose he was so convinced that we only exist as females?"

Dr. Hodgson shrugged. "Just a male chauvinist *human*."

OLD RED SHOES

Stephen Gallagher

Like the editors of this anthology, the author of the following story has taken the rather macabre tour mentioned in its pages. That tour actually exists, as does the pub the characters visit herein. Whitechapel, too, still exists, and is still a fairly poor neighborhood, one whose streets may well still be dangerous by night. Tourists don't go there, for the most part, no more than they did in the Ripper's day; when they do venture there, in fact, it's usually because of the Ripper, an irony Saucy Jack himself might well have appreciated . . .

English author and screenwriter Stephen Gallagher has become a regular contributor to The Magazine of Fantasy and Science Fiction, Isaac Asimov's Science Fiction Magazine, *and* Shadows, *and is generally regarded as one of the best of the new young horror writers. His novels include* Chimera, The Follower, *and* Valley of Lights.

Here he spins a deceptively quiet tale. After all, there's nothing frightening about a pair of old red shoes . . . is there?

"DIDN'T I EVER TELL YOU ABOUT WHEN I WORKED in a peep show up the West End?" Raymond said. "Best job I ever had, and I was only sixteen."

Sandra, the bleached blonde across the table from him, nudged Joanne. "He's winding us up again," she said. "They don't have peep shows for women. Watching blokes jiggling around starkers to disco music, you wouldn't keep still for laughing."

"I didn't say anything about being part of the show," Raymond said. "I was maintenance."

"Oh, yeah?"

"Yeah. I used to fix the peephole shutters when they got stuck, and because the management wouldn't stop the show and lose money I used to have to go in there and the girls would kind of work around me. Not a bad number for thirty quid a week."

"Thirty quid?" Sandra echoed. "That's peanuts."

"I know," Ray said, with a wink at Joanne. "But it was all I could afford to pay them at the time."

Sandra's squeal turned almost every head in the Village Snack Bar, which had about as much village atmosphere as did the City streets beyond its windows. Businessmen in dark suits, eating alone and reading their newspapers, sat like islands in a sea of secretaries. Those who didn't turn sat hunched as if in expectation of a following blow. Joanne had often thought that Sandra's voice, properly trained, could have slashed a cinema seat unaided.

"You bloody *liar*!" Sandra said, but not unhappily, and then she turned to Joanne, who was feeling about fifteen years too old for this kind of conversation. "Didn't I say it?" Sandra demanded, and Joanne smiled weakly.

"I think it's time we got back," she said. "The vans should have arrived by now."

The rain had come and gone as they'd sat in the coffee shop, washing down the paving of the narrow passageway outside and then turning the stones to silver as the sky brightened and cleared. When they emerged, Raymond led them down the passageway and out into a narrow back-street square at its end. He was a clerk in the company's shipping office, and had formerly been a motorcycle messenger for a Wardour Street courier service—and not a very good one, if his stories of falls and near-death crashes were anything to go by. But

Joanne knew that he'd probably been exaggerating these to impress Sandra, she of the chainsaw treble, just as he was exaggerating the limp that his last impromptu stunt performance had left him with.

The back of a school building and its yard crowded in on one side of the square and seemed to compress it even smaller. Ray turned as if a well-prepared thought had just occurred to him, and raising his voice over the sounds of children playing, said, "Hey, listen, no winding up, you want to hear a piece of history?"

"If it's how you helped put out the Great Fire of London," Sandra said, "it'll be about as believable as the rest of your stories."

Raymond shrugged. "Well," he said, "if you don't want to know, you don't want to know. But if these stones could only speak . . ." And he turned to walk on, with Sandra now firmly hooked and being towed along behind him.

"Why?" she said. "What happened here?"

"You wouldn't believe me, so what's the point?"

"Ray . . ." Sandra whined, and glass began to rattle dangerously in the lower-floor windows of the offices on the other sides of the square. But Ray was limping happily onward with Sandra in pursuit, and Joanne gave a weary sigh and followed on behind.

When they reached the new building only a couple of streets away, the vans had arrived and the foyer doors had been unlocked. Wiry little men were carrying library cartons up the steps as if they were weightless. Joanne and the others took a lift up to the third floor. The office fitters had been in for a month ahead of the move, and the entire suite had been decorated and then furnished in that weird business style where plywood and chipboard would lurk one layer deep under more expensive-looking finishes. It was all to be open-plan, sectioned into working areas by head-high partitions and given a human touch by occasional plant life. As Joanne headed toward the section that she'd be sharing with the three other schedules clerks, she heard Sandra saying accusingly, "Nothing happened there at all."

"If that's what you want to think," Raymond said. "Probably best, if you're the type who scares easily."

Joanne paused as she shrugged her heavy overcoat from her shoulders, and looked back. Ray was smirking and Sandra said, "Come on, *tell* us!'

Joanne was thinking that Raymond looked like a spotty schoolboy in an older brother's suit. He said, "It's one of Jack's places."

"Jack who?" Sandra said.

So then he pantomimed cutting his throat with a finger, and then repeated the gesture along the whole length of his torso, and *still* she didn't get it. So then he told her.

"All her insides raked out and pieces of her face cut away," he added. "You were standing right on the spot where they found her and you never even knew it."

"I could feel it!" Sandra insisted with something suspiciously like delight. "I did!"

"Think of it," Raymond went on, "all hot and steaming on the cobbles . . ."

"Ray!" Joanne said sharply. "Please!"

And then she turned away from their faces, blank with surprise, and went through to the scheduling area thinking that the courtship rites of the young seemed to get weirder and weirder as time went by.

Seven library boxes were waiting for her attention, and two more were added as she hung up her coat. It was her job to lay out the new department while the other three schedulers kept business going in the leaky old fifties building back on the North Circular Road, and for one moment she could feel her heart beginning to sink as she thought of the days ahead. It wasn't the work—work had never frightened her—but it was the sense of dislocation that came with the shifting of both her home and her place of employment within the space of a couple of weeks. From North Circular to City outskirts was a definite step up in professional terms, but the move from her Hammersmith flat to two rooms in the East End was something of a descent. Not that Hammersmith was any picture postcard, but at least she'd had her own bathroom. But what could she do? The money from her mother had finally run out, and now she had nothing beyond her income.

Sandra came wandering in about two hours later and seated herself at the corner desk with its half-wired computer terminal. By this time Joanne was into her third box and was starting to get over her dismay that every minor flaw in their old filing system was threatening to become a major problem in the setting up of the new. She'd also generated a good boxful of rubbish, stuff that should never have been packed and transported in the first place. Her hands were grimy and she was choking on old dust, and it wasn't without a certain irritation that she glanced up at Sandra and said, "That was quick."

"I got bored," Sandra said. "They should have somebody in to do all this."

"And then we'd never be able to make the system work again afterward. This way, we'll be straight in a week."

"I might go off sick till it's all over." Sandra tapped idly at a couple of the computer terminal keys, even though it was obvious that the board wasn't connected to anything. She said, "Ray really got you going with that Ripper business, didn't he?"

"Of course he didn't," Joanne said. "None of it's true, anyway."

"You reckon?"

"Yes, I do." And then before Sandra could pursue the subject any further, Joanne reached over to the rubbish box and lifted out a pair of dusty old red shoes. "Have you any idea who these belong to?" she said.

Sandra leaned forward to peer at them, and didn't seem to think much of what she saw. "Where did you find them?"

"In one of the office boxes."

"Well, I'd sling them if I were you. Nobody could want them."

This had been Joanne's own assessment, but it was in her nature to be cautious. "I think I'll ask around, first," she said, and put the shoes to one side.

Sandra left a few minutes later, in response to Joanne's offer to let her sort out the business directories as long as she had nothing better to do. Joanne didn't give any more thought to the old shoes until four o'clock, when she could feel herself winding down and in need of a break. She took the shoes and a couple of other strayed-in items around the adjacent areas, but nobody claimed any of them. It was Eileen in accounts who pointed out that the shoes weren't ladies' shoes at all but were actually in a small men's size, which made it pretty obvious that they had to be a removers' mistake; the Roderick and Drew males were mostly a crew of balding middle-aged men with shiny seats in their business suits, or else they were junior versions thereof, and it was difficult to imagine any of them confessing to ownership of a pair of red suede elastic-sided shoes. Besides, she noticed when she turned them over, their soles were cracking with age, and so at the end of the day she felt no guilt as she took them out into the corridor along with the broken folding umbrella and the three-year-old jar of Polish jam and deposited the entire haul in the common collection box for unpacking debris.

It was dark when she left the building a little after five, glad that the first and the worst of the days was over. The fact that she was emerging into an unfamiliar area seemed to sharpen up all of the edges and the colours of electric light on wet pavements, but the running press of people and the slow-moving crawl of vehicles that made up the rush hour were the same here as on the other side of town. She'd get used to it all, she knew; a couple of weeks, and the colours would dull again.

All the same, she'd expected to be able to find her way back to Liverpool Street Station without much problem; but she realized her mistake when she found herself facing, for the second time in the same day, the back-street square where Raymond had come up with his ''piece of history.''

She stopped for a moment. There were no cars here, but there were plenty of people cutting through on their way out to Aldgate via the passageway down which she'd walked a few hours before. The school was closed down and silent behind chained and padlocked gates, and she wondered . . . *could* Raymond have been telling the truth?

If he was, it would probably be a ''first'' worthy of the *Guinness Book of World Records*. Apart from the cast-iron railings of the school on one side, there was precious little of the Victorian about the square; new buildings had risen on two of the other sides while the old row on the fourth was in the process of being torn down for redevelopment, exposing the air ducts and the fire escapes and all the skeletal works of the buildings behind. The windows in those walls that were still standing looked down into the square from a tight angle; an old frontage with the last of the old memories, its eyes dimmed as it waited for the wrecker's ball.

But the cobbles, she noticed as she stepped down from the paving to cross the square. They looked like the originals undisturbed, old stones in shades deepened by their wetness, glazed here and there with rainbow splashes of floating oil.

So perhaps there was something in it after all. It would never have occurred to her, if it hadn't been for Raymond, but she supposed that anything was possible; an area that was a business district now could easily have swallowed up an area of sweatshops and tenement houses in almost a century of expansion, changing much of its face but also preserving the pattern and the names of the streets. But what did she actually know about the Ripper killings? No more than most people, she suspected, a half-remembered mishmash of legends in which a top-hatted figure prowled the streets of the East End and performed rapid surgical dissections on his victims under the cover of a film-studio fog.

No, she told herself, and walked quickly across the square; and her denial was not of the truth, which she was hardly qualified to judge, but of the effect which Raymond had hoped that his story might have.

She was home by six.

It didn't look much like home yet, but she was going to work on that. Her flat was on the second floor in the end house of a row of three once-genteel town houses with servants' quarters in the attic and an iron bootscraper by the door. The three had been bought up *en bloc* at some time and interconnected to make a rabbit warren of separate apartments, and Joanne's had been one of the larger bedrooms now split into two by a partition wall. Her kitchen was an alcove with a curtain across it, and her sitting room was dominated by a monster of an enameled gas fire. The main disadvantage—if you discounted the facts that it was shabby and run-down and got almost no light in the daytime—was that it was directly over the landlady's own quarters, but to someone of quiet habits like Joanne this was hardly a problem.

More boxes, more unpacking to face; it was almost as if she had nowhere to run to. As she wasted three matches to get the gas fire roaring, she told herself not to get depressed at the prospect. The place would be transformed, once she'd found space for everything, and she'd no longer find her mind flirting with the idea that she'd probably end up spending her last years in a room something like this.

She switched on her radio and drew back the curtain from

the kitchen alcove. She wasn't desperate enough to sit eating cold beans out of the can *yet*. Half an hour later she sat with her plate among the unpacking, knowing that she was going to have to turn to it in a while. She wondered what Sandra would be doing at this time. Getting ready to go out, probably, even though it was midweek. Joanne had done that kind of thing herself, years ago when there had been a bunch of them from the same department . . . but then the group had grown smaller as its members paired off and departed, finally leaving Joanne to feel beached and alone. She didn't dislike Sandra and didn't even envy her coarse and temporary good looks too much; but sometimes she ached to tell her that her vision of life was all wrong.

"I thought you already threw those out," Sandra said to her on the office steps the next morning.

"So did I, but they came back."

"What did they do, walk?"

"Possibly. They look like they've had enough practice."

Sometime during the night the building's cleaning staff had bagged up all of the trash in the office corridor and brought it down to the foyer for collection; everything except for the old red shoes, which had been lined up neatly alongside Joanne's desk when she'd walked in that morning.

The kindness of strangers could be a pain sometimes. She didn't *want* the damned things, and just to make sure that nobody else got the chance to think otherwise she'd brought the shoes downstairs and was undoing the wire tie on one of the trash bags when Sandra arrived. Sandra waited until she'd pushed the shoes inside and retied the closure, and then they walked toward the lifts together.

Sandra said, "Listen, what are you doing for lunch today?"

"I was going to get a sandwich and bring it in," Joanne said. She hadn't checked out the area properly yet but a business district had to have take-away sandwich shops; they were like fleas in an old mattress.

But Sandra said, "Well, don't. Ray's going to take us somewhere."

"*Us?*" Joanne said, her disbelief leaking through.

"Yeah, he specifically wants you to come."

"I don't think so."

"It's just a pub, that's all. But if you want to be funny about it, you can tell him yourself."

The lift arrived, its doors opening like stage curtains on a small but empty house. Three others were waiting with them by now, and they all shuffled inside. Sandra and Joanne were crowded back into a corner.

Joanne said, "But why me?"

"Ask him," Sandra said. "You're not still touchy about that Ripper business, are you?"

"I'd forgotten all about it," Joanne lied.

The computer contractors arrived about midway through the morning, and Joanne spent the next couple of hours dodging around them and trying to screen out their conversation as she concentrated on her own work. They seemed to have a mania for taking up squares of the floor and poking around in the gap underneath, and one of them cheerfully told her that the place was running with mice.

At lunchtime, Raymond and Sandra appeared.

"Get your coat on, Simpson," Raymond said, "we're going on the town."

"Honestly, Ray," she began, "I . . ."

"We're talking lunch in a market pub, that's all. Now, what's the problem with that?"

Sandra seemed to peek out from behind him, like something in a Charles Addams cartoon. "You're not nervous about those shoes turning up again, are you?" she said.

"No," Joanne said, surprised.

The market was less than ten minutes' walk away, reached by a quiet back street where cars parked bumper-to-bumper and the red metal frames of traders' stalls were dotted around like empty lifeboats abandoned by some passing ship. The market itself was a slow river of life moving across the far end of the lane, people shuffling with shoulders hunched against the drizzle among stalls sheeted with polythene. Raymond led the way, down along the backs of the stalls where the market traders had thrown sheets of cardboard to soak up the rain and the cardboard had been turned to pulp as if by the tread of a passing army. It was a world away from the glass and the concrete of the business district, but already there was a sense that it was a world whose days were numbered. Life moved in the streets but the buildings themselves were already dead; Joanne looked up and saw the name "Wentworth Dwellings" fading on a high brick wall where the lower windows had been boarded and the upper windows smashed out and replaced by plastic, the plastic then having been torn out to hang in tatters that stirred slowly in the breeze.

"Now," Raymond said finally. "Did I lie, or what?"

They'd left the market and walked barely a hundred yards down a wider street occupied by small wholesale businesses, to a point where a pub and an old church stood on adjacent corners. The church was out of use, its gates padlocked and the once-proud pillars at the top of its wide steps beginning to peel, but the public house looked bright and newly painted. Joanne looked up at the sign.

The pub was called *The Jack the Ripper*.

Sandra said, "So you mean, we're right in the area *now*?"

"Yeah," Raymond said. "Come inside, and stop acting like a tourist."

The interior layout was much as it must have been in the Ripper's day, but now it had heavy flock wallpaper and decent carpet and a jukebox that was playing Country and Western music. The tables were all taken, so they had to stand near the door where a shelf for glasses had been provided, and Ray pointed out the wall display of pages reproduced from the *Illustrated Police News* of 1888. Sandra's interest quickly dwindled, her mind having registered the reality much as she might take notice of an odd little news item tucked in among the photo stories and competitions in *Weekend*, and as she and Ray talked of other things, Joanne studied the sketches. "Identifying a missing limb" showed sober-looking gentlemen conferring earnestly over the matching of an arm to a headless, limbless female torso on a slab, its lower parts decorously covered by a drape as if it were a piece of neoclassical statuary. In "Taking the remains to the mortuary" an officer wheeled a covered handcart while a crowd of small children and the generally curious ran along behind.

If they were hoping that Joanne was going to be shocked, then she supposed that she must have disappointed them. She was the one who pointed out that one of the victims had last been seen alive in this same public house; Raymond hadn't even noticed it.

They couldn't stay for more than quarter of an hour, because they then had to walk back. Joanne's impressions now seemed to make more sense to her—she'd felt as if she was being led deeper into an area where more of the grim original fabric of the East End was exposed. Now she could understand that "original" meant as it had been in the days of the Ripper, as if everything before that era in this handful of streets had been merely preamble and everything since was epilogue—the Ripper being a shadow that, like a stain, couldn't be fully erased.

And as for Raymond and Sandra . . . well, they seemed to have forgotten about it already.

Back at the office building, Joanne saw that a refuse wagon had arrived to collect the trash bags from by the foyer. Sandra went off to the loo for her usual half-hour spruce-up and Ray headed for his own department, leaving Joanne to go up to her office alone. The computer contractors were back and they were levering up a new piece of the floor. They showed her a trail of mouse droppings that they found underneath and that was the most interesting thing that she saw all afternoon, until she looked out of the window at the end of the day and saw Raymond and Sandra walking out arm-in-arm.

When she got home that night her landlady, Mrs. Finch, caught up with her in the hallway. Joanne guessed that she must have been waiting for her.

"Evening, Miss Simpson," she said. "How are you settling in?"

"Fine, thanks," Joanne said. "Well, slowly," she amended then. "You know how it is."

"Only, I was hoping I'd see you. We've been having a lot of break-ins around here, and I wanted to warn you to be on your guard. People come in and out, and I can't always be here to keep an eye on them."

"I always keep my door locked."

"Locks don't seem to stop 'em," Mrs. Finch warned. She was a large woman, and didn't look as if she'd manage stairs easily. "Kids on drugs, a lot of it is. A lady I know surprised two of them, they tied her to a chair and set fire to her curtains with her watching. But what I wanted to say was, my son can fit you some extra security if you wanted it, only I'd have to charge for his time. You know how it is."

Joanne said, "You mean, like, dead bolts and a chain?"

"Anything you wanted. He does a good job."

"Tell him I'm interested, then."

They parted and Joanne climbed the narrow stairway up to the next landing and her own flat, but Mrs. Finch threw in a final shot, calling up the stairwell, "There was a gentleman with a yard two streets away, they killed his dog with hammers."

But Joanne wasn't listening. She was looking at the old red shoes.

They stood on the lino in the middle of the landing, leaking a wet pool of crimson. For a moment Joanne was too shocked to react, standing on the top step with her door key in her hand, but then her face set into lines of anger. Raymond with his talk about the Ripper, and Sandra with her "What did they do, walk?" As pranksters they were simply inept, but what stung her was the implication that she was just some fussy old maid who was fit for nothing more than a joke and a fright. Stepping around the shoes, she went into her flat and came out a moment later with a supermarket carrier bag. Lunch invitations and conversation, and *this* was what they really thought of her.

She placed the bag over the shoes and used it to pick them up, being careful not to get any of the red ink onto herself. Holding them well away from her body she took them downstairs and into the street, where around the corner she found a builders' brazier still smoldering. She thrust the shoes deep into the embers and bundled the bag in after. It began to blacken and melt almost immediately.

God, she was angry. She looked all around, but there was nothing and nobody to take it out on. And then she remembered that she'd left the door to her flat wide open, and this only minutes after her landlady's warning.

The stuff pooled on the lino didn't look so much like ink anymore. It had thickened and gone dark. She wiped it up with newspaper, but it seemed to have left a permanent stain.

Just wait. She'd find Raymond and give him hell tomorrow.

But she didn't.

The line of events wasn't so clear when she tried to think them through in daylight. How had they known her new address? And how had they made it there ahead of her?

And then—

How was she going to look if she made the accusation where the rest of the office could hear, and the two of them simply put on blank faces and denied everything? She didn't doubt that they'd be able to do it. During the ride in and then on the walk from Liverpool Street Station, she began to think that it had been a bad idea not to keep the shoes after all . . . they'd been her only evidence unless she planned to razor up the stained square of lino from the landing, and how would she look brandishing *that* around?

And—

Had she even looked that closely at the shoes? Could she be sure, looking back, that they were even the same ones that had reappeared in the office yesterday morning?

The answer was yes, she was sure . . . but she didn't see how she could easily convince anyone else of the fact.

So she hung up her coat and went on with her work, and she watched. Sandra didn't come over during the morning and Joanne saw Raymond only once, in the foyer at lunchtime, and he didn't see her. Joanne could feel her righteous anger leaking away as the hours went by, like acid out of a damaged battery, and as its level fell she could sense that deeper fears were being uncovered. It was terrible to know that you were a victim in somebody's eyes. It made the world a colder, bleaker place to be.

By the end of the day, she knew that she'd been singled out and picked upon. But she was no longer confident that she knew by whom; Sandra had met her eyes with a brief smile when they'd passed in the corridor during the afternoon, and had given her nothing with which to reconstruct her suspicions.

It was a relief to get home and to find that her landlady's son had been by during the day, and that she now had the extra security that she'd asked for. He'd left the extra keys and a handwritten note of his charges on the table, with a postscript asking her to pay the money to his mother. He'd put sash locks on the windows, a chain on the door, and a dead bolt a few inches below the Yale; he'd also drilled the center panel of the door and fitted a little glass spy-eye that was slightly too high for her to reach. None of the stuff was new—it was probably all demolition salvage from the slow tide of redevelopment that was still spreading outward from the city center—but it all seemed solid enough.

She locked everything, and felt better.

There were a few woodshavings to sweep up, but that was all the mess that he'd left. Joanne had managed to get the place more or less straight over the past three evenings, and tonight she intended to relax a little, if only she could get the business of the shoes out of her mind.

It took two glasses of the good sherry after dinner and an hour in the armchair with the new Catherine Cookson paperback, but she did it.

In fact, she relaxed so successfully that she woke up to find her neck stiff and the room stuffy and overwarm. She looked at her mother's clock on the mantel, and it was almost ten. The book had fallen facedown on her lap, and she marked the page and put it aside before rising stiffly. She had the dull beginnings of a headache and wanted to get some fresh air into the room. The little square key that would unlock one of the sashes was still on the ring, and the ring was hanging from the dead-bolt key in the door. She went over to get it, and heard somebody coming up the stairs outside.

Joanne froze and listened.

It could simply be a visitor, on his way to the flat above. But Joanne knew sneaking when she heard it. Whoever was coming up, he was trying not to be heard—but that was impossible, on wooden stairs in a house as old as this.

She rose onto tiptoe, and just managed to get level with the spy-eye. But when she looked through, she couldn't see anything in any detail. It took a moment for her to realize, but then she saw that it had been installed the wrong way around. The lens was looking inward instead of out. Something moved out there on the landing, but there was no telling what.

She dropped down and put her head close to the door, listening. If it *was* a visitor for upstairs, he'd now go on by; but she heard the boards creak, and knew that he was coming toward her.

A pause. Then something soft bumped against the door, once and then again, right down at the bottom edge; and then, reaching her a moment later, there came a stale, wet smell of something burned.

In one quick movement, she snapped open the dead bolt and threw back the door.

Her visitor was stooping there as if caught in a searchlight, his mouth an open *O* of astonishment; the charred remains of the old red shoes had been placed on the threshold facing into the room, and he was in the act of scattering a few ashes around them.

"You little *shit*, Raymond," she said, and seized him by the ear before he could get back out of reach; his face twisted in pain but she held on tight and wouldn't let him straighten up as she steered him around and toward the stairway. "Is this what you think of as a joke? That bike-smash must have made you sick in the head as well as anything else. I could pick your footsteps out of a hundred others."

With a hard tug she propelled him toward the stairs, and he stumbled and almost fell down them. He'd flushed bright red and seemed to want nothing more urgently than to get away and out into the night. As he reached the lower landing, arms flailing and his balance barely in check, Joanne picked up what was left of the shoes and hurried down after him. He'd run out of the door when she got there, but she followed him into the street.

"Here," she was shouting, not caring who heard, "take your red shoes with you. Keep them so you can smirk at how clever you were when you put a scare up poor daft Miss Simpson.''

He was running over to Sandra, who was waiting on the far side of the street. The two of them were looking panic-stricken, as if they'd uncapped a jar with a demon in it when they'd been expecting peanut butter. Joanne threw the first of the shoes as hard as she could, and it skittered across the tarmac before them and disappeared under a parked car. Now Raymond had Sandra by the arm, and was trying to tug her away.

"Tell your children about it," Joanne added, "if they're not too brain-damaged to understand."

"Joanne," Sandra began plaintively, "it was only a . . . ow!"

This was as the second of the shoes hit her a glancing blow on the shoulder, and Raymond finally managed to get her moving.

"Go on," Joanne shrieked, "get away from me!"

Raymond was hustling Sandra toward a large motorcycle that stood waiting alongside a builders' skip about a hundred yards down the street, but Sandra pulled away for a moment and turned her pale, hate-twisted face to Joanne.

"You dried-up old *cow*!" she screeched, and then Raymond dragged her on again.

Joanne was feeling spacey with shock, as if there was a layer of something thick and soft between her brain and her skull. She went back into the house, hardly noticing that her hands left black prints on the door and that she'd messed up her clothes with soot and ash. Her throat felt raw and there were tears drying onto her cheeks that she hadn't even been aware of. She climbed the stairs, one step for every two beats of her still-racing heart.

The door to her flat stood wide open, as she'd left it.

There was barely a moment for her to register the boy, he moved so fast. He couldn't have been in there for more than two minutes but in that time he'd jerked open every drawer and raked out the contents of every cupboard onto the floor. He didn't look old enough to shave, fourteen or fifteen perhaps, with jug-handle ears and one of those green zippered flying jackets that so many of the local youths seemed to wear. He dashed to the window, thinking perhaps that he could drop the twelve feet or so into the yard at the back, but the sash lock held firm and he spun around to face Joanne. She saw that he was so afraid he was trembling, and that seemed all wrong; but then he leaped at her and roughly shoved her aside, not looking at her as his arm swung across and she was thrown against the door before she fell.

She didn't know she'd been cut, not until she saw something squirt out across the carpet like a feeble jet from a child's water pistol, and she might not have realized it then if it hadn't continued in regular pulsing bursts that matched the pounding in her ears, spraying onto the face of her mother's clock, which lay broken just a couple of feet before her eyes. Between her and the clock she could see the knife that she'd been slashed with, a green Stanley knife with a fat handle and a stubby, triangular blade, the kind of knife that a packer or a carpet layer might use. The boy must have dropped it.

That layer of stuff between her and the world seemed to be growing thicker. Life, she was thinking; life is a train loaded up with all the good things you ever wanted, and which no one ever ran quite fast enough to catch. There was more, but there wasn't going to be time; and then she saw a shadow move over her, and realized that the boy had come back. But of course, he couldn't *leave* the knife, could he? He scrabbled to pick it up, so nervous that he could hardly get a grip on it.

And the last thing that Joanne noticed, as he stepped over her again to leave, was the colour of his faded old baseball shoes.

FROM HELL, AGAIN

GREGORY FROST

A recent review in The Washington Post Book World *put Gregory Frost in the company of J. R. R. Tolkien, Evangeline Walton, and T. H. White . . . heady company indeed for a young writer. Born in Des Moines, Iowa, Frost now lives in Philadelphia, keeps a twenty-pound cat named "Poot," and can be seen on the East River Drive at any time of the day or night, bug-eye goggles glinting rakishly, indulging one of his two admitted "obsessions," bicycling. (Frost's other obsession is with Jack the Ripper, although hopefully he doesn't do anything more strenuous than extensive research about that* one!*) His short fiction has appeared in* The Magazine of Fantasy and Science Fiction, Isaac Asimov's Science Fiction Magazine, Whispers, The Twilight Zone Magazine, Night Cry, Liavek, Faery, *and elsewhere. His novels include* Lyrec *and the well-received fantasy* Tain. *Upcoming is another fantasy novel,* Remscela, *from Ace. He is currently at work on a horror novel set in Des Moines, tentatively entitled* The Fell of Night.*

In the moody and atmospheric story that follows, he suggests that when you go fishing in the stagnant black depths of the human soul, you never know exactly what it is you'll dredge up . . .

HE PULLED LIGHTLY UPON THE OARS, STROKE UPON stroke, and his boat skimmed the black water of the Thames. Mayhew was a dredger and this his work, but no commission had ever been so strange. He pondered

what it could all mean and how it had come to be. In his
Peter boat, shallow-bottomed and easy to row, he often forgot
himself entirely. Sometimes he sang or hummed a tune.
Sometimes his thoughts just strayed, to happier times before
his wife had taken to drink and run away, when his daughter
had lived with him. But now she was back after all, and
things would be better again . . . with this commission.

He remembered Demming. Two nights before, coming out
of the fog in a frock coat, a tall toff's hat and shadow for a
face, Demming had appeared upon the quay as Mayhew tied
up his boat. Gaslight glinted off the gold of Demming's walking stick. He asked after Patrick Mayhew, and feigned surprise when he learned whom he was speaking to. "You've a
reputation as a dredger," Demming told him. And Demming
knew how lean the summer was—so lean that no sane man
could have denied his offer: a job of dredging with five hundred guineas paid in advance and a promise of an impossible
five hundred more if it proved successful. "Tomorrow night,
then," Demming said, "I'll meet you here at two." Mayhew
remembered how his footsteps faded in the fog but the sound
of the stick tapping went on and on.

It seemed to echo in the slap of the water against his
squared bow.

The second meeting. Demming had given him the heavy
purse as promised. He hadn't needed to count it to know how
much it must contain. But in the interim the questions filled
with worry had come to plague him, and these had to be
cleared up. "This is criminal, what you want me to do," he
said over the purse. "Not at all," Demming replied. "It's
dredgework that you've done a thousand times before." "Will
I need a net or grappling hooks? What is it you want me to
find?" Demming paused before answering. His face was
plainly visible now in the light of Mayhew's lantern: a long,
proud face, pouchy under the eyes, perhaps from drink. A
clean-shaven face, a powdered face. "Hooks or nets is a mat-

ter for you—I can't say. What you seek is a body. However, the corpse itself hardly concerns me. The man—for it is a man, Mr. Mayhew—stole from me a watch, a family heirloom that is irreplaceable. The mischief that befell him is of no concern. If you find money on him, you may keep it, but you may *not* turn him in to the police for any finder's fee. I'm paying you quite enough to discourage that. Nor are you to mention him to anyone. Anyone at all.'' Mayhew thought he understood this: ''You kill the fella?'' he asked. But Demming hardly balked. ''That is none of your business, either. You perform your dredgework, stick to that, and we will get on just fine.'' This left him believing that Demming had killed a man without knowing that the man carried the stolen watch on his person. An odd oversight, but not an impossible scenario to envision. And it was not much of a crime to refrain from turning the corpse in, not enough of one to overcome a small fortune.

Mayhew listened for a moment to a drunk shouting, somewhere out in the dark, near the passing quay.

Last night, on the river. With the half-built Tower Bridge a mangled horror hanging over him, he secured his weighted nets to the boat, then unshipped the oars and began the long, exhausting process. Lights on the ships at dock winked at him. He dragged and hauled nets, dragged and hauled again. His black-tarred sou'wester coat kept the sodden nets from soaking him, but made him sweat twice as hard at the oars so there was hardly a difference. As dawn came up, he called it quits with three shillings' worth of coal dredged up but nary a sign of a body.

Then the happiest moment of all in this whole adventure took place. Returning to his house, he found his daughter, Louise, on the stoop. She had come back to him out of the depths of the East End. He listened to the whole sordid story, forgiving her for her sins before he even heard them. She had lived as a whore for nearly a year, keeping with a man in

Castle Alley. He had been cruel to her, but she feared, as most of the whores did, the one the papers called "the Ripper," and her hateful prosser was at least protection against that. Soon enough she had turned to drink—ironically, to the same Dutch gin that her mother had loved. She cried as she spoke, and Mayhew held her close; she was his little girl again. He felt the weight of the money in the pocket of his coat, and he dreamed their new life. Soon he would quit the river, carry his daughter away from the squalor of Lambeth. They would take a country house, a small estate—just as soon as he found the body, and the watch.

With renewed vigor at the thought of success, he put his back to it, and the Peter boat skimmed the water like a skater across ice.

At three he was under the Tower Bridge once more, his weighted nets dragging, catching. Ship lights gleamed like will-o'-the-wisps along the banks. The first haul produced a piece of a hansom wheel and an intact lantern, also from a carriage, and Mayhew wondered if an entire cab could lie beneath him in the black depths. The lamp was worth some money to him, and it was a curious enough proposition that he dropped his nets there again to see if he would collect more fragments from a hansom. As he rowed vigorously, the nets caught again, this time holding like an anchor. He tried, but couldn't pull them free. Taking one of his grappling hooks, he stood, removed his coat, and tossed the hook out behind his boat so that it would sink beyond the nets. Down and down the rope played out, until the hook touched bottom. Then he retrieved it, slowly, letting it drag along. The hook, too, caught on something, and Mayhew pulled on that for all he was worth. He strained till his pulse was throbbing in his head. The hook tore free suddenly, sent him sprawling back into the wet bottom of his boat. He reeled in the hook. It brought up a large broken slab of wood caught on one of the spikes. When he tried the nets, he found them freed as well, and drew them in as fast as he could.

The nets brought up more broken wood and what looked to be a piece of iron rail of the sort that might garnish a driver's platform. Then there *was* a hansom on the river bottom, as unbelievable as that seemed. He sat back in wonder at how such a thing could happen, and looked right up at his answer—at the jutting promontory of the Tower Bridge. As Mayhew imagined what happened, the water behind his boat erupted in a release of bubbles. He scrambled to the rear in time to see a body flung up onto the surface of the Thames, bob there for a moment, then sink out of sight. Hastily, he grabbed his nets and flung them out where the water still rippled. Then he rotated the oars into the water and rowed hard, nearly lifting himself onto his feet. The nets took on weight and dragged. He shipped the oars quickly and started drawing the nets in hand over fist, soaking himself but too single-minded in his purpose to stop and put on the slick sou'wester.

The nets and their tangled capture bumped against the boat. Mayhew grabbed hold and pulled the whole mess in at once. The body rolled beneath the ropes, the head flopped back, and death stared up at Patrick Mayhew.

The man had been in the water much longer than Mayhew had supposed, long enough for the skin to have sloughed away from the sludge-covered bones in most places, to leave a wet, glistening visage, a moulage of mud. As much as a year, Mayhew guessed, pulling back. He had hauled corpses in every horrible state of decay imaginable, most of them obscenely bloated. This eyeless figure ought to have been insignificant by comparison, but it now sent a wave of terror shooting like an electrical discharge through Mayhew. He found himself pressed against the side, gripping one oar as if it were a weapon. This unreasoned fear lasted only moments, and then passed like a breeze continuing on downstream. Mayhew had a vision of the people on the ships at dock waking from their sleep, lifting taut faces from pints of ale, as the cadaverous wind rolled by. He wanted nothing more than to grab the nets and fling this body back into the blackness of the Thames; but he had a purpose here, and he was not finished.

He inched his way to the remains. The body wore a cloak and, beneath this, the remains of a coat, vest, and tie. Mayhew tore the cloak apart when he lifted it—the material shredded with the weight of muck to support. He dug his fingers through the slime and drew back the black coat—which looked to have been a fashionable dinner jacket—to get at the vest. At first he thought there was no watch, because the chain, covered with weedy slime, was as dark as the material. As he shifted the corpse, something in the watch pocket gleamed, and he moved the lantern nearer, then reached in and drew out the watch. Where every other part of the corpse was caked or colored from its long stay in the water, the watch case glistened as if it had been polished that morning. Mayhew turned it over, disbelieving that it could be in such condition, but the other side was just as shiny and unblemished. He could make out distinctly the smoothly molded ridges of the case and the stylized face of a Gorgon in a raised circle, even in the lantern light. He stood, and the body rolled slightly. One arm was suddenly flung out. The knuckles clacked against the side; the sharp, blackened fingers began to curl up slowly. He could bear the thing no longer. He stuffed the watch into his pocket, knelt down, grabbing the netting, and heaved the body over the side. When it did not sink right away, he grabbed a short boat hook and stabbed out, shoving the body under the surface. The hook must have caught on the corpse's coat because, when he tried to draw it back in, it snagged, tipping Mayhew off balance. He twisted around and the hook caught on the edge of the boat. All of his weight went on it as he turned, and the hook snapped.

The spot was cursed. In a panic, Mayhew threw down the broken pole, sat, and began hauling on the oars as hard as he could, desperate to escape that haunted place. Never had the Thames carried any fear for him before this, but now, even with the body back where it belonged, he could not get rid of the apprehension that had crawled into his boat with the corpse. It was as if the fear had slithered off and condensed into the muck on his clothes, at his feet. His shoulders ached and his lungs burned at the effort, but Mayhew did not slacken his pace until he was in sight of his dock. He left hooks and nets in the boat, threw the tarp hastily over everything, and set off, almost at a dead run, for home.

Louise was awake, and he could not hide his uneasiness from her. He had told her of the job, of Demming, and of what he suspected. Now he showed her the watch as he described in trembling detail his encounter with the submerged carriage and the passenger he had released, for that was how he interpreted the events. They sat at the small dinner table, Louise in her nightclothes and a shawl, Mayhew still dressed in his checked shirt and smelling of the river, the watch on display between them. Louise marveled at the etched Gorgon on the case. She reached out and picked up the watch, which Mayhew, in his loathing of it, was unable to do. He wanted to tell her to put it down, but also wanted to see inside it. Louise pressed the winding stem, and the case popped open. She opened the lid. Mayhew dragged the lamp closer.

The face of the watch amazed him; whatever he had anticipated, this certainly was not it. The watch dial, a simple dial, took up the lower quarter of the face. Around it, the gold had been etched beautifully with trumpet swirls and leaves. Above and to each side of the dial were two oval insets. These contained small photos that appeared to have been stuffed in; one of them was loose along one edge, and Mayhew peeled it down to find a painted design like a piece of foreign calligraphy underneath. The photos themselves were the only parts of the watch that showed damage from being in the river. They had gone dark and gray, and the best that Mayhew and his daughter could make out was that one of the photos was of a woman's face. The features were too vague to hint at more than that. In the top of the watch, filling that quarter, was a circle the same size as the dial below, containing another etched Gorgon ringed by snakes. Mayhew noticed now that the face was not quite human in that it had two eyes to each side of the nasal fissures where a nose ought to have been. And the teeth came to points, bared, like two rows of daggers. He closed the case to ascertain that the other Gorgon mirrored this image, and it did. He raised his eyes to Louise. She smiled at him, apparently unaffected by the horrible aspects he saw in the watch.

"Let me see something, Papa," she said as she spun the watch toward herself. She sprang open the case again, then lightly ran one fingertip around the edge of the Medusa circle. About three-quarters of the way around, she stopped and pressed with her thumb, and the circle popped up. Louise stared with momentary shock, then began to laugh. "Oh, look at this," and she held the watch out to him.

The Medusa circle had hidden a small painting. For a moment, Mayhew did not comprehend the picture, but then he understood and did not know whether to laugh or be disgusted. The painting showed a grinning priest seated on a small padded stool while a demon knelt before him, its mouth clamped around the priest's marrowbone. The demon's body was a dark green, rough with warts, and it had a second lewd face on its arse, yellow teeth and red eyes. That second face finally tipped the scales for Mayhew. "Don't laugh," he ordered Louise, "it's blasphemous. What sort of a gentleman would own a watch like that?"

"You'd be surprised as to what 'gentlemen' carry on them."

"I don't want to know. I found what's wanted and I'll give it away like I'm supposed to, nor do anything but."

"I wonder if it still runs," Louise mused. She closed the case, then began winding the stem. The watch started to tick after a moment, loud and precise.

"Put it down!" Mayhew spluttered. "The man was in the water well onto a *year* by the look of him. There wasn't a part of him that the water hadn't rotted, and yet here's his *watch*, still running like it come from a shop this morning. By what Providence can such a thing be?"

Louise put the watch down. "I don't have an idea. But there it is. Maybe that's why he wants it back, your Mr. Demming. Maybe he's got the most special watch in the world."

"Maybe so. I don't care nor I get my money, but you leave it be. I'm tired from rowing for my life, so let's get us some sleep, and today I'll take him his watch and buy you something real fine." His head swam for a moment as he stood. He shuffled off and lay down on his small bed, listening to Louise climb into hers, listening to the watch ticking on the table across the room.

The rhythmic ticking washed over him as he fell asleep and followed him down into the landscape of dream. He found himself walking through a darkened Aldgate Street. Gaslight created bubbles of clarity along the murky avenue, which contained shops that he did not recognize, many of them canted forward, looming over him, others stretching high above. Soon, he walked along Whitechapel Road. People began to appear in the pools of flickering light, their faces as distorted as the buildings. They watched him pass; most were grinning like the priest in the little painting, and their sharpened teeth held all of his attention. The rest of their features escaped him. He hastened on, found himself in a darkened lane. Someone spoke close by, and he turned to see Louise's face. At first she was the forlorn child on the doorstep but as she came to him her features distorted, her hair writhing as if alive. He stared into her eyes and found them empty, two great holes through which he could see some other place where the sky was shot through with stars. The ticking of the watch sounded like a scrabbling rat.

A weight in his hand tugged at his awareness like a child pulling on his arm. He looked down, found a huge knife there, a strange knife that looked like an immense carpenter's file. Again he faced Louise, and this time he found the features of her face fallen away, revealing muscle and bone, teeth like daggers. Her mouth hung open and he could see more of that other place between the ivory points. Her jaw clacked shut, the bared grin horrible. "Take me *here*," she said softly. Her fleshless hand slid down across his trousers. He was becoming aroused by his own daughter. The knife pulled at him, begging to be put to use. "Open the gate," a cold voice said. Could it have been him? "You don't want to do that, or the coppers will find us," Louise said. "Open the gate, let them through," the voice insisted harshly. He turned, and Louise was a skeleton poised before that other place, which now poured through the alley, suffusing every shadow with a reddish glow. Someone moved into it, and he saw Demming there, behind the living skeleton, looking accusatorily at him. Demming reached out, saying, "Give it to me," and the skeleton begged, "Papa, don't." Demming scowled and slapped the bones aside. They shattered and went tumbling; some clattered on the stones, others landed in the altered shadows without a sound and dropped into the star-shot void. "The watch," Demming demanded. With a scabrous, warty hand, he opened his cloak to attach the gold fob, which now ran from Mayhew to him. The swirling stars played in the shadows beneath his coat, too. "Papa," Louise called. "Papa." The ticking of the watch beat at his brain. He squeezed shut his eyes and tried to cover his ears.

When he opened his eyes, he was standing near the door.

Pressed between him and the wall, Louise had her palms up under his jaw as if trying to push him aside. Mayhew backed away. He saw that her nightgown was torn, purple marks on her throat. "Did I—?" he tried to ask. Tears spilled from her eyes. Mayhew could not look at her. He had known other dredgers, other men, who actually boasted of having coupled with their daughters; and once, in a pub years earlier, he had struck a man who grabbed hold of Louise. That *he* had almost done this awful thing, that the desire might live inside him as it did in those other monsters—he could hardly stand to think on it. He went and sat on his bed. Louise covered herself with her shawl and came to sit beside him.

"Papa," she said, "I ain't like that, no matter what you think. I ain't a whore for you, nor any more for any other man. I wish I'd never told you none of it." He tried to reply, to explain, but beyond her shoulder he saw the lamp on the table and beside it, the recovered watch. The watch had run down and stopped.

Demming lived in St. James's, a neighborhood far more fashionable than Mayhew's. Both the dredger and his daughter went along to Demming's house; he feared that if he left her home she would not be there when he got back. She had accepted his apology and his explanation, but he could tell that she did not truly believe any of it.

A black iron sign hung on the wall beside the door: Walter A. Demming, Doctor of Neuroses. A servant answered their knock and escorted them directly to a second-floor office. There was a single desk to one side of the room, and behind it a case containing skulls of humans and related mammals. A glass jar on the desk held for viewing a model of the brain. Mayhew went to the case and saw, on the shelf below the prominent skulls, a display of medical tools, most of them scalpels and probes. He understood only that these were tools for cutting into people. Behind him the door opened, and Demming, all in tweed, swept in.

"I dared not hope that it was you, Mr. Mayhew. With all I said to you, I maintained doubts. I—" He broke off, staring darkly at Louise.

"My daughter," Mayhew interjected by way of an introduction. He did not care for the intensity of Demming's stare.

The doctor blinked and placed a look of humor upon himself. "Of course," he said. "You have it?"

Louise reached in and removed the watch from her coat, placing it on the table. Her father had been unable to touch it, even in daylight.

Demming barely restrained himself from leaping on the watch, though from his expression he might as easily have intended to crush it as to gather it up. He seemed to forget that the dredger and his daughter still occupied the room with him; his lofty demeanor vanished, and he wrung his trembling hands and mumbled under his breath. His eyes rolled back and for a moment he struck the pose of a man lost in prayer. Mayhew noticed how dark Demming's eyelids were. Then the doctor opened the drawer of the desk and withdrew a velvet purse identical to the first one that he had given Mayhew. "You have done me an inestimable service," he said, while staring once more at Louise, this time with what might have been trepidation. "I shan't forget it." He pulled the handkerchief from his breast pocket and began rubbing at the watch case, harder than if merely polishing it.

"The watch," said Mayhew slowly, dismayed, "you sure it's the right one?" He took the purse.

"There is no doubt of that. There could be no other watch like this. And now, regrettably, I'm late for my appointments at Bethlem Hospital, so I will have to ask you to go, and take my appreciation from the money."

"Of course," Mayhew replied, goaded into recalling the class distinctions at work here. He tucked the purse away, took Louise's arm, and led her out. The liveried servant waited at the top of the stairs and showed them out onto the quiet, treelined sidewalk.

They walked down through the park to Birdcage Walk without a word traded between them. With Parliament in sight, Louise could no longer stand the silence. "He was a very impressive man, weren't he?" she asked.

Mayhew drew up short and turned her to him. "Don't you ever mention him again. Not to me, not to anyone. It's done, I'm paid, and I choose to forget everything, just like he wants. You do the same, girl."

"Papa—"

"No, damn you! Never!" He let go the moment she struggled, and watched her run ahead. She did not understand what he was trying to say. He lacked any real understanding of it himself. Perhaps the nightmare was still distorting his reason, and his hatred of Demming was due to the foul memory that he carried all too near the surface. He believed that, for reasons he could not explain, he had come in contact with something monstrous, something unholy and well beyond his comprehension. The best thing he could do, he thought, was to forget it all, to bury the memory as he had buried the corpse by tossing it back into the water. This had now been done. He hastened after his daughter, to explain the way he saw things.

Returning home, he found that Louise had not gone there. She had run off to cry, he tried to assure himself. Later she would come back and he would apologize. Later. Suddenly very weary, Mayhew lay down to sleep.

When he awoke, it was past six and still Louise had not appeared. Mayhew began to worry, but anger soon tinged his concern. This was how things had gone with her before, the last time she ran away. He suspected that she might have fled back to the East End this time, too. If whoring was all she was good for, then to Hell with her; a daughter of his should be made of better stuff than that. "This time I can't forgive her," he announced to the empty room, and buried his own loneliness beneath anger. He might have made something of her, but he saw now that she would only waste his money on drink, attracting the same filth that combed the East End. He knew he had not been rough—he hadn't hit her, and he hadn't even been yelling at her, not really. He cursed her for being like her mother, cursed her mother for everything in the world that wasn't right. He dug into his pocket, felt the weight of the coins. Well, at last something was right in the world—at least he had money enough for a long time to come. A country squire, what a great man he would become. Maybe he would marry a fine woman and raise another daughter, one of distinction this time. He went and fetched the other purse, then sat down at his table and counted his way to sleep. He awoke before dawn and took a stroll, smoking a cigarette to ward off the dampness. On Webber Row he stopped into the Frog and Peach for a pint. The few patrons were all huddled in one smoky corner and whispering excitedly. Mayhew sat up on a stool and asked the man who drew his pint what was going on.

"Well, it'll be in the papers by noon, I suppose."

"What will?"

"That the Ripper's back. Killed him a woman last night in Whitechapel, just like before."

Mayhew set down his pint. "Where? Where'd it happen?"

"Castle Alley's the street as is being given. Here, where you going?"

Running at breakneck speed, past fruit vendors, fish vendors, beggars, and drunkards, Mayhew dashed headlong across London Bridge and into the East End. The visions of the day before tinged everything he saw with evil. Louise turning from woman to carcass to bone, and in the background, Demming, always Demming. Now he forgave her, now he whined her name and begged God to forgive him for all the hateful things he had thought about her; it was really only her mother he condemned, and it always had been. Onto Whitechapel Road, shoving desperately through a line of people who waited in their own desperation outside a casual ward house to get a bed for the night. He skirted other such lines, except once to get directions to the street. The back streets were narrower and clogged with carts, wagons, and horses. He ran past row houses and the wide wooden gates of pungent stable yards, then at last into the cramped corridor of Castle Alley. Wagons and carts lined one side of the road. The smell here was much worse than that by the stables. Halfway along, three policemen stood on drier stones, on small islands in the excremental sea. Mayhew grabbed onto one of them, babbling his questions between breaths. The other two pulled him off and shoved him up against a wall with a nightstick under his jaw. Mayhew began to cry. The policemen looked at one another, embarrassed to be sharing this. The one with the nightstick eased back and said, "What's the matter, then? She your strumpet?"

"Strumpet?" Mayhew rubbed at one eye.

"Yeah, you know old 'Claypipe'?"

"You was a customer, then," suggested one of the others in the hope of lightening the mood. "Must a'been a good piece to set a man weepin'."

"I—what was the name of the woman killed?"

"Alice McKenzie. She's known round here as 'Claypipe Alice.' What, did you think it was somebody you knew?"

He nodded, wiped at his face with both hands, and tried to regain some equanimity. "My daughter. I heard that there'd been another murder—the Ripper."

"Oh, there's been that, right enough. His handiwork, all right. Through the throat, he got her, just like before. Found her between two vans, right up there." He pointed. The third policeman, silent till now, moved forward, close to Mayhew, and said, "So, you heard about a killing and you decided that it was your daughter got done. Gawd, people do go on, don't they?'' He shared a laugh with the other two.

Mayhew's hand trembled and he shoved it into his pocket. He dared not tell them about Demming, about what he suspected, about his dream. They would jail him for his part in it all, he was certain. ''My daughter, she lives on this street. Her name's Louise—Louise Mayhew.''

He sought for their recognition and got more than he wanted. One of them became beet red and turned away as if to scrutinize the alley. The policeman who had questioned him said flatly, ''Number twenty-three.'' He stepped back, rubbing his thumbs against his fingertips. None of them would meet his eyes now. They stepped from the walk and clomped off toward where the body had been found. Murder they could live with, but the father of a whore—the notion even that whores had families—was something they could not allow for.

Mayhew sniffled and moved quickly on to twenty-three. Not until he had his hand raised to knock did he hesitate, turning away suddenly in indecision, pressing again to the wall. What was he going to *say* to her, now that he had found her alive? His thoughts had been for a dead girl. Anything he said to her here would only shame her. If he left her alone, she might come home again; but if he left her *alone* . . . His wild thoughts collected like bees, and he realized for the first time what he was thinking: Demming was Jack the Ripper. How could this be coincidence—Castle Alley, of all the winding corridors in the East End? Somehow, some poor bastard had discovered this—had discovered that a gold watch helped him, or made him do it, or something that Mayhew couldn't even guess at—and Demming had been unable to continue without it. That hateful watch, everything was tied to that watch; and *he* had retrieved it. He started back out of the grimy street, ignoring the odd glances of the police.

He wandered distractedly most of the day. Mayhew was

not a man of action, nor a particularly skilled thinker. All he knew were nets and grappling hooks and the cold waters of the Thames. But he had to *do* something—if he didn't, Demming was going to kill Louise, of that much he was certain.

A drizzling rain rustled the leaves in St. James's Park and made the air smell of earth and decay. Prostitutes of a much higher class strolled by under umbrellas. One murmured to him as he passed. He kept his left arm pressed against his body to keep the item in his sleeve from slipping out. It had been a short boat hook not two days earlier; Mayhew had used a rasp file to sharpen the broken point into a needle. When a policeman appeared ahead, he ducked instinctively from sight, but in the rain Mayhew hardly looked different from anyone else in the park.

He reached Demming's street and, as he drew near the house, he saw the door open and a figure come out. The figure—a man dressed as if for a party—walked purposefully past him. Mayhew made a quick glance to determine that the man was not Demming. He glimpsed a pale, sweaty face and round, glassy eyes beneath the brim of a tall silk hat. Demming's door thumped shut. The street was silent, no one else about.

Mayhew went up to the door and rapped the knocker. A few moments passed before the door opened a crack and one eye stared out at him. It was Demming himself. The door opened wide, and the doctor stood cavalierly before him. "Well, this is a surprise. Come to hobnob, Mr. Mayhew?"

"You're Jack the Ripper!"

Demming spluttered a surprised laugh. "Am I?" He was about to go on, but paused to look past Mayhew, out into the gaslit street where Mayhew could hear footsteps. "Why don't you come in and tell me about it?" Demming let him in, then led him perfunctorily up the stairs into the same office they had stood in the day before. A chair now sat before the desk, as if he had been expected. The leather was warm, and Mayhew recalled the visitor who had passed him. "Now," said Demming, "I've done a great deal of work with lunatic delusions. Why don't you tell me yours, and let's see what I can do to help." He opened a box on the desk and with a steady hand took out a cigar, closing the box without offering one to Mayhew. He leaned back against the desk, his ankles crossed. "How am *I* the—the infamous Ripper?"

Mayhew raised his head to meet Demming's stare and said simply, "The watch."

For a fraction of a second, Demming faltered. If Mayhew had not been staring hard at him, he would have missed the twinge. Then Demming laughed and replied, "Mr. Mayhew, you are either drunk or mad. If the former, I advise you to go home and sleep it off; if the latter, you must accompany me to Bethlem this very evening." He moved around the desk and leaned for emphasis on the blotter, his cigar still unlit between his fingers.

Mayhew could only shake his head. He had entertained doubts till now, moments all the way here from Lambeth when he drew up short, thinking himself insane, his notions absurd at best. But he did not need to be a specialist in "lunatic delusions" to see that the doctor was lying, and prodding him to reveal what he knew in order to determine how he should be dealt with.

"You killed Alice McKenzie last night. But you were looking for Louise."

"Absurd, sir. I was at the theatre and a dinner party last night. A Gilbert and Sullivan musical. I went nowhere near your lovely daughter."

"You're lying."

"How many witnesses will be needed, Mr. Mayhew, to prove it?"

"The watch, then. Somehow the watch let you do it. When

Louise wound it, I went to sleep, and you were in the dream—"

"You let her wind it?" The facade was gone: first the doctor showed fearful amazement; then his eyes narrowed with determination. He drew open a drawer and pulled out a pistol, aimed it at Mayhew, who pressed back into the creaking chair as if to escape. "You saw some things, but you haven't all the facts. Still, your zeal might be enough to set the police on me, and we can't have that, not when we're so close."

"Close to what?"

"To opening the gates, to giving me some peace. What do you do on the river, Mayhew, spend hours just sitting and thinking?" He said this with an air of humor, a hint of admiration. "I'll tell you, then—as a reward of sorts.

"I've spent much of my life studying the diseases that can afflict the mind, Mr. Mayhew, while you rowed aimlessly about the Thames. I had begun working with hypnosis, Mesmerism, to treat patients. I found in a few of them a curiously recurring set of images amid their twisted fantasies—images of other worlds and their concomitant demons, much of which sounded like the reflections of some barbaric priest upon his drug-induced 'journeys.' Among those patients caged in Bethlem Hospital, I found one who was susceptible both to hypnosis and to this uncanny tapestry of images. I used a rather unusual watch to put him in a trance where he could describe his demons. It was a . . . I once *thought* it was a gift. Have you ever heard the name Cagliostro? No, of course not. He was a sorcerer who followed in the footsteps of Mesmer, in Paris. The Catholics claimed all sorts of satanic things about him—even that he had feasted with the dead. The man who gave me that watch told me that it had reputedly been fashioned for Cagliostro by a corpse, through the practice of necromancy; it subsequently had fallen into the hands of Eliphas Levi, another infamous villain, and so then passed to my

acquaintance after Levi's death in seventy-five. A *corpse*—
we joked about it. Such a wild, absurd tale. And I—I wore
the watch, here, in my vest. For years I wore it, with not so
much as a hint of its . . . God, of its *power*. It took a madman to show me that.

"What I expected, I can hardly remember. Of course I had
him stay here rather than at Bedlam. Outwardly, he was pas-
sive and I felt sure he would be safe. It wasn't until the third
murder that I discovered the—the connection. The watch
turned up missing, you see, and while searching I found that
my patient was not in his room. I did not find him that night.
But early the next morning—I could not sleep—I discovered
him unconscious in his bed. He had climbed in the second-
floor window, which still lay open. He was wearing one of
my suits, and his face, his chin and nose, had warts on it that
I could not remember him having. The watch was in his—
my—breast pocket. It was not ticking. I picked it up without
waking him, to take it, and turned the stem just a little, casually, thoughtlessly. With a cry of absolute agony, my patient snapped bolt upright. I dropped the watch and he lay
back down.

"Later that day I put him in a trance and got from him a
story that I then found hard to believe. He said that the watch
had spoken to him in his trance state, that it took control of
him, that the fantastic demons of his dreams could not compare with the real ones inhabiting the watch. They were making him perform terrible crimes. Here it was, then: I had
unleashed Jack the Ripper upon the East End. Worse, he had
worn my clothes and used *my* surgical knife. I considered
returning him to the hospital but I decided against this, mostly
out of fear that someone else might discover what I now
knew. I finally resolved to keep the watch from him while
trying to cure him of his delusion. These were only East End
trollops he had used in his aborted rituals—the world could
do without a few of them—but I had never wanted this to

happen, never. I do not know if he wrote any of the letters that the police collected.

"You will already know that I failed. He disappeared, and with him went my watch. To this day I have no idea how he escaped. My suspicion is that one of my staff unknowingly wound the watch. I sought him everywhere, discreetly of course, but had no luck. Then, after the last one, the woman Mary Kelly, he returned here. I hardly recognized him. His eyes were shot with blood, and the warts had grown in clusters across his cheek. I feared that he might actually be leprous. His mind had gone, and he babbled out that he had been moments away from completing some task, from bringing the demons of his dreams into the real world, when some other spirit, as of reason, took hold of him—which I presume means that the watch had stopped. He saw what horrors he had wrought under the demons' influence and he tried to destroy the watch in Mary Kelly's hearth. It revealed the extent of its power then, and instead of being destroyed, it erupted with some terrible energy. I still believed that this was all some dark corner of his mind, with no anchor in reality. Only later did I discover that some of the things on the grate in Mary Kelly's house had actually melted, that some unaccountable force had been unleashed. At the time, as I said, I dealt only with him. He had been burned rather severely on one arm. His mind collapsed finally even as I injected him with a soporific, careful not to touch him directly. The things he said afterward made no sense whatsoever. I could no longer keep him here, and I dared never return him to Bedlam."

"You killed him."

"In point of fact he was still alive when I pushed the rented hansom off the Tower Bridge. Your river murdered him, not I."

Mayhew shook his head at this rationalization. "Then why dredge him up when he was safely put down? And that devil's own watch,'' he said, but the realization dawned on him even as he asked it. ''You can't mean to try again?''

Demming twisted the pistol away in a sharp gesture. ''I've no *choice* now. Those vile things of his madness have come creeping into *my own dreams*. Oh, faint at first, very vague; but in the past few months I haven't dared to sleep without morphine. I would never have sought you out, except that the fiends even managed to crawl through *that* barrier. God knows what they really are. The painting in the watch hardly begins to suggest . . . Mr. Mayhew, they're like worms burrowing into your brain, eating their way right through it. If you fail them, deny them, the excrucation they can induce—Cagliostro died in a madman's anguish, in prison, and I know—I know *why*.''

After a moment, he went on more calmly. ''I knew I was going insane. All they wanted—all they *demanded*—was that I retrieve the watch and continue what had begun. For any chance at peace, I hired you, I found another at Bethlem, and I set him to it, just like before.''

''The watch,'' Mayhew said, ''the fella I passed coming in here—he's got it.''

''You don't think *I'd* carve her up. What if she looked at me, what if the image of my face were caught in her retina for the photographers to find? Let them have some other face to identify in the dead woman's gaze.''

''But why my Louise?''

''It's the damned *watch*, don't you see? You let her handle it, and it lives by these murders. I tried to clean all traces of her off the damned thing—you saw me do that! But the demons—their energy, their substance, must have drunk of her life in just those few moments. I'm sorry. It *knows* her.''

''How will you kill me, Mr. Demming? That's a gun, not the Thames, you got there.''

Demming looked down at his hand. ''Yes,'' he said in sad agreement. At that moment, Mayhew flung his short spear across the desk. It smashed an inkwell on its way, throwing blackness across Demming's face, a wide gash of shadow. The point entered him below his neck and Mayhew leaped up and shoved it with all his might. Demming sprawled back, slammed into the glass cabinet of skulls, shattering it, then fell forward across the desk. Mayhew stole the gun from his twitching fingers, then made himself withdraw the boat hook from Demming. The doctor flailed briefly, then lay on his side, gasping. Underneath him, spurting blood pooled and mixed with the ink on the desk.

Mayhew did not wait to see if the doctor died. His concern was with the monster already out and prowling the night.

He ran to Pall Mall and hailed a cab, giving the driver one of his gold coins in advance for the fastest ride to Whitechapel the man could manage. The delighted driver asked no questions, and his coach skidded every turn on two wheels, plunging through the rainy night.

No one was guarding Castle Alley; the police knew well that the Ripper did not work so regularly and never returned to the exact same location. Not before tonight.

Mayhew leaped from the coach, twisting his ankle on the ordure-slick stones. He ignored the pain and ran into the narrow street. At the other end of it, walking steadily, stiffly on, was the well-dressed man he had met outside Demming's. Mayhew slowed up, his heart and mind racing, then started ahead on the same side of the road. Twenty-three lay directly between them. He increased his pace to ensure that the Ripper did not reach it before him. With every step, he considered what to do and how to do it.

Steam rose from the sidewalk, a stench of decay. Mayhew hurriedly removed his heavy black sou'wester and balled it up around his arm. The approaching man still seemed to take no notice of him. They were close enough together now that Mayhew could see the droplets of rain on the brim of the top hat, the point of a crooked nose, the whites of shadowed eyes that continued to stare straight at number twenty-three.

The Ripper noticed him only at the last moment. Mayhew saw the face twist with hateful recognition. The Ripper's hand drew from a coat pocket a huge knife—the one that had appeared in his dream. The Ripper raised the knife and lunged at the same instant that Mayhew jumped forward and rammed his wrapped hand into the Ripper's chest. Demming's pistol made four thumping noises, quieter than if he'd knocked on a door. The Ripper stumbled back a step, staring down at himself, then up at the acrid smoke curling out from the coat. Part of his face held on to the evil scowl, but one corner of his mouth turned up as if in a grin. "Just like that," he said. He giggled, then fell over on his side. His head cracked loudly against the cobblestones, and the gold watch skittered out on its length of chain, as if trying to escape into the gutter.

Mayhew looked at the body for some time before he realized that he did not see the knife. He started to bend down to search and sensed an odd coldness in his back. Reaching up, he encountered the hilt of the knife projecting acutely above his shoulder. Bracing, he pulled it free. Strange, he thought, that there was no pain. He knew he did not want to be found outside Louise's door like this; he wanted her to come home of her own volition. And she would, he pledged, she would.

The Thames was vague behind the ceaseless drizzle. Each easy pull on the oars made Mayhew grind his teeth. His shirt, under the shiny tarred coat, was soaked in blood. He had grown tired and cold, almost as cold as the burden he carried wound about in his weighted nets. He could see the dull shine of the watch where he had tied it securely to the nets. The Tower Bridge loomed out of the rain like some great broken limb, making Mayhew think of bones rather than iron. He guessed that this was the spot more or less where he had discovered the watch. He shipped the oars and crawled back to the body. Listlessly, he took the gun, the blade, and tossed them over the side. In the coach that had carried him and his "drunken" companion to Lambeth, he had looked over at the face and wondered who the man was, what he had been. Now he no longer cared.

With the last of his energy, he grabbed onto his nets and dragged the body up over the lip of his boat and let it slide gently into the Thames. The ripples of its passing spread out across the water, disrupting all of those from the rain. Finally accepting exhaustion, Mayhew slumped back and closed his eyes, envisioning the two bodies rotting together in the coach on the bottom, the watch and the evil it contained buried in muck for all time. The tide was going out. Mayhew let it take hold of him. Slowly, he drifted beneath the jagged overhang of the bridge, cutting off the rain. He blinked the drops away like tears as the darkness crawled up him.

SPRING-FINGERED JACK

Susan Casper

How do you relax after a hard day at work? TV? A drink? A hot bath? Well, some ways might be a bit more unusual than others . . .

Susan Casper started writing in 1983, and in only a few years has become recognized as one of the most talented new writers in the field. Her short fiction has appeared in Playboy, Shadows, The Magazine of Fantasy and Science Fiction, Midnight, Isaac Asimov's Science Fiction Magazine, Whispers, Amazing, The Twilight Zone Magazine, In the Field of Fire, *and elsewhere. She is currently at work on her first novel, tentatively entitled* The Red Carnival. *She lives in Philadelphia.*

HE KNEW WHERE HE WAS GOING AS SOON AS HE walked into the arcade. He moved past the rows of busy children, blaring computer voices, flashing lights, and ringing bells. He walked past the line of old-fashioned pinball machines, all of them empty, all flashing and calling like outdated mechanical hookers vainly trying to tempt the passing trade.

The machine he wanted was back in the dimly lit corner, and he breathed a sigh of relief to see it unused. Its mutely staring screen was housed in a yellow body, above a row of levers and buttons. On its side, below the coin slot, was a garish purple drawing of a woman dressed in Victorian high fashion. Her large and ornate hat sat slightly askew atop her head, and her neatly piled hair was falling artistically down at the sides. She was screaming, eyes wide, the back of her hand almost covering her lovely mouth. And behind her, sketched in faintest white, was just the suggestion of a lurking figure.

He put his briefcase down beside the machine. With unsteady fingers, he reached for a coin, and fumbled it into the coin clot. The screen flashed to life. A sinister man in a deerstalker waved a crimson-tipped knife and faded away behind a row of buildings. The graphics were excellent, and extremely realistic. The screen filled with rows of dark blue instructions against a light blue field, and he scanned them sketchily, impatient for the game to begin.

He pressed a button and the image changed again, becoming a maze of narrow squalid streets lined with decaying buildings. One lone figure, his, stood squarely center screen. A woman in Victorian dress, labeled ''Polly,'' walked toward him. He pushed the lever forward and his man began to move. He remembered to make the man doff his cap; if you didn't, she wouldn't go with you. They fell in step together, and he carefully steered her past the first intersection. Old Montague Street was a trap for beginners, and one he hadn't fallen into for quite some time. The first one had to be taken to Buck's Row.

Off to one side, a bobby was separating a pair of brawling, ragged women. He had to be careful here, for it cost points if he was spotted. He steered the pair down the appropriate alley, noting with satisfaction that it was deserted.

The heartbeat sound became louder as he maneuvered his figure behind that of the woman, and was joined by the sound of harsh, labored breathing. This part of the game was timed and he would be working against the clock. He lifted a knife from inside his coat. Clapping a hand over ''Polly's'' mouth, he slashed her throat viciously from ear to ear. Lines of bright

red pulsed across the screen, but away from him. Good. He
had not been marked by the blood. Now came the hard part.
He laid her down and began the disemboweling, carefully
cutting her abdomen open almost to the diaphragm, keeping
one eye on the clock. He finished with twenty seconds to
spare and moved his man triumphantly away from the slowly
approaching bobby. Once he had found the public sink to
wash in, round one was complete.

Once again his figure was center screen. This time the
approaching figure was "Dark Annie," and he took her to
Hanbury Street. But this time he forgot to cover her mouth
when he struck, and she screamed, a shrill and terrifying
scream. Immediately the screen began to flash a brilliant,
painful red, pulsing in time to the ear-splitting blasts of a
police whistle. Two bobbies materialized on either side of his
figure, and grabbed it firmly by the arms. A hangman's noose
flashed on the screen as the funeral march roared from the
speaker. The screen went dark.

He stared at the jeering screen, trembling, feeling shaken
and sick, and cursed himself bitterly. A real beginner's mistake! He'd been too eager. Angrily, he fed another coin into
the slot.

This time, he carefully worked himself all the way up to
"Kate," piling up bonus points and making no fatal mis-
takes. He was sweating now, and his mouth was dry. His
jaws ached with tension. It was really hard to beat the clock
on this one, and took intense concentration. He remembered
to nick the eyelids, that was essential, and pulling the intestines out and draping them over the right shoulder wasn't too
hard, but cutting out the kidney correctly, *that* was a bitch.
At last the clock ran out on him, and he had to leave without
the kidney, costing himself a slew of points. He was rattled
enough to almost run into a bobby as he threaded through
the alleys leading out of Mitre Square. The obstacles became
increasingly difficult with every successful round completed,

and from here on in it became particularly hard, with the clock time shortening, swarms of sightseers, reporters, and roving Vigilance Committees to avoid, in addition to a re-doubled number of police. He had never yet found the right street for "Black Mary" . . .

A voice called, "Last game," and a little while later his man got caught again. He slapped the machine in frustration; then straightened his suit and tie and picked up his briefcase. He checked his Rolex. Ten-oh-five: it was early yet. The machines winked out in clustered groups as the last stragglers filed through the glass doors. He followed them into the street.

Once outside in the warm night air, he began to think again about the game, to plan his strategy for tomorrow, only peripherally aware of the winos mumbling in doorways, the scantily dressed hookers on the corner. Tawdry neon lights from porno movie houses, "adult" bookstores, and flophouse hotels tracked across his eyes like video displays, and his fingers worked imaginary buttons and levers as he pushed through the sleazy, late-night crowds.

He turned into a narrow alley, followed it deep into the shadows, and then stopped and leaned back against the cool, dank bricks. He spun the three dials of the combination lock, each to its proper number, and then opened the briefcase.

The machine: He had thought of it all day at work, thought of it nearly every second as he waited impatiently for five o'clock, and now another chance had come and gone, and he *still* had not beaten it. He fumbled among the papers in his briefcase, and pulled out a long, heavy knife.

He would practice tonight, and tomorrow he *would* beat the machine.

THE SINS OF THE FATHERS

Scott Baker

*Shakespeare said, "The evil that men do lives after them,"
and sometimes it does indeed do just that, in strange and
surprising ways . . . as the harrowing and very powerful story
coming up amply demonstrates.*

*Scott Baker is another writer who has made a large impact
with a relatively small amount of published work. Primarily
known for his short fiction, his stories have appeared in* Omni,
The Magazine of Fantasy and Science Fiction, *and elsewhere. One of his* Omni *stories, "The Lurking Duck," has
become something of a cult classic, and was published in
French translation as a book. His grisly story "Still Life with
Scorpion," first published in* Isaac Asimov's Science Fiction
Magazine, *won the World Fantasy Award as best short story
of 1985. His first novel was call* Nightchild, *and his most
recent is* Firedance. *He lives with his wife, Suzie, in Paris,
France.*

EMMA WAS AWAKENED BY A MUFFLED RATTLING SOUND,
like a tram going by some streets away. She opened
her eyes, saw a vague blur in white wheeling a table
made of steel tubes and black plastic trays past her. The table
gleamed with knives and scissors and other sharp, hard metal
things she couldn't distinguish. She reached out, groped for
her glasses with a hand so weak and heavy she could barely
move it, though at least they'd taken the tubes out of her

arms, but she couldn't find them, she couldn't even find the table they should have been on, just to the right of her bed, and for a moment she thought she was back in the operating room, they were going to have to cut into her again, open up her womb, and scrape out more of the cancer that was eating her from within, like some monstrous cannibal fetus.

"I've got your glasses on the table right here, Mrs. Blackwell."

She recognized the voice, turned her head, managed to make out another blur who must have been that young doctor who had always been so patient with her. He was standing just to the left of her bed. She liked to think her own father might have been like Dr. Knight once, when he was still young and freshly ordained and studying medicine so he could become a medical missionary in Africa. Before he'd given that all up for her mother and become just another small-town doctor to support her, and she had destroyed him.

"Dr. Knight?"

"Yes. Here, let me help you."

He held out her glasses. Her hands were trembling so badly she dropped them, but Dr. Knight just picked the glasses up and handed them to her again, let her try a second time without making any attempt to do it for her, allowing her to preserve her dignity. This time she managed to get them on. Dr. Knight came into focus, broad-faced and reassuring. Behind him she could see someone dark-skinned in a white uniform, the young Puerto Rican nurse who'd been so kind to her when the pain got too bad. She had a push table with her, but now that Emma had her glasses on she could see that the things gleaming on it were just knives and forks, glassware. Her dinner. She wasn't back in surgery after all.

But the room still wasn't right. The walls were white, not yellow, and she could see a sort of partition down at the far end, the kind they used for separating patients who had to share a room. "This isn't my room," she said.

"We've put you in another room for a while, where we can keep a better watch on you until we're sure you're ready to go back," the doctor said. "How are you feeling?"

"Better?" She hated the way her voice quavered, made a question out of it. "How should I be feeling?"

"Better." She thought he nodded. "All you need is some rest and then in a few days you can go back home."

"All I ever do is rest. Anyway, I don't have a home anymore. I live here, in the other wing."

"Of course. What I meant was, go back to your room, and your friends."

The nurse—Maria? Conchita? Emma was ashamed that she couldn't remember her name—came forward with a needle, gave her a shot.

"Here. This will help you sleep." So the dinner hadn't been for her after all.

Emma had wanted to be a nurse, too, when she was a girl, so she could help her father. She'd always read everything she could find in the papers about Florence Nightingale, and once, about a year after they'd moved to London, she had even managed to sneak out of their rooms over the Britannia Tavern, where her father kept her locked up during the day while he ministered to the beggars and lunatics at the Lambeth Workhouse, to go hear her speak, though Father had found out and thrashed her for it afterward.

Father had never approved of women spending their lives outside the home like that, no matter how much good they thought they were doing. There had been a time when he'd believed her mother was the exception, that it would be all right for her because she was working with him . . . until 1887, when Emma was twelve, and her mother abandoned them both to run off to Cleveland with that lawyer with the red face and ginger-colored mustache, the one who'd always been trying to get her father to become a Freemason and come to his lodge meetings.

Father had started drinking heavily after Mother left, putting himself in a drunken stupor every night, until the day when he'd suddenly realized that everything that had happened since he'd met her mother, all his pain, had had a purpose, that it had been no detour after all, but had instead been pointing him toward his ultimate ministry. She remembered when he'd told her that God had destined him, not to bring the faith to the savages in Africa, as he'd once thought, but to combat Freemasonry. And so he'd sold his practice and brought Emma to England, where he was convinced Freemasonry had its stronghold, to establish his ministry in Whitechapel—there to work with the poor and shiftless, the drunkards and the whores, heal their bodies with his medicines and surgeon's knives while bringing their souls to Christ and saving them from the insidious temptations of the Freemasonry that he was certain had already corrupted the British ruling classes and their puppet Church of England.

For the first year it hadn't been too bad. She'd help him sometimes during the day with his patients at the workhouses, or passing out tracts in the streets. She wanted to be with him all the time, prove to him that she wasn't like her mother, that he would always be able to depend on her. But he'd been too proud to admit how weak he was, that he could ever need help from someone, even after he'd started drinking again. On days when he couldn't keep himself sober she'd wait for him all day alone, with nothing to do after she finished cleaning their rooms but read his tracts and medical books over and over again, until it was so late at night that she finally knew once again that he wasn't going to be coming back, and that she would be forced out into the streets looking for him once again . . . to find him, when she found him at all, drunk in some tavern, buying drinks for squat, diseased whores with rotten teeth, and calling them all by her mother's name.

She'd drag him back to their rooms then—she'd been strong,

and bigger than any of the sickly English girls she saw on the streets, even if she was only thirteen—and put him to bed, watch over him, only to have him wake up the next morning hating himself, so sick with self-loathing at the memory of the women and the way he'd been pawing them, what he'd done with them, that he'd stagger over to the washbowl and vomit convulsively until there was nothing left in his stomach. And even then he'd keep trying to retch up more, as if he could tear the memory of his weakness out of his entrails and vomit it up with the gin and half-digested food. He had hated Emma, too, whenever she found him and brought him back still sober enough to be able to remember the next morning how she'd dragged him away from the whores he'd been too weak to resist, hated her for witnessing his humiliation and forcing him to remember himself as he really was.

He would beat her then, forbid her to ever go back into any of those taverns looking for him again, tell her she'd end up contaminated and diseased like the whores if she did. That had been when he'd started saying that she couldn't come with him and help him during the day anymore. He'd even begun talking about sending her away, back to some girls' school in Illinois where she would be protected. But he didn't have any money left, it all went for the gin and the whores, and so he would lock her up when he went out, though she'd taken the key from him and had a copy made once when he was too drunk to know what she was doing.

Yet he still spent his days unselfishly, trying to heal those poor souls who were too poverty-stricken and ignorant for any other doctor to interest himself in them, trying to bring them to Christ. Trying, too, to save them from the Freemasonry that he had come to England to combat, but which seemingly had vanished, though he knew that it must still be there, hidden from him where he would never be able to confront it directly—in Parliament, Buckingham Palace, the gentlemen's private clubs to which he would never be admitted. He knew that it was Freemasonry that was behind the squalor and misery all around him, that the men and women of Whitechapel were kept ignorant and corrupted and sodden with cheap gin so that their sons could provide cheap labor for the docks and the rich Freemasons' mills and factories, so that their destitute and debased daughters would have no choice but to offer themselves as whores to those richer and more powerful than themselves, to take their turn as replacements for their mothers, grown old and repulsive before their time.

Then the whores had started dying, and Inspector Abberline had come to question Father about their deaths in his polite, soft-spoken voice, not suspecting for even a moment that Father might himself be the Whitechapel Fiend . . . just hoping that with all the time he spent ministering to the worst of Whitechapel's human refuse, he might know something about somebody who could have done it, or have heard or noticed something suspicious. And then—

No. She couldn't allow herself to think about that. She tried to remember what had happened later, all the happy years afterward, when she'd gone back to Illinois to live with her uncle on his farm and had met Nathan at that tent meeting outside Naperville, how happy she'd been with him, how good her life had been from then on . . . but the shot the nurse had given her was making it impossible for her to lock the memories back into the little sealed room where she'd kept them for so many years. She couldn't shut out the way her father had looked when she'd found him hanging from the rafter, with his tongue protruding and his face all swollen as if with rage, but *white*, dead white, not the red it had always been when he was drinking. She remembered her impotent, helpless fury, how she'd burned the note he'd left for the police telling them that *he* was the Whitechapel murderer, and that he'd ended his life as the only way to stop himself from killing again, but that he was not committing the sin of suicide: he was a surgeon performing an ablation on himself, cutting a diseased element out of society before its corruption could spread any further.

She'd climbed up on the chair he'd used, taken one of his scalpels from his bag, and tried to cut him down. But he'd fallen on her when she tried to catch him, knocking her off the chair so that she'd been pinned there on the floor beneath him, with his dry, swollen tongue pressed against her cheek and his dead popping eyes staring blindly into hers, and she'd screamed and screamed and screamed, but nobody had come to help her. . . .

The injection must have finally put her asleep then, because when she opened her eyes again, she was back in her own room and her son, Teddy, was there, his silhouette recognizably like his father's, though Teddy was portlier and more pompous than Nathan had ever been. Nathan had always had his own unique dignity—that was what had impressed her so much about him, even when she first met him and he'd been only twenty years old. His natural dignity, and his kindness. Not like Teddy, who looked like exactly what he was: a moderately honest, moderately selfish, moderately successful businessman.

"Hello, Mother."

"Hello, Teddy." He was Nathan's son, her only child; she wished she could have felt something more than duty toward him. "Did you bring Mary with you?"

"Here I am, Grandmother."

"Mary?" She could make her granddaughter out now, a vague blur half-hidden behind her son. She tried to sit up.

"Let me help you, Mother."

Emma had always been a strong woman, had always hated to accept anything from anybody, but she was still too weak from the operation to refuse.

"Get me my glasses, Teddy," she told him when they'd managed to get her propped up in place. "They're over there, on the bedside table. Just far enough away so I can't get to them myself.''

She managed to stop him before he could actually push them onto her face, made him let her do it herself. Her hands seemed steadier now than when Dr. Knight had helped her put her glasses on. One glance at Teddy was enough to convince her that he was no different than ever—he just got a little stouter, a little jowlier and redder-faced every year—but Mary was growing up so fast it was always a shock to see how much she'd changed since her last visit.

Mary was twelve, just as Emma herself had been when her father took her to London. But where Emma had been tall and broad-shouldered for her day, more like girls were nowadays, Mary was slight and slender, as though Mary were the nineteenth-century girl and Emma had been the twentieth-century one. They all looked so much stronger and healthier today, yet their lives were so much easier, so much safer, despite all the nonsense people said about crime and violence and how it wasn't safe to walk the streets at night.

Father had loved Mother more than anything in the world, with the same all-consuming love Nathan and Emma had later had for each other. He would have given up anything for Mother, but she had been a cold, grasping woman who had never returned his love, and when she had left him and destroyed him, he had tried to devote himself to helping others, though he had failed at that, too. Yet unlovable, even contemptible, though Teddy was in so many ways, Mary would still have a better life with him than Emma had ever had with her own father, for all that she had loved her father in ways no one could ever love Teddy. Mary would never have to live through anything like Whitechapel, Father's hopeless spiral down into degradation and death.

"We're all sinners, Emma," Nathan had told her soon after he'd met her at that tent meeting in Naperville, where he'd so impressed her with the power and the purity he radiated when he came forward to give his testimony, call on them all to give themselves up to Christ. "One reason you're so strong is because you know who and what you are. When you commit a sin, you don't waste your strength denying it ever happened, or pretending that you're better than you are and had some perfectly good excuse. You admit you were wrong and try to do something to make things better afterward." And that was true, truer than even Nathan had ever known: she had never lied to herself, never told herself something was somebody else's fault when the blame was hers. That was why she had outlived everyone she had known when she was young, why she was still alive to provide Mary with the strength and love that Teddy would never be able to give her.

"Do you know what day it is, Grandmother?"

She squinted at the calendar. October 29.

"Of course. It's my birthday."

"Right, Mother," Theodore said, smiling fatuously. "And we've got a telegram of congratulations for you from President Johnson."

"President Johnson? I thought his name was . . ." She couldn't remember. "Some Irish name."

"That was President Kennedy, Mother. The one who was assassinated two years ago. Lyndon Johnson's president now."

"Anyway, you have to be a hundred years old before the President sends you a telegram."

"They send them to you when you're ninety now, too. Do you want me to read it to you?"

"Not now. Just put it there, by the bed." She turned to look at Mary, dismissing him, and smiled at her. "When you're an old lady like me you'll find it's a lot easier to remember things that happened when you were a little girl than things that happened just a year or two ago. How are you doing, Mary?"

THE SINS OF THE FATHERS / 239

"All right." But she wasn't all right, that was obvious, now that Emma peered at her more closely and saw the rigid way she was standing with her face closed and wooden, her hands clenched. Something was wrong. Something secret, that she didn't dare talk about in front of Teddy.

"Teddy, could you go get me a glass of water? No. Get me a Coca-Cola. Two Coca-Colas, one for me and one for Mary. They must have a machine here somewhere."

He just gaped at her.

"Well, what are you waiting for?"

"Mother, you never drink Coca-Cola!"

"How would you know? I feel like one. At my age I may die tomorrow and this will be the last chance I'll ever get to drink a Coca-Cola. Anyway, I'm sure Mary could use one. Couldn't you, Mary?"

"Yes, Grandmother."

"I just don't know if it's good for you."

"Then go ask a nurse. If she says I can't have it, just bring one back for Mary and get me whatever she says I *can* drink. But get going, *now*."

She waited until Teddy was gone, then held out her hand to Mary. Mary took it.

"What is it, Mary? I can tell something's wrong."

Mary nodded.

"Is it school? A boyfriend?"

Mary shook her head.

"Drugs, then, something like that?"

"Grandmother! Of course not!"

"Then what is it? I'm your grandmother, and I love you. You can tell me. Even if you can't tell your father."

"It's Dad. He's—you know his secretary, Miss McClure? The one with the red hair and the tight sweaters you said made her look like a prostitute?"

"What about her?"

"I hate her! Dad's *sleeping* with her. He always comes

home late and sometimes he doesn't come home at all, he just stays with her all night. He said he's going to leave Mother. He's going to get a divorce and *marry* her!''

"That's right." Emma looked up, startled. Teddy was standing in the doorway, holding two bottles of Coca-Cola.

"I hadn't planned on telling you yet, Mother. Not on your birthday, and not with Mary here like this. But as long as you had to find out, I might as well confirm things for you. I'm going to divorce Jean and marry Sharon."

"Jean's always been a good wife to you."

She tried to keep herself calm, not feel anything, stave off the rage building within her, the old, cold rage she had thought her years with Nathan had exorcised forever.

"Yes, a perfectly good wife! She cleans, she sews, she takes Mary to church on Sunday, she goes to every PTA meeting. This isn't Victorian England, Mother. You think that's what I want out of life?"

For an instant Emma was thirteen years old again, back in Miller's Court, the narrow alley where she was waiting hidden in the shadows, clutching the long knife from her father's bag as she watched Father with the whore they called Kelly, the young one who would have looked almost like her mother, if the depravity her mother had kept hidden behind her modest facade had instead been blazoned across her face for the whole world to see. Kelly was leaning back against the wall with her skirts lifted and her legs spread, taunting Father on, and he was swearing at her even as he undid his trousers and let them fall, half squatted, and pushed himself clumsily into her, shouting at her all the while that she was evil, she was filth, and calling her Margaret, calling her by *Mother's* name. But Kelly only laughed at him, told him that was *why* he wanted her, wasn't it, because she *was* filthy, she was a whore, *that* was what he wanted, not some nice clean-smelling little wife who would never take her clothes off for him except under the bedclothes in the dark with the curtains and shades drawn. And all the while Emma forced herself to watch, waiting for him to finish and pay the whore and stumble away, blind with self-loathing, so that she could use the knife, rip Kelly open and cut her father's seed out of the whore's diseased womb.

And then she was trapped back in the present, shaking with the same impotent rage she had felt when Kelly called out to a passing man just as Father was finally staggering off, forcing Emma to follow as Kelly took the other man back to the warmth of her room—though the chill November street had been good enough for her with Father—then wait outside until he, too, left and Kelly was alone again. But now Emma was ninety years old, and lying in a hospital bed with a cancer in her withered womb that was killing her more slowly, but just as certainly, as she had killed any of the whores who had tried to fatten themselves on her father's weakness, who had used that weakness to humiliate and degrade him . . . and she was as helpless to do anything now as she had been to save him in the end.

"Not now, Teddy," she managed to make herself say. "Not with Mary here. Come back some other time. Tomorrow. We'll talk about it then."

"You're sick, Mother, so I'll let you rest. And I'll come back without Mary, because that's what you want. But not because I think she needs to be shielded from any of this. She needs to understand what's going on, and it doesn't make much difference to me if she hears it with you here or on her own."

"Teddy, just go now. Take Mary home and leave me alone. Please leave me alone."

Nathan would have told her to forgive them, sympathize with them, and try to understand them, in the hope that with time she could bring them to see the error of their ways. She had never told Nathan what had *really* happened with her father, never thought it was fair to burden him with the crimes that were *her* responsibility and hers alone, but he had always known far more than she had ever told him, had perhaps even guessed most of the rest.

"Whatever you did, you did for love," he had told her once, "and for that God will forgive you."

Nathan had loved her anyway, had healed her broken life with his love, his loyalty, his devotion. He had lent her his strength and his vision of God's mercy, so different from anything her father had taught her, and together they had been whole in a way she could never have been on her own. But she was alone now, Nathan was dead and buried, and she had only his memory to guide her, help her keep her rage under control. Yet even if she *could* have been strong and generous and forgiving the way Nathan would have wanted her to be, she was still old and dying, and there would never be enough time for her to bring Teddy to see that what that woman was making him do was wrong.

Still, she had always known Teddy for what he was. She could have probably borne seeing Teddy leave Jean, watch their marriage trail off into another 1960s adultery and divorce, with nothing more than any other mother's anguished regrets, the sympathy she would feel for Jean. But Mary was different. Mary was pure, loving, she had Nathan's love and sweetness and generosity, so like her own father's but without the weakness, and Emma loved Mary the way she had loved Father, totally, without reservation, without concern for herself.

Nothing could be allowed to sully Mary. Nothing. But Emma knew she wouldn't be around to help Mary heal the wounds that would be left by a broken home, a father who would desert Mary just as Emma's own mother had deserted Emma and her father. Even with Nathan's memory preaching tolerance and forgiveness, Teddy's Miss McClure was lucky that Emma was old and bedridden and dying.

No. That was insanity. Worse than insanity: stupidity. This

was the 1960s, the era of scientific detective work, the FBI, fingerprints. They even had psychics like that Dutch man, whatever his name was, telling the police how to find murderers who had been too smart to leave any normal clues. Even if she'd been as strong as the girl she'd once been, there was no way she could kill someone and hope to get away with it again, no hope she could keep it a secret from Mary, or ever make her understand, and the knowledge that her beloved grandmother was a murderer would destroy Mary far more certainly than any outside taint Emma could shield her from.

As it had perhaps destroyed Father. Emma had never known if he really believed the note he had left for the police, if he really thought he had killed them all in fits of drunken insanity, or whether he had realized what she had done for him, and had sacrificed himself to save her.

A coward's sacrifice, if that's what it had been. If he'd just controlled himself, stopped drinking, refused to give in to temptation— But no. He'd been too weak, he'd preferred the cheap heroism of a quick, easy death to living out his life in sobriety, bearing his responsibility and his pain for himself. He would never have been able to bear his guilt, as Emma had borne her own all these years, knowing she was damned; knowing, too, that that was no excuse, that there had been no point of no return after which suicide or any other sin would have been meaningless and permissible because you were already doomed to the torments of Hell anyway. Knowing, too, that she would do it again if she thought it would save him.

But there was no way to save Mary from the Miss Mc-Clures of the world. There were too *many* of them, they were everywhere today in their short skirts and high heels, almost naked on the beaches, selling their bodies like whores in movies and on billboards and in magazines so companies could sell toothpaste and deodorants and underclothes, and if something happened to *this* Miss McClure, Teddy would just find another to take her place.

Emma was helpless, too weak to strike, tear out the evil and destroy it before it could spread any farther, even if that were possible. As helpless as the surgeons who kept opening her up, cutting out a little more of the cancer suppurating in her diseased womb, but who were unable to keep it from extending its tentacles to her liver and lungs, through her bloodstream, spreading farther and farther throughout her body, like some tree of evil taking root in her every organ and cell . . . until soon she would be only a mass of diseased corruption. Like the world had become, the evil that had once been confined to the ghettos and slums now spreading with ever-increasing speed throughout the seemingly healthy tissue of society, so that the whole thing was rotten and tainted with filth beneath its shining healthy surface, eaten away from within.

She was too weak and helpless to do anything, there was nothing anyone could have done, but that night she started spitting out all the sleeping pills the nurses gave her, and hiding them in the little purse with the jet beads on it they let her keep in her bedside table's drawer, though she never needed to use the few dollars she kept there to buy anything anymore, or ever went anywhere anymore, except when they put her in her wheelchair and covered her with blankets and wheeled her out into the garden with the others, to bask in the sun like wrinkled, senile toads and lizards.

But even with the dull pain that never really went away, and the nights she spent sleepless, worrying about Mary or lost in the past, a little of her strength was coming back.

"I'm never going to get better, am I?" she asked Dr. Knight. "I mean, better enough to go home, even for a while."

"No."

"How much longer do I have?"

He shrugged. "There's no way we can tell you. At least nother month or two, possibly a year, maybe even more. A ot of it depends on how much longer you want to hang on, nd on how hard you're willing to fight."

She had five sleeping pills saved up before Teddy came ack to see her, alone this time.

"I don't love her, and she doesn't love me, Mother. We'd oth be better off divorced."

She could tell he was lying, like she could *always* tell when e was lying to her. Trying to justify himself, pretend he was nnocent, just another helpless and blameless victim of cir- umstances, when it was all *his* fault, his and that woman's, launting her body at him every day at the office like a cheap vhore, and him too selfish and spineless to resist her or think bout his responsibilities to his wife and daughter when all e cared about was getting *her* into bed, or maybe up on his lesk after everyone else at the office had gone home—

"Mother!" To her horror she realized that she'd been numbling her thoughts out loud, that he'd heard it all. "That's nsane! You don't know what you're talking about! That's the exact kind of stupid puritan bullshit that's always kept me rom telling you about any of this. Because I knew you vouldn't even try to understand."

Emma caught her breath, tried to start over.

"Jean has always been faithful to you. Why can't you be aithful to her?"

"Because Jean isn't what I want! Any more than you were vhat Father wanted."

"What do you mean by that?"

"What do you think I mean? You think that all he was loing away from home all day, every day, that he was just working up that half-hour sermon he was going to preach over the radio? That it took him all day to set things up, prepare himself, meditate on mankind's ills and needs? Hell, he just walked in there about ten minutes before he was due to start broadcasting and made it up as he went along.''

''I don't believe you.''

''He used to take me down there with him sometimes, didn't he?''

''Yes.''

''And where do you think he spent the *rest* of that time, when you thought he was preparing his sermons?''

''You're lying. Nathan was never like that.''

''With *women*, that's where! *Whores*—isn't that what you used to call them, when you were warning me about spending my time with loose women, how they'd tempt me and subvert me and poison my life? Give me diseases?''

''Teddy—''

''Don't start telling *me* all about your father and his holy mission to England and how he hung himself to keep himself from being tempted anymore, because I don't care! He hung himself because he was a crazy drunk, not because of anything some woman did to him. And nobody poisoned my life! I've been seeing women all my life, but only because *I* wanted to, not because I was too weak to fight off some sleazy prostitute's honeyed temptations.''

''He took you *with* him? When he went to see those women?''

''A few times. I mean, not up to see them, no, but I'd wait in the park or at some lunch counter for him, and he knew I knew what he was doing. I saw one of them once, a real pretty blonde woman, when she met him at the door.''

''Teddy, stop. Please stop.'' She put up a hand, trying to ward his words off, but he wasn't listening, wasn't even looking at her, he just went on.

''I never told you before because I knew you'd never understand. I didn't want to hurt you, just like Father never wanted to hurt you. The only reason I'm saying it now is to get you to stop trying to tell me I'm committing some sort of horrible sin, just because I love Sharon and I want to get divorced so I can marry her!''

"What do you want me to do?'' She found she was suddenly calm, glacial. Nothing he could say could touch her anymore.

"Stop lecturing me about right and wrong all the time. Stop telling me what I should and shouldn't do. I'm not a child anymore. Just leave me alone.''

"And that's all?''

"No, that's not all. Stop poisoning Mary's mind against me and Sharon.''

"So now *I'm* the one poisoning people's minds?''

"You know what I mean! Sharon's going to be Mary's new mother, and she's going to have to learn to live with her.''

"What about Jean?''

"Jean and I have already worked it out. I'll take Mary for the first year, until Jean can find a job, and then we'll split her. She'll be spending the school year with Jean and her summers with me and Sharon.''

"Jean *agreed* to all this?''

"She agreed. A lot of it was her idea. She's as sick of me as I am of her, Mother.''

"Did you ask Mary about this?''

"She's just a kid. She'll do what we think is best for her.''

"Whether I like it or not.''

"Whether *either* of you likes it or not.'' He paused, seemed suddenly embarrassed. "Look, Mother, I'm sorry, I don't want things to be like this with you. I shouldn't have gotten mad like that, told you that about Father. He really loved you. It wasn't true, what I said, he never did anything like that. I was just so mad I didn't know what I was saying. You never did anything to deserve that. I'm sorry.''

He hesitated again, looking pleadingly at her, waiting for her to tell him it was all right, she forgave him, he was a good boy after all, so that they could pretend together that he'd never said anything. So that she could lie to herself and go back to believing that Nathan had always been the good and glorious and godly man whose strength she'd built her life upon and whose memory had sustained her all these years, instead of just another hypocrite like all the others.

She stared at her son, despising him for his abject cowardice, his spineless, irresponsible cruelty, as she'd never despised anyone before in her life, not Kelly or Annie Chapman or any of the others.

"Look," he said, "you've got the wrong idea about Sharon, anyway. Maybe you'll understand when you get to know her better. She's not like you think she is."

"Maybe not."

"I'll bring her with me next time I come."

"I just want to see Mary."

"I can't allow that. Not without Sharon and me there, until I'm sure you won't just make things harder for her than they already are."

"Do you want my promise that I won't 'poison her mind' against you?"

"I want you to see how things *really* are between me and Sharon first. Then when you understand, maybe you can see Mary on her own."

She lay awake that night wondering what could have happened to make Nathan change, make him into something as abject and contemptible as Teddy. Worse than Teddy, because where Teddy was just a fool who had never claimed to be anything he wasn't, Nathan had *known* what he was doing, had lied about it for years, preaching God's love on the radio every day after committing adultery with his whores, while she waited for him at home, so proud of him, so grateful.

She had thought that Nathan was so much stronger and loving than Father, when all he had been was a bigger hypocrite, living out his life of sin and luxury with the greatest of ease, lying, corrupting his son. She had always thought that Teddy's cowardice was due to his own lack of character, or perhaps to some taint that had come down to him through her from her own mother or father, but maybe he had only been too dutiful and uncritical a son, too eager to imitate the man she herself had tried to model her life after.

All the little details she had dismissed as nonsense for so many years, forced herself to explain away and forget, were coming back to her: the nights he'd been kept late at the studio, all the phone calls from women that he said were from his listeners, people who needed counseling and help so he could bring them to Christ. The retreats he went on every few months without her, so he could be alone with God. And she knew that she *must* have known somewhere, must have chosen to be blind and comfortable despite all her pride in never lying to herself.

But Nathan *had* been a good man when she met him and fell in love with him, she was still certain of that, every bit as good a man as she had gone on believing him to be. She had loved and cherished him, never complained back in the beginning when things were hard or when there wasn't enough money to pay the bills, tried to free him from day-to-day worries so he could devote himself entirely to doing the Lord's work. What had gone wrong, what could have made him into what he had become?

Perhaps if she'd been less blind, less complacent and confident and proud, she would have seen what was happening in time to stop it.

Two days later, when the attendant who was supposed to be pushing her wheelchair back in from the garden left her alone for a few minutes outside the geriatrics wing's infirmary to go answer a phone call, she managed to wheel herself in and steal a scalpel, then get back out and into place before he returned. Maybe if she killed herself and left a note for Teddy, there would be some way to use her death to put pressure on Teddy, make him feel so guilty he would give up his idea of abandoning Jean and Mary.

But to do that, she would have to abandon Mary herself. She felt confused, nothing made any sense; she didn't know what she could *do* with the scalpel, what good it could possibly do, but it made her feel a little less helpless to know it was there, hidden between the pages of a magazine in the drawer by her bed.

When Teddy showed up with his Miss McClure, Emma could see that she'd tried to dress less provocatively than usual, in discreet beiges and browns, low heels, but even so her sweater was too tight, emphasizing her enormous, cowlike breasts, and her skirt was just a little too short for the dignified effect she was trying to achieve, as if she couldn't bear not to show off her too-long legs in their sheer nylons. Her lips were covered with bloodred lipstick and she stank of perfume: musk, like some animal in heat.

Teddy made some excuse about checking with the doctor, said he'd be back in a few moments, and left them there alone together. Cowardly as always.

She seemed ill at ease. "Ted said you wanted to see me. He thought it was a good idea for us to get to know each other better."

Emma just looked at her.

"Look, I know you don't like me. Ted told me what you said. About how you think I've been flaunting my body at your son so I can steal him away from his loyal, dutiful, wonderful, devoted, but unfortunately just a bit mousy Christian little wife. Right?"

"Well, isn't that what you've been doing?"

"No! Ted and me, it's not like that at all. We want to get married, spend the rest of our lives together. Have children of our own. If he likes my body, that's his business, his business and mine, not yours or anyone else's. And as for that wife of his—You always approved of her, didn't you? Thought she was the perfect wife and mother, exactly what your son and granddaughter needed, right?''

"And you're telling me she isn't like that at all?"

"That's exactly what I'm telling you! Sure, I'm a loud-mouth and she's demure, and she's had a lot more education than I have, and she's a real whiz at church rummage sales and all that. So what?''

"And what do you have to offer that she doesn't?"

"I'm in love with Ted and she *isn't*. That's all. She's in love with being somebody's wife, having a nice house and a nice car and having people call her Mrs. Blackwell. But she doesn't care about *Ted*. She could be Mrs. Anybody, and as long as she had the house and car she wouldn't care who that Mr. Anybody was.''

She went on and on, talking about how much she loved Ted, how much Ted loved her, but Emma was no longer listening. She was just another victim like all the others, too weak and stupid to resist the corruption that had sunk its roots into her, was devouring her from within and would eventually destroy her immortal soul, too blind to see it for the cancer it really was. There was no hope for any of them.

Exactly half an hour after Ted left them alone, he returned. They must have planned it out, decided on how much time it would take his Miss McClure to lay out her true love and devotion for Teddy for Emma to see, give her her maximum chance to convince the old lady. It was *all right* to abandon Mary, destroy her home and her faith and her hopes for a future any better than they themselves had had, because they were going to do it for *love*. Like Father in the alley with Kelly, shouting Emma's mother's name as Kelly taunted him on. All for love.

But Emma knew more about love than any of them, and she loved Mary. She had sacrificed her immortal soul for love of her father, though her love had not been enough to save him; she had dedicated her life to her love for Nathan, though she had not been strong or wise enough to save him, either. This was her last chance. She could not let herself fail again.

The next time Ted returned, he had Jean and Mary with him. Jean was subdued, quiet, talking about how things were all going to work out for the best. The time on her own would give her a chance to decide what she was going to do with her life, and though it might be hard for Mary at first, Jean was sure she would be happy with her father until Jean was well enough established that Mary could come live with her. And anyway she was sure that Sharon would be a very good mother to Mary, and grow to love her the same way Jean did. It was all said in a subdued monotone, rehearsed and passionless, and, listening to her, it came to Emma that Teddy's Miss McClure was right after all. Jean never had loved Teddy, had probably never even felt much more for *Mary* than she had for Teddy: perhaps a sense of duty, of her responsibilities as a wife and mother, a respectable woman living a respectable life in a respectable way and expecting a respectable recompense in return. Nothing more.

Mary sat there, listening, not saying anything, her face closed and tight and desperately blank, while Jean and Teddy talked about her as if she weren't there, in the same tones of voice they probably used when they were talking about dividing up the furniture. As if none of them were really there, and they were all already dead, just ghosts reciting speeches that might have meant something to them when they were still alive, but that were now only empty words echoing over and over again in a void, long after even the memory of the fact that they had once meant something had faded and was gone.

She remembered the night her own mother had gone, how she had just stood there, silent, watching her pack while the carriage waited for her out front, then staring out after her as she drove away. How Father had come back from his lodge meeting to find Mother gone, and Emma had had to tell him about watching her pack, but couldn't tell him where she'd gone or why or for how long, couldn't tell him anything because Mother hadn't told *her* anything, hadn't even left a note. How she'd had to sit there with Father, holding his hand and watching him cry, and there'd been nothing she could do to make it any better, to save him. She would have done anything for him, but there was nothing he needed that had been hers to give.

And then, finally, she knew what it was she had to do, how her whole life had been leading up to this, everything, her father, Nathan, even the cancer devouring her from within. Everything.

Her father had failed his vision. She must not fail hers.

But it was a month before they allowed Mary to take a bus out from town to come see Emma on her own.

"Mary, do you remember that other time your father came here with you, when he went out and got us two Coca-Colas?"

"Of course, Grandmother. That was when he told you he was leaving Mother."

"I never got a chance to drink that Coca-Cola with you. Do you think you could ask the nurse on duty where the machine is and get us two more bottles?"

"All right, Grandmother."

"Then get me my purse. It's in that drawer."

Mary handed her the purse. Emma took two quarters out, handed them to her.

"Here. Hurry back."

She was back five minutes later with the two bottles.

"Here they are, Grandmother."

"Do you think you can go get us some cups? I know that

girls like you can drink things straight from the bottle, but I'm from another generation, and I need a cup. There should be some cups down by the water machine at the nurse's station at the end of the hall.''

As soon as Mary was gone, Emma slipped one of the green and red capsules into her bottle, watched anxiously until it dissolved. She took a cautious sip, but the capsules weren't bitter like the pain pills they gave her, and she couldn't taste anything. She put eight more capsules into the bottle, watched them as they dissolved.

They were almost gone, with only a few mushy fragments of the capsule shells left swirling around at the bottom, by the time Mary returned.

''Mary, can I ask you another favor? I know I must be a bother, constantly asking you favors like this—''

''Not at all, Grandmother.''

''Could you help me sit up? And then come up here''—she patted the left side of the bed beside her with the flat of her hand—''and sit here next to me while we drink our Coca-Colas together? Just like we were friends the same age, instead of you being polite to your old grandmother?''

''We are friends, Grandmother.''

''Good. I love you very much, Mary.''

The pills were completely gone by the time Mary crawled up onto the bed beside her. They drank their Coca-Colas together while Emma listened to Mary and asked her questions, not just about Teddy and Jean and Miss McClure, but about everything Mary felt and believed and cared about, trying to take this last chance to get to know everything she would ever know about her. And all the while she told Mary how much she loved her, and that she knew how hard things were for her now, but if she just had faith they would turn out all right in the end.

When Mary finally slipped down to sleep beside Emma, still holding her hand, she looked so beautiful, so calm and peaceful and innocent, that Emma wanted more than anything else she could imagine just to let her lie there in peace forever like that, just lie there and never wake up. But she knew that that was hopeless, that even if the nine sleeping pills in Mary's Coca-Cola were enough to give a girl her size a fatal overdose, the hospital staff would still just discover her and pump out her stomach and bring her back, to have her purity tainted and destroyed as Nathan's and her father's had been, as her own had been when her mother abandoned them.

The knife was ready, hidden beneath a magazine, and she knew how to use it. She had done it before, and though that had been more than seventy-five years ago, it was not the kind of thing you could ever forget, no matter how hard you tried. Coming up behind that drunken whore in that passage off Mitre Square and grabbing her scarf with her left hand, the scalpel already ready in her right as she yanked the whore back, slashed her across the throat—

A nurse she didn't recognize poked her head in through the door, saw Mary sleeping by Emma's side, her hand clasped in Emma's. Emma put her other hand to her lips, whispered "Shhhh!" and the nurse smiled back at her, gently closed the door behind her as she left so as to leave the two of them undisturbed.

Emma disengaged her hand gently from Mary's, picked up the scalpel, gripped it as tightly as she could. The motions, the gestures, would be the same as they had been all those other times, with all those other women, yet everything would be different. She had killed the others out of hatred and rage: that was why it hadn't been enough to just slash their throats and watch the blood come spurting out as they died, why she'd had to hack and mutilate them afterward, humiliate and degrade them in their deaths for the way they had humiliated and degraded her father in his life. But this time what she had to do she would do with love, and Mary's soul would soar free of the filth and corruption that would otherwise be her inevitable fate, ascend directly to Heaven, to that paradise of purity and innocent joy that was all that Emma had ever wanted for herself and those she loved, and that she had always known that she herself would never see.

A GOOD NIGHT'S WORK

Sarah Clemens

There's an expression current on the streets, "What goes around, comes around"—a proposition elegantly demonstrated by the jazzy little story that follows.

Although an Old Fan, Sarah Clemens is a new writer. In fact, "A Good Night's Work" is her very first sale, though we are willing to bet that it will not be her last. She lives in Mangonia Park, Florida, works at a community college, and has recently completed her first novel.

WHITECHAPEL GIRLS DON'T GO TO BED EARLY. YOU can taste the gin in the air, yearn to feel it go down and shake you and give you the warm, good times—and that's why the men come to see us, because they know we want our drams. So you wander and you search till a man turns your way and takes you off to a dark spot—darker, that is, than the streets themselves—pulls up the petticoats, and gives you a punch up the old whiskers. Then you got the money for another drink.

The nights are for drinking, make no mistake. When the times are good, you forget to be tired, but even a whore like me has got to rest when the gin runs you down. So when you feel done in, you try to get the money together for a doss, a bed for the night. It's a trick, sometimes, when you stand there, money in hand and the gin's a-calling. You sway like the wet wind has got you, then you either go for another dram, or move your feet toward rest and climb into bed with a couple of other ladies and a few hundred lovely bedbugs.

One night is like all the rest, but no one here thinks about that. All that matters is not to have the shakes, because you don't have the coppers for a dram. Next week in Whitechapel is a long way off. That's the point to be made, ducks; that one night is the same as another because in the East End you know what's important to you. That's why a woman ends up here, you know.

But not all are the same. This one night was like none of the others, and believe me, I've done things every day the likes of which would send one of them decent ladies into one of their faints—not that fainting can't be used to advantage now and again. A restless cold one it was, too, an early December night full of misted rain and pretty music and voices calling from the pubs and window light bleeding across the wet pavement. And I could not sleep.

My legs were done in. My throat was gone and my petticoats near soaked, but I could not sleep. I even found myself looking down at a ditch that had been dug by the road for a water-main repair and envying others who had been near me who had ended up resting for good in the ground. And so I walked until something came out of a shadow and moved toward me.

"I'm not so sure I need company," I said, even though the economy of the situation called for me to smile his way.

"No lady wants company these days," he said a little regretfully. "Not with Slippery Jack about."

"You're not wrong there," I agreed, and let him stop me.

"A foreigner, are you?" he asked.

"I'm a Londoner now, and have been for years. Sweden is a long way off, so don't let my accent trouble you none." If he wasn't scared off that I was taller than him, or that there's no teeth on my bottom jaw, I would take his money. Besides, old Jack could have been around, and a lady likes to have company. I looked him over a bit, and I knew this man would make the night come down easier, maybe give me some rest. He was the one I had been waiting for. You couldn't call this one a toff, quite, but he had the air about him. His clothes told the story. They were a good cut, but near as worn as my own. His eyes were pale, but full of lights, and his face a mite paler, sort of pinched, like. He was wearing one of them deerstalker caps and it was wet all the way through.

"A whore with a silk scarf," he said to me. "An old whore in a stinking sateen dress who's starving to death."

"Now, wait a bit. You down on whores?"

"I only want—"

"You only want to move on," I told him, pulling myself up. "If I am so bloody bad, just move on."

He hastened to put a hand on my arm. "Don't go. I have money. I need you."

I laughed, and his face sort of twitched. "I want to see this money."

He put down a bag, which I noticed for the first time, and reached into his coat, bringing out a real gold piece. "I'll give you enough for your own bottle and a whole bed for the night. You are tired, aren't you? Take it, whore."

Him calling me a whore again! It was a test, I know it was because I am not a fool. A whore, yes, but not a fool. Let the bloody toff do what he wanted. I snatched at the gold and he held it out of the way, tucking it into his vest.

"I won't take long," he smiled and whispered. "But it will be a good night's work for you."

And I smiled, too, though he couldn't see my smile because he was taking me into the dark, pressing his wet hands against my shoulders until we backed into a wall. His breath rolled over my face and he was very near.

"Pretty silk," he whispered, "pretty, pretty, pretty . . ."

My hands were on his arms, but they were like steel, and his fingers were coursing their way up to my throat, where they came to rest, pressing and pressing against my scarf. My windpipe caved under his grip, and gave way with a soft pop.

He laid my body down where there was more light, and glanced about quickly. A drop of sweat rolled down his nose and fell to my face. Scurrying away, he grabbed his bag and came back fumbling a bit with the catch until he got it open and brought out the knife. It was a clean stroke, the way the knife started at one side of my neck and cut through to the other. The little bugger was sharp.

The Ripper was a man who wasted no time. Up went the petticoats, and I could feel how cold the blade was as he pushed straight down into my belly and cut toward my legs, like you cut out a slice of cake. Cut, cut, cut, and away came the vitals. Slick, foul intestines to drape about my body like a frame. Bits of flesh like dark jewelry around my hands. Female organs laid cold and wet on my legs.

Then he got restless and jerked my petticoats back down. He was moving back to my face, stroking his blade over my eyelids, cutting into the eyes. I could feel him grate bone as the knife rode down my cheeks, and I suppose that was when a certain idea struck old Jack. He squatted by my head and looked by either side of my throat.

Really and truly, I had thought him a smarter man. Why hadn't he checked before to see if all the blood that is supposed to come out of a cut throat really came out? Or, for that matter, why I had felt so cold, even inside my belly. His hand touched the ground nervously, then clawed at the ground. No blood.

"I cannot bleed," I rasped helpfully.

He fell back off his heels and sat on the ground. He gripped his knife so hard his hand trembled.

"You're dead," he said hoarsely. "And I know I am insane. I'm insane! Therefore I'm imagining this."

"No doubt you're insane."

"But I'm still hearing you."

"Yes."

He skittered away from me and it was easy to feel his heart pounding. It was getting louder and louder. His old deerstalker fell off his head.

Old habits die hard, so I turned my face to him even though there were no eyes to use. "We all just thought you should finish me up. Get the job done, as it were."

He didn't move.

I suppose my voice sounded sort of bad by this time. It was hard enough talking to him as much as I had with my throat being already cut, and now with the second time, it was getting to be a trial.

"Finish you up?"

"And you done fine. It's all proper, now, though you done Black Mary more proper yet."

He wheezed a little himself now. "An accent. You have an accent."

I just waited, because he had to fit it all together sometime soon. He crawled back to me and caught up the end of my silk scarf, pulling it gently away from my throat. It was caught, though, and suddenly he couldn't be very gentle anymore. He was tearing at it, slashing away with the knife to get it away from me, and finally it did come away. Made me sad, really, because that scarf had been a friend to me for a long time.

At any rate, there he was bending over my neck. Then he touched the old cut. Sweat came splashing into the wound. Jack was proper fixed, he was.

"You're cold. You whore, you're cold. And I didn't cut your throat twice."

"Oh, yes, you did." I couldn't help but smile. He had left me with a mouth to smile with, after all. And it was a good joke, wasn't it? Me and the other girls, we had sat around for a while to think this up.

"No. I cut you once. I took m-my knife and—" He slashed the air over my face. "Once, whore. Once just now."

"And once before, off Berner Street."

He sent the knife down into my heart. "No!"

"Long Liz Stride, Jack. Remember? You got Kate Eddowes pretty good that night, but there was no time for me."

His heart was like a drum. Taking the knife out, he stuck it back in, over and over.

"Better yet, Jack. You're doing fine." My voice was like a cough full of spittle by now. I was more tired than I thought.

He fell away from me, leaving the knife in me, and pulled himself up, clutching at his forearm. "I killed you, whore."

"Yessss. Off Berner Street. You cut my throat, but that old man's pony and cart scared you off. Couldn't finish the way you wanted. So you went off and took Kate in Mitre Square."

Moaning, he slid along the wall, away from me.

"Your bag, Jack, don't leave your bag."

He actually did sort of fall forward and grab the infernal thing, pulling it with him as he ran off. It clanked a bit, because there were other blades inside. For the special little jobs, if there was time.

I could feel him making his way along the street, breathing and sweating, sweating and gasping. It was a proper good joke after all and he did understand. I'm convinced of it, and so are the girls. You know, Polly and Annie and Kate and Mary. He cut us all.

And what's a whore to do? A week before I died I told some police bloke that I could even be next. And did he listen? Well, I *died*, didn't I? I guess not, not really. So there we all were in a black sort of place. I don't think it was really heaven or hell, just a place someone had reserved for us, like the way I used to tell the fellow at the doss house to hold me a bed.

Though it seems off the subject a bit, remember that if you can't laugh, the world will shake the life out of you. We was all like that. Polly Nichols, she laughed about what a jolly bonnet she had before she went out and met Jack. Me, I told people about my husband and children, bless their souls, and maybe I told a little more than the truth, but everyone believed me. They wanted to hear my stories. And I used to fall down and act like I had gotten a fainting spell when I was brought up in front of magistrates for my drinking. That really got the laughs.

We were there in this dark place, then, and Mary Kelly, Black Mary, says, "Why, Liz, he didn't do you *near* as good as he got us. I'm thinking you don't even belong with us."

We got a good laugh out of that one, and one thing led to another.

"You're almost a whole woman," says Annie, and we laughed some more. "You ought to give Jack a chance to finish what he started, you know. Seems only right."

We near died a second death laughing.

Then I suddenly seemed to pop back into the street of Whitechapel, that dear scarf covering where he had cut my throat the first time.

And you know the rest.

Except, of course, that old Jack was having bad problems with his heart when he left me. I knew that, being dead and all, and in some way that I don't really understand, I and the girls followed him down to the Thames, where he fell in. If you ask me, he fell, but he threw himself, too, because he couldn't get the best of us. Without feeling the pain, we could feel the cold water go down into his lungs and wash the life away that the heart attack hadn't. Bless him, he took the bag along, too.

Finally, I sat up in the alley where he had taken me for his little job. It wasn't easy, putting all those wet things back into my belly, but I did my best, and after all, there was no blood. The blood all went out back at Berner Street. I scooped up everything and got myself across the street, pulling my skin and petticoats tight together, that knife still sticking out of my chest. There was that hole dug there, where the boys had been working on the water pipe, and I allowed that I would fall in.

Letting go the mess inside of me, I lay there and let my old joints get stiff the way they should. It rained a little harder after a while, and part of the dirt caved in on me. In the morning the lads came with their shovels and filled up the hole because the work was all done.

And here I am in the dark again with my sisters. It's not cold, although there are more bugs here than there are in the park or in the doss beds. They say Whitechapel life is as low as you can go, and that makes everything down here in the dark seem better than it was. It's me and the girls together again, and the earth lies over us all like a kind, warm blanket. There is rest here. I think if they dug us up now, we would all have smiles on our faces, smiles for our tired, dead bodies, smiles for old Jack, who never rested, and never will.

KNUCKLEBONES

Tim Sullivan

Born in Bangor, Maine, Tim Sullivan now lives in Phila-delphia in an apartment jampacked—appropriately enough—with horror memorabilia and monster-movie posters. To say nothing of lizard masks, rubber elephant noses, and toy di-nosaurs. A full-time writer, Sullivan has sold short fiction to Isaac Asimov's Science Fiction Magazine, The Twilight Zone Magazine, Chrysalis, New Dimensions, *and elsewhere. He also reviews regularly for* The Washington Post Book World, USA Today, *the* Cleveland Plain Dealer, Fantasy Review, Short Form, *and elsewhere, and contributed many of the horror-movie reviews for the recent* Penguin Encyclo-pedia of Horror and the Supernatural. *His most recent novel is* Destiny's End. *Upcoming are an original horror anthology he's editing, called* Tropical Chill, *and a new novel, tenta-tively entitled* Flowering Flesh, *both from Avon.*

In spite of his reputation as a major-league Party Animal and an adroit amateur Elvis impersonator, Sullivan's stories are rarely funny. This one isn't a barrel of yucks, either. But it will scare the pants off you, as Sullivan demonstrates that although knucklebones is a very old game, some games are even older . . .

"WATCH THIS," MAURICE TURNER SAID, HOLD-ing up the tiny guillotine.

The kids who weren't playing basketball gathered around him, curious about what this new kid was up to. Maurice, shorter than most of them, held the guillotine up so that the sun glinted off of it. Even the basketball game stopped for a minute, the guys who were playing wanting to see what was going on as much as the rest of the kids.

"Anybody got a cigarette?" Maurice asked.

Andy McHugh, the biggest kid in the whole school—he had stayed back two grades and was old enough to be an eighth grader, even though he was only in sixth—hooked the ball through the rattling chain hoop and walked over to the little crowd gathered around Maurice.

"I got one," Andy said, unrolling a pack of smokes from his T-shirt sleeve. With a swift downward motion, he forced a cigarette's filter tip out of the crushed cellophane package and offered it to Maurice. "There you go, kid."

"Thanks," Maurice said. Walking to the back wall of the school, he set the toy guillotine down on the highest granite step leading up to the doorway. Then he placed the cigarette in the half-inch-wide hole near the guillotine's base. Maurice waited a few seconds for effect, as he'd seen Doug Henning do on one of the rare occasions his mom let him watch something on TV besides the religious channel.

Just when they were starting to murmur, he brought the flattened palm of his right hand down hard on the top of the guillotine.

There was a noise like a paper cutter, and the cigarette was chopped neatly in half.

Maurice paused again.

"Big deal," a blonde girl said. "All you did was waste Andy's cigarette."

"Oh, yeah?" Maurice stuck his index finger in the hole. "Watch this."

He slammed the top of the guillotine down again.

The girl screamed, and the other kids all started talking excitedly. Maurice withdrew his unharmed finger and waggled it at them.

"Gnarly," Andy McHugh said. "I guess it *was* worth a cigarette."

Maurice grinned and handed him the two pieces. If Andy liked it, then everybody else would, too. The blonde girl, who had been watching Andy admiringly during the basketball game, now turned her blue eyes to Maurice. "That was really *rad*," she said.

Maurice was about to say something back to her when Bobby Feldstein drew his freckled, bespectacled face up to Maurice's. "How does that thing work?"

Annoyed, Maurice nevertheless smiled at him and held up the guillotine. "Here, Bobby," he said, "stick your finger in here and I'll show you."

Bobby pointed his finger at the guillotine, and then hesitated. "How do I know what you're going to do?" he asked.

"Oh, come *on*," Maurice chided. "Do you think I would have stuck *my* finger in there if it didn't work?"

"I guess not." Bobby smiled nervously, and put his finger through the hole.

Still grinning at Bobby, Maurice whacked the top of the guillotine as hard as he could. There was a wet, chopping sound. Bobby looked puzzled for a minute, and then began to yowl. He pulled his finger free and stared at it in amazement. Between the first and second knuckles was an ugly gash. Blood welled up and ran down his finger, crossing the back of his hand and falling onto the asphalt in bright red drops.

Clutching his hand to his chest, blood soaking into his jacket and shirt, Bobby ran off, screaming.

Maurice noted with satisfaction that nobody was watching Bobby; they were all looking straight at *him*, though none of them were making eye contact. They were *scared* of him. Even Andy—who sometimes walked right out into the street, so that cars had to go around him or even stop—looked a little pale. Only the blonde girl looked right into his eyes.

Maurice was pretty sure he would see *her* later.

* * *

When he got back from the principal's office, it was time for lunch. Maurice didn't want to eat in the cafeteria, so he started walking away from the school.

"Hey!"

Maurice turned to see the blonde girl running toward him. He waited for her to catch up.

"Are you skipping afternoon classes?" she asked breathlessly.

"No, I'm just walking to the store to get a sandwich."

"Can I come?" the girl asked.

"Sure. Why not?"

As they walked down the littered sidewalk, the girl said, "How did you get away with what you did in the school yard, anyway?"

"It was easy. I just told the principal it was an accident. She took the guillotine away, but I can get another one."

"Oh, yeah? Where do you get all your bread?"

"My dad gives it to me." Unless his mom was around, Maurice thought, but it wouldn't be cool to say that.

"Do you do a lot of errands and stuff for your dad?"

"Nah," Maurice shrugged. "Here we are."

The store—Popi's—was just a block from the school. Popi was older than Maurice's parents, maybe thirty-five or forty, and he had long, dark hair, a beard, and rimless glasses. He sold comic books, and also had video games, ice cream, and candy. He would make a hoagie to order for you for three dollars.

"Aren't you worried about being late?" the blonde girl asked.

"Nope."

"Don't you worry about *anything*?" She frowned. "You know, you haven't even asked me my name."

Maurice, leaning against the freezer case, shrugged. "Well, what is it?"

"Mary Jane Toricelli."

Maurice couldn't believe his luck, but he tried not to show his excitement. "You know something, Mary Jane," he said, "that's a great name."

"Thank you," she replied demurely.

Maurice thought about explaining why he liked her name, but just then Popi brought their hoagies out and waited for Maurice to pay him. By the time they sat down at one of the three metal tables in the place, Maurice had decided against telling her. If she mentioned it to anyone, there could be trouble later.

"I've seen you around school," Maurice lied. He had never noticed her until today, but now God had pointed her out to him.

Mary Jane blushed.

"You're one of the prettiest girls I've seen since my father was stationed here," Maurice said, taking a bite of his hoagie. He hated to say things like that, but it had to be done.

"You're an Army brat, huh?" Mary Jane's eyes widened. She had taken the compliment for granted. "Have you been around the world?"

"Germany, Japan, all over the United States."

"It must be wonderful. I've only been as far as Pittsburgh."

"Never even been to New York City?"

"No." Mary Jane was impressed. Usually she found boys to be tongue-tied. This was the first time she hadn't been the one they talked about. Maurice was really *different*.

They munched on their sandwiches and drank their cherry sodas until it was almost time to go back to school. Mary Jane grabbed Maurice's hand to get a better look at his wristwatch.

"Liquid crystal," Maurice said. He was sickened by her

touching him like that. She was a slut, just like the other Mary Jane . . . Mary Jane Kelly.

"Neat." Mary Jane frowned, letting go of his wrist. "But we better get back, or we'll be late."

"Yeah." Maurice wiped his mouth and stood up. He opened the door for Mary Jane and followed her out. On the way back to school, he stopped her by touching her elbow.

"What?" Mary Jane asked.

"Do you like to play jacks?" Maurice asked.

"I used to, but most kids our age won't play," said Mary Jane.

"I will."

"Rad!"

"You know the gas patch?" Maurice referred to an abandoned gasworks nearby, destined to be torn down by the city.

"Yeah, some kids go there after school to smoke dope."

"Right." Maurice grinned at her, as they continued walking. "What if we go there tomorrow morning, before class?"

"Why there?"

"Oh, just so we can be alone." Maurice smiled his nicest smile. "It'll be our secret."

"My bus usually gets to school a half hour early," Mary Jane said thoughtfully. "I guess it would be all right."

"Great. Don't bring anybody else, though . . . and whatever you do, don't tell anybody."

"Just you and me, huh, Maurice?" Mary Jane blushed.

"Yeah, Mary Jane, just you and me."

They were back at the school now. Mary Jane turned and smiled. "See you there."

Maurice nodded. "Yeah, see you there."

He watched her run to class, hardly able to believe his luck. Mary Jane Toricelli! Almost the same name as Jack the Ripper's fifth and final victim! The only thing he liked about her besides her name was her willingness to go along with him. They always *did*, once they saw how much money he had . . . once he got their attention. They *wanted* to be wicked, just like his mom said . . . just like Saucy Jack had said in the videotape. It wasn't like down South, Mom had told him again and again, where *she'd* grown up. These Yankee girls were all whores, all white trash, Jews and Catholics. But Maurice had found girls like that when Dad was stationed in Georgia, too. Immoral behavior was spreading like cancer. These tramps were everywhere nowadays . . . just as they had been a hundred years ago in London.

Today, as then, the Lord's work never ended.

When Maurice got home from school, he found his dad in the kitchen, starting to cook dinner. It was some kind of stew. Maurice figured he would go up to his room as soon as possible, to make plans for tomorrow. He set the table to hurry things up, so when his mom got home they could eat right away.

His mom being out this time of day wasn't unusual. It happened every time they were stationed someplace new. She was probably at the church. The first thing she did whenever they moved to a new place was find a church she liked. He could depend on her being gone a lot, working for some religious group. It made things a lot easier for him to do what he had to do.

"Maybe we can go to a movie after dinner," his dad said, "if it's not too late."

Ordinarily, Maurice would have jumped at the chance, but not tonight. He had things to do. Leave it to his father to pick the wrong time.

The stew was boiling when Maurice heard the front door open. He saw his mom in the shadowy hallway, taking off her coat. She hung it up in the closet and came into the kitchen.

"Dinner's ready, Rayette," his dad said.

His mom pursed her thin lips and nodded. She sat down

at the table. Maurice and his dad sat down, too. They folded their hands and bowed their heads over their bowls. It smelled so good, Maurice could hardly stand it, but he had to wait until the blessing was over.

"Thank you, O Lord, for these thy bountiful gifts . . ." they recited together.

"Maurice," his mom said as soon as he started eating, "you've got to spend more time on your studies. The Almighty is watching, and He knows when you're not doing your best. Right after supper, go up to your room and do your homework."

"Yes, ma'am." Perfect.

"Dear," his dad said, "I was thinking about taking Maurice to see a movie this evening."

She glared at him. "Did I hear you correctly, George?" she asked in her prim southern accent. "Do you want this boy to neglect his studies so the two of you can run off and watch some salacious filth?"

"Of course not . . . I just thought . . ."

"Keep your thoughts to yourself, if they're going to be that sinful."

His dad muttered apologetically, and went back to his stew.

As soon as the dishes were washed, Maurice went up to his room to "study." He bolted the door from the inside. Through the ventilator, he heard his mom nagging his dad. That would keep them both busy for a while. It was great to be in his own private place, he thought as he tossed his books on his desk. Except for his bed, the desk was the room's only furnishing. There were no posters on the walls, only one framed reproduction of a painting of Jesus; the Redeemer had blondish brown hair and he was looking up toward heaven. Maurice always glanced at it when he came in. His mom had put it in a place that was hard to miss, over the bed, so that it hit you right in the face the minute you walked into the room. He couldn't have any rock star posters or movie posters, even if he'd wanted them. Mom, who had given him the picture of Jesus for his fifth birthday, wouldn't allow it. It was okay, though, because Maurice only cared about those things to the extent that he would be excluded from the company of the other kids if he didn't know a little about them.

His mom said he could be anything he wanted to be when he grew up, unlike his dad. His dad didn't mind just being a captain in the Army, but Maurice was expected to do something really great. It didn't seem as if anything he did was quite good enough for his mom yet, but he was already doing the Lord's work secretly. Trouble was, only the Lord knew about it. That was okay, though, because he hated to stand out, unless he was being cooler than all the other guys, like today with the toy guillotine. What he *really* liked were the things nobody else knew about . . . the things in his collection.

Maurice pushed his bed away from the wall and reached down toward the baseboard. There was a little door down there. He opened it and crawled inside. He had gotten pretty dirty the first time he explored this secret passageway, but in subsequent trips he had swept it out with a whisk broom and removed the dead mice, throwing them down the garbage disposal while his mother was busy praying. When she was praying, Maurice could do just about anything he wanted, and she never knew. It was like she was on another planet. Maurice knew that her heart was in the right place, but all the weeping and wailing in the world wouldn't help clean up the filth on the streets that his mom always went on about. Maurice had his own ideas about how to deal with sin. Talk and prayer were not enough.

His dad had told him the secret passageway was designed for ventilation and insulation when the house was built in the nineteenth century. Today they had air-conditioning and central heating, of course, so there wasn't any real purpose for it . . . until now.

Maurice wormed his way to the two boxes where he'd hidden his collection. There was a flashlight hanging on a nail there. Maurice lifted it and wrapped its looped strap around his wrist.

He opened one of the boxes.

All of his books, magazines, and newspaper articles on Jack the Ripper were in this one, complete with a police photograph of the Ripper's last victim, Mary Jane Kelly. The name was so much like the name of the girl he'd met today that it seemed incredible.

Remembering the way Mary Jane Toricelli had touched him at lunch, he studied the photograph of her namesake, as he had done hundreds of times before. He savored the details: the legs, flayed down to the bone; the belly, slit open like a gutted fish, with the hand placed decorously inside the cavity; the breasts, cut off and laid on the table next to the bed; the intestines draped over her shoulder; the other organs, placed next to the breasts; the face, mutilated beyond recognition, a skull-like horror from an old black-and-white monster movie. He had been in love with this image for four of his nine years.

Maurice was only five when Jack came into his life. His parents had just got cable TV, so his mom could have the religious channel. While they were out, Maurice started to watch a movie showing Jack the Ripper as a minister, a holy man who was doing the Lord's work by cleaning up the filth of Whitechapel's slums. Maurice's mom had come home before it was over, and Maurice was so engrossed in the movie that he didn't hear her. He thought sure she would punish him, but she didn't. The movie had ended in a church, a shaft of sunlight illuminating the altar, and that was when she walked in. She thought it was a religious program. Not that it would have mattered, even if she had punished him. The resemblance between Jack the Ripper and Jesus had been burned indelibly into his memory. They both had the same soulful gaze and blondish brown hair, just like the picture his mom had nailed onto his bedroom wall. The scene where Jack killed Mary Kelly had reminded Maurice of something his mom said a lot: "The Lord giveth and the Lord taketh away." Maurice's heart had pounded in excitement as the camera lingered lovingly on Mary Kelly's mutilated corpse. The scene looked a lot like the police photo, one of Maurice's proudest possessions, along with the magazine articles, books, transcripts of the police reports, and the rest of the stuff in this box. But it was the other box that contained his greatest treasures.

Tomorrow morning, he would bring his treasures to school with him.

After his dad dropped him and his bundle off, Maurice slipped away from the school. It had been tough, talking and acting normal while they drove through the wet, early morning streets, but his dad hadn't noticed anything unusual. Maurice was a little worried, because he couldn't remember if he had closed the door to his little hideaway before he left the house, but he guessed it didn't matter much. He had more important things to worry about right now, anyhow.

Maurice made his way through the mist to the gas patch, where he waited for Mary Jane in the shadow of a half-destroyed old brick building. That was one of the things he liked about living in this northeastern city: the old buildings, the narrow streets, some of them paved with Belgian block pavement, reminding him of cobblestones. When a fog set in, it could have been London in 1888, the year of Jack the Ripper.

There was a thick fog this morning, rolling down the hill and spilling through the link fence that never kept the kids out. That would help, but Maurice was still nervous. He was always nervous before he did the Creator's work. To calm himself, he looked around carefully, making sure nobody was here, no kids, no old winos sleeping it off behind the brick piles. The building was partially collapsed, one wall fallen into rubble on the inside and overgrown with weeds. Huge black tanks stood just outside the ruined building, empty now but once filled with some kind of gas. Maurice had been here often enough to know that nobody could see you when you were inside, but you could see people coming down the hill that led from Warren Street. Still, he was shaking. This always happened. It wasn't just that he could get caught, and that the police wouldn't understand the importance of what he did. He was acting as God's right arm, and that was something that he had to take seriously. What he was going to do this morning was part of the same righteous quest that the Ripper had undertaken.

Mary Jane was coming now. When he saw her, Maurice's breathing was so fast and ragged that he thought he was going to faint, but he somehow calmed himself as she approached. She was wearing blue jeans and a pair of Ponys, her blond bangs hanging in her eyes as she negotiated the hillside. She found the hole in the link fence and crawled underneath it, being careful not to get her jeans dirty.

"Maurice?" she said as she stood up.

"Over here." The words sounded funny, as though they came from far away, but he was okay now. He had to be okay, or he would never pull it off. Maurice stepped out of the shadows and waved to her.

Mary Jane smiled and ran over to him. He grabbed her hand and pulled her into the ruins. It was happening, just like all the other times.

"Isn't this place neat?" he said, keeping his voice under control.

She shivered. "Kind of creepy, if you ask me."

"Nobody will bother us here."

"Good." Mary Jane grinned impishly. "Are you gonna try and kiss me?"

Maurice flushed. The idea of kissing her sickened him. She was acting like a slut. He smiled, because she was making it easier. "Maybe," he said. "But first . . . I want to show you something."

"Oh, yeah?"

Maurice beckoned for her to follow him. He led her to a dark corner where he had hidden the bundle, the leather bag wrapped up in his cape. He bent over and picked it up, unraveling the cape and then unfastening the bag's silver clasp.

"What's in the bag?" Mary Jane asked. She stood back while he put on the cape and deerstalker hat, and then asked: "Is it a Halloween costume?"

"Kind of." He turned to her, the cape swirling, the front brim of the deerstalker pulled down over his eyes. "Can you guess who I am?"

"Sherlock Holmes!" Mary Jane said, giggling.

Maurice smiled. "No."

"The King of England?" She laughed out loud.

"No." Maurice showed nothing of his anger.

"I give up. Who, then?"

"I'll tell you later," Maurice said. "First a game of jacks."

Mary Jane looked at him admiringly. She seemed to like having him be the leader. She wasn't like his mom at all.

"You go first," he said, knowing that she would do exactly as he told her.

"Okay . . . but where are the jacks?"

He held up the black bag. "In here."

Maurice snapped open the clasp and reached inside, feeling around until he found a smaller, plastic bag. He pulled it out and dumped the contents on a patch of level ground, between a pile of bricks and the wall. The red rubber ball and the silver crosses scattered at his feet.

Mary Jane looked at him for a moment before playing. "You're really weird, Maurice," she said. "I like you a lot."

She ran over to him and pecked him on the cheek.

"Play," Maurice said, gritting his teeth. His fear was shrinking now, consumed by a divine fury.

Mary Jane didn't seem to notice his simmering rage. She stooped and picked up the ball. Tentatively, she lifted it and bounced it. "Onesies!" she giggled, picking up a jack. "Twosies!" She bounced it again, her little hands snatching two more jacks off the ground. "Threesies!" This time she managed to pick up three. "Foursies!" Mary Jane moved as quickly as she could, deftly picking up the first three, but the ball fell to the ground on the second bounce, before she could get the last jack.

"Aw." Mary Jane threw down the jacks, stood, and picked up the ball, handing it to Maurice. "Your turn."

"You did real good, Mary Jane," said Maurice. He would go through the motions so that she wouldn't suspect anything. He picked up a ball and studied the random positions of the twelve jacks. Kneeling on the hard ground, he said, "Onesies!"

Maurice only got to threesies, before he failed to get all the jacks.

"Aw, too bad, Maurice," Mary Jane said, trying to sound sympathetic. She eagerly took up the red ball again, but Maurice clutched her elbow.

"Want to know something?" he said.

"What?"

"Know what they used to play jacks with? In olden times?"

"Uh-uh." She shook her head.

"Knucklebones. That's what jacks were called in the old days."

"*Bones?*" Mary Jane was astonished. "What kind of bones?"

"I told you—knucklebones." Maurice let go of her arm and reached into the bag for the scalpel as she knelt to bounce the red ball again. She was into the game. It was time.

Her back was to him now. He pulled her hair back. Before she could cry out, he slid the razor-sharp scalpel blade across the soft flesh of her throat, his hand trembling. The skin resisted and he applied so much pressure his fingers hurt. The knife poked through the skin. Mary Jane made a little moaning sound that turned into a gurgle as he cut. He forgot about everything else as the scalpel separated the flesh. He seemed to be ten feet tall. No, bigger, big as the whole universe. God. Jack the Ripper. From heaven, he looked down at the quaking body beneath him. He savored the sight for a few seconds and then he pushed her down onto the brick pile, where she flopped like a fish tossed up on shore. When she stopped twitching he bent down and turned her on her back. The blood looked black as it spilled over the bricks in the dim light. Her heart was no longer pumping, so the blood didn't spurt. He didn't have to worry about getting any on his clothes.

Maurice put on his rubber gloves and set to work in imitation of the master, God's chosen, Jack the Ripper. First he dragged the body off the bricks and laid it near the jacks, which he collected. Then he cut open the front of her jacket and blouse. Touching her bare skin excited him, even with the gloves on. He remembered that Jesus had been born unto woman, but had resisted the temptations of the flesh.

"Whore!" he cried, shoving the blade into her soft belly. He was stronger now, blessed by the Supreme Being. Using every bit of his strength, he sliced all the way to the crotch, filled with joy, cutting right through her jeans. As soon as he finished the long incision, he set the scalpel down and stuck his fingers inside, pulling the skin apart. The intestines were exposed, coiled inside the girl like a big, meaty Slinky. He reached in and pulled some of them out, juggling them from one hand to the other. They were slippery, steaming in the cool morning air. The powerful odor of her insides was a vapor, an incense to be smelled only by the Chosen One,

Jack the Ripper. He *was* the Ripper now, reveling in his holy work. He had come a long way since the first one he killed, Peggy Nicholson. Her name had been too much of a coincidence to ignore, that was for sure. It was a sign from God. Each time, he had been given such a sign, sometimes just when he felt like giving up on the whole thing. In Georgia there was Carla Edwards, a name close enough to the Ripper's fourth victim, Catherine Eddowes, that there could be no mistake. Before her, in Texas, there was Lizzie Streiz, whose name could not have been more like "Long" Liz Stride's, the Ripper's third. And in Japan, another Army brat called Annie Klazewski. (Annie Chapman, Jack's second victim, had been the mistress of a Pole, Klosowski.) Peggy Nicholson's name was almost the same as the Ripper's first, Polly Nichols. Every time, God had given them names similar to the whores Jack had done in. And every time, Maurice got better and better, always finding the ones God wanted him to take.

Before Peggy, he had only killed a kitten, not long after he had seen the movie about Jack. He had petted it out in the backyard until it trusted him. Then he went in and got a big knife from the kitchen drawer and a chicken leg from the fridge. While the little tiger kitty was eating the chicken, Maurice said a prayer and chopped down on the back of its neck as hard as he could. The cat hissed and Maurice cut it some more. It couldn't even scratch him. It couldn't do much of anything after the first chop, just lie there on the flagstone and shake while Maurice sliced it up. It was great.

Something moved behind a brick pile. Maurice snapped to attention, heart pounding in his chest. Had someone sneaked into the gas patch while he was preoccupied? He heard only the sucking of his own labored breathing, and then a scrabbling noise, the same as before. He caught a glimpse of tiny red eyes in the shadows. A rat.

Relieved, he went back to work, remembering that he

couldn't allow his rapture to interfere with what he was doing. He had almost been apprehended in Japan because he was so caught up in the sight and smell and feel of death. He had to be careful. He was getting tired, too, and sweating a lot. This was hard work. Still, the waves of pleasure washed over him as he slashed and sliced.

Mary Jane didn't have large enough breasts to cut off, and besides, there wasn't much time until the bell rang at school. That was always the problem, not enough time. Maybe ten minutes more to work. No time to cut out a kidney, as Jack would have. Maurice had to use his imagination. It was his duty to strike as much terror into the hearts of the sinful as he could.

"I know!" he said. He could actually get some *real* knucklebones. Stretching Mary Jane's limp right arm over the rubble, Maurice placed the left hand palm-upward on a brick. He withdrew a blade with a serrated edge from his bag and began to saw.

Pinkish, watery stuff oozed out of the finger. There was no danger of getting it on himself if he was cautious.

Unfortunately, the fingers were harder to cut off than he'd thought they'd be. Maurice had to work even harder to get through the bone, his hands, arms, and shoulders ached from his efforts, and he was drenched underneath the heavy cape. He discovered that it was easier, once he'd cut through the skin and sinew, to work the finger joints back and forth until they snapped off.

Each finger took about a minute, so he still had time if he hurried. He broke off eight fingers in all, leaving only the thumbs. Mary Jane looked as if she were wearing red mittens. Staring up at the broken ceiling, unblinking, she was much more beautiful than she had been when she was alive. She would never sin again.

Maurice dropped the fingers one by one into a second plastic bag, taking off the rubber gloves and putting them in with the fingers. He wrapped it all up tidily so that the fingers wouldn't leak onto the medical instruments or the jacks. He wiped the two blades off on Mary Jane's blouse and carefully placed them in their niches inside his medical bag. The two plastic sacks went in on top of the scalpels, with the deerstalker cap laid over them, covering it all. He snapped the silver clasp shut and took off the cape, wrapping it around the leather bag. It just looked like he had taken off a tweed coat and bundled it up because the weather was too warm for it.

"Good-bye, slut," he said, carrying his bundle under his left arm and saluting with his free hand. "May God have mercy on your soul."

Whistling, he walked up the hill toward the school, leaving the remains of Mary Jane Toricelli to the rats.

Right after lunch, a policewoman came to talk to Maurice's science teacher, Mr. Stubbs. The two adults left the room for a few minutes, and the place erupted in a spitball fight. Maurice joined in so that he wouldn't be conspicuous, while waiting to see what, if anything, Mr. Stubbs would say when he got back.

Mr. Stubbs was gone a long time. Finally, Buddy Hopkins said he was going to find out what was going on. He had to go to the bathroom anyway, so he would check it out.

When he came back, Buddy announced that just about every teacher in the school was gathered in the Principal's Office along with the policewoman and a black policeman. "This is big stuff," he said.

Shortly after that, Mr. Stubbs returned with the policewoman, holding up his hands for order. Something about the way he looked and sounded stopped the spitballs right away, which was unusual.

"Kids," he said, looking even older and grayer than usual, "there's been an accident."

An *accident*? What was the old fool talking about?

"Officer Cooper is here to ask you a few questions. When she's finished, you can all go home."

There was some sporadic cheering, but that soon stopped as Officer Cooper commanded their attention.

"I have to know if any of you saw a girl named Mary Jane Toricelli this morning, between seven and eight o'clock."

"That would be just before the first bell," Mr. Stubbs interjected.

There was an awkward silence in the classroom, and then a fat girl named Carmen Gifford raised her hand. "I saw her on the bus."

"Did you see her after that?" Officer Cooper asked.

"No."

"When you saw her on the bus, who was she talking to?"

"A couple of girls. She rides with them every morning."

"Are they in this class?"

"No."

"Do you know their names?"

"One of them."

And so it went. Carmen gave Officer Cooper the girl's name, Officer Cooper thanked the kids, and Mr. Stubbs, who really looked nervous and sick, told everybody to go home. Ordinarily, the kids would have been making a lot of noise, happy about getting out of school early, but they were strangely silent now as they filed out to their lockers.

"What's that?" Andy McHugh said as Maurice pulled out the bundle and slammed shut his locker door.

"What?" Maurice said, playing dumb.

"That thing you're holding there, Turner. What is it?"

"Oh, just a coat."

"Looks like a coat your father would wear." Andy kept looking at the bundle. "You got something wrapped up in it?"

"Just some books," Maurice lied.

Andy, who was more than a head taller than Maurice and more than two years older, placed one palm on the lockers on either side of Maurice, hemming him in. "I know you better than that, Moe-rees."

Maurice glared at him. He hated to be called that. Andy was making fun of his southern accent, the only kid in school who still did that.

"The teachers around here might be fooled by you," Andy said. "But I'm not. I know you're nuts."

"Get out of my way, McHugh," Maurice said angrily.

"Chill out, kid," Andy said, stepping back to let him go. "I only want to know what you're up to. Got any more of those chopping things like you had yesterday?"

"No, Mrs. Rainey took it when I was sent to her office." Maurice started walking. "I gotta go."

"You sure you don't have something in there?" Andy demanded.

"Nope. Nothing." Maurice was almost running now, out the front door and into the street, leaving Andy McHugh and his prying questions behind. He ran around the corner, past Popi's and a row of brownstones. When he was quite sure he was rid of Andy, he walked to the stop where kids who were unlucky enough to live in the Army base housing waited for their bus. It was only a little past noon. He would go to the Greyhound station, ditching the stuff he was carrying temporarily in a locker there, and walk the few blocks to the base to see his dad. Maybe he could get some money out of the old man. It usually worked.

Everything went without a hitch at the bus station, and the guard at the base was so used to seeing him that he didn't even have to show his ID to get through the gate.

He found his dad in the officers' mess, the bars on his uniform shining brightly, as he drank coffee at a table with a couple of other men. He seemed like a different person than he was at home. Kind of relaxed and important around the other officers. If only they knew what he was *really* like.

"Hello, son," his dad said, and the others said hello to him, too. "What are you doing here on a school-day afternoon?"

"They let us out early today . . . on account of an accident a girl had."

"Well, that's too bad about the girl." Dad frowned. "But I guess you aren't too unhappy about getting the afternoon off, huh?"

Maurice said nothing. HIs dad got out his wallet and gave him twenty dollars. "Catch a bus for downtown and go to that movie we missed last night . . . but don't mention it to your mother."

"Thanks, Dad," Maurice said. "Don't worry. I won't say anything."

His dad winked, and the other men all laughed. Maurice said good-bye and was off to catch his bus.

It had been a pretty good movie, entitled *Maimed*, with plenty of gory violence. It was about a guy who had been mutilated in an accident. When the people responsible got off scot-free by bribing the judge who heard the case, he went around killing them all, saving the judge for last, using chain saws, buzz saws, butcher knives, straight razors, and even a Veg-O-Matic. No one under seventeen was supposed to get in, but the sleazebag behind the ticket window didn't even look at him, just tore up the ticket and that was it.

It was three-thirty when Maurice emerged, blinking, into the daylight. He was still exhilarated from doing the Lord's work this morning. Unless Mary Jane had told one of the girls on the bus, he was home free. He had the bundle with him, which he had picked up at the Greyhound station after leaving the base. He'd better catch a bus for home right away. If his mother was there when he got in—and not on her prayer planet—he'd catch hell for being late. He wished that he had left the bundle in the locker.

Maurice got off a block from the house. When he got home, he didn't go right in. Instead, he crept up to a window. His mother was turning off the TV, no doubt having just watched *The 700 Club* or one of the other evangelist programs. She walked toward the back of the house, probably to the kitchen. She might stop him when he came in and demand to see what he was carrying. He had better find some place to hide it.

Around the side of the house, Maurice was surprised to see the car in the driveway. He checked his watch and saw that it was almost four-thirty. No, it wasn't that unusual to see his dad home this early, now that he thought about it. Maurice was the one who was late today. There was no way he was going to get the bundle past both his mother *and* his father.

Maurice tried the car door on the passenger's side. It was unlocked. He opened it as quietly as he could and placed the bundle on the floor of the back seat. Squinting with concentration, he closed it again, barely making a sound. Then he walked back around the front of the house, keeping his head down.

"I'm home," he said as he walked in the front door, deciding to take the bull by the horns.

"We're in the kitchen," his dad called to him. Maurice didn't like the sound of his voice. "Come on back. We want to talk to you."

Maurice did as he was told, finding them sitting at the kitchen table. His mother was staring at him angrily, and there on the table between her and her husband was a box. Not just any box. The box that had Maurice's Jack the Ripper books and magazines in it.

"What is *this*?" his mother demanded icily.

Maurice shrank before her withering gaze. He *had* left the door to his hideaway ajar, and his mom had gone snooping in his room and noticed it. She must have made the old man crawl in to see what was in there.

"Answer me!" she screamed. "Answer me in the name of Jesus!"

Maurice's throat felt as if it were filled with marbles. He tried to speak. "It's just . . . just . . ."

"Just *trash*, just the Devil's own *trash*!" She reached into the box, pulled out a magazine, and slapped him across the face with it.

Maurice knew better than to say anything now. He was going to get it and get it good, and the less he said the better. Did they suspect what he had done this morning? Would they turn him in?

"Look at this!" his mother raged. She held up a *Playboy* magazine. "Nine years old and he already desires to see the naked flesh of women! Filth in the eyes of God! Whores! Sluts!"

"Look at this, George!" she screamed at her husband, holding up a copy of *Gallery*. "Unadulterated, sinful garbage!"

Suddenly Maurice realized that she was raving about the skin magazines, not about the Ripper material. In her religious fervor, she didn't see what was right under her nose. Maurice couldn't suppress a smirk at this turn of events.

She smacked him with a magazine and then brought it back across the other cheek. "How dare you laugh!"

"I wasn't laughing, Mom," he whined. "I'm sorry, honest."

"Sorry! I'll teach you what sorry means." She turned on her husband. "You've been too permissive, George. How many times have I told you not to spoil this boy?"

"Maybe you're right, Rayette." Maurice's dad shook his head. "I don't know."

"Well, *I* know." She threw the magazines back into the box. "We'll take these down to the basement and burn them in the furnace."

"No, Mom!" The words were out of Maurice's mouth before he could stop them. Maurice knew that he had made a terrible mistake. Her wrath would be all the more terrible now. But what could he do? His collection was the most important thing in the world to him.

"You vile little monster," his mother said coldly. "*Order me* not to destroy this Satanic rubbish, will you?" Her hand shot out like a claw and grabbed hold of his wrist. She began to drag Maurice behind her, her free hand opening the basement door. "Bring that box with you, George."

The wooden stairs creaked under the weight of three people, and Maurice was pulled along so roughly he thought he would fall. But he somehow was still standing when they reached the concrete floor of the basement. His mother flung him away from her, and his back struck the wall, knocking the breath out of his lungs. Maurice wanted to run, but he would never get past them. Their shadows stretched toward him across the concrete floor, cast by the light coming from the kitchen door.

"Punish him," his mother said.

George hesitated. "How?"

"Take your belt off and *whup* it out of him," she said, her lips curving in a cruel smile.

"Rayette, I don't—"

"Do as I say!" she screamed.

George reluctantly unbuckled his belt and pulled it through the loops with a slithering sound. "Son, I . . ."

"Do it!"

"Bend over, Maurice," his father said.

Having no choice, Maurice did as he was told. At that moment, his mother opened the furnace grating and began to feed the magazines and books to the blue-yellow flames inside.

The belt bit into Maurice's buttocks. It stung so bad he jumped. A second blow descended, and then a third. It really hurt. Maurice didn't think he could take it. Through his tears, he saw his mother looking down at him as she crumpled pages and stuffed them into the furnace, the firelight flickering across her face.

The belt landed a little low, wrapping itself around Maurice's thigh like a snake. Each time his father hit him, it felt as if the fire were burning him, instead of his magazines and books. He screamed.

The beating stopped.

"What are you doing?" his mother demanded. "Whup him some more."

"Rayette," his Dad said imploringly.

"Do as I tell you."

George did as she told him. The stinging tongue of the belt whipped across Maurice's backside again and again. The beating continued until there was no more paper to burn.

"Come here, Maurice," his mother said when it was over.

Maurice, barely able to walk, moved painfully toward her. She reached out and embraced him, tears starting from her own eyes.

"Oh, my poor darling," she said. "It's for your own good. We must drive Satan out of your young soul."

Maurice buried his wet face in her bosom. She rocked him as if he were still a baby, until he stopped crying. Maurice had hated her only a minute ago, but now he knew that he loved his mom more than anyone on earth. She had punished him because she didn't understand that he was doing God's work, that was all. But she was the one who had taught him that the path of righteousness is strewn with thorns. How he loved her now as she stroked his hair and softly called him her baby.

Maurice was sent to bed without any supper. He lay on his stomach, whimpering, unable to sleep. He wanted to go down and get the bundle out of the car, but he didn't dare to. Fearful that his dad would be more curious about the bundle after today, he decided he would have to do it in the morning somehow, before Dad drove him to school.

After a sleepless night, Maurice was called down to breakfast. He had tried to creep down earlier, to get outside to the car. But his mom was already up, on her knees in the living room, praying. There was no way to get past her.

Maurice ate very little cereal this morning. He could actually see the back end of the car through the kitchen window. It was driving him crazy. If they found that bundle, anything might happen. He would never be able to invent a story to fool his mother—she didn't even believe him when he told the truth, usually—and with Mary Jane's knucklebones in that bag, even his dad would be hard to talk out of doing something really bad to him. He *had* to get out to the car.

His mother didn't speak to him through breakfast, seeming to be lost in thought. The only words his dad spoke came after they were finished eating, while Mom was washing the breakfast dishes. "Go get your books, Maurice."

Maurice did as he was told, running up to his room and grabbing his schoolbooks. Then he ran straight down the stairs and out the front door, shouting that he would wait outside. He came around the side of the house and peeked through the kitchen window. Seeing that his mother was still washing the dishes with her back to him, he looked around for someplace to hide the bundle. If he scooched down really low, he could sneak past the window and stuff it under the back porch steps. His mother would never notice it there, and he could figure out a way to retrieve it when he got home from school. He tried the car door.

It wouldn't open.

But how could that be? . . . Unless his dad had gone out to the car and locked it last night, it had to open. Maurice felt himself starting to sweat, and he felt kind of itchy, not on his skin, but inside. He tried the door again.

It still wouldn't open.

What was he going to do? He couldn't leave the bundle in the car. His dad would find it sooner or later. His only chance was to smash the window and stash the bundle under the steps fast, before his dad could get outside to see what was going on. Maurice could say it was an accident. He would probably be punished, but that was better than what would happen if he just stood here.

He looked around for something heavy. There were some rocks out on the strip of grass between the sidewalk and the pavement. Maurice put his books down and rushed over to get one. He picked up a big one, grubs and millipedes scurrying out of hiding, some of them crawling on his hands. He didn't care. He *had* to get into that car.

He went back and lifted the rock over his head with both hands, seeing his distorted reflection in the car window. He held it there for an instant, and—

"What are you doing, son?"

Maurice's heart froze. He dropped the rock to the ground with a dull thud. "Nothing, Dad." He looked away from his father's piercing gray eyes.

"You weren't going to break that window for spite, were you?"

"Of course not," Maurice lied. "I was just pretending I was a Ninja."

His dad smiled a little. "A Ninja, huh? That's great. Come on, get in the car, or you'll be late for school." He went around to the driver's side. "Look at that," he said, opening the door. "I forgot to lock up the car again. Your mother would kill me if she knew."

Maurice stared at his father, uncomprehending. He tried the door, and it resisted. "This one's locked, Dad."

"No, it isn't." His father was putting his keys into the ignition. "It sticks sometimes. Just tug on it a little."

Maurice put both hands on the door handle and pulled

hard. The door flew open, nearly knocking him off balance. It had been unlocked all the time!

"What's the matter, Maurice?" his father said. "Get in the car."

Maurice was staring at the open door. At the sound of his father's voice, he snapped out of it and reluctantly got inside. Right behind him, on the floor of the back seat, was the bundle. His father couldn't see it from where he was sitting, but he would find it sooner or later, unless Maurice got it out of there somehow. Maurice slowly buckled his seat belt, desperately trying to think of some way out.

"Son," said his dad, "I know that boys like to look at pictures of girls without any clothes on. I did it, too, when I was your age. But you know how your mother is. If you have any more of those magazines, put them someplace where she'll never find them. Otherwise, she'll make me punish you again, and I don't want to have to do that."

"I'm sorry, Dad." Maurice was disgusted by his dad's admission. His mom had been *right* to punish him, for all his parents knew. The old man was *so* weak.

"Well, don't let it happen again."

"I won't, Dad."

They rode on through the mist in silence. When they were within a few blocks of the school, it occurred to Maurice that he might be able to tell his dad that he needed the bundle for one of his classes. He had to do it. There was no other way to get it now.

"I left something in the back seat yesterday," he said.

"Oh? What's that?"

"It's part of a Halloween costume," Maurice said matter-of-factly, hoping that his dad wouldn't remember that he had taken the bundle with him yesterday when he was dropped off at the school. "All the kids are making them."

When his father didn't respond, Maurice unbuckled his seat belt, turned around, and reached back over the seat. His hands were shaking while he picked up the bundle. He squirmed back into a sitting position with it on his lap.

"It *will* be Halloween in a few days, won't it?" his dad said.

He bought it! Maurice could hardly believe his luck. He was going to make it now. Once he got to school he could hide it in his locker, and then take it to the bus station later. One thing was for sure, he couldn't bring it home again. Maurice looked down at the tweed cape and tried to keep from laughing out loud.

All of a sudden the car screeched to a halt and Maurice flew forward, striking his head on the dashboard. The bundle fell onto the floor.

His father honked the horn. "That kid almost got herself run over," he said angrily. "Are you all right, son?"

"Yes." Dazed, Maurice looked out the window to see a girl on a bicycle, looking very pale and scared. As his dad started driving again, she became invisible, lost in the fog.

His dad looked over at Maurice. "You're sure you're all right?"

Maurice nodded. When he looked down, he saw that the tweed cape no longer covered the black leather bag. They were both on the floor at his feet, the bag in plain sight.

"What's that?" his father demanded, still driving through the fog, but staring at the bag.

"Nothing . . . just part of the costume."

Something about the way Maurice said that made his dad suspicious. "Let me see it," he said.

"It's nothing, Dad," Maurice said, panicking. "It's just kid stuff."

"Let me see it, Maurice."

Maurice tried to pick it up. He was getting ready to jump out of the car and run away, but his dad snatched the bag from his hands and snapped open the silver clasp. "Where did you get this?" he demanded.

"I saved my money." Maurice could feel his heart thudding in his chest. His father seemed to tower over him. "You always taught me to be thrifty."

Glancing sporadically at the road, his dad pulled out the deerstalker cap and set it on the seat. Then he withdrew the bag of jacks. Next came the surgical instruments.

"Maurice," he said, fingering the scalpel Maurice had used to cut Mary Jane Toricelli's throat, "you could hurt yourself with these. Where did you get them?"

"I sent a money order to a mail-order medical supply house," Maurice said, his voice cracking. "I want to become a doctor when I grow up."

But it was too late for lies. Still holding the scalpel in one hand and steering with his elbow, his dad dumped the rest of the bag's contents onto the seat. His eyes widened when he opened the second plastic sack.

He pulled out the bloody gloves—and the knucklebones tumbled out onto the vinyl car seat.

"For the love of God, Maurice," he said, holding up one of Mary Jane's yellowing fingers, "is this what I think it is?"

Maurice was sobbing now, unable to speak at all.

"Answer me!" his father screamed, dropping the finger in revulsion.

One of the dim shapes passing by loomed out of the fog. His dad couldn't see it, turned as he was toward Maurice. Maurice started to cry out, to warn his dad, but then he saw who the car was about to hit, and shut his mouth. A tall, lanky figure challenged anyone to dare and try to run him over. Maurice grabbed the wheel and jerked it toward him.

A thump.

"*Jesus Christ!*" his dad cried, slamming on the brakes. He opened the door and leaped out of the car, still holding the scalpel. Maurice peered over the dashboard at the unmoving form of Andy McHugh sprawled on the asphalt. A serpent of blood crawled from Andy's head into the gutter and washed down a sewer grating.

Maurice got out of the car, rubbing the bruise on his forehead where he'd struck the dashboard. He called softly, "Dad."

His father turned, his eyes wide, the scalpel still in his hand. People were coming out of the fog, gathering around and staring.

"Hold it right there," a woman shouted.

His dad turned around and stared straight into the blue barrel of a .38 revolver.

"Don't move!" Officer Cooper commanded him.

Maurice saw his chance, presented to him at this last possible moment when everything seemed so hopeless, by Divine Providence. He grabbed his dad's wrist.

"Help!" Maurice screamed.

"Let the boy go!" Officer Cooper cried angrily.

His dad tried to pull his arm away but Maurice held on tight, pretending to struggle, screaming: "He's going to kill me! He's got somebody's fingers in a bag! And knives! He's crazy! He killed Andy!"

"Maurice," his dad whispered, "what are you doing?" His face was sweating, pale and confused. The blade gleamed in his other hand.

"Help!" Maurice cried. "He's choking me! He's gonna cut my throat!"

"Drop that knife or I'll shoot!" shouted Officer Cooper.

His dad didn't seem to hear her. He stared at Maurice in disbelief, as if he saw something he'd never imagined before, something out of his wildest nightmares.

Office Cooper fired twice. His dad's neat uniform blossomed into bright red flowers in two places, on the chest and belly. Maurice let go of his dad's wrist as he fell. The scalpel clattered to the pavement.

A black policeman, Officer Cooper's partner, ran across the street, his heels clacking sharply on the wet asphalt. He knelt and placed his ear over Maurice's dad's heart. Officer Cooper was looking through the windshield at the fingers lying on the front seat of the family car.

A few minutes later, an ambulance arrived. Two paramedics worked on Maurice's dad and Andy for a while. At last they gave up and zipped both of them into shiny body bags, just as three more patrol cars pulled up. The flashing red and blue lights looked very strange in the mist. As he stared at the colored lights and listened to the crackling of police radios, Maurice felt fingertips gently touch the bruise on his forehead.

He looked up into the tender eyes of Officer Cooper. She smiled at him. "It's going to be all right."

The ambulance carrying his dad and Andy wheeled into the fog and vanished. Maurice tried to look sad, but it was hard to do, as he thought about what was sure to happen now. They would trace the killings back to all the cities Captain Turner had lived in—American, Japanese, German. Maurice's mother would wail and say that the Devil had gotten into George, and she'd pray even more than she did now. Without Dad around to enforce her will, Maurice would do as he pleased, and someday he would make his mom see how much he loved her, how he did everything for her as much as for himself.

Someday he would kill for her again. Maurice knew that he would never be caught if he was careful enough, just like the original Jack the Ripper. And, unlike Jack, he wouldn't have to stop after five killings. He would carry on, protected by the All-knowing Spirit, in whose name he had slain the sinful. Nothing could stop him.

He had to agree with Officer Cooper. From now on, it really *was* going to be all right.

THE PROWLER IN THE CITY AT THE EDGE OF THE WORLD

Harlan Ellison

The Ripper has proved himself to be a most durable villain. In spite of the arrival in the media spotlight of much newer and showier mass murderers (some of them with hundreds of victims to their credit, as opposed to the Ripper's five), no one has managed to displace him as an archtypical figure in the public imagination. People have been wondering about the Ripper for a hundred years now. Anyone want to bet that they won't be wondering about him still a hundred years in the future?

One of the most acclaimed and controversial figures in modern letters, Harlan Ellison has produced thirty-seven books and over nine hundred stories, articles, essays, and film and television scripts. He is the editor of Dangerous Visions; Again, Dangerous Visions; Medea: Harlan's World; *and the forthcoming* The Last Dangerous Visions. *His short-story collections include* Partners in Wonder, Alone Against Tomorrow, The Beast that Shouted Love at the Heart of the World, Approaching Oblivion, Deathbird Stories, Strange Wine, *and* Shatterday. *A multiple award winner, he has won Nebula, Hugo, and Edgar awards, and three Writer's Guild of America Awards for Most Outstanding Television Script. "The Prowler in the City at the Edge of the World" is one of Ellison's best known tales, and perhaps the only serious rival to Bloch's "Yours Truly, Jack the Ripper" for the title of Most Famous Ripper Story.*

FIRST THERE WAS THE CITY, NEVER NIGHT. TIN AND reflective, walls of antiseptic metal like an immense autoclave. Pure and dust-free, so silent that even the whirling innards of its heart and mind were sheathed from notice. The city was self-contained, and footfalls echoed up and around—flat slapped notes of an exotic leather-footed instrument. Sounds that reverberated back to the maker like yodels thrown out across mountain valleys. Sounds made by humbled inhabitants whose lives were as orderly, as sanitary, as metallic as the city they had caused to hold them bosom-tight against the years. The city was a complex artery, the people were the blood that flowed icily through the artery. They were a gestalt with one another, forming a unified whole. It was a city shining in permanence, eternal in concept, flinging itself up in a formed and molded statement of exaltation; most modern of all modern structures, conceived as the pluperfect residence for the perfect people. The final end-result of all sociological blueprints aimed at Utopia. Living space, it had been called, and so, doomed to *live* they were, in that Erewhon of graphed respectability and cleanliness.

Never night.

Never shadowed.

. . . a shadow.

A blot moving against the aluminum cleanliness. The movement of rags and bits of clinging earth from graves sealed ages before. A shape.

He touched a gunmetal-gray wall in passing: the imprint of dusty fingers. A twisted shadow moving through antiseptically pure streets, and they become—with his passing—black alleys from another time.

Vaguely, he knew what had happened. Not specifically, not with particulars, but he was strong, and he was able to get away without the eggshell-thin walls of his mind caving in. There was no place in this shining structure to secrete himself, a place to think, but he had to have time. He slowed his walk, seeing no one. Somehow—inexplicably—he felt . . . safe? Yes, safe. For the first time in a very long time.

A few minutes before he had been standing in the narrow passageway outside No. 13 Miller's Court. It had been 6:15 in the morning. London had been quiet as he paused in the passageway of M'Carthy's Rents, in that fetid, urine-redolent corridor where the whores of Spitalfields took their clients. A few minutes before, the foetus in its bath of formaldehyde tightly-stoppered in a glass bottle inside his Gladstone bag, he had paused to drink in the thick fog, before taking the circuitous route back to Toynbee Hall. That had been a few minutes before. Then, suddenly, he was in another place and it was no longer 6:15 of a chill November morning in 1888.

He had looked up as light flooded him in that other place. It had been soot silent in Spitalfields, but suddenly, without any sense of having moved or having *been* moved, he was flooded with light. And when he looked up he was in that other place. Paused now, only a few minutes after the transfer, he leaned against the bright wall of the city and recalled the light. From a thousand mirrors. In the walls, in the ceiling. A bedroom with a girl in it. A lovely girl. Not like Black Mary Kelly or Dark Annie Chapman or Kate Eddowes or any of the other pathetic scum he had been forced to attend . . .

A lovely girl. Blonde, wholesome, until she had opened her robe and turned into the same sort of slut he had been compelled to use in his work in Whitechapel . . .

A sybarite, a creature of pleasures, a Juliette she had said, before he used the big-bladed knife on her. He had found the knife under the pillow, on the bed to which she had led him—how shameful, unresisting had he been, all confused, clutching his black bag with all the tremors of a child, he who had moved through the London night like oil, moved where he wished, accomplished his ends unchecked eight times, now led toward sin by another, merely another of the tarts, taking advantage of him while he tried to distinguish what had happened to him and where he was, how shameful—and he had used it on her.

That had only been minutes before, though he had worked very efficiently on her.

The knife had been rather unusual. The blade had seemed to be two wafer-thin sheets of metal with a pulsing, glowing *something* between. A kind of sparking, such as might be produced by a Van de Graaff generator. But that was patently ridiculous. It had no wires attached to it, no bus bars, nothing to produce even the crudest electrical discharge. He had thrust the knife into the Gladstone bag, where now it lay beside the scalpels and the spool of catgut and the racked vials in their leather cases, and the foetus in its bottle. Mary Jane Kelly's foetus.

He had worked efficiently, but swiftly, and had laid her out almost exactly in the same fashion as Kate Eddowes: the throat slashed completely through from ear-to-ear, the torso laid open down between the breasts to the vagina, the intestines pulled out and draped over the right shoulder, a piece of intestines being detached and placed between the left arm and the body. The liver had been punctured with the point of the knife, with a vertical cut slitting the left lobe of the liver. (He had been surprised to find the liver showed none of the signs of cirrhosis so prevalent in these Spitalfields tarts, who drank incessantly to rid themselves of the burden of living the dreary lives they moved through grotesquely. In fact, this one seemed totally unlike the others, even if she had been more brazen in her sexual overtures. And that knife under the bed pillow . . .) He had severed the vena cava leading to the heart. Then he had gone to work on the face.

He had thought of removing the left kidney again, as he had Kate Eddowes'. He smiled to himself as he conjured up the expression that must have been on the face of Mr. George

Lusk, chairman of the Whitechapel Vigilance Committee, when he received the cardboard box in the mail. The box containing Miss Eddowes' kidney, and the letter, impiously misspelled;

> From hell, Mr. Lusk, sir, I send you half the kidne I took from one woman, prasarved it for you, tother piece I fried and ate it; was very nice. I may send you the bloody knif that took it out if you only wate while longer. Catch me when you can, Mr. Lusk.

He had wanted to sign *that* one "Yours Truly, Jack the Ripper" or even "Spring-Heeled Jack" or maybe "Leather Apron," whichever had tickled his fancy, but a sense of style had stopped him. To go too far was to defeat his own purposes. It may even have been too much to suggest to Mr. Lusk that he had eaten the kidney. How hideous. True, he *had* smelled it . . .

This blonde girl, this Juliette with the knife under her pillow. She was the ninth. He leaned against the smooth steel wall without break or seam, and he rubbed his eyes. When would he be able to stop? When would they realize, when would they get his message, a message so clear, written in blood, that only the blindness of their own cupidity forced them to misunderstand! Would he be compelled to decimate the endless regiments of Spitalfields sluts to make them understand? Would he be forced to run the cobbles ankle-deep in black blood before they sensed what he was saying, and were impelled to make reforms?

But as he took his blood-soaked hands from his eyes, he realized what he must have sensed all along: he was no longer in Whitechapel. This was not Miller's Court, nor anywhere in Spitalfields. It might not even be London. But how could *that* be?

Had God taken him?

Had he died, in a senseless instant between the anatomy lesson of Mary Jane Kelly (that filth, she had actually *kissed* him!) and the bedroom disembowelment of this Juliette? Had Heaven finally called him to his reward for the work he had done?

The Reverend Mr. Barnett would love to know about this. But then, he'd have loved to know about it *all*. But "Bloody Jack" wasn't about to tell. Let the reforms come as the Reverend and his wife wished for them, and let them think their pamphleteering had done it, instead of the scalpels of Jack.

If he was dead, would his work be finished? He smiled to himself. If Heaven had taken him, then it must be that the work *was* finished. Successfully. But if *that* was so, then who was this Juliette who now lay spread out moist and cooling in the bedroom of a thousand mirrors? And in that instant he felt fear.

What if even God misinterpreted what he had done?

As the good folk of Queen Victoria's London had misinterpreted. As Sir Charles Warren had misinterpreted. What if God believed the superficial and ignored the *real* reason? But no! Ludicrous. If anyone would understand, it was the good God who had sent him the message that told him to set things a-right.

God loved him, as he loved God, and God would know.

But he felt fear, in that moment.

Because who was the girl he had just carved?

"She was my granddaughter, Juliette," said a voice immediately beside him.

His head refused to move, to turn that few inches to see who spoke. The Gladstone was beside him, resting on the smooth and reflective surface of the street. He could not get to a knife before he was taken. At last they had caught up with Jack. He began to shiver uncontrollably.

"No need to be afraid," the voice said. It was a warm and succoring voice. An older man. He shook as with an ague.

But he turned to look. It was a kindly old man with a gentle smile. Who spoke again, without moving his lips. "No one can hurt you. How do you do?"

The man from 1888 sank slowly to his knees. "Forgive me. Dear God, I did not know." The old man's laughter rose inside the head of the man on his knees. It rose like a beam of sunlight moving across a Whitechapel alleyway, from noon to one o'clock, rising and illuminating the gray bricks of the soot-coated walls. It rose, and illuminated his mind.

"I'm not God. Marvelous idea, but no, I'm not God. Would you like to meet God? I'm sure we can find one of the artists who would mold one for you. Is it important? No, I can see it isn't. What a strange mind you have. You neither believe nor doubt. How can you contain both concepts at once . . . would you like me to straighten some of your brain-patterns? No. I see, you're afraid. Well, let it be for the nonce. We'll do it another time."

He grabbed the kneeling man and drew him erect.

"You're covered with blood. Have to get you cleaned up. There's an ablute near here. Incidentally, I was very impressed with the way you handled Juliette. You're the first, you know. No, how could you know? In any case, you *are* the first to deal her as good as she gave. You would have been amused at what she did to Caspar Hauser. Squeezed part of his brain and then sent him back, let him live out part of his life and then—the little twit—she made me bring him back a second time and used a knife on him. Same knife you took, I believe. Then sent him back to his own time. Marvelous mystery. In all the tapes on unsolved phenomena. But she was much sloppier than you. She had a great verve in her amusements, but very little *éclat*. Except with Judge Crater; there she was—" He paused, and laughed lightly. "I'm an old man and I ramble on like a muskrat. You want to get cleaned up and shown around, I know. And *then* we can talk.

"I just wanted you to know I was satisfied with the way

you disposed of her. In a way, I'll miss the little twit. She was such a good fuck.''

The old man picked up the Gladstone bag and, holding the man spattered with blood, he moved off down the clean and shimmering street. ''You *wanted* her killed?'' the man from 1888 asked, unbelieving.

The old man nodded, but his lips never moved. ''Of course. Otherwise why bring her Jack the Ripper?''

Oh my dear God, he thought, *I'm in Hell. And I'm entered as Jack.*

''No, my boy, no no no. You're not in Hell at all. You're in the future. For you the future, for me the world of now. You came from 1888 and you're now in—'' he stopped, silently speaking for an instant, as though computing apples in terms of dollars, then resumed ''—3077. It's a fine world, filled with happy times, and we're glad to have you with us. Come along now, and you'll wash.''

In the ablutatorium, the late Juliette's grandfather changed his head.

''I really despise it,'' he informed the man from 1888, grabbing fingerfuls of his cheeks and stretching the flabby skin like elastic. ''But Juliette insisted. I was willing to humor her, if indeed that was what it took to get her to lie down. But what with toys from the past, and changing my head every time I wanted her to fuck me, it was trying; very trying.''

He stepped into one of the many identically shaped booths set flush into the walls. The tambour door rolled down and there was a soft *chukk* sound, almost chitinous. The tambour door rolled up and the late Juliette's grandfather, now six years younger than the man from 1888, stepped out, stark naked and wearing a new head. ''The body is fine, replaced last year,'' he said, examining the genitals and a mole on his right shoulder. The man from 1888 looked away. This was Hell and God hated him.

"Well, don't just *stand* there, Jack." Juliette's grandfather smiled. "Hit one of those booths and get your ablutions."

"That isn't my name," said the man from 1888 very softly, as though he had been whipped.

"It'll do, it'll do . . . now go get washed."

Jack approached one of the booths. It was a light green in color, but changed to mauve as he stopped in front of it. "Will it—"

"It will only *clean* you, what are you afraid of?"

"I don't want to be changed."

Juliette's grandfather did not laugh. "That's a mistake," he said cryptically. He made a peremptory motion with his hand and the man from 1888 entered the booth, which promptly revolved in its niche, sank into the floor and made a hearty *zeeeezzzz* sound. When it rose and revolved and opened, Jack stumbled out, looking terribly confused. His long sideburns had been neatly trimmed, his beard stubble had been removed, his hair was three shades lighter and was now parted on the left side, rather than in the middle. He still wore the same long dark coat trimmed with astrakhan, dark suit with white collar and black necktie (in which was fastened a horseshoe stickpin) but now the garments seemed new, unsoiled of course, possibly synthetics built to look like his former garments.

"Now!" Juliette's grandfather said. "Isn't that much better? A good cleansing always sets one's mind to rights." And he stepped into another booth from which he issued in a moment wearing a soft paper jumper that fitted from neck to feet without a break. He moved toward the door.

"Where are we going?" the man from 1888 asked the younger grandfather beside him. "I want you to meet someone," said Juliette's grandfather, and Jack realized that he was moving his lips now. He decided not to comment on it. There had to be a reason.

"I'll walk you there, if you promise not to make gurgling sounds at the city. It's a nice city, but I live here, and frankly, tourism is boring." Jack did not reply. Grandfather took it for acceptance of the terms.

They walked. Jack became overpowered by the sheer *weight* of the city. It was obviously extensive, massive, and terribly clean. It was his dream for Whitechapel come true. He asked about slums, about doss houses. The grandfather shook his head. "Long gone."

So it had come to pass. The reforms for which he had pledged his immortal soul, they had come to pass. He swung the Gladstone and walked jauntily. But after a few minutes his pace sagged once more: there was no one to be seen in the streets.

Just shining clean buildings and streets that ran off in aimless directions and came to unexpected stops as though the builders had decided people might vanish at one point and reappear someplace else, so why bother making a road from one point to the other.

The ground was metal, the sky seemed metallic, the buildings loomed on all sides, featureless explorations of planed space by insensitive metal. The man from 1888 felt terribly alone, as though every act he had performed had led inevitably to his alienation from the very people he had sought to aid.

When he had come to Toynbee Hall, and the Reverend Mr. Barnett had opened his eyes to the slum horrors of Spitalfields, he had vowed to help in any way he could. It had seemed as simple as faith in the Lord, what to do, after a few months in the sinkholes of Whitechapel. The sluts, of what use were they? No more use than the disease germs that had infected these very same whores. So he had set forth as Jack, to perform the will of God and raise the poor dregs who inhabited the East End of London. That Lord Warren, the Metropolitan Police Commissioner, and his Queen, and all the rest thought him a mad doctor, or an amok butcher, or a beast in human form did not distress him. He knew he would remain anonymous through all time, but that the good works he had set in motion would proceed to their wonderful conclusion.

The destruction of the most hideous slum area the country had ever known, and the opening of Victorian eyes. But all the time *had* passed, and how he was here, in a world where slums apparently did not exist, a sterile Utopia that was the personification of the Reverend Mr. Barnett's dreams—but it didn't seem . . . *right*.

This grandfather, with his young head.

Silence in the empty streets.

The girl, Juliette, and her strange hobby.

The lack of concern at her death.

The grandfather's expectation that he, Jack, *would* kill her. And now his friendliness.

Where were they going?

[Around them, the City. As they walked, the grandfather paid no attention, and Jack watched but did not understand. But this was what they saw as they walked:

[Thirteen hundred beams of light, one foot wide and seven molecules thick, erupted from almost-invisible slits in the metal streets, fanned out and washed the surfaces of the buildings; they altered hue to a vague blue and washed down the surfaces of the buildings; they bent and covered all open surfaces, bent at right angles, then bent again, and again, like origami paper figures; they altered hue a second time, soft gold, and penetrated the surfaces of the buildings, expanding and contracting in solid waves, washing the inner surfaces; they withdrew rapidly into the sidewalks; the entire process had taken twelve seconds.

[Night fell over a sixteen block area of the City. It descended in a solid pillar and was quite sharp-edged, ending at the street corners. From within the area of darkness came the distinct sounds of crickets, marsh frogs belching, night birds, soft breezes in trees, and faint music of unidentifiable instruments.

[Panes of frosted light appeared suspended freely in the air, overhead. A wavery insubstantial quality began to assault the topmost levels of a great structure directly in front of the light-panes. As the panes moved slowly down through the air, the building became indistinct, turned into motes of light, and floated upward. As the panes reached the pavement, the building had been completely dematerialized. The panes shifted color to a deep orange, and began moving upward again. As they moved, a new structure began to form where the previous building had stood, drawing—it seemed—motes of light from the air and forming them into a cohesive whole that became, as the panes ceased their upward movement, a new building. The light-panes winked out of existence.

[The sound of a bumblebee was heard for several seconds. Then it ceased.

[A crowd of people in rubber garments hurried out of a gray pulsing hole in the air, patted the pavement at their feet, then rushed off around a corner, from where emanated the sound of prolonged coughing. Then silence returned.

[A drop of water, thick as quicksilver, plummeted to the pavement, struck, rebounded, rose several inches, then evaporated into a crimson smear in the shape of a whale's tooth, which settled to the pavement and lay still.

[Two blocks of buildings sank into the pavement and the metal covering was smooth and unbroken, save for a metal tree whose trunk was silver and slim, topped by a ball of foliage constructed of golden fibers that radiated brightly in a perfect circle. There was no sound.

[The late Juliette's grandfather and the man from 1888 continued walking.

"Where are we going?"

"To van Cleef's. We don't usually walk; oh, sometimes; but it isn't as much pleasure as it used to be. I'm doing this primarily for you. Are you enjoying yourself?"

"It's . . . unusual."

"Not much like Spitalfields, is it? But I rather like it back there, at that time. I have the only Traveler, did you know? The only one ever made. Juliette's father constructed it, my son. I had to kill him to get it. He was thoroughly unreasonable about it, really. It was a casual thing for him. He was the last of the tinkerers, and he might just as easily have given it to me. But I suppose he was being cranky. That was why I had you carve up my granddaughter. She would have gotten around to me almost any time now. Bored, just silly bored is what she was—"

The gardenia took shape in the air in front of them, and turned into the face of a woman with long white hair. "Hernon, we can't wait much longer!" She was annoyed.

Juliette's grandfather grew livid. "You scum bitch! I *told* you pace. But no, you just couldn't, could you? Jump jump jump, that's all you ever do. Well, now it'll only be feddels less, that's all. Feddels, damn you! I set it for pace, I was *working* pace, and *you* . . . !"

His hands came up and moss grew instantly toward the face. The face vanished, and a moment later the gardenia reappeared a few feet away. The moss shriveled and Hernon, Juliette's grandfather, dropped his hand, as though weary of the woman's stupidity. A rose, a water lily, a hyacinth, a pair of phlox, a wild celandine, and a bull thistle appeared near the gardenia. As each turned into the face of a different person, Jack stepped back, frightened.

All the faces turned to the one that had been the bull thistle. "Cheat! Rotten bastard!" they screamed at the thin white face that had been the bull thistle. The gardenia-woman's eyes bulged from her face, the deep purple eye-shadow that completely surrounded the eyeball making her look like a deranged animal peering out of a cave. "Turd!" she shrieked at the bull thistle-man. "We all agreed, we all said and agreed; you *had* to formz a thistle, didn't you, scut! Well, now you'll see . . ."

She addressed herself instantly to the others. "Formz now! To hell with waiting, pace fuck! Now!"

"No, dammit!" Hernon shouted. "We were going to *paaaaace*!" But it was too late. Centering in on the bull thistle-man, the air roiled thickly like silt at a river-bottom, and the air blackened as a spiral began with the now terrified face of the bull thistle-man and exploded whirling outward, enveloping Jack and Hernon and all the flower-people and the City and suddenly it was night in Spitalfields and the man from 1888 was *in* 1888, with his Gladstone bag in his hand, and a woman approaching down the street toward him, shrouded in the London fog.

(There were eight additional nodules in Jack's brain.)

The woman was about forty, weary and not too clean. She wore a dark dress of rough material that reached down to her boots. Over the skirt was fastened a white apron that was stained and wrinkled. The bulbed sleeves ended midway up her wrists and the bodice of the dress was buttoned close around her throat. She wore a kerchief tied at the neck, and a hat that looked like a wide-brimmed skimmer with a raised crown. There was a pathetic little flower of unidentifiable origin in the band of the hat. She carried a beaded handbag of capacious size, hanging from a wrist-loop.

Her step slowed as she saw him standing there, deep in the shadows. Saw him was hardly accurate: sensed him.

He stepped out and bowed slightly from the waist: "Fair evenin' to ye, Miss. Care for a pint?"

Her features—sunk in misery of a kind known only to women who have taken in numberless shafts of male blood-gorged flesh—rearranged themselves. "Coo, sir, I thought was 'im for true. Old Leather Apron hisself. Gawdamighty, you give me a scare." She tried to smile. It was a rictus. There were bright spots in her cheeks from sickness and too much gin. Her voice was ragged, a broken-edged instrument barely workable.

"Just a solicitor caught out without comp'ny," Jack assured her. "And pleased to buy a handsome lady a pint of stout for a few hours' companionship."

She stepped toward him and linked arms. "Emily Matthewes, sir, an' pleased to go with you. It's a fearsome chill night, and with Slippery Jack abroad not safe for a respectin' woman such's m'self."

They moved off down Thrawl Street, past the doss houses where this drab might flop later, if she could obtain a few coppers from this neat-dressed stranger with the dark eyes.

He turned right onto Commercial Street, and just abreast of a stinking alley almost to Flower & Dean Street, he nudged her sharply sidewise. She went into the alley, and thinking he meant to steal a smooth hand up under her petticoats, she settled back against the wall and opened her legs, starting to lift the skirt around her waist. But Jack had hold of the kerchief and, locking his fingers tightly, he twisted, cutting off her breath. Her cheeks ballooned, and by a vagary of light from a gas standard in the street he could see her eyes go from hazel to a dead-leaf brown in an instant. Her expression was one of terror, naturally, but commingled with it was a deep sadness, at having lost the pint, at having not been able to make her doss for the night, at having had the usual Emily Matthewes bad luck to run afoul this night of the one man who would ill-use her favors. It was a consummate sadness at the inevitability of her fate.

> *I come to you out of the night.*
> *The night that sent me down*
> *all the minutes of our lives*
> *to this instant.*
> *From this time forward, men will*
> *wonder what happened*
> *at this instant. They will silently*
> *hunger to go back, to come to my*
> *instant with you and see my face*
> *and know my name and perhaps*
> *not even try to stop me, for*
> *then I would not be who I am,*
> *but only someone who tried*
> *and failed. Ah.*
> *For you and me it becomes history*
> *that will lure men always;*
> *but they will never understand*
> *why we both suffered, Emily;*
> *they will never truly understand*
> *why each of us died so terribly.*

A film came over her eyes, and as her breath husked out in wheezing, pleading tremors, his free hand went into the pocket of the greatcoat. He had known he would need it, when they were walking, and he had already invaded the Gladstone bag. Now his hand went into the pocket and came up with the scalpel.

"Emily . . ." softly.

Then he sliced her.

Neatly, angling the point of the scalpel into the soft flesh behind and under her left ear. *Sternocleidomastoideus.* Driving it in to the gentle crunch of cartilage giving way. Then, grasping the instrument tightly, tipping it down and drawing it across the width of the throat, following the line of the firm jaw. *Glandula submandibularis.* The blood poured out over his hands, ran thickly at first and then burst spattering past him, reaching the far wall of the alley. Up his sleeves, soaking his white cuffs, She made a watery rattle and sank limply in his grasp, his fingers still twisted tight in her kerchief; black abrasions where he had scored the flesh. He continued the cut up past the point of the jaw's end, and sliced into the lobe of the ear. He lowered her to the filthy paving. She lay crumpled, and he straightened her. Then he cut away the garments laying her naked belly open to the wan and flickering light of the gas standard in the street. Her belly was bloated. He started the primary cut in the hollow of her throat. *Glandula thyreoeidea.* His hand was sure as he drew a thin black line of blood down and down, between the breasts. *Sternum.* Cutting a deep cross in the hole of her navel. Something vaguely yellow oozed up. *Plica umbilicalis medialis.* Down over the rounded hump of the belly, biting more deeply, withdrawing for a neat incision. *Mesenterium dorsale commune.* Down to the matted-with-sweat roundness of her privates. Harder here. *Vesica urinaria.* And finally, to the end, *vagina.*

Filth hole.

Foul-smelling die red lust pit wet hole of sluts.

And in his hands, succubi. And in his head, eyes watching. And in his head, minds impinging. And in his head titillation

for a gardenia
  a water lily
  a rose
  a hyacinth
  a pair of phlox
  a wild celandine
and a dark flower with petals of obsidian, a stamen of onyx, pistils of anthracite, and the mind of Hernon, who was the late Juliette's grandfather.

They watched the entire horror of the mad anatomy lesson.

They watched him nick the eyelids. They watched him remove the heart. They watched him slice out the fallopian tubes. They watched him squeeze, till it ruptured, the "ginny" kidney. They watched him slice off the sections of breast till they were nothing but shapeless mounds of bloody meat, and arrange them, one mound each, on a still-staring, wide-open, nicked-eyelid eye. They watched.

They watched and they drank from the deep troubled pool of his mind. They sucked deeply at the moist quivering core of his id. And they delighted:

Oh God how Delicious look at that It looks like the uneaten rind of a Pizza or look at That It looks like lumaconi *oh god IIIIIwonder what it would be like to Tasteit!*

See how smooth the steel.

He hates them all, every one of them, something about a girl, a venereal disease, fear of his God, Christ, the Reverend Mr. Barnett, he . . . he wants to fuck the reverend's wife!

Social reform can only be brought about by concerted effort of a devoted few. Social reform is a justifiable end, condoning any expedient short of decimation of over fifty percent of the people who will be served by the reforms. The best social reformers are the most audacious. He believes it! How lovely!

You pack of vampires, you filth, you scum, you . . .

He senses us!

Damn him! Damn you, Hernon, you drew off too deeply, he knows we're here, that's disgusting, what's the sense now? I'm withdrawing!

Come back, you'll end the formz . . .

. . . back they plunged in the spiral as it spiraled back in upon itself and the darkness of the night of 1888 withdrew. The spiral drew in and in and locked at its most infinitesimal point as the charred and blackened face of the man who had been the bull thistle. He was quite dead. His eyeholes had been burned out; charred wreckage lay where intelligence had lived. They had used him as a focus.

The man from 1888 came back to himself instantly, with a full and eidetic memory of what he had just experienced. It had not been a vision, nor a dream, nor a delusion, nor a product of his mind. It had happened. They had sent him back, erased his mind of the transfer into the future, of Juliette, of everything after the moment outside No. 13 Miller's Court. And they had set him to work pleasuring them, while they drained off his feelings, his emotions and his unconscious thoughts; while they battened and gorged themselves with the most private sensations. Most of which, till this moment—in a strange feedback— he had not even known he possessed. As his mind plunged on from one revelation to the next, he felt himself growing ill. At one concept his mind tried to pull back and plunge him into darkness rather than confront it. But the barriers were down, they had opened new patterns and he could read it all, remember it all. *Stinking sex hole, sluts, they have to die.* No, that wasn't the way he thought of women, any women, no matter how low or common. He was a gentleman, and women were to be respected. *She had given him the clap. He remembered.* The shame and the endless fear till he had gone to his physician father and confessed it. The look on the man's face. He remembered it all. The way his father had tended him, the way he would have tended a plague victim. It had never been the same between them again. He had tried for the cloth. *Social reform hahahaha.* All delusion. He had been a mountebank, a clown . . . and worse. He had slaughtered for something in which not even he believed. They left his mind wide open, and his thoughts stumbled . . . raced further and further toward the thought of

EXPLOSION!IN!HIS!MIND!

He fell face forward on the smooth and polished metal

pavement, but he never touched. Something arrested his fall, and he hung suspended, bent over at the waist like a ridiculous Punch divested of strings or manipulation from above. A whiff of something invisible, and he was in full possession of his senses almost before they had left him. His mind was forced to look at it:

He wants to fuck the Reverend Mr. Barnett's wife.

Henrietta, with her pious petition to Queen Victoria— "Madam, we, the women of East London, feel horror at the dreadful sins that have been lately committed in our midst . . ."—asking for the capture of himself, of Jack, whom she would never, not *ever* suspect was residing right there with her and the Reverend in Toynbee Hall. The thought was laid as naked as her body in the secret dreams he had never remembered upon awakening. All of it, they had left him with opened doors, with unbounded horizons, and he saw himself for what he was.

A psychopath, a butcher, a lecher, a hypocrite, a clown.

"You did this to me! Why did you do this?"

Frenzy cloaked his words. The flower-faces became the solidified hedonists who had taken him back to 1888 on that senseless voyage of slaughter.

van Cleef, the gardenia-woman, sneered. "Why do you think, you ridiculous bumpkin? (Bumpkin, is that the right colloquialism, Hernon? I'm so uncertain in the mid-dialects.) When you'd done in Juliette, Hernon wanted to send you back. But why should he? He owed us at least three formz, and you did passing well for one of them."

Jack shouted at them till the cords stood out in his throat. "Was it necessary, this last one? Was it important to do it, to help my reforms . . . was it?"

Hernon laughed. "Of course not."

Jack sank to his knees. The City let him do it. "Oh God, oh God Almighty, I've done what I've done . . . I'm covered with blood . . . and for *nothing*, for *nothing* . . ."

Cashio, who had been one of the phlox, seemed puzzled. "Why is he concerned about *this* one, if the others don't bother him?"

Nosy Verlag, who had been a wild celandine, said sharply, "They do, all of them do. Probe him, you'll see."

Cashio's eyes rolled up in his head an instant, then rolled down and refocused—Jack felt a quicksilver shudder in his mind and it was gone—and he said lackadaisically, "Mm-hmm."

Jack fumbled with the latch of the Gladstone. He opened the bag and pulled out the foetus in the bottle. Mary Jane Kelly's unborn child, from November 9th, 1888. He held it in front of his face a moment, then dashed it to the metal pavement. It never struck. It vanished a fraction of an inch from the clean, sterile surface of the City's street.

"What marvelous loathing!" exulted Rose, who had been a rose.

"Hernon," said van Cleef, "he's centering on you. He begins to blame you for all of this."

Hernon was laughing (without moving his lips) as Jack pulled Juliette's electrical scalpel from the Gladstone, and lunged. Jack's words were incoherent, but what he was saying, as he struck, was: "I'll show you what filth you are! I'll show you you can't do this kind of thing! I'll teach you! You'll die, all of you!" This is what he was saying, but it came out as one long sustained bray of revenge, frustration, hatred and directed frenzy.

Hernon was still laughing as Jack drove the whisper-thin blade with its shimmering current into his chest. Almost without manipulation on Jack's part, the blade circumscribed a perfect 360° hole that charred and shriveled, exposing Hernon's pulsing heart and wet organs. He had time to shriek with confusion before he received Jack's second thrust, a direct lunge that severed the heart from its attachments. *Vena cava superior. Aorta. Arteria pulmonalis. Bronchus principalis.*

The heart flopped forward and a spreading wedge of blood under tremendous pressure ejaculated, spraying Jack with such force that it knocked his hat from his head and blinded him. His face was now a dripping black-red collage of features and blood.

Hernon followed his heart, and fell forward, into Jack's arms. Then the flower-people screamed as one, vanished, and Hernon's body slipped from Jack's hands to wink out of existence an instant before it struck at Jack's feet. The walls around him were clean, unspotted, sterile, metallic, uncaring.

He stood in the street, holding the bloody knife.

"Now!" he screamed, holding the knife aloft. "Now it begins!"

If the city heard, it made no indication, but

[Pressure accelerated in temporal linkages.]

[A section of shining wall on the building eighty miles away changed from silver to rust.]

[In the freezer chambers, two hundred gelatin caps were fed into a ready trough.]

[The weathermaker spoke softly to itself, accepted data, and instantly constructed an intangible mnemonic circuit.]

and in the shining eternal city where night only fell when the inhabitants had need of night and called specifically for night . . .

Night fell. With no warning save: *"Now!"*

In the City of sterile loveliness a creature of filth and decaying flesh prowled. In the last City of the world, a City on the edge of the world, where the ones who had devised their own paradise lived, the prowler made his home in shadows. Slipping from darkness to darkness with eyes that saw only movement, he roamed in search of a partner to dance his deadly rigadoon.

He found the first woman as she materialized beside a small

waterfall that flowed out of empty air and dropped its shimmering, tinkling moisture into an azure cube of nameless material. He found her and drove the living blade into the back of her neck. Then he sliced out the eyeballs and put them into her open hands.

He found the second woman in one of the towers, making love to a very old man who gasped and wheezed and clutched his heart as the young woman forced him to passion. She was killing him as Jack killed her. He drove the living blade into the lower rounded surface of her belly, piercing her sex organs as she rode astride the old man. She decamped blood and viscous fluids over the prostrate body of the old man, who also died, for Jack's blade had severed the penis within the young woman. She fell forward across the old man and Jack left them that way, joined in the final embrace.

He found a man and throttled him with his bare hands, even as the man tried to dematerialize. Then Jack recognized him as one of the phlox, and made neat incisions in the face, into which he inserted the man's genitals.

He found another woman as she was singing a gentle song about eggs to a group of children. He opened her throat and severed the strings hanging inside. He let the vocal cords drop onto her chest. But he did not touch the children, who watched it all avidly. He liked children.

He prowled through the unending night making a grotesque collection of hearts, which he cut out of one, three, nine people. And when he had a dozen, he took them and laid them as road markers on one of the wide boulevards that never were used by vehicles, for the people of this City had no need of vehicles.

Oddly, the City did not clean up the hearts. Nor were the people vanishing any longer. He was able to move with relative impunity, hiding only when he saw large groups that might be searching for him. But *something* was happening in the City. (Once, he heard the peculiar sound of metal grating on metal, the *skrikkk* of plastic cutting into plastic—and he instinctively knew it was the sound of a machine malfunctioning.)

He found a woman bathing, and tied her up with strips of his own garments, and cut off her legs at the knees and left her still sitting up in the swirling crimson bath, screaming as she bled away her life. The legs he took with him.

When he found a man hurrying to get out of the night, he pounced on him, cut his throat and sawed off the arms. He replaced the arms with the bath-woman's legs.

And it went on and on, for a time that had no measure. He was showing them what evil could produce. He was showing them their immorality was silly beside his own.

But one thing finally told him he was winning. As he lurked in an antiseptically pure space between two low aluminum-cubes, he heard a voice that came from above him and around him and even from inside him. It was a public announcement, broadcast by whatever mental communications system the people of the City on the edge of the World used.

OUR CITY IS PART OF US. WE ARE PART OF OUR CITY. IT RESPONDS TO OUR MINDS AND WE CONTROL IT. THE GESTALT THAT WE HAVE BECOME IS THREATENED. WE HAVE AN ALIEN FORCE WITHIN THE CITY AND WE ARE GEARING TO LOCATE IT. BUT THE MIND OF THIS MAN IS STRONG. IT IS BREAKING DOWN THE FUNCTIONS OF THE CITY. THIS ENDLESS NIGHT IS AN EXAMPLE. WE MUST ALL CONCENTRATE. WE MUST ALL CONSCIOUSLY FOCUS OUR THOUGHTS TO MAINTAINING THE CITY. THIS THREAT IS OF THE FIRST ORDER. IF OUR CITY DIES, WE DIE.

It was not an announcement in those terms, though that was how Jack interpreted it. The message was much longer and much more complex, but that was what it meant, and he knew he was winning. He was destroying them. Social reform was laughable, they had said. He would show them.

And so he continued with his lunatic pogrom. He butchered and slaughtered and carved them wherever he found them, and they could not vanish and they could not escape and they could not stop him. The collection of hearts grew to fifty and seventy and then a hundred.

He grew bored with hearts and began cutting out their brains. The collection grew.

For numberless days it went on, and from time to time in the clean, scented autoclave of the City, he could hear the sounds of screaming. His hands were always sticky.

Then he found van Cleef, and leaped from hiding in the darkness to bring her down. He raised the living blade to drive it into her breast, but she

van   ished

He got to his feet and looked around. van Cleef reappeared ten feet from him. He lunged for her and again she was gone. To reappear ten feet away. Finally, when he had struck at her half a dozen times and she had escaped him each time, he stood panting, arms at sides, looking at her.

And she looked back at him with disinterest.

"You no longer amuse us," she said, moving her lips.

Amuse? His mind whirled down into a place far darker than any he had known before, and through the murk of his bloodlust he began to realize. It had all been for their amusement. They had *let* him do it. They had given him the run of the City and he had capered and gibbered for them.

Evil? He had never even suspected the horizons of that word. He went for her, but she disappeared with finality.

He was left standing there as the daylight returned. As the City cleaned up the mess, took the butchered bodies and did with them what it had to do. In the freezer chambers the gelatin caps were returned to their niches, no more inhabitants of the City need be thawed to provide Jack the Ripper with utensils for his amusement of the sybarites. His work was truly finished.

He stood there in the empty street. A street that would *always* be empty to him. **The people of the City had all along been able to escape** him, and now they would. He was finally and completely the clown they had shown him to be. He was not evil, he was pathetic.

He tried to use the living blade on himself, but it dissolved into motes of light and wafted away on a breeze that had blown up for just that purpose.

Alone, he stood there staring at the victorious cleanliness of this Utopia. With their talents they would keep him alive, possibly alive forever, immortal in the possible expectation of needing him for amusement again someday. He was stripped to raw essentials in a mind that was no longer anything more than jelly matter. To go madder and madder, and never to know peace or end or sleep.

He stood there, a creature of dirt and alleys, in a world as pure as the first breath of a baby.

"My name isn't Jack," he said softly. But they would never know his real name. Nor would they care. *"My name isn't Jack!"* he said loudly. No one heard.

"MY NAME ISN'T JACK, AND I'VE BEEN BAD, VERY BAD, I'M AN EVIL PERSON BUT MY NAME ISN'T JACK!" he screamed, and screamed, and screamed again, walking aimlessly down an empty street, in plain view, no longer forced to prowl. A stranger in the City.

THE LODGE OF JAHBULON

COOPER McLAUGHLIN

*As we mentioned a bit earlier, there have been a multitude
of attempts to explain why Saucy Jack did the terrible things
that he did. One recent theory explains the Ripper murders
in terms of a conspiracy among the richest and most influential men in England, a conspiracy so widespread and per-
vasive that it touches the Royal Family itself, a conspiracy
protecting a secret important enough that the conspirators
would do anything, go to any lengths, to keep that deadly
secret under wraps.*

*New writer Cooper McLaughlin—a frequent contributor to
The Magazine of Fantasy and Science Fiction—bases the sus-
penseful and evocative story that follows on this particular
theory . . . but uses it as a springboard to take us even deeper
into the realm of nightmare.*

THE YOUNG WOMAN PUSHED HER WAY THROUGH THE
night crowds of Whitechapel High Street. Under the
flaring gaslights, hansom cabs and four-horse drays
clattered over the cobbled street.

A ragged man blocked the woman's path, holding a wet,
silvery fish in front of her face. ''New mackerel . . . Six a
shilling, missus . . .'' She brushed past him, almost tripping
over a sallow-faced boy of seven. A tray hung from his neck
and the red-and-green lithographed sign on his chest read
''Bryant and May's Alpine Vesuvius.''

"Fusees, mum? Fusees, milady?" His voice cracked. He held up a box of matches. The woman reached out to push him away. The boy's arms were like sticks and his bare feet were scabbed with sores.

Marie Jeanette Kelly looked into his eyes. "God save us . . ." She took out a shilling.

"Have this, *gossoon*. Fill your belly. Don't take it home or it'll be spent on the drink." She moved away.

The boy tugged at her long brown dress. "Yer fusees, milady . . ."

Marie Kelly smiled. "Boy, I've no need of matches," she said in her light Limerick brogue. "There'll be fire enough for me, in time." She touched his head. "Off with you, now." She pulled her French shawl over her upswept red hair and draped it on her bonnet, hiding her eyes. "Say a prayer for me, then."

Fifty yards on she paused, then turned into the dark of Old Castle Street. Halfway up the lane she stepped into a doorway and looked back. Her heart pounded. Had it been *him* she'd seen on the Aldgate omnibus? The man with the neat mustache. Him with his clever, clever hands. Quick hands they were, she knew. She could see him sitting on the edge of the bed, his cold blue eyes studying her naked flesh. His hands, the clever hands, moving like spiders. She took a deep breath. There were hundreds of young men like that, checked coats and mustaches all the same.

The full August moon shone through the yellow-brown clouds which hovered over London, and a faint, hot breeze blew up from the Thames, bringing with it the smell of sewage and coal smoke.

Her body was damp with sweat under her woolen clothes. French clothes . . . *He* had bought them. She closed her eyes. *Mother Mary. I should have known. The joy of it was not for the likes of me.* She remembered the beach at Dieppe. Hold-

ng her skirts up as she ran over the strand, little Maggie in
 her fresh frock and her pink bonnet, laughing at her side.
And himself, eyes like cold blue stones, sitting on the sea-
wall, a proper English Milord, the spider hands moving over
the pages of his string-bound book. Her throat tightened.
Where are you now, Alice Margaret? My sweet little Maggie
. . May God protect you from the likes of *him*.

She stepped from the doorway and turned her back on the
lights of Whitechapel High Street. Her footsteps echoed from
the shuttered facades as she hurried toward the dark warrens
of Spitalfields.

Spitalfields. Where the blue-coated Peelers came only in
force. She walked past Thrawl Street, Flower & Dean, then
Fashion Street, turning into Dorset, a narrow thoroughfare
known to the Metropolitan Police as "Do As You Please
Street."

Smoke-darkened brick buildings, three and four stories
high, rose on either side. Yellow light filtered from the slitted
windows. Under the gas lamps, twelve-year-old whores
waited for custom. Worn-out hags of thirty sat in the doorways, talking, nursing their brats, and passing square-faced
bottles of gin. Behind the crumbling brick walls of the common lodging houses lived pickpockets, footpads, and razor-
men. Generations of thieves sleeping ten to a room.

Here she had friends. Long Liz would help her. She thought
of little Maggie's mother. There was no one to help Annie
Crook when she was dragged away from her lover and her
child, and taken off in the shuttered coach. Poor Annie. Too
late for her, but not for little Maggie. Somehow she'd get
Maggie back and take her away to Ireland. To the wilds of
County Galway, where they'd never be found.

At the corner of Dorset and Crispin, a faded blue and yellow sign marked the Britannia, a pub called "Ringer's" by
the locals. Marie pushed through the soot-streaked oak doors

and stepped inside. The smells of tobacco, stale beer, and sweat surrounded her.

The room was low-ceilinged and blackened by smoke. The webbed silk mantles of gas jets burned above the long row of coat hooks which lined one wall.

Mrs. Ringer stood behind the bar, her purple-veined face shiny with sweat. " 'Allo, Dearie . . . New here, are you?''

"It's . . . it's me, Missus Ringer . . . Marie Kelly.''

The old lady peered at her myopically. "Well, so it is, Dearie. Didn't know you in them fancy clothes. Found a rich one, 'ave you?''

Marie ignored the question. "Is Long Liz here?''

"Liz? Not yet, she isn't. But Polly and Dark Annie is back at the ladies' table.'' She looked closely at Marie. "You don't look so good, love . . . You go back and I'll send Jenny to you. You needs summat' to put the roses on yer cheeks.''

At a table under a flaring light sat four men wearing silk scarves and tight-fitting coats, their fingers glinting with gold rings as they played cards. "Dolly-mops,'' veteran pimps, razor-scarred from the incessant Piccadilly turf wars. They watched silently as she passed. The men understood the house rule of no pandering or soliciting on the premises. By Mrs. Ringer's decree, the "ladies' table'' was both a club and a refuge for off-duty whores.

Polly Nichols looked up. "Marie, is it you? I never . . .''

Dark Annie Chapman put down her half-finished glass of ale and turned in her seat. "Well, aren't you the swell in them clothes . . . Wherever have you been?''

Marie sat at the table, facing the door. "I've been away. In the country. Has . . . has anyone been asking for me?''

"Not a soul,'' said Annie Chapman. She was a short woman with fair skin and blue eyes, called "Dark Annie'' because of her fits of melancholia, brought on by alcohol and opiates.

"God, Marie. You look a sight. You need a drink, you do," Polly Nicholls said. She was a dark-haired woman with skin like a Gypsy. Her eyes were bright, and her cheeks had the feverish blush of tuberculosis.

Marie looked at her two friends in their frayed clothes and their shabby bonnets. If it hadn't been for Annie Elizabeth Crook, she, too, would be a worn-out street slut like them, selling herself for the price of a drink or a night's lodging. Perhaps, she thought, that would have been a better fate. If she had not gone to work in the tobacco shop at number 22 Cleveland Street, she would never have met the man who frequented the house opposite at number 19. But then she would never have known little Maggie either. She sighed as Jenny came to the table, wiping her hands on her greasy apron. "Wot'll you lot have?"

"Give us purl, all around."

"Purl, is it? 'Ow nice. Who's going to pay?"

Marie threw a half crown to the table. "Keep a civil tongue, slut, or I'll have Ma Ringer take a stick to you."

Polly and Dark Annie laughed as Jenny turned away, her back stiff. Marie leaned forward. "Have you seen Long Liz? She was to meet me here this night."

"Saw her half an hour ago," Polly answered. "Taking some sotted bargeman up to her bed . . . She'll be back soon."

Jenny returned with three mugs of purl and slammed them to the table. Marie lifted the pint of hot beer, ginger, and sugars, and took a long swallow. At the far end of the room the door opened and a tall, thin woman entered. She wore a printed shawl draped over her bonnet. The woman walked unsteadily to the table where the four men sat.

Marie put down her mug. "Who's that?"

Dark Annie turned her head. "Cathy Eddowes . . . John Kelly's her fancy man. A hard one, he is."

As Marie watched, Cathy Eddowes bent to speak to Kelly.

He held out his hand and Cathy emptied her purse into it. Kelly spoke to her in a low voice, then gave her a shove toward the door. As she staggered out, the other men at the table laughed and picked up their cards.

Polly touched Marie's arm. "What do you want with Liz?"

"I saw her two days ago. In Covent Garden. I'd a room there, but it's too dangerous . . . I asked her to find me a place to stay . . . Somewhere I won't be found."

"Have you money, then?" Dark Annie asked.

Marie hesitated. "I've some. Little enough to do me for a few days."

A tall woman made her way toward them. She wore a black worsted jacket trimmed with rabbit fur and a dress of rusty sateen. Beneath her black crepe bonnet, her face was waxy and honed by hunger. "There you are!" She bent and kissed Marie's cheek, then slumped into a chair. "The bugger . . . tried to do me out of sixpence, he did." Her accent was a curious mixture of cockney and Swedish.

Dark Annie smiled at her. "You needs a drink, Liz. Marie's giving us purl. Warm your heart, it will."

Long Liz laughed and took a half-empty bottle of Godfrey's Cordial from her pocket. She took a drink of the opium and treacle mixture, then shoved the bottle toward Polly. "Pass it about. Better than booze, that is."

Marie turned to Liz. "Did you find a place for me?"

"Of course I did, love. It wasn't easy . . . a room to yourself around here. Got its own door, so you can come and go as you please. It'll cost a bit though. M'Carthy what owns the place wanted six shillings a week. But I got him down to four-and-six."

"I don't care. I've enough until I can settle my business. But I mustn't be found . . . They'll do me like they did Annie Elizabeth."

Long Liz drank from the bottle of cordial. Her eyes were

unfocused and her speech slurred. "Wha-What do you mean? Did you find her?"

"I did that. I found her at the Marylebone Workhouse."

"How did you know where she was?"

"The man I was in France with . . . the one who took Maggie away. I heard him talking to one of his friends about where they had Annie Elizabeth. I didn't know then . . ."

Marie took a drink of her purl and shuddered. "I wish I hadn't seen her. I know the matron there . . . from my own parish, in Limerick. She got me in. Poor misfortunate Annie. They've got her trussed like a goose. She didn't know me at all. The matron said Annie'd been sent from St. Guy's Hospital with a great bandage on her head, and she's been there ever since. Like an animal. They did it to her, the bloody bastards."

"They? Who's 'they'?" Polly asked.

Marie glanced at Long Liz. "The man I went to France with. Him and his friends . . . Walter Sickert, he is."

Dark Annie looked up. "Sickert? I knows 'im. Hangs about that Cleveland Street house across the way from where you and Annie Crook was in the tobacco shop."

"That Cleveland Street house," Marie said. "It's the Devil himself that lives there. Desperate men all of them, in that place."

"Aah. Come off it, Marie." Polly laughed. 'I've seen the fancy gentlemen what goes in and out of that house. Mary-Anns, the lot of them. They've got little boys in wigs and dresses running about."

Long Liz reached forward and touched Polly's arm. "You don't know the half of it. I've been inside . . . in the rooms below." She dropped her voice. "A crown they paid me . . . I wouldn't go back for a hundred guineas. It was that Netley took me there."

"The one what brings the gents in his coach?"

"That's him. Put a cloth over my eyes and took me around

the back. Oh, I knew where I was, all right. Netley stripped me down and washed me all over." She paused and took a drink from her bottle. "Then he rubbed me with some 'orrible-smelling stuff. Made me dizzy, the stink of it. Next I knew I was tied to some kind of stone table. Then . . . one of them had me . . . Big as a horse he was, and like ice inside me. I fainted away. When I came to I was in Netley's coach. He took me to Whitechapel and pushed me out. Said if I breathed a word of it, he'd cut out me liver."

Marie slammed her hand on the table. "God forgive me. I'd do them all in if I could. Sickert, Netley, the lot of them. After what they did to Annie Elizabeth. Now they've got little Maggie away from me. That Sickert. 'You're her mother now,' he says to me the day they took Annie off. 'She needs to be taken care of . . .' he says. You should see the way the man looks at her. And her an innocent of three years."

"What will you do?" Long Liz asked.

"Do? I'll go to Fleet Street and tell the story to the newspapers, I will. Either they give little Maggie back to me or I'll tell the whole of the world who the father is."

"And who is that, then?"

Marie leaned back in her seat. "Prince Albert Victor Edward, that's who. Pretty Prince Eddy. Him with his soft ways and his face like a girl's. God save the Empire if the likes of him comes to the throne. Worse than his father, the Prince of Wales, that one is."

Dark Annie laughed. "So you'll tell the penny papers? Fat lot of good that'll do. Think of all the shopgirls in London what 'as bastards by lords and dukes and such. The Prince of Wales himself has dollies all over the City."

Marie looked at her. "That's not the whole of it. It's not just another baby on the wrong side of the blanket. Annie Crook and Prince Eddy are man and wife in the eyes of God. For wasn't I the witness to it? I made my mark in the register at St. Saviour's Infirmary when the priest joined them to-gether.''

Polly gasped. "St. Saviour's? A priest? You mean a *Roman* priest?''

Marie glared at her. "What else, then? Annie was a good girl . . . Not a heathen, like some.''

"God's blood!'' Polly whispered. "He's to be King, after his father . . . And married to Papist! If the penny papers got that, there'd be riots in the streets. Old Queen Victoria would have Prince Eddy's head on a pike.''

"What'll you do?'' Long Liz asked Marie.

"Wouldn't Prince Eddy help? I mean if he loved Annie, married her and all . . .'' Polly said.

Marie laughed. "Him? He's weak in the head, that one is. The man who came to see Sickert told him that the old Queen had wind of some scandal. She's got Prince Eddy locked up in Marlborough House. And how would the likes of me get to him? I can't knock on the gate and introduce myself as his bastard daughter's nanny, now, can I? I've got to find Sick-ert and make him give up the baby.''

Long Liz untied her bonnet and put it on the table. "Net-ley. Netley would know where Sickert is . . . Thick as fleas, the pair of them.''

"Netley's the one who took Annie away,'' Marie said. "If he knows I'm making trouble he'll have me off and cut up my brain, like they did hers.''

Long Liz tapped her fingers on the table. "Look . . . all of you . . . There's a way to get at the buggers. Send them a letter. Tell them what will happen if Marie doesn't get the babby back.''

Polly pushed back her chair. "I don't want nothing to do with that lot.''

"Suppose there was something in it for you? Besides help-ing Marie?'' Liz smiled. "We could send a letter to Sickert

. . . through Netley. Tell him he'd better give up little Maggie
. . . Maggie and . . . a hundred pounds."

Marie turned toward her. Her face was flushed. "I'll not
touch his blood money. I want the child, that's all."

Liz looked at her. "Rich, are you? How are you going to
get Maggie and yourself to Ireland? What will you live on?
A few pounds is nothing to men like that."

Marie bent her head. "You're right, Liz. I know you are.
If I'd fifty pounds I could take the baby to Galway and live
for a year . . . until I could find decent work."

"That's the way, Marie. It's owed to you." Liz looked at
the other two women. "We'll send a letter telling Sickert to
give over the baby and the money . . . or else."

"How will you do that?"

"Like I said. Pass it to Netley. He's sure to be hanging
about Cleveland Street. Marie can't be seen, so one of us
must do it."

"Not me," said Polly. "That man gives me the shivers."

Liz frowned. "Better if two of us take it. He wouldn't try
anything funny with a pair of us. A hundred pounds, we'll
ask." She looked around the table. "Ten pound each to us,
and seventy for Marie and the baby."

The three-story brick house was set back from the road,
surrounded by a small, formal garden. A polished brass plate
by the door pull read:

CHRISTIAN SPIRITUALIST CENTER
PECKHAM
R. J. Lees

Inside the house, the library was large. Two walls were
covered from floor to ceiling with bookcases containing volumes on theology, metaphysics, and the occult.

Robert James Lees sat at the carved oak desk which had

been a gift from his friend, the late Benjamin Disraeli, making notes in the margin of his book, *The Astral Bridegroom*. He was a pale man with a broad forehead and deeply set dark eyes. At thirty-eight, he was unfashionably thin and athletic, given to long, solitary walks.

He put down his pen and turned to his wife, who sat at a gate-legged escritoire, working out the monthly accounts for the Center. "I say, Laura, I really must speak to the publisher about a new edition of this book. There are some frightful errors in it."

Laura laughed. "It's that you're such a perfectionist, Robert. It's a beautiful book . . ." She rose and went to the tea cart which sat by the hearth. "Will you have more tea?"

He took the cup from her and placed it on the desk next to the gold-framed photograph of Queen Victoria, which was inscribed "To a loyal and most helpful Subject. Victoria, R."

He leaned forward and picked up the cup. This time there was no warning. His muscles stiffened in a clonic seizure which slammed him back against the chair. The bone-china cup shattered against the desktop. His face tightened and cataleptic tension pushed his eyes back in their sockets. A strangled cry came from his throat.

Laura moved quickly to his side. She had seen him like this many times . . . but never before without warning. She took a deep breath and reached inside herself, fighting to calm the fear. Then she placed her hand gently on the top of his head, letting her own vital force flow into him.

He slumped in the chair, then slowly sat up, pressing his hands to his head. "Laura . . . Laura . . ."

"What is it, my dear? What did you see?"

"I . . . I don't know . . ."

Laura went to the sideboard and brought him a large brandy. He took a slow sip and shuddered.

"It was nothing, nothing that I could 'see.' It was a sense of evil . . . Some hellish miasma that seemed to surround us all. Like nothing I've ever felt. I had the feeling that it involved the Queen. I was looking at her picture just before it happened.''

Laura mopped the spilled tea with a cloth. ''Was there nothing else?''

Robert Lees paused. ''There was a word . . .'' He picked up the pen and wrote on a pad.

Laura looked at the paper. '' 'Jahbulon.' Whatever can that mean?''

Sir William Withey Gull, Bt., M.D., F.R.C.P., F.R.S., Physician in Ordinary to Her Majesty the Queen, looked out of the window of his office in St. Guy's Hospital. In the distance, across St. Thomas Street, he could see the glint of sun on the gray-brown waters of the Thames. As he watched, a red and black barge passed under London Bridge, headed east toward the channel.

He smiled to himself. If it had not been for his tenacity and drive he might be on that vessel, a bargeman like his father. Instead, he was at the top of his profession, a medical genius, a master of the healing arts. The man who saved the life of the Prince of Wales.

He caught his reflection in the soot-grimed window. Heavy-set and broad-shouldered. His hair was brushed forward and he was clean-shaven, a calculated enhancement of his resemblance to Napoleon Bonaparte.

He turned to his desk and glanced down at his notes. Tomorrow he would lecture his third-year medical students. He enjoyed the lectures and the demonstrations themselves, if not his audience. Most of the students these days seemed to be inattentive, lazy dolts. Products of the weakening moral fiber of society. He flipped the notebook closed. Fabians and Socialists. Corrupted by the likes of that bloody Irishman, George Bernard Shaw, or that effete poet, William Morris. He knew who they were. Let them study as much as they iked. He would see that they never passed the examining boards.

There was a soft knock at the door. "Come!" Gull sat at his desk.

An elderly *commissionnaire* came in. He touched his black cap and stood at attention. "Message for you, Sir William." He handed Gull a heavy white envelope. "The coachman says I should ask if there's a reply, sir."

Gull ignored him. He broke the red wax seal which was embossed with a compass and level insignia. The letter bore no date or salutation:

> A matter of great importance has come to my attention. We will meet tonight at nine. Be prepared for the Working of Invocation.

> S. 33°

The paper shook in his hands. From the Grand Inspector General. Not just a letter, a command.

"Very well, Maguire. Tell the coachman that no reply is necessary." He reached into his waistcoat and took out a coin. "This is for you . . ."

"Thank *you*, sir." Maguire touched his cap and turned smartly toward the door.

"Oh, Maguire . . . tell Matron Henley to come in, if you please."

Maguire found Martha Henley bent over a long, flat drawer of anatomical charts. He gave her bottom a pat. "Ah. You're a lovely one, you are. A man wouldn't need two mattresses with the likes of you."

Martha straightened up and slapped his hand. "Get away . . . you." She gave the old man a half smile and pushed her iron gray hair up under her nurses's cap. "You'll draw back a bloody stump one of these days, you will."

Maguire jerked his head toward the office. "Himself requires your presence in his Royal Chambers."

Martha retied the strings of her spotless white apron. "What kind of humor does he have?" She had been with Sir William for twenty-five years and was well aware of his erratic temper.

"Ah. The sun is shining on him this day." He flipped the coin in the air and caught it. "Lit up like a Guy Fawkes when he got that letter. Must have been from a sweet young thing like yourself, not a dried-up biddy like his lady wife."

Martha gave his arm a punch. "Get away, before I have the police on you for a common nuisance." She went to Sir William's door, knocked and entered.

Gull looked up from his notes. "Mrs. Henley. I . . . I've decided to give . . . a demonstration tomorrow, in place of my lecture."

Martha nodded. "Yessir."

"Are there . . . any new cases in the mortuary?"

"Well, sir. There's one came in two hours ago. Died in Reception. 'Death under suspicious circumstances.' A young woman. Mr. Ellis is to do the autopsy."

"What damage?"

"Blow to the head, I believe."

"Tell Mr. Ellis I'll do it myself. He can prepare the slides for the second-year practicum students."

"Very well, sir."

Gull waited until the door closed behind her, then took a brass key and unlocked the bottom drawer of his desk. He lifted out a heavy silver box and placed it on the desk, admiring the ornate symbol on its top. He laughed. The Grand Inspector General had decreed an invocation. He, William Gull, Grand Inquisitor Commander, Freemason of the Thirty-First Degree, would preside.

* * *

Sir William turned into the mews which backed on number 19 Cleveland Street. He went down the steps and unlocked the rear door, pushing it closed behind him with the heavy Gladstone bag he carried. He crossed the flagstone floor and walked down a long, dimly lit corridor.

The Grand Inspector General opened the door at his coded knock. He was a heavy man, his head bald to the crown, his beard full and graying. "Ah, William. Good to see you . . ." They exchanged the ritual handshake of the Brotherhood.

"Robert." Gull smiled. "Delighted to get your message. It's been a long time since . . ."

"Too long, perhaps. But do come in. Netley's gone to fetch Sickert, there will be only the four of us. We've time for a drink. I've an excellent single-malt my son sent down from Scotland."

The Robing Room was brightly lit by four gas jets. Along one wall a wooden rack held a dozen dark blue ceremonial robes, each embroidered with a silver symbol over the left breast. At the far end of the room a carved door led to the Inner Temple.

The two men sat in heavy Spanish-leather chairs by the small fireplace. The Grand Inspector took a sip of his whiskey. "Sorry to call you on such short notice. Were you able to . . . make preparations?"

"I was most fortunate." Gull opened the bag at his feet and took out the silver box. He passed it to the other man.

The Grand Inspector opened the box and looked in. "Excellent. We shall have a good invocation, I'm sure."

"Why an invocation now? It isn't the usual time."

The Grand Inspector leaned back in his chair and lit a cigar. "We have a problem that makes it necessary to consult the Master of the Lodge."

Gull sat up abruptly. "What matter is so important?"

The Grand Inspector blew a cloud of smoke at the ceiling. "The matter of Annie Crook and her daughter."

''Crook and the girl! That's been settled.''

''Not quite, my dear fellow. It seems some of Crook's . . . associates . . . led by Sickert's good friend, one Marie Kelly, have cobbled up a blackmail scheme. I've had Netley look into it. There are at least three, besides the Kelly woman. Netley has their names. They want the child, and a sum of money.''

Gull cursed under his breath. If it hadn't been for that soft-headed Prince Eddy, the mother and her royal bastard would have been properly taken care of. He looked at the Grand Inspector. ''It would be dangerous to repeat the Annie Crook solution.''

''You did a fine job there, William, but you're right. Fortunately we don't have to consider Prince Eddy's wishes this time. We shall know what is required after the invocation.''

''Who knows about this blackmail scheme?''

''General Warren, of course, but his duties lie elsewhere.'' The Grand Inspector smiled. ''Other than that, only Sickert and Netley.''

''Can we trust Netley?'' Gull asked.

''To a *degree*.'' Both men laughed. ''He is the Tyler of the Lodge and responsible for security. He's well paid for the work he does. For the present we need him. When this is over . . . Well, he's not really one of *us*, is he?''

''And Sickert? Even if he is initiated . . .''

The Grand Inspector studied the pale yellow whiskey in his glass. ''He had friends in high places. When this is done I think he will go into exile.'' He took a sip of his drink. ''He's motivated by fear and ambition. If his role in this scandal came out, if would be the end of his popularity as a painter among those who count. Besides he's been charged by the Prince to see to the little girl. He is rather fond of her.''

Gull gave an explosive laugh. ''Fond of her, yes. Overly fond, I'd say.''

''Whatever the Master wishes, William. You will be in

charge. General Warren and I will do all we can, but obviously we cannot be directly involved. There is too much at stake. I hardly need remind you that our hold over this government is tenuous. These are perilous times . . . riots and discontent. Socialists in the streets pandering to the rabble. In fifty or a hundred years we will have consolidated the power of the Brotherhood throughout the world. But this is a crucial time. The fall of the Monarchy would destroy our power in this country. This scandal could lead to a republic . . .''

"A republic . . ." Gull spat the word. "Surely the Queen could . . .''

The Grand Inspector frowned. "The *Queen*. That fat, senile doyenne." He got up and stood with his back to the fire. "The Queen is the chief of our problems. Shut up in Balmoral, communing with the ghosts of the Prince Consort and her paramour Brown. The Prince of Wales with his doxies is no better. Prince Eddy is our hope. He is, ah, malleable. His father's reign, when it comes, will be a short one. When dear Eddy inherits the throne, we shall control the Empire." He held up his glass. "We serve the Master of the Lodge."

Gull returned the salute. "The Master of the Lodge."

There was a knock at the door. The Grand Inspector moved quickly and drew the bolt. A short dark man in a coachman's cloak stood in the doorway. He wore thick-heeled boots which added an inch to his height. His hands were gnarled and abnormally large, as if made for a man twice his size.

"Mr. Sickert is here, milords," he announced.

"Thank you, Netley," the Grand Inspector said.

Walter Sickert entered the room. At twenty-eight he was much younger than the other men. His face was pale and thin and his fair hair was curly. He wore a long checked coat which hung nearly to his ankles. A red handkerchief was stuck in his breast pocket.

He touched his mustache with a shaking hand. ''Good evening, gentlemen.''

The Grand Inspector came forward and shook his hand. ''Ah, Walter. I believe we can start now.'' He turned to Netley. ''Tyler . . . Secure the Lodge.''

''Yessir.'' Netley left and closed the door behind him.

The three blue-cloaked men entered the Temple of the Inner Lodge in single file, their hoods shielding their faces. Each wore a small goatskin apron tied about his waist.

The room was large, its floor tiled with black-and-white squares. On each wall, three sets of seven-branched candelabra gave off a flickering, smoky light. At the far end of the room was an arched alcove in which sat a massive black wood throne on a dais. Ten feet in front of the throne stood two tall brass pillars engraved with a pattern of leaves and intertwined snakes. The pedestal of the right pillar bore the letter ''J,'' that of the left the letter ''B.''

Between the pillars was a long stone table with guttered edges. Leather straps hung from each corner. In the center of the table a brass brazier filled with hot coals gave off an intense heat.

The three men knelt. From under his cloak the Grand Inspector drew a leather-bound book. He opened it and in his resonant voice began to read the ancient Aramaic script.

Sir William Gull, Grand Inquisitor of the Lodge of Jahbulon, took the silver box from the hands of Walter Sickert. He rose and went to the table. Behind him came the chanting voices of the other two men.

Gull stopped and raised the box. In the alcove a faint coruscating blue light hovered over the throne. The room chilled. The air filled with a rank, rotting smell. Walter Sickert shivered and gasped for breath. The voice of the Grand Inspector rose as the ancient words echoed in the chamber.

Gull opened the box and took out the fresh, human heart.

As he dropped it into the fire, he was blinded by the red light which flashed from the throne.

The Grand Inspector leaned back in his chair and watched Sickert hang his robe on the rack. Sickert's face was pale and he mopped his brow with his red handkerchief.

"Pull yourself together, man. You're not a schoolboy. Have a bit of whiskey to steady your nerves." The Grand Inspector smiled at Gull, who sat opposite him. "Well done, William. A fine invocation. Our instructions are clear. You will be in charge and Sickert and Netley will help. We don't know who those silly sluts may have talked to. Make clear examples of them."

Sickert drained his glass and poured himself another. "Couldn't we . . . Wouldn't it be easier to *buy* them off? After all . . ."

The Grand Inspector flushed. "Mr. Sickert! You are under oath to the Master of the Lodge. You *will* follow instructions. Don't be a fool. Would you give them the girl as well?"

"I . . . No . . . Of course not. But what about her, the girl?"

"She is your ward. When this is finally settled you will be free to . . . educate her . . . as you will. If the job is not properly done, other arrangements will be made for her. Where is she now?"

Sickert looked at the floor. "I've sent her to the country. To relatives in Dorset. I shall do my part, naturally."

The Grand Inspector rose. "William, you will keep me informed. Call on General Warren for any help you may need, but be discreet. Now, I must go. I'm sure you gentlemen have plans to make. Netley will take me home."

John Netley flicked his whip, urging the horse to a faster pace. He smiled to himself. If only his old dad could see him now. Driving for gentlemen and even Royals. Made more in a day than the old man did in a month. Another year, maybe two, there'd be enough money. Buy a pair of new Hansom Patented Safety cabs. Hired drivers. He could put his feet up and count the money.

He whistled to his horse and slapped the reins as they passed the dark bulk of the Admiralty Building. The steel rims of the coach wheels echoed over the deserted cobbles of the Horse Guards Parade. He turned left, past the Foreign Office. Near the end of the street he halted and opened the coachman's trap. " 'Ere we are, sir."

Robert Arthur Cecil, Third Marquis of Salisbury, Grand Inspector General of the Lodge of Jahbulon, stepped down. He crossed the walk and went up the polished white steps.

The uniformed officer at the door saluted. "Good evening, Prime Minister."

The Grand Inspector nodded. "Good evening, Constable."

The door of Number 10 Downing Street closed behind him.

Robert James Lees sat up in his bed. He fumbled in the dark, then struck a light to the night candle. Beside him, his wife came awake.

"Robert? What is it?" She glanced at the carriage clock on her night table. "It's three in the morning . . ."

"Nothing, my dear. I . . . I had a dream." He swung from the bed and groped for his slippers. "Something came to my mind. I must go down to the library. Go back to sleep, my dear." There was no point in disturbing Laura. The dream had been vague but filled with menace. Again the mysterious word *Jahbulon* had come to him.

In the library he lit the oil lamp on his desk, then began to search through his wife's neatly indexed catalog of his books. It took him nearly an hour to find it. He placed the thick, leather-bound quarto volume on his desk and opened it to the title page.

Heresies of the Several Secret Orders
Being an Account of the Beliefs & Rituals of
The Inner Circles of Such Bodies
by
Fr. Gilberto Suarez, S.J. (c. 1632 A.D.)
Translated from the Portuguese
by
R. S. A. Lytell-March, M.A. Oxon.

He consulted the index, then turned to page 118 and began to read.

First among Dangerous Heretics are those Initiates of the Lodges of Jahbulon. These Lodges are an inner Working of that Society called Freemasons. The Workings of these Lodges are unknown to those Ordinary Members of Masonic Orders who are called Craft Masons and even to those initiates called Royal Arch Masons. The Lodges of Jahbulon are an Elect Society within a Society, given to the Secret Worship of Evil. The word Jahbulon derives from the Unholy Trinity: Jahweh—Baal—Osiris. The Chief of this Trinity being the Devil-god Baal. The Ceremonies which . . .

Robert Lees pulled a sheet of foolscap toward him. He wrote the date, 31 August 1888. He began to make notes.

Polly Nicholls stumbled up the steps of # 56 Flower & Dean Street. She pushed her way through the door with its broken mortise lock and went down the long hall toward the community kitchen. The air was thick with the smell of boiled cabbage, bloaters, and stale urine. From the floors above came the night noises of the common lodging house, where men and women slept two and three to a bed.

She steadied herself against the wall, then entered the communal kitchen. A low fire burned in the hearth and the room was lit by a single gas jet. Ragged clothes hung on ropes stretched from wall to wall. At the far end of the room, beneath a sign which read "No Washing on Sundays," a fat man with a gray-stubbled face drank ale from a bottle. Billy Eames, the lodging house deputy, looked up as Polly came in. "Eh, Polly. Wotcher want?"

She held on to the back of a chair. "Billy . . . I needs a place to doss. My legs is weak."

Billy cleared his throat and spat on the floor. " 'Ad your nose in the gin, you has."

Polly blinked against the smoke. "Ah, Billy. I could lie down forever . . . I need a doss, Bill."

"You got fourpence, Polly? Fourpence to share, eightpence if you wants a bed to yerself."

She shook her head. "Bill, I'm falling off my feet. I've not tuppence. But . . . I've money coming. Ten quid, I'll have this week. For sure, Bill . . ."

Bill glared at her. Ten quid! Not likely. Bloody whores. Slopping booze and begging for pity. "You 'ad the price, didn't you? Made it twice over up against the wall, I'll wager." His face flushed. "Down your throat, it went. Well, this isn't an almshouse. I don't play no favorites here. Worth my job, it is. Get on down to High Street and find some gent what'll give you sixpence for what you've got."

Polly straightened up and looked at him slyly. "What about you, Bill?" She raised her skirts above her laddered stockings.

Bill stood up, knocking over his bottle of ale. "Get out! You bloody cow!"

Crying, Polly fled down the dark corridor.

The black coach turned from Brick Lane into Flower & Dean Street. Sir William Gull stretched his cramped legs and held up a paper parcel. "Have some grapes, my dear Sickert. Excellent for the liver."

Walter Sickert hunched in the seat opposite. "No, thanks. I have no appetite."

Gull laughed. "Bit of nerves, eh? Like shootin' grouse, one must have patience. These women are night birds. Have to catch them on the wing. Our good Netley knows where the coveys are."

Sickert said nothing. They'd been patrolling the streets for hours. He closed his eyes and thought of little Maggie. When this was over he'd take her away. Far away.

The coach jolted to a halt and the driver's trap opened. "I see one of them, sir. It's Polly Nicholls for sure." Netley's voice was low.

Gull patted the leather bag by his side. "Excellent. Drive past her and stop at the next cross street." As the coach started up he turned to Sickert. "You, my dear fellow, shall act the bird-dog. Fetch her to us. I'm sure a man of your charm will not find it difficult."

The night air had cleared Polly's head, and her steps steadied as she walked toward Whitechapel High Street. Ahead, she noticed a man in a long checked coat standing under the streetlamp. She smiled. Perhaps she wouldn't have to go so far. He appeared to be a young man, and what she could see of his face under his cap seemed vaguely familiar. As she approached he stepped into her path.

"Uh. Good evening, miss."

Polly smiled. "Looking for a friend, are you?" She could tell from his nervousness that he wasn't used to picking up women on the street.

"Uh. Yes, I am . . ." He stepped into the shadows.

Polly touched his arm. An easy one, this one would be. A gent, from his voice. Good for six shillings at least. She looked up at him. "Like a bit of fun, would you?"

"Well, yes. I . . ."

She could feel his arm tremble. A Nervous Nellie. Probably come off before he had it out of his trousers. "Six shillings, then," she said. Get the money first. Couldn't trust a man even if he did look like a gentleman.

"Six shillings?" The man looked puzzled. "Oh. Yes. I see . . ." He fumbled in his pocket and pulled out a wadded note.

Polly looked at it under the light. A pound. A whole bloody pound! This was her lucky night. She stuck the note into her pocket and waited to see if he asked for change.

"Come on, then." She took his arm.

He pulled back. "Come . . . Where?"

The simpleton. What did he expect? A four-poster bed? Probably didn't know that you could do it as well standing against a wall. She gave him a professional smile. "There's a lane over there, no one to see, love."

He hesitated, then seemed to make up his mind. He took her firmly by the arm. "I've a carriage. Just down the road. It'll be . . . more comfortable."

He led her to the black coach. The driver sat silent and hunched on the box, the collar of his cloak pulled up around his ears, his hat tipped over his eyes.

Sickert opened the door and handed her up. "Just like a lady," she thought.

Sir William Gull pulled her forward and clapped the chloroformed cloth over her face. The coach creaked on its springs, then was still. He tapped twice on the ceiling with his gold-headed stick. Netley's voice floated down from the trap. "Sir?"

"Cleveland Street. The mews. And be quick about it."

Gull wrapped his instruments in a chamois cloth and closed the bag. He looked across the Robing Room at Sickert, who sat slumped in a chair, his head in his hands.

"Act the man, Sickert." Gull poured himself a whiskey

and smacked his lips in appreciation. "That went well. The Master was pleased. Only sorry that the woman couldn't tell us where Marie Kelly is . . . She's at the root of this. Once we've dealt with her, the matter will be finished."

He walked to the door and touched the canvas-wrapped bundle with his foot. "You and Netley get rid of this . . . thing."

Sickert raised his head. "What shall we do?"

Gull looked at him in disgust. "Do? Dump it in the Thames. No, wait. Dispose of it in Whitechapel. Some dark lane." He smiled. "Just be sure you're not seen."

The coach clattered down the narrow confines of Buck's Row, and past Barber's slaughterhouse. The air reeked of blood and offal from the knacker's yard. Red-eyed rats scuttled in the gutters.

Netley halted and jumped down from the box. " 'Ere's a good place, sir. Be quick."

He grunted as Sickert shoved the bundle out and slammed the coach door shut. Netley dragged the corpse to the walkway and unrolled the tarp. He glanced at the coach, then bent and took the crumpled pound note from Polly Nicholls' pocket.

Chief Inspector Frederick G. Abberline hung his bowler on a wooden peg and looked around his office. The small room in Scotland Yard was cluttered with boxes of papers and his desk was buried under a mountain of red-taped files.

He was a tall man with the square, flushed face of his Saxon ancestors. He touched his pocket to be sure that his daily ration of four cigars was in place, then pushed aside a stack of papers on his desk. Next week he'd get organized, if only for appearance's sake. He patted his ample stomach. But, then, thirty-two years of struggling up through the ranks gave a man some privilege. Two more years and he'd have enough put by to retire to a cottage in Bournemouth. Sit back with a pint and watch his beloved roses grow. A sense of sadness swept over him. It wouldn't be the same without Cynthia. Since his wife had died, life had lost its savour. "Soup without salt," he muttered. "Soup without salt."

The door opened and Sergeant Hughes came in, carrying a mug of tea in one hand and a file of reports in the other. The buttons of his uniform gleamed and his boots were spit-polished. He looked at Inspector Abberline's desk and frowned. "Here you are, sir." He put the mug on the only open space available.

Abberline took a sip of the sweet, black, police-issue tea. "And what's on the docket today, Sergeant?"

Hughes looked for a place to put the files, then handed them to the Chief Inspector. "The usual, sir. A smash-and-grab in Aldgate Street. Threat-and-menace to a shopkeeper in Edgeware Road, thought to be by one of the Gallowglass gang . . . And a report from Inspector Spratling of J Division on a woman killed in Whitechapel."

"All right, Sergeant. I'll look them over and make the assignments. That's all, then."

"Sir!" Hughes wheeled in a smart about-turn.

He pulled the folders toward him and glanced at the murder report. "Mary Ann (Polly) Nicholls," it read. He sighed and lit one of his cigars. "The usual," as Hughes said. Last year. What was it? In the Home counties alone. Seventy-six homicides including infants. Women . . . beaten, crushed, stabbed, stomped, eviscerated, doused with acid. He tapped his cigar against the desk. Out of that they'd gotten eight convictions. He looked out the window. Soon he'd be out of it. The clean, fresh air of Bournemouth. Smell the roses and to hell with the bloody C.I.D. He began to read.

P.C. 97J Neil reports that at 3:45 A.M., 31st inst. (August), he found the dead body of a woman lying on her back with her clothes a little above her knees, with her throat cut from ear to ear on a yard crossing at Buck's Row, Whitechapel. P.C. obtained the assistance of P.C.s 55H Mizen and 96J Thain. The latter called Dr. Llewellyn, No. 152 Whitechapel Road. He arrived quickly and pronounced life to be extinct. He directed her removal to the Mortuary, stating he would make a further examination there.

Upon my arrival and taking a description I found that she had been disemboweled, and at once sent to inform the doctor of it. He arrived quickly and on further examination stated that her throat had been cut from left to right. Two distinct cuts being on the left side. The windpipe, gullet, and spinal cord being cut through. The abdomen had been cut open from the center of the bottom of the ribs on the right side, under the pelvis to the left of the stomach . . .

Abberline laid Spratling's report on the desk. Another case. One of hundreds. Done in by a lover or her pimp. He pushed the folder aside. Yet there was something disturbing about this particular case. The mutilation. Parts of the body gone missing. The absence of blood at the scene. He looked again at the report. Considering the nature of the woman's wounds the site should have looked like an abattoir. He took the copy of the assignment sheet Hughes had brought. Twenty years as a detective had taught him the value of his intuition. There was something odd here. He put the file aside. This case he'd look into himself.

The three women sat at the table at the rear of Ringer's. Marie's shawl was pulled over her head, shadowing her face. "It was them that did it. Those men from Cleveland Street."

"Don't be daft, Marie," Long Liz said. "They're gents. They wouldn't dirty their hands with that sort of work. More like it was one of that lot . . ." She nodded at a pair of pimps drinking rum at the table behind them. "Them with their razors . . ."

The women were silent. Violent death was no stranger to them.

Dark Annie leaned forward. "Cut her up in bits, I heard. Mrs. Martin in Thrawl Street knows a man what saw poor Polly 'fore they took her away. He said . . ."

Marie clenched her fists. "Shut your gob, Annie. I don't want to hear it."

"Ah. Marie. I was only . . ."

Long Liz interrupted. "Look. It's a terrible thing about Polly. But naught to do with us. We've other business to take care of. Netley was supposed to leave a message with Mrs. Ringer. It's been ten days now . . ."

Marie rocked back and forth in her chair, her eyes hidden. "It's me they're after." Her voice broke. "I don't know where little Maggie is. My money's gone and M'Carthy's after me for rent."

"Don't worry, Marie. They're putting us off. We'll build a bit of a fire under them. Annie and I will see Netley. Tell him to get a move on or it's off to Fleet Street with the whole story."

"I don't trust him, that Netley. Creepy little bugger," Dark Annie said.

Long Liz laughed. "He's not big enough to hurt anyone. Step on him like a roach, I will. He'll be busy in Cleveland Street tonight. Bringing those Mary-Anns to visit their little boyfriends. Annie and I will go there tonight. Give him the bloody 'or else.' Marie stays out of this." She turned to Dark Annie. "We'll meet at the chandler's shop in Dorset Street at nine."

Dark Annie stood in the darkened doorway of the chandler's shop. The shop had closed at eleven, and still no sign of Long Liz. Annie shifted her weight to ease her feet. Liz had forgotten, or more likely was so sotted she couldn't walk. Annie pulled the shawl around her shoulders and started toward Ringer's. She hadn't enough money for a drink or a doss and had hoped to get some from Liz. "Bloody hell!" she muttered. Have to find a customer before the night was out.

She saw a woman staggering toward her. As she passed under the streetlamp the woman cried out, "Annie . . . Annie . . ." Long Liz lurched against the bricks of a building and held out her arm.

"Ah. For God's sake, Liz. Where have you been?"

Liz pulled a bottle of opium cordial from her pocket. "Havin' a bit of fun, love. Take some of this . . . do you wonders." The bottle with its half inch of liquid slipped from her hand and shattered on the walk. Liz giggled. "Oh, dear . . . Never fear . . . We'll all soon find sweet Heaven's cheer . . ." she crooned.

"Come off it, Liz." Annie shoved her away. The tall woman backed against a shop front and slid to the ground. Her head slumped forward. Dark Annie knelt beside her. Liz let out a drugged snore.

"Ah, Christ!" Annie looked up and down the street, then quickly went through Liz's pockets. Not tuppence. The slut had drunk it up. She stood. There was money to be had. Netley. She could get some from him. An advance. Without Liz there, who was to know? She turned and walked away, heading for Cleveland Street.

Dark Annie stood across the street, in front of the tobacco shop where Annie Elizabeth Crook and Marie Kelly had once worked. She watched as John Netley's silk-hatted passengers dismounted and went into number 19.

She crossed the street. "You. Netley!"

The little man looked down from the box. "What you want, you?"

"You know what I want, you windfucker. You had a letter ten days ago about the baby and the . . ."

Netley dropped his whip and jumped from the carriage. He grabbed Annie and slammed her against the coach. "Shut your bloody face, you!" He raised his fist, then glanced down the street. Too many people about.

Annie pushed at his chest. "Where's the money? Why hasn't we heard?"

Netley smiled, showing yellowed teeth. "Ah . . . the principals in the matter . . . Takes time, this sort of thing does . . ."

"It won't take no time for us to go to the papers."

Netley released his hold on her. "Well. Might be I could take you to one of the gents involved. It ain't far." He reached to open the coach door.

Annie pushed him again. "I'm not going anyplace with you. We wants the money."

Netley smiled again. "I'll see what I can do. Tomorrow night by the Rose & Crown in Whitechapel Street. You and your friends, eh? I'll bring part of the money, fifty quid . . ."

"What about the baby?"

"Ah, the man who has her will want reassurances, like. From your friend Marie. Then he'll give over the baby and the rest of the money."

Fifty pounds! Dark Annie thought. God! A bloody fortune. "All right. But be there. Nothing funny or you'll read about it in the papers." She hesitated. "How about a bit in advance? For me trouble."

Netley reached in his pocket. "Where is Marie Kelly living?"

"None of your business."

He took out a half crown and flipped it in the air, catching it on the back of his hand.

Annie licked her lips. "Ah, I don't know. Not really. She's got a room from a man named M'Carthy, that's all I know."

"Tomorrow night, then. Eleven o'clock." Netley dropped the coin into the gutter at her feet and turned away. He smiled to himself. They'd meet the "principals," all right. Finish the job all at once.

Annie picked up the coin and walked away. Fifty quid. She fingered the half crown in her pocket. With that much money she could get away from this filthy city. Liverpool, maybe. Live like the Queen. She turned into a pub, holding Netley's coin in her fist. Have a drink and think it out. There was no reason the others had to know. Long Liz was sleeping it off and Marie was in hiding. So much the better.

Robert Lees pushed away the remains of his breakfast. He felt a sense of apprehension which spoiled his appetite. He had not slept well, disturbed by a series of dreams which he could not remember. He poured a third cup of tea and began to read the *Times*. An item in the lower left corner of page three caught his attention.

WHITECHAPEL MURDER
BRUTAL SLAYING OF WOMAN IN BUCK'S ROW

His heart pounded and he lowered the paper. He tried to remember his dream of last night, but the images evaded him. He read on. The article gave few details, but implied that the murder was a particularly grisly one. Police were seeking witnesses.

Laura came into the room. She looked at his half-eaten breakfast. "Are you not feeling well, Robert?"

He smiled at her. "I'm all right, my dear. I didn't sleep well last night."

She touched his shoulder. "I know. You were up all hours."

He turned sharply. "What do you mean?"

"I woke at four o'clock and you were gone. I came down-stairs and there you were, scribbling away. You were so intent that I didn't want to startle you."

Lees stood up, almost knocking over his chair. He went to the library. On his desk were three sheets of foolscap covered with his neat, copperplate handwriting.

Laura watched from the doorway as he sat down and read them.

Two men in a room lighted by candles. The room is beneath a house in which many men come and go. Both men are cloaked and hooded. Before them is a stone table to which a woman is bound. The shorter man has a silver knife. He cuts the woman and plunges his hand into her.

The two men are in a black coach. The taller one is wearing a long checked coat with a red handkerchief in the breast pocket. They take the body of the woman from the coach. She is dressed in a black jacket and a black skirt. There are great wounds on her body, and her throat has been cut. There are many boxes and crates nearby. The number "29" is prominent.

Laura looked at her husband sitting stiff and pale at his desk. "What is it, Robert?" She came toward him.

Robert Lees folded the notes and put them in his pocket. He rose. "I must go out, Laura."

"Where? Are you certain you're not ill?"

"I'm perfectly well. But I must see someone at Scotland Yard."

Chief Inspector Abberline looked regretfully at the last inch of his cigar. He stubbed it in a saucer as Sergeant Hughes came in.

"There's a gentleman, a Mr. Lees to see you, sir." He gave Abberline a card. "Says it's about the Whitechapel murder. Insists on seeing the officer-in-charge."

Abberline caught the emphasis on "gentleman." A "man" who insisted on seeing the Chief Inspector would have been summarily dealt with. He looked at the engraved card. "Mr. Robert James Lees. Christian Spiritualist Center, Peckham." He recognized the name.

"Send him in, Sergeant."

Abberline rose as Lees came in. "Do sit down, Mr. Lees. The sergeant told me you might have some information."

Lees sat on the edge of the chair. "Perhaps . . . This is a difficult matter for me to explain, Inspector. You see, I am very much involved in spiritualist matters . . ."

Abberline nodded. "Yes, Mr. Lees, I'm aware of that. My late wife attended several of your public lectures. She enjoyed your books . . ." Abberline did not say that he was also aware of the rumor that Lees enjoyed Her Majesty's Grace and Favor in spiritualist matters.

Lees sat back in his chair. "This may sound strange, sir. But I had a dream which I believe may relate to the recent Whitechapel murder."

Abberline studied the man. A dream. What he needed was a witness. But no harm in listening to the man. At least he *seemed* normal. He recalled the multiple murders in Blackpool which had been solved by information from a psychic reader. He pulled a notepad toward him. "Do tell me about it, Mr. Lees."

Sergeant Hughes came in with another cup of issue tea. "Did the gentleman have anything useful to offer, sir?"

Abberline thrust his notes into the ziggurat of papers by his elbow. "Afraid not, Sergeant. Seems he had a strange dream, but what he saw didn't related to the facts of our Whitechapel case. The gory bit was similar, but his description of the woman and the scene where the body was found didn't fit at all.''

"A dream, sir?"

"Yes, indeed." Abberline smiled. "Probably caused by too much claret and bad beef."

Sergeant Hughes handed him a memorandum and pointed his finger toward the ceiling. "From on high, sir. The Commissioner. Seems he's taking an interest in us."

"That's either good news or bad news, Sergeant." He unfolded the note.

"Be advised that as of this date, you will submit to me personally, daily investigation reports on the Whitechapel murders.''

Abberline noticed the last word. Murders? A misspelling. There was only one Whitechapel murder. The note was signed "Sir Charles Warren, Metropolitan Police Commissioner." He frowned. Major General Sir Charles Warren was no friend of the C.I.D. In his Annual Police Report of 1887 he had not even mentioned the existence of the detective division.

Laura Lees met her husband at the door as he returned from his afternoon walk.

"Robert, there are two gentlemen to see you. From the police. They wouldn't tell me what it's about."

Abberline and Hughes stood up as Lees came into the library. "Good day, gentlemen. Please sit down. How can I help you?" Lees took a chair facing the two officers. "May I offer you sherry?"

"No, thank you, Mr. Lees. This is official business." Abberline glanced at Hughes, who opened his notebook.

"Ah. Was the dream I told you of some use?"

Abberline rested his hands on his knees. "Can you give me an account of your whereabouts last evening, Mr. Lees?"

"My whereabouts? I'm not sure I take your meaning, Inspector."

"Mr. Lees . . . A woman fitting the description you gave was murdered last night in Hanbury Street. Number twenty-nine, to be exact. The yard of a box factory. Your 'dream' was very explicit."

Lees paled. "I see. And you suspect I did it?"

Abberline's face was impassive. "Just a routine inquiry, Mr. Lees."

"I was here all evening. Our regular meeting lasted until almost midnight. After that I was with Lord Hallowell, the chairman of our finance committee, going over expenditures. Hallowell left about two A.M., and I went straight up to bed."

"Your movements can be verified, then."

"Of course, Inspector . . . I understand your difficulty. But I am no stranger to psychic experiences, as you know. This murder. Is it connected to the other one?"

Abberline hesitated. "Almost certainly. The nature of the mutilation . . ."

Lees lowered his voice. "I *know* these cases are connected. Not of course in any way I can prove. There are forces at work here . . . Some great evil which is a threat to our nation . . ."

"Mr. Lees . . . These two women were common prostitutes. I hardly . . ."

"Do you know the word 'Jahbulon,' Inspector?"

Abberline looked at Hughes. "No, I do not."

"It refers to a secret society within the Order of Freemasons . . . Given to the worship of the devil-god Baal."

"Freemasons?" Abberline was startled. He was one of the few ranking police officers who was not a Mason. General Warren himself was known to be a high-ranking member of that organization. Indeed, there was a room in Scotland Yard which was reserved for the use of Masonic officers.

"Mr. Abberline, what possible connection could there be between the Royal Family and these killings?"

Abberline stared at him. First the Masons, now the Royal Family. If the man weren't so obviously sincere, he'd think him out of his senses. "None at all, I'm sure."

"There is, Inspector. I'm not certain what the connection is, but assuredly there is one."

"Yes. Well, Mr. Lees, if you have any more 'dreams,' or any information whatsoever, please contact me personally." He handed Lees his card. "It might be better if you reached me at home, rather than at the Yard."

Lees watched through the window as the two men crossed the garden. He sat down at his desk and began a letter to his good friend Colonel Hamilton, the Queen's Equerry, at Balmoral Castle.

At the garden gate Abberline paused. "What do you think, Sergeant?"

"I think he's daft. Ought to be in Bedlam."

"Perhaps. In any case, check with Lord Hallowell and verify his presence here last night. And Sergeant . . ."

"Sir?"

"I think we will not mention our visit to Mr. Lees in the daily report to General Warren."

As their cab clattered into the cobbled court known as Scotland Yard, they saw a crowd of reporters gathered on the steps of the building. Fleet Street was about to create the man known as "Jack the Ripper."

Three men sat at the polished oak table in a small room in the rear of 10 Downing Street. The Prime Minister filled his glass and pushed the decanter of port to Sir William Gull. "Gentlemen, this matter must be brought to a close quickly. The penny-dreadful press is fostering panic with this Jack the Ripper nonsense. I am informed that the Queen herself has taken an interest in the case."

Police Commissioner General Warren cleared his throat. "The Queen? I say, why should the Queen be concerned with a pair of dead whores?"

"I don't know. But I mean to find out. In any case we must carry on with the plan."

"The Kelly woman's the crux of the matter," Sir William said. "With her out of the way . . ."

"What success have you had, so far?" the Prime Minister asked.

"None, so far. Netley and Sickert are searching for her this minute . . . And the other one as well."

General Warren interrupted. "I've put out a discreet word to our Brethren in the police. If Kelly's seen or arrested I shall get notice immediately."

The Prime Minister rested his blunt hands on the table. "What about this fellow of yours . . . Abberline? Is he one of us?"

General Warren smiled. "Not our sort. Up from the ranks. A plodder . . . good enough in his way, but serving time until he retires. I have him reporting directly to me."

Sir William looked at the Prime Minister. "This fellow Netley. He's not trustworthy. When this is done . . ."

Robert Arthur Cecil, Marquis of Salisbury, Prime Minister of the United Kingdom, Grand Inspector General of the Lodge of Jahbulon, held up his hand. "My dear William, I'll leave that matter to you. We must put the spurs in and finish this matter quickly."

Dorset Street was nearly deserted. The gory murders detailed in the illustrated penny press had produced a Ripper panic among the people of Whitechapel. The few women on the streets traveled in twos or threes, or were guarded by their razor-toting pimps.

Long Liz hurried up the street, glancing at the darkened doorways. She turned into the narrow confines of Miller's

Court. She did not see the man in the long checked coat step from the doorway halfway up the street. Walter Sickert quickened his step to follow her.

Liz stopped and tapped softly at the door of number 13. "Marie . . . Marie . . . It's me, Liz." There was no response. She went to the window at the side. It was covered with a dirty cloth curtain. Two of the panes in the lower part of the window had been smashed out. She pushed back the curtain and looked in. A small deal table was pushed against the door. In the light of the single candle she saw Marie Kelly crouched against the far wall.

"Marie . . . It's me. Let me in . . ."

There was a scraping sound as Marie pulled the table from the door and drew the iron bolt. "Liz. Come in quickly." She slammed the door behind her and shot the bolt.

The room was a twelve-by-twelve square. Against the right wall was a low wooden bed piled with a heap of tattered bedclothes. In the far corner, an open cupboard contained broken crockery, a half-dozen empty bottles, and a dried end of bread. Opposite the door, the small, soot-blackened hearth was cold. Above the hearth hung a cheap print, entitled *The Fisherman's Widow*.

"God! Like a bloody coffin, this is."

Marie pulled her shawl tight around her shoulders. "Don't say that! Sure, I'll be in my grave soon enough if I'm found. Liz . . . What'll I do? I'm out of money. Two days it is since Annie was killed and I haven't been out of this room. M'Carthy's after me for the rent, and I've nothing to eat but a crust of bread, and that hard as the stones of Connaught."

Liz put a canvas bag on the table. "Cheer up, Marie. It's your imagination what's doing you in. Just bad luck that the Ripper got Polly and Annie. He's a lunatic. Could have been anybody."

She reached into the bag and pulled out a bottle of gin, a small loaf, and a hard round of cheese. "A bit to eat is what you need. But first . . ." She went to the cupboard and took down two cracked teacups. She pulled a bottle of cordial from her pocket and poured an inch into each cup, then filled it with gin. "Drink this. Make you right as rain. Don't you worry, old Liz will take care of you. I'll find that Netley and make him give over. Tries it on with me and he'll get a knee in his coalsack."

The gin and opium mixture hit Marie like a hammer. A warm lethargy spread through her body. She took another sip.

Long Liz smiled at her. "Puts the world right, doesn't it? I'll see Netley tomorrow, then come back here. I'll knock like this so you'll know it's me." She rapped twice on the table, then three times.

Marie steadied herself with one hand. "I'm afraid, Liz. Will you stay the night with me?"

"Of course I will, love. Now, have a bite . . ."

Walter Sickert leaned against the brick wall outside number 13. The voices which had come through the broken window had long stopped. He waited, staring into the blackness, thinking of Marie and little Maggie. He reached through the broken window and cautiously pushed aside the curtain. The two women slept side-by-side. In the dim light Marie's face was serene. There was a half smile on her lips. His artist's eye caught the look of innocence. Perhaps if they had stayed in France . . . She had been kind and loving to little Maggie. He let the curtain drop.

The late afternoon sun was bright and the yellow-brown cloud of coal smoke which hung over London had blown away on the westerly August wind.

Robert and Laura Lees sat on the open upper deck of the omnibus as it clattered down Edgeware Road. Robert balanced the wicker picnic basket on his lap. Their Sunday outing to Regent's Park had been a success. Now he leaned back in his seat, feeling slightly drowsy from the wine he had consumed at lunch.

At the Marylebone stop, a heavy-set man came up the stairs and made his way to a seat at the front. Lees felt a sudden shock. A cold *frisson* seized him.

"What is it, Robert?" Laura looked at him with concern. Since those policemen had come to the house he had seemed so preoccupied.

He patted her hand. "Nothing, my dear. That man . . . For a moment I thought I knew him." He stared at the back of the man's head.

Ten minutes later the 'bus halted at the Marble Arch stop. The man rose and came down the aisle toward them. Their eyes met. Robert paled. *That's him.* The man stopped short, and gave Robert a look of hatred. He pulled his hat down over his eyes and moved on. *He knows that I know.* Robert gave the basket to Laura as the man pushed through the passengers coming up the stairs.

"Laura! That's the man in my dream. One of the men in the blue cloaks. He's the Ripper!"

"Robert! Where are you going?"

"I've got to follow him. You go home, Laura . . ." He brushed through the startled passengers. From the top of the steps he saw the man turn left into the crowds of Oxford Street.

Lees followed. He was certain that this was the man in his dream, the one who had plunged his hands into the woman. He had spent hours meditating on the image. There was no question about it. It was him, the man with the uncanny resemblance to Bonaparte. Lees kept his distance as the man weaved through the crowds. That look . . . Somehow the man knew he had been recognized for what he was.

Abruptly, the man crossed Oxford and hurried down Regent Street to Piccadilly. Lees wondered what to do. If only Abberline were here. A police constable came toward him, swinging his stick. He was tempted to stop the officer and tell him that the man ahead was Jack the Ripper. But what could he say? "I saw him in a dream"? He hurried on, catching a glimpse of the heavy, black-coated figure turning into Berkeley Street. The man was directly ahead, not more than twenty feet. He stopped suddenly and looked in a shop window.

It was the wrong man. This man had a mustache. Lees leaned against a lamppost and searched the street. No sign of his quarry. Yet he knew he was right, the man had come this way. He took a deep breath and forced his body to relax. Follow the psychic spoor. The man was somewhere ahead.

He crossed Berkeley Square, then paused, uncertain. He closed his eyes for a moment, feeling for the vibrations, then hurried toward Grosvenor Square. He stopped and surveyed the people milling about. At the top of the square he caught a glimpse of a man in a black coat. This time he was certain. He began to run.

The man in black turned and disappeared into the side street. Lees sprinted after him. Halfway down the narrow street he saw him.

The man went up the stairs and let himself in with a latchkey. Lees stopped and caught his breath, then walked slowly toward the house at 74 Brook Street. He looked up at the fashionable brick facade with its graceful Palladian windows. To the right of the fanlighted door was a small brass plaque:

William W. Gull, Bt., M.D., F.R.C.P.

Lees steadied himself against the wrought-iron railing. Unbelievable. He knew Gull by reputation. Everyone did. The man who was credited with saving the life of the Prince of Wales. One of the Queen's personal physicians.

He walked on. Perhaps he was wrong. Perhaps his psychic

powers had failed him. But he knew otherwise. Whatever Gull was in the eyes of society, he was a vicious killer.

Robert Lees reached into the inner pocket of his waistcoat and took out a card. "Frederick G. Abberline, 52 Hans Crescent." He stepped into the street and flagged a cab.

Chief Inspector Abberline knocked the dottle from his pipe and looked at the notes he had made. Unlike his office, the room was spare and neat. Starched antimacassars graced the overstuffed chairs, and the wooden sideboard gleamed with polish.

"It's a serious charge, Mr. Lees. A man like that . . ."

"Do you believe me, Inspector?"

Abberline paused and refilled his pipe. "That's not the point, is it? What I believe is of no matter. There's no evidence. Nothing one could take to a jury."

Lees sighed. "I know, Inspector. But there will be more violence unless this man and whoever is with him are stopped. Something must be done." Lees thought about mentioning his letter to Colonel Hamilton at Balmoral, then decided against it. Abberline might think he was being accused of not doing his job.

"I'll do what I can, Mr. Lees. If anything more comes up . . . Whatever its source, let me know immediately. Perhaps it would be better if you call on me here, at home. Not at Scotland Yard."

"Why is that, Inspector?"

Abberline smiled. "There is something peculiar about this case. While not as vivid as yours, I, too, have my intuitions."

Sir William Gull paced the floor of the Robing Room. He pulled a heavy gold watch from his waistcoat and snapped it open. Eleven P.M. Bloody Netley! Should be back by now. It was Sickert's idea to have Netley drop him off in Whitechael, then return for Gull to make his nightly foray. Have a etter chance of finding Marie Kelly on his own, the man aid. Leave Gull and Netley to look for Long Liz.

Gull read again the unsigned note from General Warren. "Kelly is in custody at Bishopsgate Police Station. She will be released shortly after midnight."

Kelly. The source of their problems. Gull crumpled the note and threw it in the fire. She would pay, the filthy slut. The door opened and Netley burst in, a grin on his wrinkled monkey's face. "I've got her, sir . . ."

"Where have you been, you fool? What do you mean, you've got her?"

Netley's grin faded. "Long Liz, sir. Found her in the street after I let Mr. Sickert off. Sotted with the drink, she was."

Gull moved toward him and Netley backed up. "Got her? Where?"

"In the coach."

"You left her out there, you idiot?"

Netley lowered her voice. He held up half a vial of laudanum. "Poured this in her. What with the load she had, she won't come round for a day."

Gull hesitated, then picked up his bag. "Put that tarp in the coach. Be sure the seats are covered. We'll take care of this one on the way."

"Where to, sir?"

"Bishopsgate Police Station. They've got the Kelly woman and they're going to release her anytime." Gull laughed. This would be a most enjoyable evening.

The coach stopped fifty yards from the lights of the Police Station. Gull dismounted and looked at his watch. Almost one o'clock. There was still time. "You stay here, Netley. The woman knows you. When she comes out, I'll follow her. You stop the coach ahead of us and leave the door open. When I have her, drive on. I'll do the rest." Gull moved up the street and stood in a darkened doorway where he could observe the station.

Ten minutes later the woman came out. She pulled the shawl over her bonnet and went down the street, weaving slightly. Gull followed, walking softly. The coach passed them and stopped. Netley opened the door, then climbed back on the box. He pulled his collar up, hiding his face.

As the woman approached the rear of the coach, Gull moved closer. "Missus Kelly . . ."

The woman turned and looked at him. A well-dressed gent. Probably one of the plainclothes rozzers from the station. "Wotcher want?"

"Just this . . ." Gull smiled and stepped closer. The silver knife flashed. The woman doubled over with a grunt. Gull caught her and shoved her into the coach, slamming the door behind them. He pushed her against the cushions. His face was hot and flushed. He felt the ecstasy come as he raised the knife. "Bitch . . . Filthy bitch . . ."

Gull slumped back against the seat. He relaxed, feeling a warm lethargy. He stroked the silver box at his side and looked at the inert figure on the seat opposite. It was a good night's work.

He tapped on the roof of the coach. The trap opened. "Where are we?"

"Mitre Square," Netley replied.

Mitre Square. How appropriate. *The Mitre and the Square.* The most important of all Lodge symbols. "Find a likely spot, Netley."

A job well done. Two of them in one night. It was his triumph, his accomplishment. He would make it a monument to his genius. He felt in his pocket for the piece of chalk he had carried away from today's lecture. The Master would be pleased.

Netley stopped by the deserted entrance to the Goldstone

Buildings. There was no one in sight. Gull opened the coach door and stopped under the brick archway. "Drag it in here, out of sight." He began to write on the wall.

Netley grabbed the woman under the arms and pulled her out. In the faint light of the coach lamp he saw her face.

"This ain't Marie Kelly!"

Gull turned. "What do you mean?"

"It's not *her* . . . This is the Eddowes woman. I knows her." He dropped the body in the entrance.

Gull grabbed Netley by the coat. His face flushed with rage. "It's Kelly! It is!"

Netley struggled free. "Not so loud, sir. It's not *that* Kelly. This one . . . Her old man is Kelly. She sometimes goes by that name."

Gull turned abruptly. "Get us out of here."

Netley stood by the door of the Robing Room. He shifted his feet uneasily and watched Gull. The man sat hunched forward in his chair, fingering the silver box, his lips moving in an inaudible litany. Going round the bend, Netley thought. Him and his little knife. Be after me next. Netley felt no qualms about the killings. It was like putting down a diseased dog. No loss to the world. But this man . . . Gets off on the slashing. Enjoys it.

Netley cleared his throat. "Will you need me, sir?"

"Need you? Ah." He looked at Netley as if he'd never seen him before. He got up and began to pace back and forth, holding the box before him. "Must find the Kelly woman before it's too late. We haven't a clue. If you and Sickert were doing your job properly . . ."

Netley stared at the floor. "I done my best, didn't I? I was the one what found out about M'Carthy . . ." And not so much as a bloody thank-you from either of them.

Gull stopped. "M'Carthy? Who's he?"

"The man what rents a room to Kelly."

"Rents her a room! Why didn't you tell me?"

Netley gave him a sullen look. "I told Mr. Sickert. He said he'd take care of it."

"Did he? Where is this M'Carthy?"

"I don't know. Whitechapel's full of Paddys and half of 'em is named M'Carthy."

"So. Mr. Sickert is looking into it, is he?"

Netley backed up as Gull came closer. "Just between us, Netley . . ." Gull smiled affably. "I'd like you to keep your eye on Mr. Sickert. See where he goes." He took a gold sovereign from his pocket and pressed it into Netley's hand. "Just between us, you understand?"

Netley looked into the mad, dark eyes. The meaning was clear.

Walter Sickert slipped into the night shadows of Miller's Court. A faint light showed behind the tattered curtains of number 13. He tapped softly on the door. Two times, then three more. There was movement in the room. The bolt slid back and the door opened.

"Liz, I . . ."

He pushed the door wide and stepped in. Marie Kelly backed away. "You!"

"Marie, please . . ."

"Get out. I'll scream." She reached behind her and grabbed an empty bottle. "Not one step, Sickert."

"I only want to talk to you." He closed the door behind him.

"Talk, is it? All I want from you is the child. I've no need to talk to you or your murderous friends. You killed Polly and Annie. Now you want to kill me."

"Marie, believe me. I only want to help you. You're in danger here."

"Danger indeed. From the likes of you."

Sickert leaned against the door. "Maggie . . . Maggie misses you. She asks when you're coming back."

"Does she? She hasn't forgotten me?" Marie brushed at her eyes. "The poor darlin'."

"Marie. I want you to come away. You and Maggie. We'll go to France. A place in the country where I can paint. You can take care of her. She loves you."

Marie watched him, controlling her hatred. This man. This *monster*. To think that she would stay with him. If she agreed, there would be a chance to escape. To take little Maggie with her. She put the bottle down. "What is it you want of me?"

Sickert relaxed. "Look. It will take me two or three days to arrange matters. Maggie is . . . in the country. I'll fix it for us to go abroad. You stay here, out of sight."

"I've no money for food or rent, and the M'Carthy is ready to throw me in the street. I've no clothes except what's on me back."

He reached in his pocket and pulled out a pound note. "That's all I have with me now. I'll be back tomorrow night and bring you more. Will you come with us?"

She gave him a long, hard stare. "I will that."

General Sir Charles Warren stabbed the pile of newspapers on the table with a blunt finger. "Look at this, will you. They criticize me . . ."

The Prime Minister folded his hands primly. "And me as well, dear Charles."

Warren's face was purple. "It's Gull's fault. He's got the whole City in an uproar. Vigilantes in the streets . . . The police, *my police*, held up to mockery. Not only did he do the job in the most disgusting way, the fool got the wrong woman!"

"Calm yourself, Charles. He is under instruction by the Master of the Lodge . . . As we are . . ."

Warren settled back. "Yes. Of course. But you haven't

heard the worst. I've managed to keep it from the papers. The idiot left a message. With the Eddowes woman. Chalked it on the wall like a schoolboy.''

"What message?" The Prime Minister looked startled.

"Some illiterate cant . . ."

"He is a physician, my dear fellow. You can hardly expect literacy from him."

"The point is he used the word 'Juwes.' Fortunately I got to the scene and wiped it out before it could be photographed in evidence. Told my men that it referred to 'Jews' and I didn't want to chance any riots against the Semites.''

The Prime Minister bit his knuckle. "That was inexcusably stupid of him." They both knew that the word "Juwes" was a reference to the three Masonic Apprentices who killed Hiram Abiff. A mythical allusion that any ordinary Mason would recognize.

"That's not the end of our troubles," Warren went on. "Colonel Hamilton, the Queen's Equerry, has been snooping about. Hasn't been to see me personally, but he's called on some of his friends in Scotland Yard asking about Abberline. Wants to know what sort of a man he is . . .''

"I'm aware of Colonel Hamilton's presence. He was to see me this morning. Our good Queen is concerned that we are not doing enough to protect her loyal subjects. She wants my assurance that we will find the killer and stop him.''

"That Gull is a madman," Warren said. "Should be in a lunatic asylum. I've given orders that in any further cases I must be called immediately. My men will touch nothing unless I'm there.''

The Prime Minister gave him a thin smile. "Excellent, but I must counsel patience, Charles. There is one more obstacle. When she is removed, I'm certain that Jack the Ripper will disappear.''

* * *

Inspector Abberline looked out the open French doors of the Lees library. To his right was a sweep of clipped green lawn and beyond that orderly rows of white, red, and yellow roses. It seemed strange that he should be in this room discussing four murders when there was such beauty to be found in the world. He turned back to Lees, who was paging through the work by Father Suarez. "Did you have any premonitions about these last two?"

"No. But it is clear to me that this is not the end of it. Did you learn anything about Gull?"

Abberline drew on his pipe. "I've been making inquiries. Strange fellow, but he has powerful friends. Excellent professional reputation, but he's given to moods. Apparently he can be very blunt, even cruel at times; at others, the soul of affability. There are some reports of strange incidents. He has been known to remove parts of bodies from his autopsies. Once several years ago, he was seen to drop a human heart in his pocket and walk off."

"A human heart!"

"Yes. He explained this rather odd behavior by saying he was doing some private medical research at his home. But discreet inquiries among his servants indicate that he has no laboratory or other medical facilities in the house."

"Surely they'd notice if he had bits and pieces of bodies about the place."

"Quite so. It is reported that he frequently has blood spots on his clothing, but, then, he is a physician."

"No evidence, then?"

"None yet. He doesn't keep his own carriage. I checked the nearest cab rank, in Grosvenor Square. The drivers say that he frequents a place in Cleveland Street. Usually returning by private coach. I checked the address. The place is a known male brothel. He doesn't seem to be a customer, he goes into the mews, to a place underneath the house."

Lees stood up. "That's what I saw! 'Rooms beneath a house where men come and go.' That's it."

"Yes. I thought you might be interested. I propose we go there tonight, to see if you get any, ah . . . feelings about the place."

"You need more than my 'feelings.' "

"Yes. Well, we shall see, shan't we? Perhaps we might find an opportunity to take a look inside."

"Do you have a warrant?"

Abberline smiled and blew a cloud of smoke. "Of course not. But if I saw a back door standing open in the night, it would be my duty as a police officer to have a look. I might catch a footpad in the act."

Laura opened the door. "Colonel Hamilton is here to see you, Robert."

Lees rose as a tall, slim man came into the room. His hair was cut *en brosse* and his clipped mustache and bearing marked him as a Guard's Officer. "Tom! How good to see you." Lees extended his hand. He turned to the Inspector. "Colonel Hamilton, this is Chief Inspector Abberline."

Abberline stood up and shook the Colonel's hand. "Sir."

"Ah. Inspector Abberline. You're in charge of these Ripper murders, I've heard." Hamilton glanced at Lees.

"Yes, he is. Mr. Abberline and I have been . . . consulting about them."

Colonel Hamilton sat down and crossed his long legs. "I see. I gather, then, I may speak freely."

"Most certainly. I take it you had my letter."

"I did. I must say Her Majesty is most concerned about this matter." He paused. "Her feeling is that the police, ah . . . are not pursuing this case to the fullest."

Abberline looked him in the eye. "Perhaps *some* police, sir."

"Yes, Inspector. But you and Mr. Lees have some views on this case? I've been commanded by the Queen to look into this matter. You can be assured that what you say will find Her Majesty's ears only."

Abberline sucked on his pipe. "Well, Colonel, we've no hard evidence to go on. Only Mr. Lees's . . . conjectures . . . and my observations. Nothing that would stand in court."

Hamilton smiled. "I'm familiar with Mr. Lees's 'conjectures.' I speak from my own experience when I say they are very 'real.' I'm not a judge. Suppose you tell me what your conjectures are."

"This is a very delicate matter, Tom. The people involved . . ." Lees said.

"The Queen is aware of that. There have been stories, rumors, from other sources." The Colonel looked from one man to another. "If the Crown is involved in any way . . . These are troubled times. We've had enough scandals. One of this apparent magnitude might destroy the monarchy. The Queen has authorized me to say that if, as she suspects, Prince Eddy is in any way connected with this, he will never succeed his father to the throne. We must discover whatever influences are active here . . . and neutralize them. But this cannot be done in the conventional way. Do you agree?"

"I agree." Lees looked at Abberline.

"Perhaps, Mr. Lees, it would be best if you told the Colonel what we know about the Lodge of Jahbulon."

Gull stood by the hearth. Firelight glinted from the silver symbol on his hooded blue cloak. "Well, what did you find out?"

Netley looked at him nervously. "I did what you said. I followed him. You was right. He went to her, the Kelly woman. He went inside and I listened at the window. It was her voice, all right, a bloody Paddy, she is. They was making plans. 'E's got the baby here in London. Tomorrow, first thing, the three of them does a flit to France. It's all fixed."

"Traitor! Oath breaker!" Gull paced the room, his robe

swirling behind him. He stopped and grabbed Netley by the coat and shook him. "You know what happens to traitors?"

"Honest, sir, I . . ."

Gull gave Netley a shove that sent him staggering. "Where is she? The woman?"

Netley circled, keeping the chair between him and Gull. "Miller's Court, sir. Number thirteen."

Gull stopped and pulled out his watch. "I instructed Sickert to be here at ten o'clock." He gave a high-pitched laugh. "For a most important meeting. Yes. Most important. He should be here directly. Where is the Rod?"

"The Rod, sir?"

"The Rod of the Tyler, you fool!" Gull shouted.

"Oh. That Rod." He went to a cupboard and took out a thick, three-foot-long stick carved with a pattern of snakes and leaves. It was the club he carried when he "secured the Lodge." Part of the mumbo-jumbo these gents were so fond of. To him it was a stick. If someone tried to get in, he'd give them a bash. Simple as that.

He watched Gull fumble in his leather bag. "When Mr. Sickert gets here I'll let him in," Gull said. "You stand behind the door. When he comes in, *strike the traitor down!*"

"You mean hit Mr. Sickert?"

"That's what I mean, Netley." He lowered his voice. "Unless . . . you, too, are a traitor."

"No, sir. Whatever you say." Loonies, these gents. The lot of them should be shut away.

There was a knock at the door. Gull jumped. "That's him. Tyler, take your post!"

Netley looked at him, puzzled.

"Get behind the door," Gull hissed. "Strike him down!"

Gull unlocked the door and swung it open. "Come in, my dear Sickert." He made a sweeping gesture with his arm. As Sickert entered, Gull stepped behind him and closed the door.

Netley closed his eyes and brought the club down. It caught

Sickert above the left ear. Blood spurted and he fell to his knees.

"Again! Hit the traitor again!"

Netley swung and hit Sickert on the back of the neck. He sprawled forward, groaning. Gull knelt and took a bottle and a cloth from under his cloak. He rolled Sickert over and clamped the chloroformed rag to his face.

Gull rose and looked at the limp body. "Ah. Well done." He clapped Netley on the shoulder. "The Master will be pleased. Now take his feet, I'll take his arms." They carried Sickert into the Inner Temple and swung him onto the stone table. Gull strapped his arms and legs down.

"Excellent." He rubbed his hands together. "He'll keep. Now we shall pay a call on Mistress Kelly."

The two men stood in front of the darkened tobacco shop at 22 Cleveland Street. Abberline pointed across the street to number 19. "What about it, Mr. Lees?"

Lees shivered. "That's it. No question. I can feel it from here. Evil . . ." Heavy draperies covered the windows. There was the faint sound of music and laughter in the air.

"Nearly midnight," Abberline said. "Let's go round to the mews."

"Why did we come so late?"

Abberline smiled. "Ah. I learned the breaking-and-entering trade from experts. For a footpad, the later the better. No one about, master and servants, all in their beddie-byes. Let's take a look."

"Yes, let's get on," Lees said. As they walked past the streetlamp he touched a hand to his breast.

"What's that hanging about your neck?"

Lees looked embarrassed. "It's . . . a Crucifix. My wife got it in Malta. Very old. Made of iron." He smiled at Abberline. "Said to have been worn by a Crusader. Sort of a good-luck charm."

Abberline grunted. "Good luck it is, then. I've my own charm." He reached in his overcoat pocket and pulled out a Webley & Scott Mark I. "A .455-caliber charm. Newest thing. General Warren likes to keep the police armories up to date . . . in case the peasants get out of line."

"I thought the police didn't carry weapons."

"We don't. Except with special permission. I was going to ask General Warren, but he wasn't at home."

Abberline held out his arm as they came to the mews entrance. "Let's be quiet like." A single gas lamp cast shadows over the cobbles. Halfway down the mews stood a driverless black coach.

At the rear of number 19 they slipped down the stairs to the servants' entrance. The windows were dark. The door was locked. Abberline took out a small leather case. "Another example of my misspent youth." He bent to the keyhole. "Simple lock, this is . . ." he whispered. He inserted the pick. The second try got it. He eased the door open and motioned to Lees.

The room was dank. Along the right wall a set of stone tubs gave off the smell of stagnant water. Underfoot, the flagstones were slippery with damp-mold. Straight ahead was a long corridor. Light seeped from the cracks of the door at the end.

Abberline tugged at Lees's sleeve and moved forward. Behind them Netley rose from his seat in the dark corner. He swung the club at Abberline. The blow hit the taller man's shoulder and struck his head. He fell forward, and crashed into the wall.

Lees threw himself on the dark figure. The club clattered on the stones. Netley grabbed for his throat and Lees slammed his fist into the man's stomach. Netley fell back. Lees stepped in and swung blindly. His fist hit Netley on the temple. Netley bounced off the wall and fell to one knee. He jumped up and fled down the corridor.

Lees went after him. He tripped over Abberline's outstretched legs and sprawled headlong. Netley threw open the door of the Robing Room as Lees struggled to his feet and ran down the corridor. He hit the closing door with his shoulder. The force carried them both into the room. Netley landed on top of him. The little man grabbed Lees's hair and slammed his head against the floor. Netley's gnarled jockey hands closed on his throat. He gasped for air. A red film blurred his vision. Lees arched his back and drove his knee into Netley's crotch.

The little man fell back with a scream. Lees sucked in air and clutched the sideboard, pulling himself up. Netley charged, his yellow teeth bared. "Bastard!" he screamed. "I'll kill you!" He pulled a razor from his pocket and flicked it open.

Lees saw the heavy silver box on the sideboard. He picked it up and threw it as Netley swung the razor. The box hit Netley in the forehead.

The lid flew open. There was an explosion of blood. Netley dropped to his knees and the razor fell from his hand. He slumped forward in the pool of gore. Lees looked down, unable to believe what he saw. His legs trembled. He shook his head to clear his vision. Then he understood. The bile rose in his throat.

He wiped his mouth on his sleeve and backed away. At the far end of the room he saw the door to the Inner Temple. He touched the crucifix on his breast. A faint sound came to him. A distant voice, rising and falling in a discordant chant. He turned his mind inward seeking an inner source of power. He went to the Temple door and threw it open.

In the flickering light he saw the man in the blue robe. The man in his dream. The man on the 'bus. The hood of his cloak was thrown back and a blue light played on his coarse features. Sir William Gull raised the silver knife over the bound body of Walter Sickert. His saliva-flecked mouth spoke the ancient words. Blue light crackled from the throne before him.

"Stop!"

Gull turned his mad eyes on the intruder. "Infidel! Desecrator!" He rushed at Lees, slashing with the knife. Lees crouched, then kicked out at the man's body. Gull turned and took the blow on his hip. Lees grabbed his arm, trying to twist the knife from his hand.

A thundering rumble came from the alcove. The blue light was shot through with streaks of red. Lees felt his strength weakening as Gull pushed the blade toward his face. His foot slipped and he fell backward. Gull gave a cry of triumph and raised the knife.

A clap of thunder filled the room. Gull spun around and struck the wall. He dropped the knife. His right hand turned red as the blood poured from his sleeve. Gull screamed, not a scream of pain, but a scream of hatred.

Lees looked up. Abberline sagged against the door, the Webley dangling from one hand.

"Abberline!" Lees shouted as he saw Netley come up behind him. Netley swung the club and Abberline went down. Gull lurched to his feet, clutching his arm. "Tyler! Tyler! Secure the Lodge!" Before Lees could move, Gull was out the door, following on the heels of Netley.

The lights in the alcove flashed brighter, yellow streaks shot through with red. A sharp, metallic smell filled the room. On the table, Walter Sickert stirred, his head thrashed from side to side. Foam flecked his lips.

Lees fought off his instinctive fear. He picked up the knife and moved to the table. Cut the man free. Get out. He looked down at Sickert's thrashing form. The red mass filled the alcove, tendrils of flame interweaving in a primordial pattern. Sickert groaned.

Lees stood immobile. A sense of warmth filled his body, an ecstatic, surging power. He could feel the strength in his arms, his vision was clear. He could see the world as it *really* existed. The man before him was a *traitor* . . . The man had broken his oath to the Master. He must be punished . . . He must die . . . A red-yellow ray shot from the throne and touched his arm. Kill! The arm moved as if it were a separate entity. Lees fought to control it. Desperately, he sought that secret spring within himself, some refuge in a corner of his soul. A hiding place from the power that seized him. Kill! came the command. The Master will be pleased . . .

"Laura! Laura!" Lees cried out. His body shook as he fought for control. The touch came. Laura's touch. Like cool fingers in his mind. The Connection. The power of the Great Mother flowed into him. He forced his left hand to move to the iron crucifix which hung at his breast. He ripped it from its chain and threw it into the roiling red mass.

The explosion blew him off his feet. He felt a searing heat on his face, then a freezing chill. He rose to one knee. The walls of the alcove were blackened and the throne was shattered. The red flames shrunk on themselves, falling inward, an eye-searing pinpoint. There was a whistling sound, as if air were being sucked from the room. Then silence.

Lees picked up the knife. The once bright blade was black and pitted. He moved to the stone table and cut Sickert's bindings. The man moaned and his eyelids fluttered.

Abberline was on his knees in the doorway. He clutched the door and pulled himself up slowly. "Lees . . . What happened? I came to and saw you standing there with that knife . . . The expression on your face . . . Then it was like a bomb went off."

Lees put an arm around Abberline and steadied him. "It was . . . An old enemy . . . An ancient Adversary. It's gone now. For the moment. Come on, old man, let's get out in the air. We need to get help."

* * *

They came out into the mews. The night air was crisp, and the stars seemed intensely bright. ''What happened to Gull and Netley?'' Abberline asked.

Lees looked down the mews. The black coach was gone. ''It appears they made their escape.''

Abberline leaned against the railing. ''Gull won't get far. Not with that bullet in him. I expect he'll go to ground in his house. I saw what was in that box. There's another woman dead, for sure. I'll see the bastard hanged.''

Lees took a deep breath. ''I suppose I'd better see to Sickert.''

''Do that. I'll find a constable and get some help.''

Lees went down the steps. When he reached the Inner Temple it was empty. At the far end a hidden door stood open. The steps led upward. Walter Sickert was gone.

The three men sat in Robert Lees's library. Colonel Hamilton sipped his sherry and looked at Lees and Abberline. ''It's been more than a week now since Marie Kelly's murder and the newspapers are still at it.'' He sighed. ''But there'll be no more Ripper murders. If we can believe what we've made out of Gull's incoherent ramblings.''

Abberline rose and went to the French doors. He looked out into the garden. ''I know all about that lunatic's story. And I know who was in this with him. In all my years of police work I've never seen anything like what was done to Marie Kelly. What's to be done about *that*? Will they hang him?''

''There will be no trial. The matter is too delicate. The Queen has instructed me . . .''

Abberline whirled and faced him. ''I thought not. In thirty years I've sent nine men to the gallows. Tuppence pimps and men that killed for a loaf of bread. Not a rich man in the lot. Nobody is hanged with a silken rope in this country.''

Lees leaned forward, his elbows on his desk. "Exactly what has been done, Tom? This isn't the sort of thing my conscience would allow me to overlook, simply to save a Royal reputation."

"I understand your position, gentlemen. But the matter is out of our hands. The issues are too large. Arrangements have been made. I must remind you that in the interest of the nation your knowledge comes under the rubric of 'Official Secret.' "

"What 'arrangements' have been made? Put them all on the bloody Honors List?" Abberline gave Hamilton a look of disgust.

"Gull is totally insane," Hamilton said. "The word has been put out that he's suffered from a stroke. When he recovers from your gunshot wound . . . he will die of natural causes."

Abberline looked astonished. "Die? You mean you're going to do him in?"

Hamilton raised his hand. "Nothing so crude, Inspector. He will have a public funeral. Arrangements have been made to confine him in an asylum, for life." Hamilton gave a wry smile, "Under the name 'Thomas Mason.' "

"What about Netley and Sickert?" Lees asked.

"Ah. Poor Mr. Netley. Seems he had an unfortunate accident. Fell from the box of his coach and was crushed under the wheels . . . Happened near Clarence Gate, I believe. There were no witnesses. As for Sickert, we've no real evidence against him. He's fled to the Continent and taken the girl with him."

"And the others? Warren and the P.M. ? They're the real villains in this," Abberline said.

"Warren has resigned, as you know. As for the P.M., well . . . politicians come and politicians go . . ."

"And that's it?"

"That's it."

Abberline turned back toward the doors. The blooms of the roses were bright against the green grass. "I'm getting out. Out of the police trade." His voice was low. "Thirty years of chasing villains, for what? The *real* villains are never caught. The men who kill for power. I'm off to Bournemouth to grow my roses, and damn them all."

Major General Sir Charles Warren sat slumped in his chair. "I told you not to trust that maniac Gull. He brought the Temple down around our ears, didn't he? My job is gone . . . The Queen would have taken our heads in the Tower if she could."

The P.M. made a steeple of his fingers. "Dear Charles. We may have lost a battle, but not the war. There is always the Brotherhood."

"The Temple was desecrated."

"That's not the end of it, Charles. The Lodge of Jahbulon is being moved abroad."

"Abroad? Not France, I hope." General Warren was one who firmly believed that "Wogs start at Calais."

"Not France. But this country is finished. Another fifty years and it will be a backwater. Keir Hardie and his socialist Labour Party will see to that. No, the Lodge is being moved to Germany."

Warren looked up. "Germany! Well . . . They may be barbarians, but at least they have a sense of *order*."

"It is the Master's wish, Charles. If all goes well, Germany will one day rule the world . . . and the Brotherhood will rule Germany."

Epilogue

Walter Sickert lived for many years in France, where Lord Salisbury was his sometime houseguest. A student of Whistler and a friend of Degas's, he was a major English painter in his time. One of his biographers notes that he could not paint without the presence of a certain red handkerchief. He did several paintings concerning the murders of women. His works hang in major museums, including the Tate.

GAME IN THE POPE'S HEAD

GENE WOLFE

Gene Wolfe is perceived by many critics to be one of the best—perhaps the *best—science fiction and fantasy writers working today. His tetralogy,* The Book of the New Sun— *consisting of* The Shadow of the Torturer, The Claw of the Conciliator, The Sword of the Lictor, *and* The Citadel of the Autarch—*is being hailed as a masterpiece, quite probably the standard against which all subsequent science fantasy books of the eighties will be judged; ultimately, it may prove to be as influential as J. R. R. Tolkien's* Lord of the Rings *or T.H. White's* The Once and Future King. The Shadow of the Torturer *won the World Fantasy Award.* The Claw of the Conciliator *won the Nebula Award. Wolfe also won a Nebula Award for his story "The Death of Doctor Island." His other books include* Peace, The Fifth Head of Cerberus, *and* The Devil in a Forest. *His short fiction—including some of the best stories of the seventies—has been collected in* The Island of Doctor Death and Other Stories, Gene Wolfe's Book of Days, *and* The Wolfe Archipelago. *His most recent books are* Soldier of the Mist *and* The Urth of the New Sun. *Wolfe lives in Barrington, Illinois, with his wife and family.*

Here he suggests that if we are the roles we play, then we'd better be damned careful what roles we choose.

"**A** SERGEANT WAS SENT TO THE POPE'S HEAD to investigate the case." (From the *London Times*'s coverage of the murder of Anne Chapman, September 11, 1888.)

Bev got up to water her plant. Edgar said, "You're over-watering that. Look how yellow the leaves are."

They were indeed. The plant had extended its long, limp limbs over the pictures and the sofa, and out through the broken window; but the weeping flukes of these astonishing terminations were sallow and jaundiced.

"It *needs* water." Bev dumped her glass into the flowerpot, got a fresh drink, and sat down again. "My play?" She turned up a card. "The next card is 'What motion picture used the greatest number of living actors, animal or human?' "

Edgar said, "I think I know. *Gandhi*. Half a million or so."

"Wrong. Debbie?"

"Hell, I don't know. *Close Encounters of the Third Kind*."

"Wrong. Randy?"

It was a moment before he realized that she meant him. So that was his name: Randy. Yes, of course. He said, "Animal or human?"

"Right."

"Then it's animals, because they don't get paid." He tried to think of animal movies, Bert Lahr terrified of Toto, *Lassie Come Home*. "*The Birds*?"

"Close. It was *The Swarm*, and there were twenty-two million actors."

Edgar said, "Mostly bees."

"I suppose."

There was a bee, or perhaps a wasp, on the plant, nearly invisible against a yellow leaf. It did not appear to him to be exploring the surface in the usual beeish or waspish way, but rather to be listening, head raised, to their conversation. The room was bugged. He wanted to say, This room is bugged; but before he could, Bev announced, "Your move, I think, Ed."

Ed said, "Bishop's pawn to the Bishop's four."

Debbie threw the dice and counted eight squares along the edge of the board. "Oh, good! Park Place, and I'll buy it." She handed him her money, and he gave her the deed.

Bev said, "Your turn."

He nodded, stuffed Debbie's money into his pocket, shuffled the cards, and read the top one.

You are Randolph Carter. Three times you have dreamed of the marvelous city, Randolph Carter, and three times you have been snatched away from the high terrace above it.

Randolph Carter nodded again and put the card down. Debbie handed him a small pewter figure, a young man in old-fashioned clothes.

Bev asked, "Where did the fictional American philosopher Thomas Olney teach? Ed?"

"A *fictional* philosopher? Harvard, I suppose. Is it John Updike?"

"Wrong. Debbie?"

"Pass."

"Okay. Randy?"

"London."

Outside, a cloud covered the sun. The room grew darker as the light from the broken windows diminished.

Edgar said, "Good shot. Is he right, Bev?"

The bee, or wasp, rose from its leaf and buzzed around Edgar's bald head. He slapped at it, missing it by a fraction of an inch. "There's a fly in here!"

"Not now. I think it went out the window."

It had indeed been a fly, he saw, and not a bee or wasp at all—a bluebottle, no doubt gorged with carrion.

Bev said, "Kingsport, Massachusetts."

With an ivory hand, Edgar moved an ivory chessman. "Knight to the King's three."

Debbie tossed her dice onto the board. "Chance."

He picked up the card for her.

You must descend the seven hundred steps to the Gate of Deeper Slumber. You may enter the Enchanted Wood or claim the sword Sacnoth. Which do you choose?

Debbie said, "I take the Enchanted Wood. That leaves you the sword, Randy."

Bev handed it to him. It was a falchion, he decided, curved and single-edged. After testing the edge with his finger, he laid it in his lap. It was not nearly as large as a real sword—less than sixteen inches long, he decided, including the hardwood handle.

"Your turn, Randy."

He discovered that he disliked Bev nearly as much as Debbie, hated her bleached blond hair, her scrawny neck. She and her dying plant were twins, one vegetable, one inhuman. He had not known that before.

She said, "It's the wheel of Fortune," as though he were stupid. He flicked the spinner.

"Unlawful evil."

Bev said, "Right," and picked up a card. "What do the following have in common: Pogo the Clown, H. H. Holmes, and Saucy Jacky?"

Edgar said, "That's an easy one. They're all pseudonyms of mass murderers."

"Right. For an extra point, name the murderers."

"Gacy, Mudgett, and . . . that's not fair. No one knows who the Ripper was."

But he did: just another guy, a guy like anybody else.

Debbie tossed her dice. "Whitechapel. I'll buy it. Give me the card, honey."

He picked up the deed and studied it. "Low rents."

Edgar chuckled. "And seldom paid."

"I know," Debbie told them, "but I want it, with lots of houses." He handed her the card, and she gave him the dice.

For a moment he rattled them in his hand, trying to imagine himself the little pewter man. It was no use; there was nothing of bright metal about him or his dark wool coat—only the edge of the knife. "Seven-come-eleven," he said, and threw.

"You got it," Debbie told him. "Seven. Shall I move it for you?"

"No," he said. He picked up the little pewter figure and walked (passed) past Holborn, the Temple (cavern-temple of Nasht and Kaman-Thah), and Lincoln's Inn Fields, along Cornhill and Leadenhall streets to Aldgate High Street, and so at last to Whitechapel.

Bev said, "You saw him coming, Deb," but her voice was very far away, far above the leaden (hall) clouds, filthy with coal smoke, that hung over the city. Wagons and hansom cabs rattled by. There was a public house at the corner of Brick Lane. He turned and went in.

The barmaid handed him his large gin. The barmaid had Debbie's dark hair, Debbie's dark good looks. When he had paid her, she left the bar and took a seat at one of the tables. Two others sat there already, and there were cards and dice, money and drinks before them. "Sit down," she said, and he sat.

The blonde turned over a card, the jack of spades. "What are the spades in a deck of cards?" she asked.

"Swords," he said. "From the Spanish word for a sword, *espada*. The jack of spades is really the jack of swords."

"Correct."

The other man said, "Knight to the White Chapel."

The door opened, letting in the evening with a wisp of fog, and the black knight. She was tall and slender and dressed like a cavalryman, in high boots and riding breeches. A pewter miniature of a knight's shield was pinned to her dark shirt.

The barmaid rattled the dice and threw.

"You're still alive," the black knight said. She strode to their table. Sergeant's chevrons had been sewn to the sleeves of the shirt. "This neighborhood is being evacuated, folks."

"Not by us," the other man said.

"By you now, sir. On my orders. As an officer of the law, I must order you to leave. There's a tank car derailed, leaking some kind of gas."

"That's fog," Randolph Carter told her. "Fog and smoke."

"Not *just* fog. I'm sorry, sir, but I must ask all of you to go. How long have you been here?"

"Sixteen years," the blonde woman said. "The neighborhood was a lot nicer when we came."

"It's some sort of chemical weapon, like LSD."

He asked, "Don't you want to sit down?" He stood, offering her his chair.

"My shot must be wearing off. The shot was supposed to protect me. I'm Sergeant . . . Sergeant . . ."

The other man said, "Very few of us are protected by shots, Sergeant Chapman. Shots usually kill people, particularly soldiers."

Randolph Carter looked at her shirt. The name *Chapman* was engraved on a stiff plastic plate there, the plate held out like a little shelf by the thrust of her left breast.

"Sergeant Anne Chapman of the United States Army. We think it's the plants, sir. All the psychoactive drugs we know about come from plants—opium, cocaine, heroin."

"You're the heroine," he told her gently. "Coming here like this to get us out."

"All of them chemicals the plants have stumbled across to

protect us from insects, really. And now they've found something to protect the insects from us." She paused, staring at him. "That isn't right, is it?"

Again he asked, "Don't you want to sit down?"

"Gases from the comet. The comet's tail has wrapped all earth in poisonous gases."

The blonde murmured, "What is the meaning of this name given Satan: *Beelzebub*."

A tiny voice from the ceiling answered.

"You, sir," the black knight said, "won't you come with me? We've got to get out of here."

"You can't get out of here," the other man told them.

He nodded to the knight. "I'll come with you, if you'll love me." He rose, pushing the sword up his coat sleeve, point first.

"Then come on." She took him by the arm and pulled him through the door.

A hansom cab rattled past.

"What is this place?" She put both hands to her forehead. "I'm dreaming, aren't I? This is a nightmare." There was a fly on her shoulder, a blowfly gorged with carrion. She brushed it off; it settled again, unwilling to fly through the night and the yellow fog. "No, I'm hallucinating."

He said, "I'd better take you to your room." The bricks were wet and slippery underfoot. As they turned a corner, and another, he told her what she could do for him when they reached her room. A dead bitch lay in the gutter. Despite the night and the chill of autumn, the corpse was crawling with flies.

Sickly yellow gaslight escaped from under a door. She tore herself from him and pushed it open. He came after her, his arms outstretched. "Is this where you live?"

The three players still sat at their table. They had been joined by a fourth, a new Randolph Carter. As the door flew wide the fourth player turned to look, but he had no face.

She whispered, "This is Hell, isn't it? I'm in Hell, for what I did. Because of what we did. We're all in Hell. I always thought it was just something the church made up, something to keep you in line, you know what I mean, sir?"

She was not talking to him, but he nodded sympathetically.

"Just a game in the pope's head. But it's real, it's here, and here we are."

"I'd better take you to your room," he said again.

She shuddered. "In Hell you can't pray, isn't that right? But I can—listen! I can pray! *Dear G—*"

He had wanted to wait, wanted to let her finish, but the sword, Sacnoth, would not wait. It entered her throat, more eager even than he, and emerged spent and swimming in scarlet blood.

The faceless Randolph Carter rose from the table. "Your seat, young man," he said through no mouth. "I'm merely the marker whom you have followed."

MY SHADOW IS THE FOG

Charles L. Grant

Like riding a bicycle, there are some skills that you never forget. Some skills, however, are better off forgotten . . .

As both writer and editor, Charles L. Grant is one of the most influential and respected figures in the horror genre today. As editor, Grant is responsible for creating the long-running original anthology series Shadows, *now in ten volumes, and arguably the finest horror anthology series of the seventies and eighties. Grant also created the Greystone Bay series of chronicle novels, and has edited a long string of important non-series horror anthologies:* Fears, Terrors, Midnight, After Midnight, Nightmares, The Dodd, Mead Gallery of Horrors, *and many others. In fact, an argument could be made that Grant is the most important horror fiction editor of his day, at short-story lengths. As a writer, he's no slouch either, as attested to by his two Nebula Awards and his three World Fantasy Awards (one for editing* Shadows, *but two for his own writing). His stories have appeared just about everywhere, and have been collected in* Nightmare Seasons, Tales from the Nightside, *and* A Glow of Candles. *His novels include* The Nestling, Tea Party, *the Oxrun series,* Nightsongs, *and, most recently,* The Pet. *Grant lives in New Jersey with his wife, writer Kathryn Ptacek.*

THE WIND WAS STRONG THAT DAY. I REMEMBER THAT much. It was strong. And it was cool.

The fog wasn't there.

Not at first; not until later.

But there were whitecaps on the bay and great masses of white clouds and a distant white haze that veiled the low hump of South End from the beach where I sat and threw handfuls of pebbles into the dark water. The chair that I used was of the folding kind, and the coat that I wore was barely enough to keep me warm though it was still September and the walk from my room had put a mirror of nervous sweat along the ridge of my brow.

I had arrived just after noon, and stopped in front of a low deserted building whose function I've never learned, not in all the years it's waited for me, doors nailed shut and windows shut with nailed planks. Facing the water was a wide platform—a loading dock, I think—raised above the beach and walled with concrete. I have no idea what was beneath it; I only knew that I was higher by at least a yard than the land around me, and it was a chore to climb up there, to hoist myself from the stony beach to the battered wooden flooring with its whorls and sighs and scrabblings of blown sand.

No one who saw me paid me any heed. I was, after all, only another old man come to take in what there was of a pale, waning sun. Nothing special, nothing different. A face scraped with the chisel of too many decades living, hair the color of old straw thinned in useless harvest, shoulders slightly rounded. My hands were gloveless, my feet in light-weight boots, and the cardigan I wore under the caped black coat was one I've had for what seems like a hundred years.

I remember the wind, and the bay, and the feel of Whitstable at my back, aged enough, I suppose, to rightfully want a bit of peace at the end. I don't really know. I never asked, and the people never told me.

But dammit, I do remember the wind, and I remember

sitting in the death of the summer sun most of the afternoon throwing pebbles into the water and nearly falling out of my chair when I heard someone say, "Hello."

I looked over, looked down, and there was a little girl with short brown hair, and a short tartan skirt blowing about her legs snug in white tights. A red sweater a size too large, hanging to the middle of her thighs, billowing and slapping when the wind slipped beneath. She smiled at me, her eyes squinting from the sun's glare.

"Hello," I said.

"Are you waiting for him, then?" she asked, her head slightly tilted to one side.

"I don't know," I answered with a smile. "Am I?"

"You look as if you are."

My smile widened. "Then I suppose I am."

She turned to face the bay, one hand to the side of her red-cheeked face to protect it from the wind. "I don't think he's coming."

"Oh?"

"Oh, no, I don't think so. May I throw one of your stones, please?"

I handed one over—it was round, sea-smooth, mottled, and dry. Without a word of thanks, she raised her arm, sighted, and threw it as hard as she could. It didn't go very far, barely past the first waves, but it was far enough to make her giggle and ask if she could do it again.

"You hands will get dirty," I said in gentle admonition as I handed another one over. "Your mother will be angry."

"No, she won't," the girl said. "She never gets mad at me."

I raised an eyebrow. "Never?"

She threw the second stone, a bit farther than the first. "No."

A gust made me close my eyes, and when they opened again she was staring closely at me, like a bird trying to decide if I was part of the chain that provided it with meals at the end of a spring shower.

I waited for her to say something.

A gull cried overhead.

At last she shrugged and jumped down to the beach, walking very carefully over the stones to the edge of the water. Though the waves here were quite low because of the wood-and-rock breakwaters spaced along the shore, I wanted to call a caution to her. Instead, I only watched, marveling at the way she kept her balance while the wind kicked at her skirt, at the loose ends of her sweater, and lifted her hair until she turned a youthful gorgon.

She pointed then to the eastern horizon and, without turning around, called, "Do you know France is over there?"

"I do," I called back, cupping a hand to the side of my mouth.

"Do you know a lot, then?"

I smiled. "I used to," I said. "I don't remember it all now."

"Pity," she said. Just like that—pity.

"I suppose it is."

"He doesn't always remember either," she said, not sadly. "He's terribly old, you know." She looked at me, an odd look, and I wondered if she was comparing my age with her friend's. "Terribly old. Sometimes, when he's lost, I think he doesn't remember me at all." The look changed then, from odd to almost sly. "Do you remember?"

I was getting weary of shouting, but she showed no inclination to turn around, and I didn't have the strength to climb down beside her.

"This man," I said then. "Who is he? Is he from around here?"

She nodded. "Yes. But you're not, are you? You talk funny."

I had to smile. "You're right. I'm not. I'm from a long way away."

I had to smile, because I wasn't sure.

"America," she decided, and nodded once to agree with herself. "I could tell. I'm good at telling things like that, I'm almost always right." Then she looked at me over her shoulder and gave me the brightest, most loving smile I had ever seen. "He's a cleaner, you see."

I wasn't sure I heard her properly and shook my head. She lifted her hands in a sigh and came back to me, leaned on the top of the wall, and repeated herself, her tone telling me frankly that I should have known that.

"I see," I said. "And just what does he clean?"

"Everything, I guess. For goodness' sake, don't you remember anything?"

I frowned. Her cheerfulness was gone now, replaced by the impatience a child has for one like me, who has nothing but patience left and no way to use it. I didn't care for her company anymore. I was like that, a dubious privilege of old age—judgments that come and go like the nightmares that warn me just how much longer I have to live, how much more I have to endure before I can have peace. They aren't premonitions, I don't believe in things like that, but it's why I returned to Whitstable—an old town and an old man, waiting for someone to decide what should be done with them before they turn into embarrassments for the future.

But I do remember the wind, and the sun, and the matter-of-fact way she looked at me again, then walked to the near breakwater and climbed it, looked back at me and grinned before walking out to the end.

It was narrow.

It couldn't have been more than a foot or so wide, and there she was, out at the tip and balanced on one leg.

I was so stunned I couldn't move, and I didn't dare breathe lest she lose her balance and fall.

Fool, I thought; you stupid little fool, you'll kill yourself out there.

She laughed. Her arms spread wide, her fingers spread to the wind, and she glanced over her shoulder and called something to me. I couldn't hear. My ears were stoppered in anticipation of her falling screams. She called again, and spun around, and I found myself rising, though my legs were too weak to carry me fast enough, my voice too weak to call out for help, for someone to stop her. I looked frantically behind me but there was no one in the parking lot beside the pub where I'd had an early lunch, no one in the narrow streets, no one in the windows. My arms flapped uselessly at my sides, my mouth opened, closed, opened again, and when I reached the breakwater's edge I kept stepping forward, stepping back, a fearful dance of indecision that soon dropped me to my knees.

The wind brought the clouds, hid the sun, and I watched her little game, gasping, until she tired of it and came back as easily as if she were walking a wide pavement. I leaned forward anxiously, one hand thumping against my chest to force my lungs to work, the other reaching out as if to help her.

"Can you do that?" she said when she reached me at last. "It's not very hard."

I rolled and staggered to my feet and backed away from her. My chair had toppled over and I fumbled for it, with it, cursed it until I could set it right again and drop into it, panting.

"Who are you?" I asked, wiping my mouth, brushing back my hair.

"Delia," she said. "Delia Travers."

I looked away from her, into the sun.

"Who are *you*?" she asked quickly.

"Jack," I said finally. "Jack Light." My voice sounded hoarse, and distant, certainly not my own, so I cleared my throat and gave my name again. And as I waited for a response, and for my heart to calm and my lungs to take air without burning inside, I glanced at her from the corner of my vision.

And blinked because suddenly I thought I knew who she was. I had seen her before.

But only in fog.

She giggled.

I looked at her sharply.

"The cleaner's name is Jack," she said.

"Yes," I said slowly. "I know." And frowned because I wasn't sure I was right.

She nodded, crossed her arms on the top of the wall, and tucked her chin on one wrist. "That's two Jacks I know," she said. "Do you know two Jacks?"

I shook my head.

For a moment the sun again pulled a cloud over its face, and the beach grew too cold for me to endure. As I fumbled into a pair of worn black gloves, I thought of leaving, of heading for the pub where I could go downstairs, to the back corner, and drink myself to nightfall. I could think just as easily in there, with the warmth and the chatter and the laughter all about me, certainly more easily than I could out here, in the cold and the wind-silence, where the waves slanted away from me as if they knew who I was.

Footsteps on the stones, then.

The girl turned as I did, to watch a quartet of young people walking awkwardly toward the water, holding each other, laughing in each other's shoulders, glancing at us once and grinning as if to include us in their fun. Delia waved shyly; I nodded and looked away.

I didn't want to watch them.

There was too much noise, too much life, and I didn't like the way the little girl kept watching me not watching them. Her expression was knowing, and finally it was sly again, and I couldn't help wishing her friend would come along and take her away.

She made me nervous.

I didn't know why.

But when the laughter and squealing grew, I watched the young people anyway, and squinted so hard there were tears in eyes. A hand brushed hard over my face, and I looked away from the setting sun. Time to go, I told myself; you'll catch your death if you wait.

"Do you know," the girl said suddenly, turning her back on the others, "that Jack is even older than you?"

"Is that possible?" I said, smiling.

"Oh, yes. He's older than everybody!"

She grunted and puffed her way to the top of the wall and sat cross-legged, her back to the drop, rocking on her bottom. "Did you know what he did when he was a man?"

"No," I said, curiously uneasy because I thought I knew and didn't much care for the way she'd put the question.

Old men, you see, aren't men at all; they're relics in museums, ghosts that walk the earth to remind real men of what they would become, because once they got there they never would remember.

The sun dropped to the horizon; the warmth and wind died. The bay was empty, South End gone in a twilight shadow, and there was only one of the young people left on the beach. A woman, kneeling at water's edge and poking at something with a pale stick.

The girl hunched her shoulders and leaned forward, her secret obviously not for anyone but me. "He killed people." Then she looked side to side, up to the clouds, back to my face. "He really did. He was *horrid*."

And she crossed her eyes and laughed.

The young woman looked up, startled, and returned to her prodding.

I pushed out of the chair and walked over to the girl, stiffly, in anger. I crouched in front of her and pulled off my left glove. She stopped laughing when she saw my hand thrust at her face.

"Do you see that?" I said.

She nodded, slowly.

It was an old hand, liver spots and high veins and the knuckles more prominent than the fingers they started.

The wind pushed at my back, pushed hair into my eyes, and I used my free hand to balance me on the platform.

"A hand can kill, little girl," I said grimly, softly, holding her gaze with mine and pleased at the fear I saw there at last. "A hand with a gun, a knife, a razor, a club . . . it can kill, and it isn't something to laugh at. Not now. Not ever. A hand *kills*. Do you understand me?" I took a breath; she didn't speak. "It is horrible, to kill. I don't care how young you are, child, it's not right to laugh."

My hand trembled, from the cold, from my anger, and I watched it trace a pattern in front of her eyes before I jammed it back into its glove and dropped the rest of the way to my knees.

The girl blinked, wiped a hand over her eyes, and blinked again. "I'm sorry, Jack," she whispered, and looked over her shoulder. "I'm sorry," she said again, and ran over to the woman, knelt beside her, and watched her until the two of them were laughing, sharing a secret and once in a while glancing over at me.

I felt the fool.

And I felt a stirring. A remembering. As intangible as the fog that now drifted in behind me. I hadn't noticed it before, sneaking and ducking behind the swells, filling the hollows, waiting until the wind died and the sun died before climbing into the twilight. Touching the back of my neck like the kiss of an old friend, curling around my throat like the caress of an old lover.

When I looked to my left, the village was gone, gray in its

place and shimmering blotches of light where the pub's windows ought to be, echoes of footsteps and the muffled cough of an engine.

Delia and the young woman were nearly invisible when I looked back; all I could see was the red sweater, all I could hear was the laughing—soft, and low, and a comfort to my ears, so much so that I managed to climb down to the stones without embarrassing myself by falling.

I straightened.

The fog deepened, and I took a deep breath.

The fog held me, and I swayed, and spread my fingers to catch it.

Spread them. And flexed them. Felt the strength return, and the knowing.

And the light was nearly gone when Delia came back and took my hand.

"Jack," she said. "I have a new friend."

I nodded.

"Do you remember?"

It was only a few seconds before I nodded again.

She gave a small cry and threw her arms around me, hugged me, pressed her cheek to me, burrowed into me, then looked up to show me the tears filling her eyes. "I didn't think you would," she said.

I didn't always want to.

That was something she couldn't understand, could never understand—that it took more than a wishing to make a dream come true, that it took more than a wanting to make a friend come to stay, to save you from dying when dying should have been.

"I'm so glad you're back," she whispered. "To meet my new friend."

The wind had been strong that day, strong and cool.

I remember that much.

As I remember the look on the young woman's face, the

same look on all their faces when they see me and wonder and wonder at my smile, and the odd little girl standing at my side, and the way I hold out my hand to help her to her feet.

"Good evening," I said politely. I remember that; I always do.

Delia stirs and wriggles with the impatience of her kind.

"The fog is bad tonight," I said further. "Come with me, I'll show you home."

And she followed. They always do.

Into the fog.

Into the dark.

Where I remember all the rest.

And Delia hands me the knife.

LOVE IN VAIN

Lewis Shiner

The old cold creatures still exist deep inside us. Occasionally, something will happen to stir them, those creatures that we'd rather not have awakened, those creatures that most of us would like to pretend are not there at all.

In the brutal, brilliant story that follows—one of the most powerful pieces of fiction you're likely to read this year—Lewis Shiner not only stirs those ancient creatures, he hits them a couple of good licks with a stick and really gets them riled. He wakes them up, all right. Take a good look at them, now that they're awake and staring unblinkingly at you with their cold, hard eyes. You probably won't like the look of them—but we bet that you can't turn away, either.

Lewis Shiner is widely regarded as one of the most exciting new writers of the eighties. His stories have appeared in The Magazine of Fantasy and Science Fiction, Omni, Oui, Shayol, Isaac Asimov's Science Fiction Magazine, Wild Card, The Twilight Zone Magazine, *and elsewhere. His first novel,* Frontera, *appeared in 1984 to good critical response. Upcoming from the new Foundation line is a new novel,* Deserted Cities of the Heart. *Shiner lives in Austin, Texas, with his wife, Edith.*

For James Ellroy

I REMEMBER THE ROOM: WHITEWASHED WALLS, NO WINdows, a map of the U.S. on my left as I came in. There must have been a hundred pins with little colored heads stuck along the interstates. By the other door was a wooden table, the top full of scratches and coffee rings. Charlie was already sitting on the far side of it.

They called it Charlie's "office" and a Texas Ranger named Gonzales had brought me back there to meet him. "Charlie?" Gonzales said. "This here's Dave McKenna, from the D.A. up in Dallas?"

"Morning," Charlie said. I could see details, but they didn't seem to add up to anything. His left eye, the glass one, drooped a little, and his teeth were brown and ragged. He had on jeans and a plaid short-sleeved shirt and he was shaved clean. His hair was damp and combed straight back. His sideburns had gray in them and came to the bottom of his ears.

I had some files and a notebook in my right hand so I wouldn't have to shake with him. He didn't offer. "You looking to close you up some cases?" he said.

I had to clear my throat. "Well, we thought we might give it a try." I sat down in the other chair.

He nodded and looked at Gonzales. "Ernie? You don't suppose I could have a little more coffee?"

Gonzales had been leaning against the wall by the map, but he straightened right up and said, "Sure thing, Charlie." He brought in a full pot of coffee from the other room and set it on the table. Charlie had a styrofoam cup that looked like it could hold about a quart. He filled it up and then added three packets of sugar and some powdered cream substitute.

"How about you?" Charlie said.

"No," I said. "Thanks."

"You don't need to be nervous," Charlie said. His breath smelled of coffee and cigarettes. When he wasn't talking, his mouth relaxed into an easy smile. You didn't have to see anything menacing in it. It was the kind of smile you could see from any highway in Texas, looking out at you from a porch or behind a gas pump, waiting for you to drive on through.

I took out a little pocket-sized cassette recorder. "Would it be okay if I taped this?"

"Sure, go ahead."

I pushed the little orange button on top. "March 27, Williamson County Jail. Present are Sergeant Ernesto Gonzales and Charles Dean Harris."

"Charlie," he said.

"Pardon?"

"Nobody ever calls me Charles."

"Right," I said. "Okay."

"I guess maybe my mother did sometimes. Always sounded wrong somehow." He tilted his chair back against the wall. "You don't suppose you could back that up and do it over?"

"Yeah, okay, fine." I rewound the tape and went through the introduction again. This time I called him Charlie. Twenty-five years ago he'd stabbed his mother to death. She'd been his first.

It had taken me three hours to drive from Dallas to the Williamson County Jail in Georgetown, a straight shot down Interstate 35. I'd left a little before eight that morning. Alice was already at work and I had to get Jeffrey off to school. The hardest part was getting him away from the television.

He was watching MTV. They were playing the Heart video where the blonde guitar player wears the low-cut golden prom dress. Every time she moved, her magnificent breasts seemed to hesitate before they went along, like they were proud, willful animals, just barely under her control.

I turned the TV off and swung Jeffrey around a couple of times and sent him out for the bus. I got together the files I needed and went into the bedroom to make the bed. The covers were turned back on both sides, but the middle was undisturbed. Alice and I hadn't made love in six weeks. And counting.

I walked through the house, picking up Jeffrey's Masters of the Universe toys. I saw that Alice had loaded up the mantel again with framed pictures of her brothers and parents and the dog she'd had as a little girl. For a second it seemed like the entire house was buried in all this crap that had nothing to do with me—dolls and vases and doilies and candles and baskets on every inch of every flat surface she could reach. You couldn't walk from one end of a room to the other without running into a Victorian chair or secretary or umbrella stand, couldn't see the floors for the flowered rugs.

I locked up and got in the car and took the LBJ loop all the way around town. The idea was to avoid traffic. I was kidding myself. Driving in Dallas is a kind of contest; if somebody manages to pull in front of you he's clearly got a bigger dick than you do. Rather than let this happen it's better that one of you die.

I was in traffic the whole way down, through a hundred and seventy miles of Charlie Dean Harris country: flat, desolate grasslands with an occasional bridge or culvert where you could dump a body. Charlie had wandered and murdered all over the South, but once he found I-35 he was home to stay.

I opened one of the folders and rested it against the edge of the table so Charlie wouldn't see my hand shaking. "I've got a case here from 1974. A Dallas girl on her way home from Austin for spring break. Her name was Carol, uh, Fairchild. Black hair, blue eyes. Eighteen years old."

Charlie was nodding. "She had braces on her teeth. Would have been real pretty without 'em."

I looked at the sheet of paper in the folder. Braces, it said. The plain white walls seemed to wobble a little. "Then you remember her."

"Yessir, I suppose I do. I killed her." He smiled. It looked like a reflex, something he didn't even know he was doing. "I killed her to have sex with her."

"Can you remember anything else?"

He shrugged. "It was just to have sex, that's all. I remember when she got in the car. She was wearing a T-shirt, one of them man's T-shirts, with the straps and all." He dropped the chair back down and put his elbows on the table. "You could see her titties," he said, explaining.

I wanted to pull away but I didn't. "Where was this?"

He thought for a minute. "Between here and Round Rock, right there off the Interstate."

I looked down at my folder again. Last seen wearing navy tank top, blue jeans. "What color was the T-shirt?"

"Red," he said. "She would have been strangled. With a piece of electrical wire I had there in the car. I had supposed she was a prostitute, dressed the way she was and all. I asked her to have sex and she said she would, so I got off the highway and then she didn't want to. So I killed her and I had sex with her."

Nobody said anything for what must have been at least a minute. I could hear a little scratching noise as the tape moved inside the recorder. Charlie was looking straight at me with his good eye. "I wasn't satisfied," he said.

"What?"

"I wasn't satisfied. I had sex with her but I wasn't satisfied."

"Listen, you don't have to tell me . . ."

"I got to tell it all," he said.

"I don't want to hear it," I said. My voice came out too high, too loud. But Charlie kept staring at me.

"It don't matter," he said. "I still got to tell it. I got to tell it all. I can't live with the terrible things I did. Jesus says that if I tell everything I can be with Betsy when this is all over." Betsy was his common-law wife. He'd killed her, too, after living with her since she was nine. The words sounded like he'd been practicing them, over and over.

"I'll take you to her if you want," he said.

"Betsy . . . ?"

"No, your girl there. Carol Fairchild. I'll take you where I buried her." He wasn't smiling anymore. He had the sad, earnest look of a laundromat bum telling you how he'd lost his oil fortune up in Oklahoma.

I looked at Gonzales. "We can set it up for you if you want," he said. "Sheriff'll have to okay it and all, but we could prob'ly do it first thing tomorrow."

"Okay," I said. "That'd be good."

Charlie nodded, drank some coffee, lit a cigarette. "Well, fine," he said. "You want to try another?"

"No," I said. "Not just yet."

"Whatever," Charlie said. "You just let me know."

Later, walking me out, Gonzales said, "Don't let Charlie get to you. He wants people to like him, you know? So he figures out what you want him to be, and he tries to be that for you."

I knew he was trying to cheer me up. I thanked him and told him I'd be back in the morning.

I called Alice from Jack's office in Austin, thirty miles farther down I-35. "It's me," I said.

"Oh," she said. She sounded tired. "How's it going?"

I didn't know what to tell her. "Fine," I said. "I need to stay over another day or so."

"Okay," she said.

"Are you okay?"

"Fine," she said.

"Jeffrey?"

"He's fine."

I watched thirty seconds tick by on Jack's wall clock. "Anything else?" she said.

"I guess not." My eyes stung and I reflexively shaded them with my free hand. "I'll be at Jack's if you need me."

"Okay," she said. I waited a while longer and then put the phone back on the hook.

Jack was just coming out of his office. "Oh-oh," he said.

It took a couple of breaths to get my throat to unclench. "Yeah," I said.

"Bad?"

"Bad as it could be, I guess. It's over, probably. I mean, I think it's over, but how do you know?"

"You don't," Jack said. His secretary, a good-looking Chicana named Liz, typed away on her word processor and tried to act like she wasn't having to listen to us. "You just after a while get fed up and you say fuck it. You want to get a burger or what?"

Jack and I went to U.T. law school together. He was losing his hair and putting on weight but he wouldn't do anything about it. Jogging was for assholes. He would rather die fat and keep his self-respect.

He'd been divorced two years now and was always glad to fold out the couch for me. It had been a while. After Jeffrey was born, Alice and I had somehow lost touch with all our friends, given up everything except work and TV. "I've missed this," I said.

"Missed what?"

"Friends," I said. We were in a big prairie-style house north of campus that had been fixed up with a kitchen and bar and hanging plants. I was full, but still working on the last of the batter-dipped french fries.

"Not my fault, you prick. You're the one dropped down to Christmas cards."

"Yeah, well . . ."

"Forget it. How'd it go with Charlie Dean?"

"Unbelievable," I said. "I mean, really. He confessed to

everything. Had details. Even had a couple wrong, enough to look good. But the major stuff was right on.''

''So that's great. Isn't it?''

''It was a setup. The name I gave him was a fake. No such person, no such case.''

''I don't get it.''

''Jack, the son of a bitch has confessed to something like three thousand murders. It ain't possible. So they wanted to catch him lying.''

''With his pants down, so to speak.''

''Same old Jack.''

''You said he had details.''

''That's the creepy part. He knew she was supposed to have braces. I had it in the phony-case file, but he brought it up before I could say anything about it.''

''Lucky guess.''

''No. It was too creepy. And there's all this shit he keeps telling you. Things you wish you'd never heard, you know what I mean?''

''I know exactly what you mean,'' Jack said. ''When I was in junior high I saw a bum go in the men's room at the bus station with a loaf of bread. I told this friend of mine about it and he says the bum was going in there to wipe all the dried piss off the toilets with the bread and then eat it. For the protein. Said it happens all the time.''

''Jesus *Christ*, Jack.''

''See? I know what you're talking about. There's things you don't want in your head. Once they get in there, you're not the same anymore. I can't eat white bread to this day. Twenty years, and I still can't touch it.''

''You asshole.'' I pushed my plate away and finished my Corona. ''Christ, now the beer tastes like piss.''

Jack pointed his index finger at me. ''You will never be the same,'' he said.

* * *

You could never tell how much Jack had been drinking. He said it was because he didn't let on when he was sober. I always thought it was because there was something in him that was meaner than the booze and together they left him just about even.

It was a lot of beers later that Jack said, "What was the name of that bimbo in high school you used to talk about? Your first great love or some shit? Except she never put out for you?"

"Kristi," I said. "Kristi Spector."

"Right!" Jack got up and started walking around the apartment. It wasn't too long of a walk. "A name like that, how could I forget? I got her off a soliciting rap two months ago."

"Soliciting?"

"There's a law in Texas against selling your pussy. Maybe you didn't know that."

"Kristi Spector, my God. Tell me about it."

"She's a stripper, son. Works over at the Yellow Rose. This guy figured if she'd show her tits in public he could have the rest in his car. She didn't, he called the pigs. Said she made lewd advances. Crock of shit, got thrown out of court."

"How's she look?"

"Not too goddamn bad. I wouldn't have minded taking my fee in trade, but she didn't seem to get the hint." He stopped. "I got a better idea. Let's go have a look for ourselves."

"Oh, no," I said.

"Oh, yes. She remembers you, man. She says you were 'sweet.' Come on, get up. We're going to go look at some tits."

The place was bigger inside than I expected, the ceilings higher. There were two stages and a runway behind the second one. There were stools right up by the stages for the guys that wanted to stick dollar bills in the dancers' G-strings and four-top tables everywhere else.

I should have felt guilty but I wasn't thinking about Alice at all. The issue here was sex, and Alice had written herself out of that part of my life. Instead I was thinking about the last time I'd seen Kristi.

It was senior year in high school. The director of the drama club, who was from New York, had invited some of us to a "wild" party. It was the first time I'd seen men in dresses. I'd locked myself in the bathroom with Kristi to help her take her bra off. I hadn't seen her in six months. She'd just had an abortion; the father could have been one of a couple of guys. Not me. She didn't want to spoil what we had. It was starting to look to me like there wasn't much left to spoil. That had been eighteen years ago.

The D.J. played something by Pat Benatar. The music was loud enough to give you a kind of mental privacy. You didn't really have to pay attention to anything but the dancers. At the moment it seemed like just the thing. It had been an ugly day and there was something in me that was comforted by the sight of young, good-looking women with their clothes off.

"College town," Jack said, leaning toward me so I could hear him. "Lots of local talent."

A tall blonde on the north stage unbuttoned her long-sleeved white shirt and let it hang open. Her breasts were smooth and firm and pale. Like the others, she had something on the point of her nipples that made a small, golden flash every time one caught the light.

"See anybody you know?"

"Give me a break," I shouted over the music. "You saw her a couple months ago. It's been almost twenty years for me. I may not even recognize her." A waitress came by, wearing black leather jeans and a red tank top. For a second I could hear Charlie's voice telling me about her titties. I rubbed the sides of my head and the voice went away. We ordered beers, but when they came my stomach was wrapped around itself and I had to let mine sit.

"It's got to be weird to do this for a living," I said in Jack's ear.

"Bullshit," Jack said. "You think they're not getting off on it?"

He pointed to the south stage. A brunette in high heels had let an overweight man in sideburns and a western shirt tuck a dollar into the side of her bikini bottoms. He talked earnestly to her with just the start of an embarrassed smile. She had to keep leaning closer to hear him. Finally she nodded and turned around. She bent over and grabbed her ankles. His face was about the height of the backs of her knees. She was smiling like she'd just seen somebody else's baby do something cute. After a few seconds she stood up again and the man went back to his table.

"What was that about?" I asked Jack.

"Power, man," he said. "God, I love women. I just love 'em."

"Your problem is you don't know the difference between love and sex."

"Yeah? What is it? Come on, I want to know." The music was too loud to argue with him. I shook my head. "See? You don't know either."

The brunette pushed her hair back with both hands, chin up, fingers spread wide, and it reminded me of Kristi. The theatricality of it. She'd played one of Tennessee Williams's affected Southern bitches once and it had been almost too painful to watch. Almost.

"Come on," I said, grabbing Jack's sleeve. "It's been swell, but let's get out of here. I don't need to see her. I'm better off with the fantasy."

Jack didn't say anything. He just pointed with his chin to the stage behind me.

She had on a leopard skin leotard. She had been a dark blonde in high school but now her hair was brown and short. She'd put on a little weight, not much. She stretched in front of the mirrored wall and the D.J. played the Pretenders.

I felt this weird, possessive kind of pride, watching her. That and lust. I'd been married for eight years and the worst thing I'd ever done was kiss an old girlfriend on New Year's Eve and stare longingly at the pictures in *Playboy*. But this was real, this was happening.

The song finished and another one started and she pulled one strap down on the leotard. I remembered the first time I'd seen her breasts. I was fifteen. I'd joined a youth club at the Unitarian Church because she went there Sunday afternoons. Sometimes we would skip the program and sneak off into the deserted Sunday school classrooms and there, in the twilight, surrounded by crayon drawings on manila paper, she would stretch out on the linoleum and let me lie on top of her and feel the maddening pressure of her pelvis and smell the faint, clinically erotic odor of peroxide in her hair.

She showed me her breasts on the golf course next door. We had jumped the fence and we lay in a sand trap so no one would see us. There was a little light from the street, but not enough for real color. It was like a black-and-white movie when I played it back in my mind.

They were fuller now, hung a little lower and flatter, but I remembered the small, pale nipples. She pulled the other strap down, turned her back, rotating her hips as she stripped down to a red G-string. Somebody held a dollar out to her. I wanted to go over there and tell him that I knew her.

Jack kept poking me in the ribs. "Well? Well?"

"Be cool," I said. I had been watching the traffic pattern and I knew that after the song she would take a break and then get up on the other stage. It took a long time, but I wasn't tense about it. I'm just going to say hi, I thought. And that's it.

The song was over and she walked down the stairs at the end of the stage, throwing the leotard around her shoulders. I got up, having a little trouble with the chair, and walked over to her.

"Kristi," I said. "It's Dave McKenna."

"Oh, my *God*!" She was in my arms. Her skin was hot from the lights and I could smell her deodorant. I was suddenly dizzy, aware of every square inch where our bodies were touching. "Do you still hate me?" she said, pulling away.

"What?" There was so much I'd forgotten. The twang in her voice. The milk chocolate color of her eyes. The beauty mark over her right cheekbone. The flirtatious look up through the lashes that now had a desperate edge to it.

"The last time I saw you you called me a bitch. It was after that party at your teacher's house."

"No, I . . . believe me, it wasn't like . . ."

"Listen, I'm on again," she said. "Where are you?"

"We're right over there."

"Oh, Christ, you didn't bring your wife with you? I heard you were married."

"No, it's . . ."

"I got to run, sugar, wait for me."

I went back to the table.

"You rascal," Jack said. "Why didn't you just slip it to her on the spot?"

"Shut up, Jack, will you?"

"Ooooh, touchy."

I watched her dance. She was no movie star. Her face was a little hard and even the heavy makeup didn't hide all the lines. But none of that mattered. What mattered was the way she moved, the kind of puckered smile that said yes, I want it too.

* * *

She sat down with us when she was finished. She seemed to be all hands, touching me on the arm, biting on a fingernail, gesturing in front of her face.

She was dancing three times a week, which was all they would schedule her for anymore. The money was good and she didn't mind the work, especially here where it wasn't too rowdy. Jack raised his eyebrows at me to say, see? She got by with some modeling and some "scuffling," which I assumed meant turning tricks. Her mother was still in Dallas and had sent Kristi clippings the couple of times I got my name in the paper.

"She always liked me," I said.

"She liked you the best of all of them. You were a gentleman."

"Maybe too much of one."

"It was why I loved you." She was wearing the leotard again but she might as well have been naked. I was beginning to be afraid of her so I reminded myself that nothing had happened yet, nothing *had* to happen, that I wasn't committed to anything. I pushed my beer over to her and she drank about half of it. "It gets hot up there," she said. "You wouldn't believe. Sometimes you think you're going to pass out, but you got to keep smiling."

"Are you married?" I asked her. "Were you ever?"

"Once. It lasted two whole months. The shitheel knocked me up and then split."

"What happened?"

"I kept the kid. He's four now."

"What's his name?"

"Stoney. He's a cute little bastard. I got a neighbor watches him when I'm out, and I do the same for hers. He keeps me going sometimes." She drank the rest of the beer. "What about you?"

"I got a little boy too. Jeffrey. He's seven."

"Just the one?"

"I don't think the marriage could handle more than one kid," I said.

"It's an old story," Jack said. "If your wife put you through law school, the marriage breaks up. It just took Dave a little longer than most."

"You're getting divorced?" she asked.

"I don't know. Maybe." She nodded. I guess she didn't need to ask for details. Marriages come apart every day.

"I'm on again in a little," she said. "Will you still be here when I get back?" She did what she could to make it sound casual.

"I got an early day tomorrow," I said.

"Sure. It was good to see you. Real good."

The easiest thing seemed to be to get out a pen and an old business card. "Give me your phone number. Maybe I can get loose another night."

She took the pen but she kept looking at me. "Sure," she said.

"You're an idiot," Jack said. "Why didn't you go home with her?"

I watched the streetlights. My jacket smelled like cigarettes and my head had started to hurt.

"That gorgeous piece of ass says to you, 'Ecstasy?' and Dave says, 'No thanks.' What the hell's the matter with you? Alice make you leave your dick in the safe-deposit box?"

"Jack," I said, "will you shut the fuck up?" The card with her number on it was in the inside pocket of the jacket. I could feel it there, like a cool fingernail against my flesh.

Jack went back to his room to crash a little after midnight. I couldn't sleep. I put on the headphones and listened to Robert Johnson, "King of the Delta Blues Singers." There was something about his voice. He had this deadpan tone that sat down and told you what was wrong like it was no big deal. Then the voice would crack and you could tell it was a hell of a lot worse than he was letting on.

They said the devil himself had tuned Johnson's guitar. He died in 1938, poisoned by jealous husband. He'd made his first recordings in a hotel room in San Antonio, just another seventy miles on down I-35.

Charlie and Gonzales and I took my car out to what Gonzales called the "site." The sheriff and a deputy were in a brown county station wagon behind us. Charlie sat on the passenger side and Gonzales was in the back. Charlie could have opened the door at a stoplight and been gone. He wasn't even in handcuffs. Nobody said anything about it.

We got on I-35 and Charlie said, "Go on south to the second exit after the caves." The Inner Space Caverns were just south of Georgetown, basically a single long, unspectacular tunnel that ran for miles under the highway. "I killed a girl there once. When they turned off the lights."

I nodded but I didn't say anything. That morning, before I went in to the "office," Gonzales had told me that it made Charlie angry if you let on that you didn't believe him. I was tired, and hung over from watching Jack drink, and I didn't really give a damn about Charlie's feelings.

I got off at the exit and followed the access road for a while. Charlie had his eyes closed and seemed to be thinking hard.

"Having trouble?" I asked him.

"Nah," he said. "Just didn't want to take you to the wrong one." I looked at him and he started laughing. It was a joke. Gonzales chuckled in the back seat and there was this cheerful kind of feeling in the car that made me want to pull over and run away.

"Nosir," Charlie said, "I sure don't suppose I'd want to do that." He grinned at me and he knew what I was thinking, he could see the horror right there on my face. He just kept smiling. Come on, I could hear him saying. Loosen up. Be one of the guys.

I wiped the sweat from my hands onto my pant legs. Finally he said, "There's a dirt road a ways ahead. Turn off on it. It'll go over a hill and then across a cattle grating. After the grating is a stand of trees off to the left. You'll want to park up under 'em."

How can he be doing this? I thought. He's got to know there's nothing there. Or does he? When we don't turn anything up, what's he going to do? Are they going to wish they'd cuffed him after all? The sheriff knew what I was up to, but none of the others did. Would Gonzales turn on me for betraying Charlie?

The road did just what Charlie said it would. We parked the cars under the trees and the deputy and I got shovels out of the sheriff's trunk. The trees were oaks and their leaves were tiny and very pale green.

"It would be over here," Charlie said. He stood on a patch of low ground, covered with clumps of Johnson grass. "Not too deep."

He was right. She was only about six or eight inches down. The deputy had a body bag and he tried to move her into it, but she kept coming apart. There wasn't much left but a skeleton and a few rags.

And the braces. Still shining, clinging to the teeth of the skull like a metal smile.

On the way back to Georgetown we passed a woman on the side of the road. She was staring into the hood of her car. She looked like she was about to cry. Charlie turned all the way around in his seat to watch her as we drove by.

"There's just victims ever'where," Charlie said. There was a sadness in his voice I didn't believe. "The highway's full of 'em. Kids, hitchhikers, waitresses . . . You ever pick one up?"

"No," I said, but it wasn't true. It was in Dallas, I was home for spring break. It was the end of the sixties. She had on a green dress. Nothing happened. But she had smiled at me and put one arm up on the back of the seat. I was on the way to my girlfriend's house and I let her off a few blocks away. And that night, when I was inside her, I imagined my girlfriend with the hitchhiker's face, with her blonde hair and freckles, her slightly coarse features, the dots of sweat on her upper lip.

"But you thought about it," Charlie said. "Didn't you?"

"Listen," I said. "I got a job to do. I just want to do it and get out of here, okay?"

"I know what you're saying," Charlie said. "Jesus forgives me, but I can't ask that of nobody else. I was just trying to get along, that's all. That's all any of us is ever trying to do."

I called Dallas collect from the sheriff's phone. He gave me a private room where I could shout if I had to. The switchboard put me through to Ricky Slatkin, the head of my department.

"Dave, will you for Chrissake calm down. It's a coincidence. That's all. Forensics will figure out who this girl is and we'll put another 70 or 80 years on Charlie's sentence. Maybe give him another death penalty. What the hell, right? Meanwhile we'll give him another ringer."

"You give him one. I want out of this. I am fucking terrified."

"I, uh, understand you're under some stress at home these days."

"I am not at home. I'm in Georgetown, in the Williamson County Jail, and I am under some fucking stress right here. Don't you understand? He *thought* this dead girl into existence."

"What, Charlie Dean Harris is God now, is that it? Come

on, Dave. Go out and have a few beers and by tomorrow it'll all make sense to you.''

"He's evil, Jack," I said. We were back at his place after a pizza at Conan's. Jack had ordered a pitcher of beer and drunk it all himself. "I didn't use to believe in it, but that was before I met Charlie."

He had a women's basketball game on TV, the sound turned down to a low hum. "That's horseshit," he said. His voice was too loud. "Horseshit, Christian horseshit. They want you to believe that Evil has got a capital *E* and it's sitting over there in the corner, see it? Horseshit. Evil isn't a thing. It's something that's *not* there. It's an absence. The lack of the thing that stops you from doing whatever you damn well please."

He chugged half a beer. "Your pal Charlie ain't evil. He's just damaged goods. He's just like you or me but something died in him. You know what I'm talking about. You've felt it. First it goes to sleep and then it dies. You know when you stand up in court and try to get a rapist off when you know he did it. You tell yourself that it's part of the game, you try to give the asshole the benefit of the doubt, hell, somebody's got to do it, right? You try to believe the girl is just some slut that changed her mind, but you can smell it. Something inside you starting to rot."

He finished the beer and threw it at a paper sack in the corner. It hit another bottle inside the sack and shattered. "Then you go home and your wife's got a goddamn headache or her period or she's asleep in front of the TV or she's not in the goddamn mood and you just want to beat the . . ." His right fist was clenched up so tight the knuckles were a shiny yellow. His eyes looked like open sores. He got up for another beer and he was in the kitchen for a long time.

When he came back I said, "I'm going out." I said it without giving myself a chance to think about it.

"Kristi," Jack said. He had a fresh beer and was all right again.

"Yeah."

"You bastard! Can I smell your fingers when you get back?"

"Fuck you, Jack."

"Oh no, save it for her. She's going to use you up, you lucky bastard."

I called her from a pay phone and she gave me directions. She was at the Royal Palms Trailer Park, near Bergstrom Air Force Base on the south end of town. It wasn't hard to find. They even had a few palm trees. There were rural-type galvanized mailboxes on posts by the gravel driveways. I found the one that said Spector and parked behind a white Dodge with six-figure mileage.

The temperature was in the sixties but I was shaking. My shoulders kept trying to crawl up around my neck. I got out of the car. I couldn't feel my feet. Asshole, I told myself. I don't want to hear about your personal problems. You better enjoy this or I'll kill you.

I knocked on the door and it made a kind of mute rattling sound. Kristi opened it. She was wearing a plaid bathrobe, so old I couldn't tell what the colors used to be. She stood back to let me in and said, "I didn't think you'd call."

"But I did," I said. The trailer was tiny—a living room with a green sofa and a 19-inch color TV, a kitchen the size of a short hall, a single bedroom behind it, the door open, the bed unmade. A blond-haired boy was asleep on the sofa, wrapped in an army blanket. The shelf above him was full of plays—Albee, Ionesco, Tennessee Williams. The walls were covered with photographs in dime-store frames.

A couple of them were from the drama club; one even had me in it. I was sixteen and looked maybe nine. My hair was too long in front, my chest was sucked in, and I had a stupid smirk on my face. I was looking at Kristi. Who would want to look at anything else? She had on cutoffs that had frayed up past the crease of her thighs. Her shirt was unbuttoned and tied under her breasts. Her head was back and she was laughing. I'd always been able to make her laugh.

"You want a drink?" she whispered.

"No," I said. I turned to look at her. We weren't either of us laughing now. I reached for her and she glanced over at the boy and shook her head. She grabbed the cuff of my shirt and pulled me gently back toward the bedroom.

It smelled of perfume and hand lotion and a little of mildew. The only light trickled in through heavy, old-fashioned venetian blinds. She untied the bathrobe and let it fall. I kissed her and her arms went around my neck. I touched her shoulder blades and her hair and her buttocks and then I got out of my clothes and left them in a pile on the floor. She ran on tiptoes back to the front of the trailer and locked and chained the door. Then she came back and shut the bedroom door and lay down on the bed.

I lay down next to her. The smell and feel of her was wonderful, and at the same time it was not quite real. There were too many unfamiliar things and it was hard to connect to the rest of my life.

Then I was on my knees between her legs, gently touching her. Her arms were spread out beside her, tangled in the sheets, her hips moving with pleasure. Only once, in high school, had she let me touch her there, in the back seat of a friend's car, her skirt up around her hips, panties to her knees, and before I had recovered from the wonder of it she had pulled away.

But that was eighteen years ago and this was now. There had been a lot of men touching her since then, maybe hundreds. But that was all right. I lay on top of her and she guided me inside. She tried to say something, maybe it was only my name, but I put my mouth over hers to shut her up.

I put both my arms around her and closed my eyes and let the heat and pleasure run up through me.

When I finished and we rolled apart she lay on top of me, pinning me to the bed. "That was real sweet," she said.

I kissed her and hugged her because I couldn't say what I was thinking. I was thinking about Charlie, remembering the earnest look on his face when he said, "It was just to have sex, that's all."

She was wide awake and I was exhausted. She complained about the state cutting back on aid to single parents. She told me about the tiny pieces of tape she had to wear on the ends of her nipples when she danced, a weird Health Department regulation. I remembered the tiny golden flashes and fell asleep to the memory of her dancing.

Screaming woke me up. Kristi was already out of bed and headed for the living room. "It's just Stoney," she said, and I lay back down.

I woke up again a little before dawn. There was an arm around my waist but it seemed much too small. I rolled over and saw that the little boy had crawled into bed between us.

I got up without moving him and went to the bathroom. There was no water in the toilet; when I pushed the handle a trap opened in the bottom of the bowl and a fine spray washed the sides. I got dressed, trying not to bump into anything. Kristi was asleep on the side of the bed closest to the door, her mouth open a little. Stoney had burrowed into the middle of her back.

I was going to turn around and go when a voyeuristic impulse made me open the drawer of her nightstand. Or maybe I subconsciously knew what I'd find. There was a Beeline book called *Molly's Sexual Follies*, a tube of KY, a box of Ramses lubricated condoms, a few used Kleenex. An emery board, a finger puppet, one hoop earring. A short-barreled Colt .32 revolver.

* * *

I got to the jail at nine in the morning. The woman at the visitor's window recognized me and buzzed me back. Gonzales was at his desk. He looked up when I walked in and said, "I didn't know you was coming in today."

"I just had a couple of quick questions for Charlie," I said. "Only take a second."

"Did you want to use the office . . . ?"

"No, no point. If I could just talk to him in his cell for a couple of minutes, that would be great."

Gonzales got the keys. Charlie had a cell to himself, five by ten feet, white-painted bars on the long wall facing the corridor. There were Bibles and religious tracts on his cot, a few paintings hanging on the wall. "Maybe you can get Charlie to show you his pictures," Gonzales said. A stool in the corner had brushes and tubes of paint on the top.

"You painted these?" I asked Charlie. My voice sounded fairly normal, all things considered.

"Yessir, I did."

"They're pretty good." They were landscapes with trees and horses, but no people.

"Thank you kindly."

"You can just call for me when you're ready," Gonzales said. He went out and locked the door.

"I thought you'd be back," Charlie said. "Was there something else you wanted to ask me?" He sat on the edge of the cot, forearms on his knees.

I didn't say anything. I took the Colt out of the waistband of my pants and pointed it at him. I'd already looked it over on the drive up and there were bullets in all six cylinders. My hand was shaking so I steadied it with my left and fired all six rounds into his head and chest.

I hadn't noticed all the background noises until they stopped, the typewriters and the birds and somebody singing upstairs. Charlie stood up and walked over to where I was standing. The revolver clicked on an empty shell.

"You can't get rid of me that easy," Charlie said with his droopy-eyed smile. "I been around too long. I was Spring-heeled Jack and Richard Speck. I was Ted Bundy and that fella up to Seattle they never caught." The door banged open at the end of the hall. "You can't never get rid of me because I'm *inside* you."

I dropped the gun and locked my hands behind my head. Gonzales stuck his head around the corner. He was squinting. He had his gun out and he looked terrified. Charlie and I stared back at him calmly.

"It's okay, Ernie," Charlie said. "No harm done. Mr. McKenna was just having him a little joke."

Charlie told Gonzales the gun was loaded with blanks. They had to believe him because there weren't any bullet holes in the cell. I told them I'd bought the gun off a defendant years ago, that I'd had it in the car.

They called Dallas and Ricky asked to talk to me. "There's going to be an inquest," he said. "No way around it."

"Sure there is," I said. "I quit. I'll send it to you in writing. I'll put it in the mail today. Express."

"You need some help, Dave. You understand what I'm saying to you here? *Professional* help. Think about it. Just tell me you'll think about it."

Gonzales was scared and angry and wanted me charged with smuggling weapons into the jail. The sheriff knew it wasn't worth the headlines and by suppertime I was out.

Jack had already heard about it through some kind of legal grapevine. He thought it was funny. We skipped dinner and went down to the bars on Sixth Street. I couldn't drink anything. I was afraid of going numb, or letting down my guard. But Jack made up for me. As usual.

"Kristi called me today," Jack said. "I told her I didn't

know but what you might be going back to Dallas today. Just a kind of feeling I had."

"I'm not going back," I said. "But it was the right thing to tell her."

"Not what it was cracked up to be, huh?"

"Oh yeah," I said. "That and much, much more."

For once he let it go. "You mean you're not going back tonight or not going back period?"

"Period," I said. "My job's gone, I pissed that away this morning. I'll get something down here. I don't care what. I'll pump gas. I'll fucking wait tables. You can draw up the divorce papers and I'll sign them."

"Just like that?"

"Just like that."

"What's Alice going to say?"

"I don't know if she'll even notice. She can have the goddamn house and her car and the savings. All of it. All I want is some time with Jeffrey. As much as I can get. Every week if I can."

"Good luck."

"I've got to have it. I don't want him growing up screwed up like the rest of us. I've got stuff I've got to tell him. He's going to need help. All of us are. Jack, goddamn it, are you listening to me?"

He wasn't. He was staring at the Heart video on the bar's big-screen TV, at the blonde guitarist. "Look at that," Jack said. "Sweet suffering Jesus. Couldn't you just fuck that to death?"

FURTHER READING

ANTHOLOGIES

Barnard, Alan, ed. *The Harlot Killer.* Dell

Parry, Michael, ed. *Jack the Knife.* Mayflower Books

REFERENCE BOOKS

Rumbolow, Donald. *The Complete Jack the Ripper.*

Spiering, Frank. *Prince Jack.*

Jack the Ripper, The Final Solution.

When London Walked in Terror.

SHORT STORIES

Benson, Theodora. "In the Fourth Ward," *The Harlot Killer.*

Bloch, Robert. "A Toy for Juliet," *Dangerous Visions.*

Boucher, Anthony. "A Kind of Madness," *Jack the Knife.*

Campbell, Ramsey. "Jack's Little Friend," *Jack the Knife.*

Lowndes, Marie Belloc. "The Lodger," *The Harlot Killer.*

Pumilia, Joseph F. "Forever Stand the Stones," *Jack the Knife.*

Utley, Stephen. "The Maw." *The Magazine of Fantasy and Science Fiction,* July 1977.

Waldrop, Howard. "The Adventure of the Grinder's Whistle." *Chacal* 2.